The Siren Sea

By

Brian R. Pellar

Cover design and drawing of Mt. Fuji by Brian R. Pellar

USS Midway cover photograph NH 72657 courtesy of Naval History and Heritage Command

2nd Printing

Table of Contents

Acknowledgement

No artist creates in a vacuum—particularly when it comes to a first novel. I would like to thank the following people who helped me along the way:

Thomas Keneally
Judith Grossman
UC Irvine's MFA Program in Fiction
Kate Besser
William Caldarelli
Community of Writers in Olympic Valley
Eve Wood
Araceli Peñafuerte
Richard Martel
Ronald Pellar
Nadine Hall
Tim Gospodnetich
Neal Shusterman
M. Scott Carhart

About the Author

Brian R. Pellar is the author of the non-fiction book *Moby-Dick and Melville's Anti-Slavery Allegory* (Palgrave Macmillan, 2017). He has also published six papers on the Origins of the Alphabet in the academic journal *Sino-Platonic Papers* (SPP 196, SPP 219, SPP 246, SPP 263, SPP 296, and SPP 328). After serving four years in the US Navy—with two years aboard the aircraft carrier USS Midway (CV-41) in Japan—he attended UC Irvine as a double major and then earned an MFA in English from UC Irvine in 1996. He is also an artist and has a life-size figurative bronze sculpture, *Form No. 2*, permanently installed in the Chancellor's Rose Garden at UC Irvine. He also designed UC Irvine's anteater-head ceremonial graduation mace. He currently resides in Arizona and is working on several writing and art projects.

"Come hither, as thou farest, renowned Odysseus, great glory of the Achaeans; stay thy ship that thou mayest listen to the voice of us two. For never yet has any man rowed past this isle in his black ship until he has heard the sweet voice from our lips. Nay, he has joy of it, and goes his way a wiser man. For we know all the toils that in wide Troy the Argives and Trojans endured through the will of the gods, and we know all things that come to pass upon the fruitful earth."

-The Sirens. Homer, *Odyssey*

"What are they seeking? The whites always want something; they are always uneasy and restless. We do not know what they want. We do not understand them. We think that they are mad." I asked him [Ochwiay Biano, Chief of the Taos Pueblos] why he thought the whites were all mad. "They say that they think with their heads," he replied. "Why of course. What do you think with?" I asked him in surprise. "We think here," he said, indicating his heart.

-Carl Jung, *Memories, Dreams, Reflections*

Prologue

On July 11, 1984, I was processed out of the Navy at Treasure Island in San Francisco after having served four years. My first few months in the service were spent in Boot Camp at the Naval Station Great Lakes, Illinois, and then GMT "A" School on Coronado Island, California, where I graduated first in my class. I then spent two years aboard the aircraft carrier USS Midway, CV-41, which was homeported in Yokosuka, Japan. My last year and a half in the Navy were spent at the naval weapons magazine on the island of Guam, where I helped repair, replace, and move nuclear weapons.

While in Guam, I had the good fortune to meet up with a Chief who, for now, I choose to keep anonymous. At that time, I had discovered Carl Sagan's book Cosmos, *and I carried it around like an extra stripe on my sleeve. I read and then re-read it and babbled on about it and my proposed university exit from the Navy to whoever would listen—as I had just been accepted into the University of California, Irvine as a political science major for the fall of 1984. I had been bitten by the "rage to know" (to borrow from Horace Judson's* The Search for Solutions, *a book I found in the library on the USS Midway), and my unusual enthusiasm for all things intellectual seemed to have caught the attention of this particular Chief.*

It was close to my departure from Guam, with much talk of trying to get me to stay in the Navy when this Chief suddenly and unexpectedly invited me over to his home for dinner. At first, I was reluctant to do so, as this Chief was greatly feared by the entire crew. He was a large and muscular man with protruding cheeks, battleship grey beard and hair, both perfectly trimmed to regulation length, dark, deep-set eyes, and abnormally large hands, and he quickly instilled a sense of absolute authority to anyone unlucky enough to fall beneath his rank and gaze. Thus, when the invitation first went out, I was filled with trepidation and loathing, not sure what his motives or intentions were.

However, when I went over to his house and knocked on his door, I was pleasantly shocked when he greeted me with oversized black spectacles and a warm smile. I never expected that and never thought that the likes of someone like him would ever own a pair of glasses, let alone wear them. He quickly ushered me into his home, where I was introduced to his wife and two daughters. We exchanged pleasantries, ate a quiet chicken and broccoli dinner, and then he excused himself from his family. He said that it was time to introduce me to "Sophia." At first, I thought that he was going to show me a dog or cat or parakeet or something that needed to be fed and hugged, but instead, he escorted me into a small bedroom off the main hallway of his house. As he walked into the room, he slowly raised his arms and calmly said, "Sophia . . . my library."

I was stunned.

All around him, from the floor to the ceiling, were books—books in shelves, books in piles, books in piles leaning into shelves and corners. There were even books crammed between the ceiling and the shelf and between the shelves themselves.

I couldn't believe it, and I could still see him smiling intently at me as I gazed dumbfounded around the room. In one hand, he held out a bottle of wine, and in the other, two glasses. He said that the real reason that he had invited me over was to discuss literature, which we then proceeded to do, in between wine refills, till all hours of the night. We discussed Edgar Rice Burroughs, Arthur C. Clark, Robert E. Howard, Melville, Faulkner, and, of course, his favorite, Conrad, whose book Heart of Darkness *he particularly delighted in. The next day I really thought that it had all been a dream, for when I next saw him at the weapons magazine, he was back to being his normal self—glaring, scowling, and quick to bark out the day's orders. He barely spoke or acknowledged me at all.*

However, the next weekend I received another invite. And again, I was met at the door with his glasses, a bottle of wine, and a

3

welcoming smile. This time, however, he apologized and told me that he needed to keep up appearances at the magazine, and he could never divulge to the crew this intellectual side to him. And once again, we drank and talked all night and then remained silent and detached from one another at work. This went on for a few more times, with each encounter as jovial, thought-provoking, and spirited as the one before.

But on the third or fourth visit, it appears we drank too much, and he mistakenly crossed a line. While discussing the classified work we do on weapons, he suddenly sat up, serious, and asked me something that he probably shouldn't have. He asked if I'd ever heard the words "Fuji Jiken" mentioned among the other GMTs, particularly the ones I had served with on the USS Midway.

I said no.

He then lowered his head in thought, looking down at a small pile of National Geographic magazines splayed out on the floor as though he was debating with himself as to whether to open that hatch or not. In the end, though, and I'm not sure why, as it still haunts me to this day, he leaned back in his chair, placed his thick fingers softly around his glass of red wine, and then spoke in a low but carefully directed voice. He defined "Fuji Jiken" and then proceeded to provide context.

A ton of it.

I was shocked at what I was hearing. At first, I thought he was kidding, but the tone and manner in which he told the story quickly extinguished any doubts that fired forth. He went on for a long while, but I never took notice of the time, as it was quite a fascinating story. When he finally finished, it was late in the evening, and he set his glasses down, stared straight into my eyes, and told me never, ever, under any circumstance, repeat what he had just mentioned. I remember looking at the sun-baked flesh that was deeply folded in on itself between his brows, a peculiarity, no doubt, naturally brought about by the repetition of the daily discharge of orders amidst an intermittent spray of silent warning. He had transformed back into that authority figure that everyone feared, and he sat hulking before me, his eyes in shadow, and I was petrified. I stammered out that, of course, of course, I would keep quiet. And indeed, until just recently, when I heard of the Chief's passing, I never said a word to anyone.

But now that he is gone, I feel that the events that he described should be made known, for, as will be seen, I strongly feel that it's in the public's interest to know what had transpired back in 1977, as it resonates so strongly with those American values that we hold so dear, particularly to something so much bigger than oneself, and above all, the sustained conviction of doing the right thing, though damnation and self-deception tear at the toil. Thus, the following story, though fictionalized in many places and in most of the dialogue, is based on what the Chief related to me that night. I helped create motivation through the addition of several fictional incidents (including the illegal use of drugs, hate for W-Division, and the illegal behavior and procedures regarding classified weapons), and I substituted several of my own experiences of shipboard life to try to bring some authenticity to a story that, though tinged with intent, is rather short in detail and specificity. Though he spoke at length, it was impossible in those few hours amidst several glasses of wine for him to uncoil such a long tale. But what he was able to convey seemed to ring true to me. And at times, too true. That is, I'm not sure if it was the manner in which he told it, with small breaches of emotion that imparted to me the feeling that he was somehow involved in it in some way, either personally or he knew someone who was—as I later learned that he, too, had served on the USS Midway prior to me—but, either way, I was lucky to get some documents to substantiate what had happened. To this end, I'm indebted to Ms. Ann Redding at the Department of Defense and Mr. Jonathan F. Griswold at the State Department for steering me in the right direction and for getting me in touch with not only the right people but the appropriate FOIA (Freedom of Information Act) forms that needed to be filled out.

Receiving a copy of the journal of Taylor was more than I ever could have imagined. I have placed as much as I could of the journal entries between each of the chapters of my book, and though limited, it provides enough information to fill in many of the important gaps and dates that the Chief left out. Whether purposeful or from a faulty memory or lack of information, I'll never know. But I thank him for what he was able to provide. And provide he did, for those nights that we laughed and drank together and spent deep in thought were easily the highlight of my four-year naval career.

:t the following in _____
(Type in plaintext or code)

AIRTEL   AIR MAIL   SECRET

(Priority)

TO: DIRECTOR, FBI   ATTENTION: FBI LABORATORY

FROM: ADIC, LOS ANGELES/ Orig: Naval Intelligence, Suitland, MD

SUBJECT: Unsub;
Joseph Taylor, Seaman, U.S. Navy
Co-conspirator: Fuji Jiken (The Fuji Incident)
Unauthorized access/theft/damage to nuclear weapon
OO: LA

Enclosed for the Bureau is one copy each of (1) ▮▮▮▮▮▮
▮▮▮▮▮▮▮▮▮▮▮▮▮▮▮▮▮▮▮▮▮▮▮▮▮▮▮▮▮▮▮▮▮▮▮▮
(2) 3.5x6 personal journal of Joseph Taylor, handwritten, beginning,
9/25/77, "I am neither in air nor on earth . . .", and ending 11/25/77,
". . . buttressing the blackness just beyond"; (3) ▮▮▮▮▮▮▮▮▮▮▮

▮▮▮▮▮▮▮▮▮▮▮▮▮▮▮▮▮▮▮▮▮▮▮▮▮▮▮▮▮▮▮▮▮▮▮▮▮▮
▮▮▮▮▮▮▮▮▮▮▮▮▮▮▮▮▮▮▮▮▮▮▮▮▮▮▮▮▮▮▮▮▮▮▮▮▮▮
▮▮▮▮▮▮▮▮▮▮▮▮▮▮▮▮▮▮▮▮▮▮▮▮▮▮▮▮▮▮▮▮▮▮▮▮▮▮
▮▮▮▮▮▮▮▮▮▮▮▮▮▮▮▮▮▮▮▮▮▮▮▮▮▮▮▮▮▮▮▮▮▮▮▮▮▮
▮▮▮▮▮▮▮▮▮▮▮▮▮▮▮▮▮▮▮▮▮▮▮▮▮▮▮▮▮▮▮▮▮▮▮▮▮▮
▮▮▮▮▮▮▮▮▮▮▮▮▮▮▮▮▮▮▮▮▮▮▮▮▮▮

③- Bureau (Encls.-8)   ENCLOSURE   DE-B
2- New York (Encls.-4)   619796
2- Los Angeles
TMK:fet   REC-83
(7)   STA114   AUG 20 1978   7 AUG 13 1978   SENT

pproved: _____   Sent _____ M   Pet _____
Special Agent in Charge   ☆ U. S. GOVERNMENT PRINTING OFFICE : 1969 O - 348-659 (II)

SECRET

3.5" x 6" Journal of Joseph Taylor

The Fantail

The air was cut through with the scent of coconut, and Daniels hated coconut. But it was the only sun tan oil that he had, and he really needed it. Though it was early evening, the heat was unrelenting, and he could feel it shimmering up in waves all around him from the black non-skid of the fantail deck of the aircraft carrier USS Midway, which was steaming southwest in the Pacific towards Kenya. His eyes were shut, and even though his beach towel was thick and sizeable, it felt as though his back and legs were being skewered over a barbeque.

Daniels sat up to relieve himself from the heat. But as he did this, he suddenly thought of sipping an ice-cold Asahi Super Dry in the Zigzag club in Yokosuka with Yuki, his Japanese girlfriend. He smiled. In fact, he couldn't help but smile every time he thought of her and that permanent and perpetual grin of hers that was glazed over with that soft pink lipstick that smelled of peach and drove him wild. Her sense of humor always seemed to jet-fuel her personality. It began on his first date with her at the New York, New York club in the Shinjuku district of Tokyo, where she sat curled up close to him in a booth, very much at ease, with one of her slender legs dangling towards the floor, the other raised with her foot on the padded seat, and her right hand resting high up on her knee. Her long black hair softly swayed in rhythm to her head as she nodded and listened intently to him drone on about the Navy and the USS Midway. But while he was talking, he accidentally touched her leg with his hand. And what she said next he'll never forget—without flinching or missing a beat, she smiled, opened her palm to him, and said, "One penny, please!" His heart melted. He leaned into her, returned her smile, and said, "Honey, you're soon going to be one rich woman." He then kissed her lightly on the cheek.

That was a year ago before he had committed to getting out of the Navy and going to college. But the thought of her not being with him back in the States was too much. While visiting the Philippines a month ago, her absence really hit home. After a night of drinking with his shipmates and the "buy me drink" girls at the Buffalo Beer House in Olongapo, he stumbled back to the ship, alone and depressed, and immediately wrote her a letter—telling her how much he missed her and that he loved her. And with his fingers in tune with his heart and with them flying faster than his thoughts, he suddenly ended the letter with the words, "Will you marry me?"

When he fully realized what he had just written, he put the letter down, took a deep breath, and asked himself if it was just the alcohol and loneliness propelling the pen. But the immediate answer he received from his heart was perfectly clear and concise—he loved her and couldn't imagine living without her. With this realization, he jumped down from his rack, zipped over to the post office on the Midway's second deck, placed a penny in the envelope, and mailed it.

He had first met Yuki at a tiny traditional wooden teahouse squeezed in between two larger modern shops in the bustling Shinjuku district of Tokyo. She was walking out the door, and he was walking in. She smiled at him, and he immediately turned and introduced himself. She was a bit shocked at this, as the Japanese do not typically meet strangers in passing. Most dates and meetings are set up through friends. But as Daniels was a foreigner, he was excused from their almost strict etiquette. It wasn't long before he invited her to join him at the New York, New York dance club that evening. To his surprise, she said yes. The next week, she came to the Naval base in Yokosuka, and she took him to the nearby Kotoku-in temple to see the Great Buddha of Kamakura, a massive 13th-century bronze statue of Amitabha that is 43 feet high and weighs over 100 tons. It wasn't long after that they were regularly seeing each other while the Midway was in port. He would join her at Byblos in the Roppongi district, with its unique DJ glass elevator that zipped up and down its three floors just next to the dance floor, its DJ spinning groove after groove, their bodies moving tightly in rhythm to the beat. And, of course, they always seemed to end up at the Zig Zag Club next to the base. It was Daniels' favorite, and they would end up drinking, talking, and listening to music until about 11 p.m., as the trains stopped running at midnight. They would then wander over to a small shop near the train station that served stir fry rice to drunk sailors heading back to the base. Daniels had no idea what was dumped in it other than chicken, some random vegetables such as peas and onions, and, of course, soy sauce. Maybe it was the alcohol, but it always seemed to taste amazing and hit the spot.

But more recently, they stopped wandering over to the rice shop. Instead, they made their way over to a special hotel called a "Love Hotel" that only rented out its rooms by the hour—and which always seemed to upset him. He couldn't take her back to his ship, and she couldn't take him to her mother's apartment in Tokyo, where she lived, and she wouldn't allow him to take her to a regular hotel. Thus, he was never allowed the luxury of waking up with her the next morning and feeling the warm press of her palm, the tender tug of her toe, the lush lengthening of the far eastern light. These hourly hotels were always timed exactly, and he was forced to get up after an hour or two and head over to the station so she could catch the train. But their time in the station always seemed to make up for it. It was the long goodbyes. Particularly their last one. It was late in the evening, and he just didn't want to let her go, and they stayed pasted together for what seemed like an eternity, softly swaying in each other's arms.

That night the platform was surprisingly empty, except for a lone sailor standing off to Daniels' right. When the train finally approached, its lights illuminated the curved twin line of the track.

Daniels leaned forward and kissed Yuki on her forehead. "I love you," he said.

She pulled back, looked up at him, and smiled. "Really? You really?"

"Yes, silly. More than you can imagine."

11

"Why?"

The question startled him. "Why? What do you mean why?"

"You heard. My imagine not good."

"Mmmm. . . Well, for starters, you have such a kind and loving personality."

She smiled, her right knee dipping slightly as she pressed both of her palms into the back pockets of her tight jeans.

"And I love your polite etiquette and your, ah, gentle heart." He ran a finger over the thin white blouse covering her breast and then gently placed it on her mouth. "And, of course, those lustrous lips and pretty face of yours, plus your smile, silky hair, beautiful skin, and body." He wrapped his arms around her waist, trapping her arms behind her. "And, of course, your passion!" He pulled her tight and then kissed her on the forehead. Just a hint of peach lipstick drifted up, and he kissed her again.

The train slowed, its wheels screeching.

Yuki pressed her cheek against his chest. "I love you, Chris," she said. "Please write letter." She broke free and walked over toward the edge of the platform. The train stopped, but instead of stepping on, she suddenly spun and ran back into his arms, tears streaming down her cheeks. His body fused into hers. But it was only for a second. She quickly pulled away, gave him one last look, and hurried over to the open door of the train, her hand wiping her face, disappearing into the maze of motionless and silent bodies.

The train pulled away, and as the red lights of the last car reached the far end of the station, the sailor standing next to Daniels suddenly leaned over and said, "You're lucky. You've got yourself a real angel there."

Daniels nodded and stared at the empty platform and the darkness just beyond. "I know," he whispered. "I know."

That was over a month and a half ago, and he still hasn't heard from her. He was getting increasingly worried. He hoped she would agree to marry and go to California with him while he attends college. But what if she says no? He still had another six months left with her in Japan. But what about when he left Japan forever? Without her? Could he endure that? That loneliness?

Daniels looked at his textbook, *Oceanography*, and then down at the small photograph of Yuki jutting out from the top as a bookmark. He had yet to open the book today, or for that matter, all week. For some reason, he couldn't quite comprehend, perhaps over his fear of her response to his drunken but honest rambling in that letter, he kept putting off the reading assignments and was now rapidly falling behind. The thought scared him. He was falling into the same pattern as high school, sliding down from "A"s in his first year to "D"s and "F"s in his fourth—just barely graduating. *What the hell's wrong with me?* His courses were his ticket out of the Navy, and college could catapult him and Yuki to a much better life. Four years was enough, and he recoiled at the thought of being called a "Lifer." The Navy was flying professors onto the USS Midway from Chapman College in California to teach classes to young sailors such as himself in the PACE program—Program for Afloat College Education. The classes were held on the O-2 level just below the flight deck and within the pilot's ready rooms. Up there, they had large comfortable leather seats with swivel fold-up trays for the textbooks and notepads. Everything about the room was comfortable and resonated with complexity, intelligence, and university learning and experience. He loved it. He particularly enjoyed sitting there with his open book and open mind high up on the ship in front of a lecturing and passionate college professor, taking in the historic news of the world that he had missed out on in his limited schooling. It was there . . . there . . . up towards the light and just under the slick bulleted F-4 phantom planes that catapulted the highly trained university professionals off the steel decks of the Midway where he felt so far removed from the turmoil and the dark auto-pilot, high school mentality of the swarming spaces many decks below him.

Daniels lay back down and grabbed his Oceanography book, but as he did, the faint sound of an approaching jet buzzed into his ear. His attention suddenly turned to the F-4 Phantom, and he let go of the book. He knew he wasn't supposed to be here sun tanning on the fantail—the extreme aft end of the aircraft carrier during flight ops—but the hell with 'em, he thought. He had heard that the stress a pilot experienced from trying to land his plane, which has been described as a controlled crash, was even higher than what a soldier experienced in combat. So he knew that a pilot wouldn't even notice him as he struggled to contain his nerves while trying to land his plane at full thrust in the hopes of hooking one of the three arresting cables on the flight deck of the USS Midway.

This time, he thought, he would try to keep his eyes shut. The last time, when the jet was directly over him, the noise was so intense and explosive that it seemed as if the fighter was going to flame right into him.

As the jet neared, the buzz slowly gave way to a dull roar, then a heavy thunder, and then finally to an explosion that overwhelmed him and forced his eyes open once again—just in time to see the tail of the phantom zip past the start of the ship's runway, which wasn't very far above his head. The roar was actually painful, and he rubbed his ears. He then eyed the grey metal mass of runway that began just above him, and he wondered just how far away it and the flames of the jet were from his body.

He did a quick calculation. The fantail deck that he was lying on, which jutted out a bit past the runway, was part of the first deck of the carrier. This deck was called the hangar bay deck, for if he stood up and walked back into the ship, he would walk through a passageway and then step into a massive metal-clad cavern in the middle of the ship that was used to store and maintain planes and helicopters. The hangar bay height was about 17.5 feet in clearance, with another foot to the overhead or ceiling. That makes it 18.5 feet. Then add another 8 feet for the O-2 deck, which was the deck where all the pilot-ready rooms were, as well as the Captain's and Admiral's in port staterooms. This would then make the three-inch armored flight deck, the O-3 deck, close to 27 feet above his head. Now add another 15 feet or so for the plane, and that places 30 tons of flaming steel about 42 feet just over his head in the middle of the Indian Ocean.

Cool, he thought and smiled. The odds that one of the planes would come in too low and obliterate him in a fireball were pretty small. He shut his eyes again and focused on the far-off buzz of another phantom approaching. He'd try again.

As the plane neared, he could feel the sound ripple through his legs and up into his chest. Just a bit more, he thought, just a bit. He tightened his eyes and braced for the roar and vibration. But just as the sound ripped into him, something struck his right shoulder.

He opened his eyes. Leaning over him stood a Chief. His hands were on his hips, his eyes narrowed, and his mouth was opening and closing in flashes of yellowed teeth. But Daniels couldn't hear a thing due to the noise of the jet, and he could only watch the Chief's lips flare open and shut as the jet screamed just above them.

The sound soon subsided, and Daniels sat up and smiled. Though he couldn't remember his name, he recognized him. It was the Master Chief of the ship, and his office was right next to the fantail on the port side of the Midway.

"Hi, Master Chief."

"What the fuck's wrong with you! Get your ass out of here! Now!"

Daniels rolled and jumped to his feet, then bent over and picked up his towel, oil, book, and keys. "Sorry, Chief, just needed to get a little sun and some studying in. . . that's all."

The Master Chief stepped back, his eyes locked on the next phantom that was fast approaching. The Chief wasn't that tall, maybe a ball bearing or two shy of five foot six. But what he lacked in stature, he certainly made up in presence. His voice was resonant and yet seamy, as though he gargled each morning with JP-5 jet fuel. "You know," he said, "when I heard there was someone out here, at first, I

15

didn't believe it. I thought, what damn fool would kill himself over a little sun?"

"Sorry, Chief, I just thought . . ."

"You thought! I don't give a fuck what you thought! Get the fuck off my fantail! Now!"

Daniels nodded and quickly sidestepped the Chief and headed over towards the open door on the starboard side of the ship. But before he could slip through the door, the Chief suddenly yelled, "What division you in?"

Ignoring the question, Daniels quickly hopped through the opening. Then ran.

If the Master Chief put a call into Chief Saxton, he was a dead man. Saxton was already pissed off at him for the false security alarm that Daniels and his Tech had caused that morning while opening the division spaces. And to get a phone call from the Master Chief Petty Officer of the ship, the one man who had a direct line to the Captain of the ship, would put him over the edge—even pull him from the inspection team, the PRP, or Personal Reliability Program, and screw up his chances of taking any more college classes.

Daniels eyed the long passageway and realized he wouldn't make it. Noticing a hatch a few feet away, he quickly slid down the ladder, carefully cocking his head to the right to avoid hitting any metal from the lip of the hatch. It was a coop, a large berthing compartment where up to 60 men slept. It appeared empty, and he couldn't hear anyone nor the typical nighttime sounds he was accustomed to—radios, TVs, talking, snoring, etc. It was unusually quiet, so the men assigned there must work the day shift. The smell, however, was palpable—stale, with a hint of athlete's foot wafting up from boots hung up and hidden from view.

He raced to the other side of the coop and bounded up the ladder to the opposite passageway on the port side of the ship. Near the top, he stopped and stuck his head up, and scanned the passageway. Nothing. Only the typical splash of pipe, circular gauges, and massive bundles of coiled wire snaking down the length of the overhead.

He waited. Still nothing. He scurried up through the hatch and into the passageway. He made his way over to the door that entered the hangar bay. He stopped, peered in, and froze. The Master Chief was over on the port side by aircraft elevator number three. He was talking to a sailor, and he looked agitated.

Daniels retreated into the passageway and bolted over to a head, a bathroom—named for the toilet area in the very forward part, or head, of an old sailing ship. He quickly found an empty stall, shut the door, and sat down on the seat. This is perfect, he thought. It would buy him the time he needed. More than once, an empty stall came to his rescue! There was no way that he was going to piss off Chief Saxton twice in one day. Once was bad enough.

He settled in, put his oceanography book down on his lap, and opened it. May as well get in some studying time. But after a minute or two, he suddenly felt uneasy for some reason that he couldn't quite explain. He scanned the stall. It was solid aluminum, cheap and lightweight, with a flimsy high door. But no one was there outside the door, nor did he hear someone walk in. He was sure of it.

But something was wrong. A shiver suddenly swept down his spine, and the hair on the back of his neck stood up. He leaned forward again to listen but still didn't hear anything. But just then, a slight sound above him caught his attention. He looked up and froze.

A sailor, standing on the toilet in the next stall, was peering down at him! As their eyes locked, the sailor quickly disappeared.

You're kidding me, thought Daniels. *Of all the hundreds of damn stalls on the ship, I pick the only one with a damn Peeping Tom! What are the odds?*

Daniels started to panic, closed his book, and reached for the door, but the thought of running into the Master Chief quickly overrode his instinct. He settled back and then quickly scanned the sides. The aluminum that connected his stall with the next one didn't reach all the way to the floor. He could see the shadow of the sailor's boots. He leaned back and considered his options. Should he keep quiet, leave, or say something? A small movement from an empty screw hole to his right suddenly caught his attention. An eyeball was targeting him!

It then disappeared, and he could only see blackness.

Daniels started to panic now. His heart raced. What to do? Leave, stay put, yell? But at this thought, a hand suddenly materialized from beneath the side of the stall and touched Daniels' leg. *My God!*

Instinctively, Daniels grabbed his Case knife from his belt holster, flipped open the blade, and placed the razor-sharp edge on the sailor's exposed wrist. Neither one moved. Then the sailor's hand slowly slipped down and away from the blade and disappeared back into the stall.

Enough, thought Daniels, I'll take my chances with the Chief. He grabbed his book and bolted back into the passageway. It was empty. He wondered if he should report that sailor to the Master of Arms, the ship's police. Instances like this were sporadic on a ship. Still, if they did happen, or if someone was caught exhibiting any form of homosexual behavior, he heard that they would be immediately sent to see the Captain, bypassing the Executive Officer. They would be flown off the ship the next day. They would also be in handcuffs with an armed escort—the escort providing protection, as this type of behavior was not only frowned upon by the ship's crew but caused a lot of anger and even violence.

Daniels looked around and wondered where the Master of Arms office was. He knew it was in the aft part of the ship, not far from where he was, but its exact location could take a while to find. Also, to head down there right now could be trouble. What if the Master Chief was there reporting the actions of a stupid sailor sun tanning himself on the fantail beneath landing jets?

On second thought . . . no. Leave it be. Better get some supper and then get back to the forward SASS spaces where he worked during the day and prepare to take the magazine night temps with his tech, Stoker. Maybe if they got down to the weapons magazine early enough, they could fire up a joint and chill out.

Yes, a joint would be nice. He smiled. A nuclear weapons magazine is probably the safest place on the planet to smoke marijuana.

Journal of Joseph Taylor

25 Sept. 1977

I am neither in air nor on earth but sail the shifting boundary between. Flew in as a passenger on a mail cod from Diego Garcia early this morning and reported aboard the USS Midway (CV-41) at 0700 hours.

Must have fallen asleep before landing. Last thing I remember was the mail cod softly banking into a cloud and then seeming to fall forever through an ocean of white. Then intermittent images of darkness, massive pine swept mountains, and molten fire. Then the plane touched down in a controlled crash landing at sea—full thrust—hitting heavy the grit-sand deck of the carrier, engaging the arresting cable, abruptly waking me, fracturing my dream. Even now, pen moving, I can still feel the hard jolt and swift tremor through my fingers.

Given a list for checking in. Walked what seemed miles and miles through echoing passageways obtaining the appropriate signatures from the various departments. Weapons. Post Office. Personnel. Past countless compartments, offices, workrooms, fuel pipes, fire hoses, and an infinite network of electrical cables twisting across every overhead and bulkhead. Past the countless men hunched in grease-blotched shirts, over desks, equipment, engines, eyes flitting, yet strangely vacuous, hands nimble and automatic, hastened by the scheduled shift to sea.

Entering Medical, I smashed my shin on the low, steel lip of the door frame. An old Chief glanced up at my pained face, his stare empty and remote. He leaned from the bulkhead, his belly straining towards the deck. His face was thick and pink and buried in the starched collar of his pressed shirt. He took my check-in sheet, mumbling something incoherent, and scribbled his name. I hobbled out, the smell of isopropyl alcohol clinging to me and mixing with the lingering layers of machine oil and paint, floor wax, sweat, and other exotic extras emanating from each of the one thousand feet of the carrier.

Will have to wait a few days in order to go down into W-Division's work spaces where the ship's nuclear weapons are kept.

The Magazine

Petty Officer Second Class Daniels exhaled the smoke of his joint into the emergency blowouts of the ship's forward nuclear weapons magazine. The deck plugs beneath his feet seemed to shimmer. Thousands of them dotted the orange magazine floor before him like spots on a leopard rug. He took another hit from the joint as his eyes raced over the pitted surface of the deck. The shimmering intensified, vibrated, almost alive, each dot appearing and disappearing as if eyes, blinking and staring. Studying him. He glanced over at the 30MC, the ship's intercom system that connected this magazine to the Division Office and Chief Saxton two decks above him, then he swung around and exhaled the smoke into the grille. *Too many plugs*.

Each plug was threaded and had a large Phillips screw embedded in the middle to remove them so that bolts and chains could be screwed into the deck to tie down and secure the carrier-dropped nuclear weapons and various equipment. Glancing over row upon row of these plugs, he entertained the thought of how many holes filled the weapons magazine—*No, Albert Hall*. The holes suddenly reminded him of the Beatles' "four thousand holes in Blackburn, Lancashire." The THC was really starting to kick in, and he smiled. He stared blank-eyed at the small dots before him and pondered over their exact number. *Surely have to know, must know*. He mused that in a top-secret file somewhere in a top-secret room in top-secret Washington, there must be printed in regulation ink the exact number of holes in this nuclear weapons magazine floor, the number having been calculated long ago over steaming cups of black coffee and crushed cigarettes to account for maximum space efficiency. He started to laugh as he suddenly felt the overwhelming urge "to count them all." Feeling light-headed and buzzed, the perfect state for efficient hole counting, he thought, he started to count in the corner next to the blowouts, counting in groups of three as he made his way down the line over to the door.

When he reached hole 102, directly below the magazine's fire station, he cursed and frantically flipped his fingers up and down like a paper fan. The roach, forgotten, had burned his left index finger and thumb. He stared down at it, lying on top of a plug while rubbing his fingers against his pants in a futile attempt to smother the pain. *Stupid! You're gonna blow it.* The air reeked of marijuana. He looked to the blowouts and then picked up the roach. He filled his mouth with saliva, and by carefully aiming and refining, he targeted drool with a large glistening bubble, slowly downward until it hit the red tip and extinguished the fire.

He eyed the soggy roach for a moment. He then walked over to the emergency blowouts, which were used to discharge radioactive particles from the space he stood in, and with a casual flip of his wrist, jettisoned the roach into the large grille where the suction from the fans propelled it through hundreds of feet of pipe to a hole in the fantail of the aircraft carrier. He let the blowouts run for a while, feeling the strong rush of air cool over his face and hands. When he was certain that the magazine was clear of smoke, he pushed the red "off" switch and listened intently as the soft metallic echo ringing deep within the pipes subsided. He looked at his watch. *Gotta take the temps. I'm wasting time.* Daniels grinned as he thought of the Chief, who was only two decks above him, oblivious to the illegal activities taking place right under his feet in a nuclear weapons magazine. *Madman, if you only knew.*

The urge to light up had pulled at him. The incident on the fantail with the Master Chief and then the stranger in the head had stressed him out, but this morning's ass chewing by the Chief had really seared his nerves. Stoker, his technical assistant, who was now screwing around in the back of the same magazine, had accidentally set off a false alarm this morning while trying to open the spaces. He gave the wrong number code. Several division members, the Division Officer, and an entire mess deck filled with swarming sailors were all put face down on the deck by Marines—all armed with flak jackets and helmets and M-16s. And all itch'n to inflict as much pain as possible on a sailor, or squid, as they called them.

Since Daniels was senior and in charge, a petty officer second class, the Chief blamed him. But worse still, pot quenched his uneasiness with the cramped spaces, which always seemed to suffocate him. Press in on him. Daniels hated being confined to the steel caverns of the ship, the division offices, and deep, warm magazines, where he felt claustrophobic, *unaware*, cut off from the sun and the cool breeze many decks above. He was uneasy with the fact that he was forced to work in a small steel room that was situated beneath the ocean surface. Looking around at the painted white walls, he could almost sense all of that dark water pressing in against him. Covering him.

He forgot about counting the plugs beneath his feet as he made his way over to a stack of B61 thermonuclear bombs. Its textbook stats filled his head. *The B61 is a lightweight, multipurpose weapon used primarily for air strikes against cities or tactical targets. Dull silver in color, weighing approximately 800 pounds. It's between 10 and 500 kilotons.* Then there was the stack of B57s that stood to his right. *Weighing in at slightly over 500 pounds, two men could lift the warhead or tail of it if disassembled and separated. A generic weapon in the 10 to 20 kiloton range that could be used for almost anything: freefall high or low altitude burst, retarded, high or low altitude burst, ground burst, or water burst—its depth pressure fuse to be used against submarines or naval task forces.* Though not in this magazine, in the aft magazine, there was also the B43—*an aging monster, a one-megaton goliath used primarily for blockbusting cities and large targets. Solid white, it weighs in at an excess of 2000 pounds.*

Daniels stepped toward the stack of B57s. He resented working on them. *Hell, it was a forced position.* When he signed up for the Navy, he was excited that he would get to go to Beep School to study electronics. He was told by his recruiter that the rate he chose, Gunner's Mate Technician, would allow him to do this. The recruiter said that a GMT was a technical rate and that he would be working on the advanced electronics within missiles and the large guns on ships. This sounded exciting, and Daniels jumped at it, particularly since the rate would allow him a lot of leeway in choosing ships and getting the chance to be stationed overseas. However, by the time he was told in GMT "A" school that he was being trained to work on nuclear weapons, it was too late to switch schools. At first, he was excited by what he was learning. Top secret clearances, access to weapons and information, barb-wire seclusion, and secrecy from curious eyes glancing in from without—it was all high drama. But after graduation and transfer to the fleet, the "one out of many" exclusive club feeling slowly melted from him. The reality and horror of the weapons seeped into him like the radiation they emitted. In "A" school, he was lectured about tools, exposure rates, yields, components, and some of the effects of these weapons. He was shown slick charts with numbers on Nagasaki—73,884 deaths, 74,909 injuries, 11,574 houses burnt down, 1,326 ruined, 5,509 half-ruined, 50,000 partly damaged.

However, the books he checked out from the base library showed something different. From behind safe grainy black and white photographs, he stood witness to the pain of aftermath, where grandparents, mothers, fathers, children, and newborn kittens instantly vanished: cracked, charred concrete, twisted metal, a piece of fallen temple, campfire bodies, red bubbled flesh, a smashed wall clock, its hands rigidly pointing to 11:02 A.M., a shadow of a ladder and a man on a seared side of a building— the image having been set up, burned on wooden film, developed, and preserved in a local museum, a true nuclear photograph.

And he, Petty Officer Daniels, felt burdened with the maintenance and care of these devices to ensure that when called upon, they detonated and killed with the utmost efficiency.

Daniels inched closer to the stack of B57s, his elbow touching the cradle of the middle weapon. Everyone in W-Division handled this responsibility differently. Most did what they were told and refused to think about it. Others glorified it. Pictures of nuclear explosions hung

25

everywhere in the division's spaces. Morbid catalysts for impetuous remarks and lustful wide-eyed reverence. Each year, all W-divisions in the Navy mailed out to one another Christmas cards with a cheery "Merry Christmas" over a slick mushroom cloud. The last card he worked on himself, spending several days carefully drawing in a small skull within the smoke of the explosion. He felt a rush drawing it, particularly afterward, when everyone congratulated him on it. But thinking on it now, his stomach churned in disgust at how he could have been so taken in by the groupthink that glorified such weapons of horrific power and devastation.

Daniels placed his hand on the skin of the bomb. It was cool. The majority of the men simply numbed themselves to the weapons and the destruction they stood for. They just simply chose not to think about it. This "psychic numbing" resulted in a blatant disregard for safety, rules, and operating procedures—notably, the failure to keep a minimum distance and time away from the weapons resulted in high levels of radiation exposure. It almost seemed that the crazier they attached themselves to them, the more bragging rights they had, and the more respect from the others was instilled.

Daniels glanced out over the magazine. Heavy lead radiation shields capped each stack of bombs like manhole covers. Daniels wondered how many times he had seen his fellow shipmates not only sit and rest upon them but even sleep on them! By mandate, everyone in the division had radiation badges affixed to their belts. These badges were monitored monthly, and the exposure levels were recorded in each individual's medical record. If the Division Officer knew the real reason why some came back with levels so high that it was necessary to keep them out of the magazines for a while, shit would fly. Or would it? He sometimes thought they were all used as guinea pigs in some grand experiment to determine the long-term effects of radiation exposure on unsuspecting sailors—or rather, on "government property." He had been told many times that all military personnel were the property of the United States Government. If a terrorist group were to gain access to the spaces, the Marines had orders to retake them at all costs—hostages be damned. Sailors were men, were pawns, expendable, as with all military. They would happily blow his brains out onto the white bulkheads and then glorify what they did. By signing a six-year contract with the Navy, he had been relegated to the domain of statistics and numbers, of waste, prime for disposal by clean unseen hands, far, far removed from the dirt and grime of actual working logistics and tragic consequence.

Daniels ran his finger along the cool aluminum skin of the front of the B57 bomb. The warhead. *Deceptive. It's hot within, like Rogers... me.*

He hated many of the men entrusted to work on these warheads. The lying, cheating, fighting, psychotic behavior, and stupidity that took place within the confines of these spaces sickened him. So did his own contributions because it was hard to quit smoking pot when it was so freely available in his department.

He stepped back and studied the stack of B57s before him. The three of them lay bolted, one on top of the other, secure in their dark green handling gear. They were small, 9 ft. 10 in. long, a dull white like week-old snow. He felt the urge to touch them again. He saddled up to the bomb and let his fingers hop and skip along the side of a weapon, playfully aware of the cool aluminum surface that formed a graceful arc up to the blood-red nose cover protecting the radar within. Ah, such an accursed child, he thought as he touched its pale skin. The coolness of the weapon felt good against his burned fingers. He placed his mouth next to the weapon, took a breath, and exhaled. A thin layer of condensation bubbled up on the weapon's surface. "God, such elegance, power—enough to boil deserts into glass to drink the rain from."

The opiated Thai stick had fully gripped his mind now. He felt light, buoyant, as if he could float above the many rows of nuclear zeppelins bound before him. It wasn't fair. He really felt the urge to fly, to jettison his many encumbering thoughts, emotions, and physical body if need be, and lift off from the billions of plugs beneath his feet, up and through the many ocean-pressured decks above him, and burst free from this naval vessel, naval world, to a far-away crystal clear sky above some California college with lots of palm trees and smiling faces hurrying from lecture hall to lecture hall.

He suddenly thought of Yuki and that consummate smile of hers. He could see it now, shimmering just above him, softly calling to him. Pulling him. Up and away. But as quickly as her image surfaced, it vanished, and he looked up at the white overhead, littered with white padded pipes and slick steel tracks for hoists. She was several thousand miles away, and he was here. Now. Alone.

The thought of her not in his life after the Navy made him suddenly sick. He looked to the bulkhead and suddenly felt all of that water beyond it pressing in on the sides of the ship. On the compartment. On him.

No, she'll agree, he thought. *Must agree. Of course, she loves me.* He could feel it deeply, and he smiled at how he could even question it. Daniels felt suddenly animated. He now had another purpose and goal to work towards in his last six months. *Marriage.* He just needed to focus. To try and stay relaxed. If she is reluctant to marry and leave Japan, he'll just need to keep plugging away.

He looked at the rows of white bombs. They shimmered like ghosts. He muttered, "Bubble, bubble, to death, we struggle." He smiled. He had been warned away from marriage by several of the older sailors in his division, including the Chief. But marriage was more than just a balm to help ease the pain that lingers long after that first lance of love. Yes, it was definitely something more. *It's the flushed softness of the morning horizon—the cradle of the sun itself.*

He touched a B57, and it once again felt cool to the touch. *No, cold.* He could hear a hum and feel a slight vibration running up his legs from the ship's engines as he stood riveted before the weapons. The weapon vibrated slightly beneath his fingers. They all seemed to animate, to breathe in their green cradles. They were small creatures tangled in seaweed, like small white whales, hungry, struggling, blindly struggling to lose their bonds, their noses red and bloodied from lashing out at one another, at the sea floor, at the very earth herself.

25 Sept. 1977 (2005 hours)

Interesting first day. Until my full top secret clearance is approved, I'll have to be escorted down into and back out of the classified spaces—via a large steel booth welded to the bulkhead called "the cage," an armed entry/exit point extending out from the passageway bulkhead like a steel bubble, like the stretched skin of an expectant mother. Sailors walking down the ship's long second deck passageway must veer around it and keep moving when they enter the red security zone. They can't stop. I was told that at first, it was just a scream—a warning to move along. Then it's an alarm, with twenty armed Marines charging in, slamming the unfortunate sailor to the deck.

Just heard they had an accidental alarm this morning that put the Division Officer and a bunch of sailors on the deck. Chief Saxton was highly upset—that being the second false alarm in a week. He visited me after I had my sign-in sheet completed and ordered me to sit down on a trash can in the berthing compartment. I almost crushed it under my weight. Saxton's a large man—African American, six feet, strong grip, deep-set eyes. His voice has a raw edge to it, powerful and deep. It reeks of coffee and turbid nights. He told me not to "argue"" but to "listen" very carefully to whatever the Marines say while either in the cage or outside of it during an alarm because it's dangerous. Again, listen, listen. Do not argue, do not disobey, "listen." Not much different here than from boot camp. However, the consequences are more severe. UC Berkeley just seems so unreal to me now. Just wisps of Professor Wilmington, his physics, the bustle and lively chatter of Sather Gate, picking blackberries beneath it next to the creek—the fumble, the funeral. Professor Stevens' remark, warning—his insistence that if I dropped out, they wouldn't allow me back. How if I was determined to join the service, I should finish school and then enlist as an officer. But I needed out, needed time.

Anyway, I'm now confined to the damned coop, mostly cleaning. Visited the ship's library and checked out a few books. Also visited the weight room—crowded. The USS Midway is 6 days out from Mombasa, Kenya, a couple of months out from Japan, and exactly 16 days out from one of the strangest ceremonies I've ever heard of.

The Cage

The law of rare events. The thought shot into Daniels' mind, incongruous with a gun barrel quivering two inches from his head. *They tend to clump*.

Daniels stood within the "cage" with his hands flat against the bulkhead of the tiny steel compartment welded inside a seven hundred-foot second deck passageway. The pot he had just smoked in the magazine was still strongly affecting him. The red light above his head seemed to pulse as if alive, and the slight sounds, such as the shuffling of shoes and the exhalation of breaths slipping into his ears, seemed heightened and yet surreal, each flowing into the next in continuous waves that seemed all foam and no crest.

The cage jutted out into the passageway several feet, its round corners and steel sides enclosing Daniels, Stoker, and the Marine, its bulletproof mirrored windows reflecting the blur of sailors that shuffled past on their way to the mess deck, berthing, or to the hundreds of other compartments in the area. Daniels' face hovered five inches from the alarmed door that led down to his division offices and the weapons magazines. Beads of sweat bubbled out from the back of his hands, reflecting the red bulb above him. He could barely make out the face of his watch -- 2017 (8:17 p.m.), Sunday, 25 September. Laughter mixed with the chime of forks and knives against aluminum trays could be heard coming in from the ship's mess area through an open door in the passageway next to the cage. The strong, delectable aroma of steak drifted through the interior of the space. His stomach growled.

Daniels lifted his head slowly toward the Marine. Lance Corporal Collins remained motionless but for the pendular shifting of his .45-caliber pistol as it alternated from Daniels' head to Petty Officer Third Class Stoker's. Collin's bald head swiveled in the same delicate arc as his gun. Keeping his eyes fixed upon the two sailors, the Marine took a step back and flipped a switch above his desk. A soft click could be heard despite the clanging and skidding of boots against the decks of the USS Midway.

Meticulous, by the book, and damn redundant. Just had to push it, didn't you? Daniels knew the Corporal of the Guard in central had already alerted the ship's Marines. A minute ago, Stoker had again given the wrong number combination while closing the forward weapons spaces. *Why now? Again—the blame will fall on me.* This was the second alarm his Tech had caused today, the third this week, and the third time he would have to take the heat for Stoker's mistakes. *Shit.* He eyed his Tech.

Stoker was spread out a few feet away from him, half submerged within the shadow cast by Collins. His eyes were swollen, and they quivered. With his thin arms, wiry hands, and bloated belly, Stoker looked like a rat. A caged rat.

A movement outside the cage caught Daniels' attention. Through the one-way window, Daniels watched a large man enter the security zone and approach the cage. *Shit! He's back! Must have forgotten something.* He turned to Stoker and whispered, "The Chief."

"Keep your mouth shut," said Collins.

"Jesus, let me warn him," said Daniels. "There's still time."

The Marine grinned and placed the barrel of his gun against the back of Daniels' head. It was cold. "I don't give a rat's ass if you're a second class or not. I said to keep your mouth shut. Hear me?"

Daniels clenched his teeth. His eyes followed the clinking footfalls of the approaching Chief. The Chief stopped in front of the cage. He eyed the un-padlocked door. Appearing confident that the spaces were still open, he inserted his ID into the slot and then glanced at his watch.

Daniels smiled at his bad luck, his thoughts effervescent. The Chief resembled an old and sagacious oak, gnarled and hard—the kind of oak the eighteenth-century Royal Navy had entrusted to lay down as the keel, the backbone, for an immense 120-gun ship of the line of the first rate. His rust-stained eyes seemed to shimmer in the dim light, to stare straight at the deck as if nailed in place. His dark brown arm swung low past his barreled belly. His right arm lay rudder straight against his side, his fist tapping his thigh, an action he only carried out while waiting to enter. His gaze was riveted to the mirrored cage, which extended into the ship's main passageway like a monstrous steel cyst. *Must suspect something's wrong by now. Shit, he's going to be pissed.*

Daniels stretched and leaned upright against the armored watertight door. He could hear Collins shift as well, then sit down, taking in and expelling short, fast breaths. By now, he was getting used to loaded guns pointed at his head, but he worried that one might be held by a trigger-happy Marine who'd get a rush out of blowing some sailor's brains out of his skull and onto the bulkhead. The grunts always joked about the possibility with a smile, and he wondered how many deep down, from the pit of their boots, would actually do it if given a chance. He looked at the quivering shadow of the .45 on the bulkhead, a black blade that repeatedly cut into his silhouette, and decided that Collins was unquestionably a risk.

Daniels turned his head slowly in a circle, stretching the muscles of his neck, his eyes scanning the bulkhead next to him, then following a huge cable as it coiled up to the red bulb hanging hypnotic like a great serpent's head, then rotating to the window, stopping at the Chief. He tensed. The Marine and the guns didn't frighten him half as much as the man who stood before him on the other side of the glass and steel, the man everyone—

"Hit the deck!" The command from one of the ship's Marines blasted its way through the passageway. *Shit, they're here.*

The clatter and clamor of falling trays, utensils, and men flew from the dining hall as the Marines charged down the second deck passageway and set themselves precision-like throughout the mess deck, compartments, and passageways that led to and surrounded the cage.

"Goddammit." It was barely a whisper. The Chief drew out his arms, took in a heavy breath of air, turned his head towards the cage, and settled his large bulk on the red steel deck. He lay flat, hands and feet outstretched, head directed toward the mirrored cage, eyes tight and focused, as if he'd melt the steel to get at the two figures within. Daniels thought he could make out a faint growl escaping from the Chief's lips over the scuffle of military boots.

Silence.

Daniels leaned over toward the window to give himself a better view.

A quick movement near a hatch in the passageway caught Daniels' attention. A well-built Hispanic Marine stood crouched, his M-16 pressed firmly against his flak jacket like an infant at its mother's breast.

The Marine leaned forward and scanned the security zone to see if the area was secure. Satisfied, he fingered his rifle and carefully made his way up to Chief Saxton. The Marine stopped, his boot an inch from the Chief's hand, but the Chief ignored him.

The Marine understood the game and played it well. Daniels knew he was aware that it was another false alarm, as did the Chief, but divine regulation and procedure dictated, and Marine spirit did the rest. The Marine searched the Chief with his eyes for any hidden weapons or threats and then lightly stepped forward, like a wolf sensing prey, keeping the gun barrel pointed up and towards the cage.

Daniels and Collins watched the tip of an M-16 inch up past the bottom of the window. The barrel hole, as black and ready as an ink well, vibrated back and forth in tight circles as the Marine crouched hidden against the steel side. Collins turned to Petty Officer Second Class Daniels, "Posse's here."

"Delta one, all secure?" The Marine screamed up at the cage.

Lance Corporal Collins stood up, looked intently around the cage twice, paused, and then screamed, "Affirmative." Daniels smirked. *Unbelievable. Trace to retrace. The game goes on.*

The Marine stood up. He cupped his hand to the glass, blocking the

35

light, and peered in at Daniels. His nose spread flesh flat against the glass, his eyes large and milky as they peered within. Seeing that Collins was not being held at gunpoint, he turned and yelled, "All clear," to the contingent of Marines crouched throughout the corridors like Pitbulls. A chain reaction of shouts filled the air as each Marine bellowed "Stand down" and rose up.

The Marine turned to the passageway door and scanned the tangle of bodies strewn about the mess deck. Sailors climbed to their feet. Typical Marine, thought Daniels, as he watched him clear out with the rest of them.

The Chief rose and brushed off his uniform with precise, short swipes. He glared at the cage for a second, spun around, and left. Daniels' uneasiness deepened. Since the Midway took to sea from Yokosuka, the sociability and tolerance of the Chief had slowly corroded like iron in the long passages of time and elements. *Tempest and sea. Eating into his gut, the churning slick blue lining of life, no longer absorbing but absorbed.* It was rumored that when Saxton was promoted to chief, he stopped playing cards, quit all gambling, and started playing solitaire alone, against himself.

Collins tapped Daniels on the arm with the phone. Daniels swung around, grabbed it, and placed it to his ear.

"Hello?" said Daniels. A few seconds of silence passed. "I said hello."

"Yo," came the reply from the other end. "Go ahead."

"This is the PO, Gunner's Mate Technician Petty Officer Second Class Daniels. I would like to engage the alarms to forward security zone one."

"Okay, Daniels, we'll try again, standby."

Daniels clenched the phone handle. The remark carried a sarcastic bite. He closed his eyes for a second and then reopened them, focusing past the bars to a long pipe that seemed to sag down from the overhead. His head felt suddenly heavy, and his pulse picked up. THC usually calmed him, but now, suddenly, he could almost feel anger

36

seep through his body like gasoline through a rag. He looked up to the red bulb above him; its heat seemed to intensify the mood. *How can so many things go so wrong in just one week?* As if in answer, the light flickered in the cage, and the words of his father once again sounded off. *"They tend to clump."*

Images flared before him. A sea captain's house on Pleasant Street in Dorchester. A tall chestnut tree rising up from the front, its branches fanning the pointed four-windowed tower or widow's walk. He could see his father showing him the Geiger counter assembled from spare parts in the tiny rock basement of the 130-year-old house in Boston's suburb. A single bulb swayed above the cluttered workbench, sending light creeping toward the corners. A rusted water main sagged down from cobwebbed beams and ran into the rock wall beside them.

Explaining the physical principles to him, his father stressed the importance of the Law of Rare Events. To demonstrate, he turned the Geiger counter on and made Daniels listen carefully to the pattern of the clicks.

Click...Click,   Click...Click...Click,   Click...Click,   Click, Click...Click, Click, Click, Click...Click...

Daniels glanced up at his father's straight nose and intense eyes, a steamy blue, bloodshot, it seemed, from the furnace of thoughts within. His father asked that he describe the pattern. After several attempts, Daniels gave up, lowering his head.

"They tend to clump, don't you see? They clump," he said. "You will never hear a Geiger counter go click, click, click, click, at even-spaced intervals. It's random. Nothing is perfect. Nothing. If a plane crashes in Chicago one week, another might crash soon after the first. The same with train wrecks, earthquakes, bad luck, or any other thing. They are completely separate, yet linked by this law."

He reached down with his right index finger and raised his son's chin, who stared at the floor. "Furthermore, small variations in input could lead to major variations in output. Do you understand?"

His father leaned forward. Daniels instinctively eased back, slightly unbalanced. His father continued, his tone softening.

"The build-up of snow on a mountain reaches a critical point where something such as vibrating molecules from shouting could trigger an avalanche. From sharp ice to soft man to abstract wisps of knowledge, all rise and fall in the flow of order and chaos. Do you hear me? You must be able to see this underlying order. Events not only clump but pave the way for larger events to catalyze and unfold at a magnitude exponentially larger. If you grasp these concepts—listen to me—if you grasp these concepts, you will understand the intricate workings of a chaotic world, of society, of *events* in society, of *nature* herself, and how she works, how she speaks, how she can move *with* you—not against. Do you see?"

Daniels' eyes met his father's. For a brief second, both pairs held tight—one trying to impart vision, reason, and desire into the makeup of a chaotic world; the other, trying to share a moment, an understanding of heart—*coalescence*. His father sensed his son's perplexity and turned away.

His father marched over to the wooden staircase, his back straight, his head up high. He grabbed the wooden ball on the rail with his left hand and stopped as if he had forgotten something, something important. But he continued his ascent, finally disappearing into the enclosed stairwell, not once looking back, leaving his son staring at the cracks running together on the cold cement beneath his feet. That was twelve years ago when he was nine. The years had compressed into one big...

"Daniels?"

...*headache.*

"Answer me. Seven?" the voice on the phone demanded.

Seven. Seven. God, the day's number is twelve. Seven plus what is twelve? "Five," replied Daniels. Stoker, now leaning against the door, avoided his eyes. It was still hard to believe that Stoker had given the wrong number. *He should have looked at his number tables in his pocket notepad. What the hell was that moron thinking?*

"Affirmative."

"Great, can you please alarm Mag one and two and the forward cage."

"Now, just hold a minute. I need to speak to the Tech first. We sure don't need *three* surprises today, do we?"

"Sorry," said Daniels.

He handed the phone over to Stoker, who pulled out his pad to Daniels' relief and responded correctly this time.

Stoker handed the phone to the Marine and shuffled out from the cage. As Daniels turned to follow, his eye caught the faint outline of letters penciled onto the door that led down into the spaces. He peered closer, trying to read the scribbled words. He couldn't make out the first line but recognized the next three. "I am the way to a forsaken people. I am the way into eternal sorrow. Abandon all hope ye who enter here."

Someone has a sense of humor. He turned, walked out into the passageway, and headed down to the coop, trying to get some sleep; his mind on the ass-chewing he was sure to get in the morning. The Marine slammed the door shut behind Daniels, the echo blasting out, resonating through his bones.

26 Sept. 77 (0735)

Just came back from breakfast with some of the guys—got the lowdown on the division and on everyone. But had to take some medicine, courtesy of sick bay, to alleviate a case of sickness from the heavy seas this morning. I don't know if I can get used to the perpetual motion of the ship. Between this and the scurrying men, mountains of machines, and endless compartments, it seems at times worse than home. Was told by the Chief that in a few days, I would be fine— should be lucky I wasn't assigned to a small boy (destroyer). The motion there is worse. Took a walk to the stern before breakfast. It was nice, my first chance to really clear my head since reporting aboard. The waves peaked and pitched, the strong wind throwing streams of foam and bubbling spray up into the sky. Two screaming gulls beat the air and rode the currents, and shimmered across the horizon. I watched as one of our tiny escort destroyers rose up on the crest of a wave and then plummeted down into the trough as if swallowed, almost disappearing from view. For an instant, only a gray dot vibrated on the white-capped sea, then gradually grew, stretching outward and elongating forward, spitting into recognizable naval form. The sailors on board her must be strapped to their bunks at night in seas such as this. The Midway, huge, plows right through.

She is just over a thousand feet long and displaces over 65,000 tons. A floating city. Her stats are impressive: Her electrical power could serve a population of one million, and her fuel supply could heat 3,000 homes for a year. She has twelve conventional boilers, which churn out 200,000 horsepower to turn four twenty-two-ton apiece propellers. She has 80 aircraft, 2,000 compartments, 2,000 electric motors, 1,500 telephones, 200 miles of pipes, 3,000 miles of copper conductor, 4.5 miles of fire hose, 2.23 million gallons of fuel, 1.3 million gallons of jet fuel, and produces 240,000 gallons of fresh water daily. To feed her crew of 4,500, over 13,000 meals are served every day. Daily food requirements are 1,000 loaves of bread, 5,000 pounds of vegetables, 4,500 pounds of meat, 20,000 pounds of dry provisions, and 3,000 pounds of potatoes. She also carries in her magazines more firepower than all the bombs dropped in World War II.

Taylor

"And another thing," said the Chief, his thick eyebrows weaving together, "If you're so determined not to show any leadership, you can forget your dream of college—you'll never make it. The only place you're heading to now is back to Petty Officer Academy."

Daniels shut his eyes. The academy was the last thing he wanted to see: Petty Officer Towers—his mustache perfectly trimmed, his shoes shined to a mirror finish, the hair above his small, pink forehead greased back in thick grooves, one arm behind his strained and straight back, pointing to charts with giant bold letters screaming: "LEADERSHIP," "ACCOUNTABILITY," "RESPONSIBILITY," "ATTITUDE," "PERSONAL GROOMING," etc., etc., ad nauseam.

"Did you hear me?" The Chief put down his coffee cup and took a step forward. Daniels opened his eyes.

"Yes, sir. Petty Officer Academy."

"What did I tell you about calling me, sir? Do I look like a fucking officer?"

"No, Chief. Won't happen again."

Saxton turned and picked up his coffee. "I don't want to hear about another alarm. And I don't care who caused it. Now get the hell out of here, and that storeroom had better be spotless."

"Yes, sir, I mean Chief." Daniels turned, eyes shut, his back and arms tensing for a backlash. None came, just a guttural growl and then the sound of the Chief gulping the rest of his cup. Daniels stepped out of the office and, without turning his head, walked by the open door of the division pub room. Though he couldn't see them, he could feel the stares cutting into him from the men within and could hear the chuckling of Stoker and another second class named Rogers.

"Stoker!" screamed the Chief. "Get your ass in here."

Daniels smiled as he climbed the ladder, glad that he was first. The Chief's temper always hit a high on the last person to have his ass chewed. Daniels stepped up onto the next deck, rounded the corner, walked past the division's bathroom, and then entered the cage. He exchanged his badge for his ID card and then headed down to the coop. He wanted to get an hour of rest before cleaning out the storeroom below M-3, the aft weapons magazine.

He jumped down the ladder to the coop and walked toward his rack. The air was cool, the light dim. As usual, the smell of sweat and old socks and open boots overwhelmed the cramped compartment. The racks were stacked three high on both sides of the main aisle and end-to-end along it. Space was short and overcrowded, and aisles were barely negotiable. There were no walls or partitions, only one dark, cramped space. To Daniels, it was a riveted tomb. Ever since Rogers slipped him a picture book of submarine warfare in World War Two, Daniels walked differently throughout the ship, an eye always looking to nearby hatches and ladders. It was the second week after reporting aboard that Rogers checked the book out of the ship's library and placed it beneath his pillow. The book was littered with graphic, grainy black-and-white pictures taken by trophy U-boat commanders through their periscopes. They showed ships sinking in seconds, ships not unlike his own, each with vast steel spaces and an affinity for filling, for water, for death, filling to the brim with hundreds of submerged desperate sailors with no numbered chance, men like himself, like Petty Officer Second Class Daniels, drowned and crushed in collapsing steel spiraling a mile down to the soft sand in an immense, cold ocean. *Damn him.*

Daniels turned from the main aisle and walked toward his rack, his face toward the deck, but he was suddenly startled by a large hand that dropped in front of him, a black king chess piece clutched tightly between two white fingers hanging an inch from his brow.

"Chess?"

Daniels stepped back, startled by the deep yet sonorous voice. He looked up. It was the new guy, Taylor. He lay outstretched on his rack, smiling, a chessboard before him, an open book, *Winning Chess,* to his right. His herculean 6-foot 4-inch frame shifted, and the metal struts creaked. His body seemed to swallow up the bed. The mass of muscle in his arms bristled as he shifted and sought comfort, and his slick shaved skull formed a pocked pale dome whose muscled undulations twitched and flickered in the light around his ears and hairline. His thick jaw hung slack as he scanned the racks around him and then shut as he faced Daniels.

"I'm not really up for it right now." Daniels stepped toward his rack.

"A good game of chess will clear the head," said Taylor.

Daniels stopped. "I'd need a million of 'em."

"No, just one." Taylor leaned forward. "Provided you can win, of course."

"Don't even try. I've got Chief on the brain."

"You mean ass."

"Jesus, you just got here. Where'd you hear that?"

Taylor shook his head. "Word spreads quick. Particularly when the Division Officer and Chief get put on the deck."

"Yeah, well, screw 'em. It wasn't my fault."

Taylor rolled his huge body over on his side. "One game?"

"What makes you think that I even know how to play?"

"Again, word."

"I don't know," said Daniels, "I'm tired."

Taylor leaned over and extended the chess piece to Daniels, his eyes wide, his head gesturing to climb up. "Activate the intellect, the body follows. I hear you're really into that."

"Where'd you hear that?"

"Again, word," said Taylor.

"So what's it to you?"

"A chance to practice against someone challenging."

"Why not Roberts or Sanchez?" said Daniels.

"Do you see anyone around?" said Taylor, his hand sweeping out before him.

"Besides," said Taylor, "Roberts wasn't shit."

"My God, you just arrived, and you already played him?"

"Yes. But he said he gives you a run for his money."

"Bullshit. He's never beaten me."

"Didn't say he did."

Daniels took in a deep breath.

"One game?"

Daniels looked up at Taylor. Taylor nodded, gesturing to hop up.

"One, huh?"

"One."

Daniels kicked off his boots and hopped up onto the empty rack next to Taylor's. They placed the chessboard so that it straddled the two racks. Taylor handed Daniels the white pieces, and they set up the board. Daniels studied his men.

"It's your move, just in case you weren't sure," smiled Taylor.

"Fuck you."

"Just checking."

Daniels picked up a pawn, then set it back down. He bit his lip, not sure what opening move to make.

"Where you from?" asked Taylor.

Daniels looked up. "Boston. What about you?"

"LA."

"LA, huh? What brings you here? I heard you played football at college but left before you finished."

"Fuck," whispered Taylor, his head dipping down.

"Must be true." Daniels smiled.

"That's none of anyone's fuck'n business."

"Cool it. The grapevine's nothing but bitter leaves and sour grapes anyway." Daniels took in a deep breath, "So, what university did you go to?"

"Does it matter?"

"Just curious." He moved his king's pawn up two squares. Taylor did the same.

"So I heard you're taking a college class," said Taylor. "What is it?"

"Oceanography."

"Peace of cake."

"Actually, it is," said Daniels. "Can you imagine a better place to take it?" Daniels swept his arms towards the water beyond the bulkheads.

"Actually, yes."

"Really. . . better than here?"

"I said yes."

They both studied the board for a moment, and then Daniels shook his head and chuckled.

"What's so funny?' said Taylor.

Daniels eased back and smiled. "You."

"Me?"

"What'd you study?" asked Daniels. "Football?" Daniels moved his knight three squares above his King's Bishop.

"Actually, it was physics." Taylor also moved his knight three squares above his Queen's Bishop. "UC Berkeley."

"Berkeley?" said Daniels. "That's where my father went! He wouldn't shut up about it. He loved it there." Daniels looked at Taylor in what would only amount to awe and a bit of pride.

They both studied the board, each lost in thought. After a long silence, Daniels finally spoke. "You're telling me . . . that you went to Berkeley and studied physics. And now you're here . . . here." He looked around the coop. "Playing chess with me . . . an enlisted squid? I don't fuck'n believe it."

"Believe what you want."

"Belief is a luxury around here. It's knowing that counts," said Daniels.

"Ok, then what's Newton's third law?" asked Taylor.

Daniels shook his head. "Please. I thought you'd ask me something hard."

46

"Well?"

"Something exerts a force upon something, that second something exerts a force upon the first. The forces are equal and, ahh, opposite." He smiled.

"Hmm, we've got us a real Encyclopedia Brown here."

"Encyclopedia Brown? I loved Encyclopedia Brown!"

Taylor eyed him.

"Honestly, when I was just a kid," said Daniels, "there was nothing better than curling up with one of his stories and trying to figure out who did what and when."

"Just a kid? Moved on to slightly bigger mysteries, huh?"

"Yeah, actually . . . I did. Poe, Doyle, Melville, Darwin . . ."

"Melville?"

"Yeah, love him. My favorite's . . ."

"*Moby-Dick.*"

"Exactly," said Daniels, excited. "That book blew me away. You read it too?"

"Of course," said Taylor. "Why do you think I'm here."

For a second, they eyed one another, and Daniels suddenly felt a sense of deep joy in seeing that Taylor seemed to feel that same way about his love for Melville. Though Taylor didn't show it, Daniels could sense that Taylor was excited.

"My God . . . so what was is like at college? Hell, at Berkeley! That must have been so cool to be with so many brilliant students and professors on such a beautiful campus. My dad went on about how he used to just sit next to Strawberry Creek not far from Sather Gate and read—far removed from everything."

"Actually, it's not what you think."

"Bullshit. Don't tell me that. Look, look around you . . . Berkeley. . . fuck, any school would be heaven compared to this shit."

"Again, it's not what you think."

"Then, what?"

"If you think that everyone will be having hourly intellectual

47

conversations on the state of matter, the evolutionary rise of consciousness, and our '*place* in an ever-expanding universe,' you're crazy."

"I don't believe it," said Daniels. "My father told me—"

"Your father?"

"Yeah, my father, a biology professor. He studied biology at Berkeley for grad school."

"Grad school? Impressive. That's where I wanted to end up." Taylor lowered his head and shut his eyes for a moment. "Then what you doing here?" he suddenly asked, raising up.

"I don't know. What the fuck are you doing here?" Daniels smiled.

"You know, you're a slow player," said Taylor, suddenly shifting in his rack. As Daniels picked up his knight, a loud clambering shot into the coop as Stoker bounded down the ladder and shuffled up to them. At the sight of Stoker, Daniels frowned.

"Daniels, it's time."

"Bullshit. We have almost an hour."

"Nope. The Chief just told me, quote, 'Get his fuckin ass down and clean that room, *now*.'"

Daniels looked over to Taylor. "Shit."

"We'll finish tonight," said Taylor.

Daniels slipped off the rack, put his boots back on, and followed Stoker up the ladder. As he stepped onto the mess deck and walked forward, he could hear Taylor's deep voice drift up and out of the coop. He was singing.

26 Sept. 77 (2243)

Interesting second day. Mixed feelings. I haven't seen the insides of the magazines yet, and not sure how I'd react to finally seeing a real weapon. Hope the radiation badges give us an accurate reading. If they are even slightly higher than what they told us in "A" school, then I'm not long for here. I should have backed out when they finally told me at the start of school what I'd be working on. No one knew, and I didn't want to be the first to become a lowly Boatswain's Mate, swabbing decks and painting for four years if I objected. The stories they told of that one sailor who drew a peace sign in the letter "O" of the Nuclear Weapons Training Group Pacific sign when he found out what he'd be actually doing. They immediately shipped him off to Nam as a front gunner on a PBR. He was killed shortly after. They say to trust them, but I don't. Can't. Of all the rates in the Navy to enter and I end up in this one. What irony. I need to bide my time, put in my four years, and then get the hell out of here. Somehow back to school.

Went down to the division offices this afternoon for five hours, studying and signing off my orientation and training booklets. I found them to be fascinating. I particularly like the sections on security, and yet it seems funny as to the many precautions taken to prevent unauthorized entry into the spaces. But are this many Marines necessary, with this much firepower? An aircraft carrier seems so removed from a terrorist or fanatic's threat.

There was another alarm last night in the cage. Again it was Daniels. He blames his Tech. As usual, the niceties of all new environments prove to be paper thin after a few days as the lower layers seep up and solicit attention. A few strange individuals in this division. Stoker for one. He's small and skinny and has shifty eyes. They're constantly moving as you talk to the man. His twitching nose is buried a foot up Rogers' ass.

Rogers is the cool-collected "leader" of the pack. He laid into me today because I'm a "wog." Not a "shellback" like him. I understand that the closer we approach the eleventh of October, the more excited

49

everyone will become. Particularly the shellbacks. For most of the wogs, it's more like terror. What an exotic ceremony. "Crossing the line—the earth's equator. The more I hear about it, the more strange and surreal it all seems. If I wrote home about it, no one would believe it. Nor should they. I still can't imagine a United States Aircraft Carrier, all her "shellback" officers, captain and admiral included, and shellback enlisted men, dressing up as pirates, flying a skull and crossbones from the radar tower, setting up a royal court—complete with "beauty queen"—and then sending thousands of wog officers and enlisted men through a ceremony that would gross out most college fraternities. Strange. But interesting.

Just finished my first game of chess with Daniels, who I hear is also a wog. Began the game earlier but had to postpone it till tonight. It was a good battle, but I won. I am looking forward to playing more chess with him. He's smart, and he's really excited about getting out of the Navy and going to school.

Me too. But not sure if they'd let me back.

Just started Conrad's Heart of Darkness.

The Trial of Sword in Steel

"Pick it up," said Rogers, his grin razor sharp. "Should be nothing to a man your size." His dark black hair stood up straight and oiled above his wide forehead. He leaned his thick five-foot, 11-inch frame against the bulkhead in M-3, the aft SASS spaces on the Midway, his eyes targeting Taylor's. They both stood next to a tail of a B-57 bomb that housed the warhead's parachute. A trainer. Daniels and Stoker stood off to the side watching.

"One minute. That's all. Every newbie must do it, or at least try," said Rogers.

Taylor put his hand on Roger's shoulder and looked at the B-57 tail. "That ain't shit. But don't fuck with me."

"Watch your tone, seaman," said Rogers, removing Taylor's hand, a slight tremor in his fingers. "I ain't fucking with you. Everyone in this division did it. Ain't that right, Daniels?"

Daniels shook his head in agreement.

Daniels remembered Rogers telling him he had to do it, and after a few sneers from everyone, he finally bent down into the "hump position" and lifted it a few inches from the deck. He held the one hundred and twenty-five-pound tail aloft for a few seconds and actually felt great for doing it afterwards. But why he was asking Taylor to do it was a mystery. Everyone could see that Taylor would simply lift it like it was a bag of balloons. Had to be a power play, which Rogers excelled at.

"Look at it this way, university man; it's an initiation of toil and sweat into the mysteries of the nuclear rate—the high priests, the 'Lightkeepers of Leviathan.'"

Taylor smiled and shook his head. "Bullshit."

"You game or chicken shit?"

Taylor straightened up, his huge chest expanding out. Rogers instinctively leaned back but then inched forward.

"Ok, if that's what you want," said Taylor.

Together, Rogers and Taylor stood the tail up on end, and then, looking at his watch, Rogers said, "Go." With an ease that startled Daniels, Taylor dipped and clenched and rose up in one smooth motion. It appeared to Daniels as if the tail had just floated up.

Taylor set it down and then backed away from it.

"Whoa, not so fast," said Rogers. "That wasn't shit. Everyone, even Daniels here, done that." Stoker smiled.

Daniels ignored the comment.

Rogers continued. "What very few in the history of the rate have been able to do, however, is what's called 'The Trial of Sword in Steel.'"

"Wow, really impressive," said Taylor, smiling.

"Ain't fuckin round. It's why we're really here."

Taylor looked over to Daniels again, who again nodded in agreement.

"Whether one fails or not," said Rogers, "everyone must at least attempt to lift a 300-pound warhead. To fail to do so would shame not only the division but all lightkeepers around the nuclear world."

Taylor leaned back, his eyes rolling, and laughed, deep and easy.

"Hey," said Rogers. "This ain't funny, seaman." He signaled Daniels to help him out.

"He's right, Taylor," said Daniels reluctantly. "Everyone's got to try."

Taylor straightened up but still smiled. "You guys are fuck'n nuts."

"Watch the insubordination, Seaman," said Stoker. "Don't want to start with your ass at Captain's Mast, now do you?"

"Sure," said Taylor. "And the charge? Refusing to lift a nuclear warhead with my hands? I'm sure that will go over great with the Captain."

"Don't get smart with me, Seaman," said Stoker sheepishly. "It's only a trainer." He puffed up his petulant chest and stepped forward and backward like a Chihuahua trying to best a bulldog. "Remember, there can be made plenty of opportunities for you to see the Captain."

"Are you threatening me, Stoker?" Taylor loomed up before him. Stoker quickly stepped back, staring at the deck.

"Taylor, let it alone," said Daniels, stepping forward. "Everyone's done it. Or at least tried."

"That's right, Seaman," said Rogers. "But no one has succeeded in this division, ever. But me. They were all pussies."

Taylor eyed him.

"You see, Seaman," said Rogers. "The Trial of Sword in Steel's a test of blood. Of nobility. Worthy of only a king. You, if you can, must lift a B57 warhead and keep it aloft for three minutes."

"Fuck you," said Taylor.

"What's up, can't hang, Seaman?" said Rogers.

"If Sanchez or the Chief were to walk in," said Taylor, "and see me holding a warhead up, even a trainer, then I *would* be seeing the Captain, maybe even the brig or prison."

"What are you scared of," said Rogers. "It's a rite of passage. Only cowards wouldn't try it."

"What'd you say?" Taylor stepped forward, his fists clenched at his sides.

Rogers jerked back but then, suddenly gaining confidence, stepped forward, his eyes on Taylor's hands. "Holster those, Seaman." He then pointed to his second-class chevron, his finger twitching. "See this. You better respect it, wog. Because if you don't, we'll have two beauty queens in the crossing-of-the-line ceremony. Hear me? You and . . . and—" He looked over to Daniels. "Someone else in this division."

Daniels suddenly felt sick. He couldn't imagine they'd grab *him*.

"Sorry, won't do it." Taylor turned and slowly walked toward the door of the magazine, his fingers clenching and unclenching.

"Stop!" said Rogers. "I mean what I said. You're not so big that ten of us, including Sanchez and Chief, couldn't tie you down, shave every hair on your body, and put a dress on you for wog queen. And you should know by now, Seaman, that ain't an idle threat."

Taylor turned and looked at Daniels. Daniels nodded.

"But if you were to lift that warhead," Rogers continued, "and prove that you are indeed a king and not a queen, then I'd say it would be just someone else in a dress strutting his stuff alone." He smiled and glanced over to Daniels.

"Fuck you, Rogers," said Daniels. "I ain't a seaman you're talking to."

"Who said I was talking about you?"

"Cut the shit," said Daniels.

"Remember," said Rogers. "There's no rank on that day. You being senior to me by just the hair of a rat's ass won't mean nothing."

"Fifty bucks says you can't lift it," chipped in Stoker.

"There you go," said Rogers. "Additional incentive."

"Fuck you, Stoker," said Taylor, suddenly walking forward, eyebrows knotted. "Keep your money." Taylor approached the training warhead in its handling gear next to the tail. He stared down at the warhead, his eyes gleaming in intensity.

"No, not the trainer," said Rogers, smiling. "For a true king, you must lift the real thing." He pointed toward a live warhead set up on a stand next to the tool bench. Everyone turned and looked. The warhead stood up vertically from the deck in its handling stand, large steel bands running round it at the top and bottom, securing it in place for an operation to replace a component within. The dull white finish of its surface blended in with the off-white paint of the magazine wall.

"No, don't do it," said Daniels. "Now he's bullshitting. Everyone used the trainer."

"Bullshit," said Rogers. "I didn't."

"Bullshit yourself," said Daniels, "I'm not going to allow it. Period."

"What, are both you chi—"

"Let it go, Daniels," said Taylor suddenly. "Trust me. I can lift it and set it down gentle as a baby." He turned and stared at the real warhead. Daniels noticed a slight tinge of fear surface in Taylor's eyes, but as soon as it showed, it disappeared.

"It's too dangerous," said Daniels. "If it slipped, we'd all be—"

"Shhh," said Taylor, putting his finger to his mouth. "Trust me. We need to shut this fucker up."

"I said no," said Daniels. "It's the trainer or nothing. I don't care if Rogers says he used a live one or not; I will not allow it—period!"

Taylor nodded, and both Rogers and Stoker lowered their heads. Daniels eyed the training warhead next to him. It's two, thirty-inch suspension lugs lay folded neatly into its white skin. The ready/safe and access windows stared out like two twisted black eyes.

Rogers and Stoker quickly undid the clamp holding the trainer vertical; then, both walked behind Daniels towards the door to keep an eye out just in case someone showed.

The warhead of the trainer stood up straight on the deck before them. Daniels stared at the large sloping surface, seeming to angle down and cut into the stretch of deck plug steel at Taylor's feet. Taylor took a huge breath, bent down, wrapped his arms tightly around the white skin of the warhead, set his legs firmly, counted to three, and then lifted.

The warhead rose quickly, and Daniels was surprised at how easily it elevated. But what surprised him even more was the image before him of the B57 warhead cradled like a baby in the arms of a man—its aluminum radiating coldly against Taylor's huge chest—an image no civilian on the planet has ever seen. Daniels stood amazed, watching the huge muscles expand on Taylor's massive arms. The seconds ticked on, and though the tremendous weight showcased the strain of muscle, only a thin bead of sweat broke out across Taylor's forehead. His face remained strangely calm and devoid of any struggle.

As Daniels called out thirty seconds to go, a voice suddenly shot out from behind him—"What the fuck you doing!"

Taylor and Daniels turned. It was Sanchez, the leading petty officer of the division. A first class. He was a big man himself, about 6 foot, two hundred pounds. He had short black hair and a carefully trimmed mustache that hid a small scar just above his lip.

Stoker and Rogers were surprisingly nowhere to be seen, somewhere in the back of the magazine, no doubt.

Taylor set the weapon down lightly, shy of the time needed. He let out a deep breath and smiled.

"You're fuckin kidding me!" said Sanchez, moving quickly. "You insane! Get it secured before the Chief shows!"

They scrambled and quickly secured it. Sanchez then bellowed, "In the office, now!"

Daniels followed Sanchez and Taylor into the aft office that was situated just outside the magazine. Just as they sat down, the Chief walked by with the Division Officer and entered the magazine. All three looked at one another, surprised. A touch of fear and then relief registered in their eyes. Sanchez shut the door, and Daniels quickly explained what had happened.

Sanchez listened and then sat in silence. On the other side of the door, in the aft pub room, came the murmur of men and then low laughter that Daniels knew was directed toward Taylor and himself.

At last, Sanchez stood. "I've seen some damn fools in my day. But you take the cake. Did you see who just walked by? You're lucky I went in when I did. You'd be in the brig right now waiting to see the Captain." His gaze shifted from one to the other. "But if I wanted to fuck you royally, I could. But I won't, 'cause I'd be screwing myself. Rogers and Stoker and particularly you Daniels, I need for the upcoming inspection, and I can't replace. But you, Taylor, I can."

He rose and placed his arm on Taylor's shoulder. "I'm going to do you a favor, son. I like you. So, I'm going to keep my mouth shut about what I saw. As you're new and naive, it's not really your fault."

Taylor glared at him, then looked away.

Sanchez continued. "Though I don't find Roger's sense of humor very funny, we don't use violence here to solve our problems. So don't think about touching those boys. They're also my drinking partners, as we all should be. Now get the fuck out of here and learn some fucking common sense!"

Taylor got up to leave, but as he did, Sanchez suddenly said, "Oh, in case you're wondering about 'The Trial of Sword in Steel.' They really were bullshitting you. Rogers never passed that test nor used a real warhead, and he ain't no damn king. Nor will you ever be. That warhead is not a football. You understand. Here you don't just lose a game if you fumble."

Taylor glared at him.

"Yes, I know about your little mishap at Berkeley. Hell, everyone does. You fuck'd up and cost your team a trip to the Rose Bowl and title game. I won't have you do that here; you understand me. We don't need high-minded college intellects and fuck ups here, Taylor. We need players. *Good* team players. We have an upcoming NTPI inspection that could make this ship unfit to carry nukes and sink the Captain if we fail. I need you to step down and re-wire that fucking head of yours to start thinking about your fellow sailors. We are a team. Understand that?"

Taylor didn't react to this. He only stared at the deck, the muscles in his neck twitching.

Sanchez continued, his voice low but intense. "This is not a game. It's for real, and you'll end up in the fucking brig. Or worse. Do I make myself clear?"

Taylor turned to leave. But as he did, Sanchez quickly added, "No one is king but the weapon itself. That's why we're here. To serve it. And the rules. And don't for a second think that you're better or smarter than any of us. Because you're not."

Taylor stood still, his back to Sanchez. But after a long pause, he turned and spoke, a trace of anger to his voice, "How long did *you* hold it up, Petty Officer Sanchez?"

Sanchez appeared startled by the question but remained silent.

"Didn't think so," said Taylor. He turned and walked through the door but then suddenly stopped, swinging around again. "And you're wrong. It is a football. The only difference here is that the uniforms are government issue with no padding."

He then disappeared into the trunk and headed up the ladder to the second deck. Daniels followed.

29 Sept. 77

It's two in the morning. Can't sleep. This place is crazy.

The day started off pretty well. Played some chess. First, two games were evenly fought, but I won both. The third—a draw. I was tired. I mostly sat on a laundry bag in the coop all morning and read. I am still only a blue badge and still have to be escorted down into the spaces until my clearance comes in. That shouldn't be too long. Went down into M-3 today during a lunch break on a B57 operation (I don't know what the rules are on keeping journals. Where that line on discussing certain topics is, I don't know, nor do I want to compromise this journal, and ask. But I'll write about it anyway).

I found today's experience intensely interesting and yet, intensely troubling. "A" school didn't prepare me for this. Row after row. An incredible power. It was numbing to be standing next to such a destructive force. Felt very uneasy. I could almost feel the radiation bleed into me. Unseen. A silent assassin.

The look is the same as the trainer's we worked on in "A" school, and so the feeling should have been the same. But it wasn't. What I can't see, penetrate with my eyes; my mind does. To know! The curse of knowledge. The intellect, the supreme sense, is far keener than the eye. Not as sharp, pervasive, and clear as the heart, but powerful nonetheless. And maybe too powerful. For it can eclipse the heart. Why did I do this? Work with such mass destruction? I had a chance to be an HM, a hospital corpsman, a healer, but no, I was tricked into choosing this rate. And I didn't realize it till too late. I'm seriously worried about radiation exposure and the very idea of maintaining such weapons of tremendous destruction.

As I stood there today looking over the weapons with Daniels, both Rogers and Stoker approached and soon conned me into a game of initiation. Being the newbie, I went along with it. First, it was just holding up a tail, which I did easily. Then it was some bullshit "Trial of Sword in Steel," a challenge to pick up a two hundred and fifty-pound training warhead for five minutes. According to Daniels, no one assigned to the Midway has ever done it. At first, I thought it was all crazy and couldn't believe that men working on nuclear weapons did such things. But not wanting to get off on the wrong foot with the guys, I gave in and tried. But Sanchez showed before I finished. I think he knew about it from the start. Don't like that they're messing with me like that. This is a far cry from the hallowed halls of UC Berkeley. And the stadium—the fumble. I couldn't believe he brought it up. Only aboard a few days and everyone and their mother knows. I thought that by being a thousand miles away—in the middle of the fucking Indian Ocean—I could finally find some solitude and peace. But I just can't seem to. Shame is transcendent—it knows no border!

Daniels, so far, is the only one who seems somewhat normal. He's medium height, stocky, with brown unruly hair, blue eyes, and uncharacteristically knowledgeable. He also has a wild streak in him, is a talker, and is a good but agonizingly slow chess player. After finishing a few games with him this evening, I had a long discussion before going to bed about Thoreau's "Civil Disobedience." It was great, and we seemed to communicate on a certain level that I really miss. No one around here seemed to have got beyond a high school education—even the chiefs. And even if they did, no one I've met is particularly interested in talking physics, history, or writing. Here, it's just beer, breasts, and bullets. The officers are in a world of their own and, according to protocol, can't bridge the gulf between themselves and the enlisted.

Since leaving Berkeley, I feel as though my mind has shifted down a few gears, but after talking and arguing, with Daniels, I get a certain rush that I haven't felt in quite a while. His father went to Berkeley as well. Grad school. My dream. Or, at least, was. However, I'm not sure about him yet; he seems to be in trouble all the time and on everyone's shit list. No one seems to respect his authority, and he seems to be waging an internal battle over it, but I think the disrespect's mostly his own doing. I have a feeling they're really gonna hit him hard for the crossing of the line ceremony. I overheard Rogers and Stoker discuss how they were going to ambush him and put a dress on him for the beauty queen contest the night before the crossing of the line. I mentioned it to Daniels, but he didn't seem to take it too seriously. He said the night before, he would hide out in his favorite spot, the 0-7 level until the contest was over.

He needs to be careful when we cross that line. They almost crossed it with me today.

The Game

Taylor walked up to Daniels' rack and watched as Roberts moved his knight two squares up and one over to attack Daniels' queen. Daniels searched the board for any weaknesses in his own attack. A smile advanced across his face as he realized Roberts had indeed made a fatal miscalculation. Daniels moved his bishop across the board, stopping on a square in line with Roberts' king.

"Checkmate," said Daniels. Roberts, a bony seaman apprentice with a flat nose and stringy brown mustache, looked to the board puzzled. He studied it, still not believing what he had just heard.

"Should've paid attention to what he was doing with his knight and bishop and not his little diversion with the queen," said Taylor.

"Shit." Roberts rolled over and off his rack. "That's it, no more. Damned if I can win." He grabbed his work shirt, quickly put it on, and walked away.

Taylor smirked. "Chatauranga?"

"Chatauranga?"

"Chess. It's the oldest known name for chess in existence."

"What's it mean?"

"It refers to the four branches of the Indian Army—foot soldiers, horses, chariots, and elephants."

"Not bad for a wog." Daniels smiled.

"We're equal there, aren't we?"

"Guess so. Rank don't mean shit then."

"Or the night before," said Taylor, his voice cutting through with caution.

"Fuck the night before. Like I said, they won't find me."

"I hope you're right. Cause you might enjoy wearing that dress so much you might never wear a uniform again."

"Funny. Are we going to play a game or what?"

"Weren't we?" said Taylor.

"That's not my idea of one."

Taylor stood for a second studying Daniels, tossed his copy of *Heart of Darkness* on his rack, and then swung up and faced Daniels, who was laying against his pillow, the game board straddling the bar separating the two bunks, propped up by two pillows on either side of it. Daniels placed two tight fists out in front of him. "Take your pick."

"Sorry," Taylor shook his head.

"Again? You've chosen black since we started playing. That's not fair, now, is it?"

"What ever is?" said Taylor.

"All right, I'll be white this time, but I need the practice of moving second against you, so next time I'd like to be black."

Taylor ignored him and set up his pieces. Daniels did the same. When all the pieces were in position, Daniels picked up his king's pawn and moved it up two spaces. Taylor responded by doing the same. Daniels then moved his king's bishop's pawn up two spaces in the traditional king's gambit opening, fully expecting Taylor to bring his queen down and put him in check as he had been doing. He instead traded pawns.

"Hey, what's up? You just nuked my pawn. That's not like you."

"The struggle is for the expansion of the center," said Taylor.

Daniels knew he was referring to one of the basic rules of all opening play—to control the center of the board.

"However," said Daniels, "it might begin in the center, grow in the center, but it sure as hell matures and terminates any place it wants to."

"Or has to. Let's finish this game in a decent hour." Taylor forced a smile, but the edges didn't quite make it.

Daniels moved his bishop to four spaces above his queen's bishop. Taylor then swung his knight to the third space above his king's bishop, attacking Daniels' pawn. Daniels moved his knight out to protect it.

"What is it about the game that makes you play with such ferocity?" asked Daniels.

Taylor moved his bishop's pawn up one space. "Winning."

"But why chess?" Daniels moved his queen up to strengthen his besieged pawn.

"Nothing compares," said Taylor. "It's pure. It has a beginning and an ending—a finality to it. You can only win or lose, and to win, you need to be intellectually superior." Taylor moved his queen's pawn up to attack Daniels' bishop and pawn.

"You can draw."

"Yes," he paused, "but just temporarily. The mate will happen." He smiled.

Daniels took Taylor's pawn with his own. "Okay, but if perfection and intellect are so important to you, why the Navy? Why? Why enter something so flawed and chaotic? Why didn't you just take some time off from Berkeley and then go back?"

Taylor slid his bishop up two spaces in front of his queen, then stared at the board. "There is truth and perfection in all that we see and do. But we must carve it out, like David from the marble. The Navy called to me. It was my marble."

"Oh, yes, oh wise one." Daniels moved his queen's pawn up a square to strengthen his King's bishop and unlock his other bishop. "But what about the nukes we work on? They sure as shit might be technologically perfect, but don't you think they're a far cry from the purity of Carrara marble?"

Daniels could see that his question troubled Taylor. Taylor took his time thinking about it and then finally replied, "Yes. In a strange way, I think they embody the perfection of laws, of nature, of God." Taylor moved his bishop five spaces above his king's knight's square, attacking Daniels' queen. "They all have probabilities of achieving an intended end state. Yet, human, mechanical, or electronic, and other types of error can disrupt those states."

"Great end state. Kaboom, and millions vaporize. Where's the perfection in that?"

"Depends on who's the target. But that's another question altogether."

"Really?"

"Truth be told . . . I wish they were never made."

"That so," said Daniels.

"Look, we all rationalize it as best we can. I'm just as stuck here as you . . . and they didn't have to lie to me about what we'd be working on. If I had known, I never would have done it. Now move!" The suddenness of Taylor's anger surprised Daniels.

Daniels moved his queen back one space. He swallowed. He wished the game was over. "Look, Taylor, I think we're getting a little bit off the deep end here."

Taylor studied the board. His next move surprised Daniels. He castled and took advantage. Daniels sighed. He couldn't decide on a plan of attack. He stalled.

"In terms of this striving for perfection, what would you say is the weak link in the system then?" Daniels threw the question out, bait to buy time.

"What do you mean, what system?"

"Any system. I don't know...the system we work with. Is the weakest link mechanical, electronic, or human?"

Taylor glanced around him. "Not sure we can discuss that."

Daniels tensed, suddenly understanding the meaning and implication of his own question. He scanned the coop to see if anyone was listening. Satisfied, he lowered his head. "Fuck it. Fuck them. I can talk."

"Move, please."

"I will. Just give me a minute." Daniels put his head between his hands and pondered the pieces before him. But each time he tried to concentrate, a rebellious thought pushed itself up, forcing him to take notice, like an itch on his back he couldn't quite reach. *Is the weakest link mechanical, electronic, or human?* He shoved it back down again and tried to concentrate. The thought popped up again. Taylor fidgeted with a captured pawn, eyebrows knitted.

"What are you thinking about?" asked Daniels.

Taylor put the pawn down. "Are you going to move, or are we going to sit here all night?"

"Dammit, I'm stuck. Give me another two minutes, and I promise I'll move. Okay?" They both picked up their pawns and twirled them in their fingers. After a couple of minutes, Daniels threw his pawn down. The thought wouldn't go away.

Taylor flicked his piece at Daniels. "Move, or I'll move the piece for you."

"Okay, I'll move." He moved his forward pawn and knocked Taylor's pawn off the board. It tumbled over the edge of the mattress and hit the deck. "Well, at least I moved."

Taylor ignored the comment and the fallen piece and, with his queen's knight, took Daniels' pawn.

Again Daniels took a while to ponder his next move; this one thought dominating him—a small seed blown in by fierce winds of Clotho, Lachesis, and Atropis. A small seed destined to root.

Daniels moved his queen's bishop up and took Taylor's pawn. *He's thinking what I'm thinking; I know it, feel it.*

"Hey, Taylor."

"If you're going to ask what I think you're going to, then don't."

"Aaha, then you *were* thinking about it, weren't you? I knew you couldn't let it go."

"We're going to end up in the brig."

"Hey, no one can hear us, and besides, we really aren't doing anything wrong, just thinking, and there's no harm in that." He stared hard at Taylor. "And fuck 'em, they may control our actions, but not our thoughts."

This comment seemed to stir Taylor. His eyes suddenly sparkled. He studied the board. Daniels swallowed. After what seemed to Daniels an hour, Taylor lifted his head. He spoke, his deep voice slow, serious. "All right, but keep it down. We'll discuss it for a few minutes, then never again. Okay?"

Daniels grinned. "Okay." *Damn them and their sense of control and discipline. Brick by brick, they fall.*

Daniels inched forward, the excitement clear in his countenance. Taylor looked around the coop.

"The question," said Daniels, "will be to figure out the weakest link in our system. A thought experiment, of course."

"No," replied Taylor. "The question is, how can we talk *and* finish this game in a reasonable hour? Move."

"If I'm not mistaken, it's your move." Daniels looked at his watch.

Taylor checked each piece. "Hmmm."

Taylor moved his king's bishop up five spaces above his queen's knight so that it sat next to Daniels' bishop.

"We need to narrow and define a system," said Daniels.

"Anything and everything pertaining to the security of the weapon's spaces," said Taylor.

"We need to concentrate on access points into the spaces and security procedures. Maybe there's a flaw. Or better yet, we should find and concentrate on the weakest link given those parameters."

"Keep defining, refining until we expose the flawed link," said Taylor. "There's always a flaw."

"The entry points to the spaces would not be a good place to start. They would be the strongest. So the place to start, then, would most likely be the emergency exits or elevators."

"Both of those points are watertight. Anytime watertight integrity is broken, Damage Control Central would be alerted."

"Not bad for a—"

"Wog?" said Taylor.

"A beginner," said Daniels, slightly irritated.

"As I was saying, all doors, hatches, and elevator doors are alarmed. Weapons Office, Ordnance Control, and the Marines would be alerted."

"On board less than six days and you got security down," said Daniels.

"Gunner's Mate Security booklets. Been reading them and having

67

'em signed off."

"Oh, yeah, forgot about those damn things."

"Plus "A" school is still fresh in my head."

Daniels moved his king's knight out in front of his queen. Taylor immediately moved his knight up three spaces in front of his queen.

"However," said Taylor, "if trying to get in, the best way might be when the weapons are being moved. They're out of the magazines and accessible, the alarms are not a factor, and you deal strictly with Marines."

"Oh, only fifty Marines armed to the teeth and itching to shoot someone. No, you need to get it before it reaches the eyes of the Marines."

"How?"

Daniels thought for a minute. The game was starting to get exciting to him, and from Taylor's look, he was enjoying it more. The excitement was not only from the intellectual stimulation and the mental rebelliousness but from the risk. The danger. They both knew this conversation could get them court-martialed.

"The machinery room," said Taylor.

"What about it?"

"The machinery room sits inside the weapons elevator trunk at the top," said Taylor. "Gain access to the room, open the inner door, climb down onto the platform with the upcoming weapon during a weapons offload at sea."

"And pick up a 1000 or 2000-pound bomb and carry it up to the room. No way," said Daniels.

"Break it down as we did in "A" school."

"Yeah, and use the small 57; it weighs only 500 pounds. Break it down, then use a hoist or a "come along" hand wrench to lift the warhead up to the room. That warhead only weighs about 250 to 300 pounds. Two strong men could do it."

"Replace it with a bomb dummy unit," said Taylor, "hidden in the machinery room in a container."

"Like a jet engine container or bag," said Daniels.

"Keep the real bomb hidden in the room until later that night, and then pull her out. No one will know." A faint smile crept up his cheek.

"No," said Daniels, "After receiving any weapon, there is an immediate receipt inspection. They will check the serial numbers and see that it has been switched."

"Hmmm." Taylor paused, his face blank. "Disguise the bomb dummy unit to match the one taken, or gct rid of it immediately."

"An easier way would be to take one in port instead of during an offload at sea," said Daniels.

"Path of least resistance," said Taylor. "Keep narrowing. In port would be easier. Civilian shipyard workers going on and off would disguise your activities. The weapon could then be taken off unnoticed with a crane or forklift and crate."

"They'd never know," said Daniels. "Shipyard workers sometimes work all night long hauling equipment and supplies on and off this ship. Hell, you probably could walk one right off the afterbrow if it was disguised well enough."

"Maybe," said Taylor. His face grew serious. "And what would you do with it once it was off?"

"Hell, I don't know." Daniels lowered his head, then raised it. "Actually, I do. I'd embarrass the fuck out of the military. Hell with 'em. Like you, thcy conned me into this, and I'd love to see them con their way out of the world's newspapers."

"So purely as a demonstration," said Taylor.

"Definitely." Daniels smiled. "A protest. Considering the insane amount of destructive power I'm now witnessing, plus the radiation, I'd call it a humanitarian protest. Then give it back."

"Hmm. . . sure," said Taylor, "and then spend the rest of your life in a brig. Say goodbye to university and your freedom. Now move."

"Yeah. Give me another minute. It's all just bullshit anyway."

"Please move," said Taylor.

It was hard to concentrate on the game. Weapons dominated

Daniels' mind. Also, everyone on the ship was feeling a bit jumpy from the long cruise, particularly with Africa only a day away. He moved his bishop up a square on his king's side, pinning Taylor's knight against his queen.

"You guys still playing?"

Daniels jumped. It was Roberts. *Should have been listening.*

Roberts had a spot of sauce on his upper lip. "Spaghetti for dinner," Daniels asked.

"How'd you know?" Roberts instinctively wiped his lip, then brushed his hand on his pants.

"Yeah, we're still playing," said Taylor, annoyed.

Roberts climbed onto Brewster's rack since Taylor was still in his. "I'll wait," said Roberts.

"Let's finish the game," said Taylor. Daniels nodded.

Taylor moved his rook out one square. "Check," he said, drawing out the word.

"What!" Daniels examined the board.

"Mate," said Taylor, smiling. "I win."

"Shit." Daniels climbed down from his rack. He flipped open the top of his bunk, exposing a large storage compartment beneath it. He grabbed his oceanography book and some paper and then slammed it shut. But as he started to walk off, he stopped and turned. "You win, you win. Why do I put up with this anyway?"

Taylor smiled. "You know why."

"Why?"

Taylor leaned over the rack, his huge head seeming to hover in mid-air. For a brief second, it reminded Daniels of the way his father would stare down at him. Daniels eased back.

"Cause deep down you enjoy it," said Taylor.

"So. What's so fun about losing?"

"So? Look around you." Taylor turned and gestured with his hand. "Look."

Daniels followed his broad fingers as they targeted the back of the

70

coop and several empty racks, a few sleeping men, a sailor reading a playboy, another polishing his shoes, another staring blankly up at the overhead.

"I think you understand," said Taylor.

Daniels nodded, catching Taylor's drift. He stared at him for a moment and then started to shuffle off.

"One more thing," said Taylor.

Daniels stopped.

"Watch your back, huh."

Daniels nodded and bolted up the ladder, leaving Taylor hunched over the board. He ambled down the second deck passageway, thinking of chess, of Taylor, and of winning. He headed for the library to catch up with the reading for his oceanography course. He was way behind again. He suddenly felt more determined than ever to get a high grade and then get the hell out of the Navy.

Towards the aft end of the ship, he zipped into a side passage and entered the library. It was a fairly small compartment that was located about mid-ship, and given the blank steel bulkheads, the profusion of pipes, and wound wiring, it still looked like a library—there were the usual parallel rows of tall aluminum bookcases brimming with all sorts of books and journals, and in the center, near the checkout counter, there was a small area filled with tables for sailors to relax and read. Daniels made for a table in the empty room and plopped down.

He pulled out his oceanography book and started to read. But every time he got about halfway down a page, he found his mind wandering to Yuki. He still hasn't heard from her. *Why?* Panic suddenly seized him, and he shut his book. *She's taking her time because she's not sure. What if she says no?!*

He grabbed a sheet of paper and quickly began to write:

Dear Yuki,

How are you? I miss you so much.

I wish we were sitting in the Zig Zag Club right now, drinking a nice cold beer, listening to some awesome music, and enjoying the soft pleasure of each other's company. But instead, I find myself sitting here alone in the library of the USS Midway, trying to study. But I can't. I'm finding it hard to concentrate when I haven't heard back from you. Are you okay? Did you receive my letter?

Yuki, please listen to me very carefully. Though I probably rambled on a bit in my last letter—I MEANT EVERY WORD! Yes, every single letter. Particularly the last few where I mention marriage. I know it was rather abrupt and not the perfect nor romantic setting for such a question, and I hope I didn't scare you. But I can't imagine leaving the Navy without you! I know you have your mother to attend to, but I feel that we can somehow work it out. Maybe once we're married, you can sponsor her, and she can move to the States with us. I know it can work out for all of us. So please consider my proposal and write to me as soon as you can. Okay?

Again, I miss you terribly, and I can't wait to see that beaming smile of yours—which is nothing more than the light of dawn dispelling the dark demon of night. I'm truly reborn every time your lips rouse and rise.

I love you!!

Christopher

PS. We're pulling into Africa tomorrow! I signed up for a real African safari, and I can't wait to go on it and see some lions! I'll tell you all about it when I see you.

PSS. I was thinking of all the pennies that I sent you and what would happen if one never made it, or if one ever fell out of that lovely hand of yours. At first it troubled me, but the more I thought about it, the more I realized that it would be okay. It's important to spread the luck! Here's a poem I wrote for you:

In dropping a penny
I let it be.
In my misfortune,
Is luck for thee!

Daniels carefully folded the letter, placed a penny in it, and then kissed it for good luck. He slipped it gently into his book and then bolted out of the library. He headed for the ship's post office, his mind on Yuki and her answer, Yuki and her answer . . .

1 Oct 1977 (0627)

Pull into Mombasa, Kenya, today. Have signed up for a safari with Daniels and Henderson. It will cover parts of Tsavo and Amboseli parks. I'm looking forward to it. It feels strange to be going to Africa to visit the land that gave birth to all humans. The mother continent.

Pulling into Mombasa reminds me of a story I heard many years ago. My parents have not had detailed access to our family history, only bits of knowledge passed down orally, finally written down by my father, the first of our extended family to go to college. All of his learning he then imparted to me, sitting me down, night after night, year after year, telling me that education, learning to read, to write, and write well, was the only real and honest investment a man could make for his future, for his family's. Yet, for all of this, he never finished college. He was severely beaten in his last year at UCLA. After watching UCLA win a football game against USC, a group of students from USC got into a verbal altercation with him and a friend as they walked across the stadium parking lot. It soon turned to fists. His skull was fractured, resulting in an epidural hematoma. He was comatose for two weeks and hospitalized for over a month. The incident left him with slight aphasia—language disorder, from which he partially recovered. He never got over it, nor let me forget it.

As a result of his disorder, he had to see a speech therapist for many years. When I was a young child, he visited one by the name of Dr. Dennis Freedman, an African American. When the session finished, my father and the doctor got into a discussion about a piece of African sculpture in the lobby. The conversation soon shifted to Africa itself and the doctor's personal history. He said that he was able to trace his ancestors to the Gold Coast, where eight or nine generations ago, a Denkyira warrior, his ancestral tribe, was captured by the Asante tribe on the Gold coast, was sold to the English, and was then forcefully sent to America from Cape Coast. He said that over half the ship's slave cargo perished on the journey over.

That story shocked my young and naive mind then and still does. I mull it over and over how one can be violently uprooted from one's home, sold into bondage by another tribe, and shipped to a strange land in horrendous conditions to do the unconscionable and relentless barbaric bidding of another race.

Dr. Freedman's horrific story of chattel slavery, coupled with the Midway's arrival to Mombasa, has suddenly prompted me to consider the negative aspects of my own less severe (on every conceivable level) military servitude within a highly inflexible and inherently violent martial system. That is, I feel now, myself a stranger, bound to martial law and custom for four years—where I've voluntarily and unwittingly traded my freedom and humanity for unthinking robotic service to an extreme, though qualified, violence (isn't it always qualified?). If ordered to take part in a nuclear holocaust, a truly unimaginable prospect, I have no choice but to obey. None! Thus, I find myself in a system worse than the martial system that Melville found himself in and that he attacked in White Jacket, *as my robotic service to extreme violence now incorporates an almost religious devotion to those highly radioactive weapons of unimaginable horror and destruction—just one of which, whether purposeful or accidental, could easily kill more people than the collective total of all humans that existed in Africa over 50,000 years ago.*

Daniels was right. I should have never left Berkeley.

I fucked up again.

I truly hate it here.

Africa

The monotonous trill of the battery-powered alarm woke Daniels. He slammed the top of the clock taped to a water pipe slithering up the side of his rack. It stopped. His eyes opened. Sleep drained from his mind, and a metallic world materialized. "Shit." The word was barely audible. In fact, he wondered if his lips had moved at all.

He coughed and wiped his eyes and then stared up at the white piece of foam glued to the bottom of Henderson's rack above him. He tried to focus his eyes on the grooves creeping in and out of the depressions on its surface. He had been told by Petty Officer Second Class Stewart that a sailor named Talbot used to sleep in this rack. He would occasionally wake in the middle of the night and bolt upright, smashing his head into the bunk above. After a few cuts and bruises, padding was placed above him to soften the blow. Talbot was finally discharged after losing it at a division picnic a year ago. He had downed a couple of six-packs of beer and demanded that the Chief follow him over to a heavily forested hillside to check for traces of "Charley." He had served as a Marine in Vietnam in 1967-68 and then worked as a clerk for a shipping company two blocks from the naval station on 32nd Street in San Diego. He then re-enlisted in the Navy after an unsettling situation in which he'd been attacked and beaten by a co-worker. Daniels always chuckled at the thought of someone re-enlisting into the military after being scared half to death by a fight. But then again, everyone had their wayward reasons, and Daniels was no exception.

As far back as he could remember, he had loved the sea, its breadth, and its openness. When he was ten, he stood on the dark sanded shore at his grandfather Fredrick's house in Salem, the cool ocean breeze caressing his face. He gazed at the cloud-covered horizon, the ceaseless march of wave washing up and over his feet, gently pulling him downward, soaking him in the cold and distant remnants of exotic ritual. His heart pounded as his grandfather, who had served in the Navy during and after WWI, quoted Conrad, Melville, and Dana and, pointing his bony finger far beyond the offing, gave direction and repeated emphasis to rich and exciting tales of strange, uncharted lands, mysterious tribal dances, and savage lions crouching—their sharp teeth and long claws glistening in the glare of the searing sun, their taut iron muscle coiled to spring. Daniels listened and took it all in, the skin of his own feet stretched tight from the continual cold pull of the Atlantic—but instead of feeling repelled, he welcomed it, as he felt in that chill a confirmation of his own youth, vitality, and eagerness to face the hardships that he knew would eventually come. As his grandfather related, there was always a price to pay for comprehension. Thus, prepare oneself, he would say— cultivate and finesse the prep. Mind it, and don't forget.

Skipping a grade in elementary school presented him a chance to enlist at seventeen, just after high school graduation—but at an age where he would still need his parent's consent to join. Without letting his parents know his intentions, he rode down in his recruiter's car to the naval office, where he spent many euphoric hours going through the various books, pamphlets, and videos. The first film he saw had dramatic appeal—a tall, clean-cut Captain, voice deep and trusting, walking across a modern carrier, pointing out each warplane that was pregnant with 500 or 1000-pound bombs and Sidewinder missiles. He talked of launch, air combat, and recovery statistics. The film would then cut to him walking across the wooden deck of a battleship, running his index finger along the gray skin of a sixteen-inch gun turret, remarking that it could fire a shell weighing as much as a Volkswagen almost thirty miles. At the film's end, the Captain stood on the bridge of the battleship, his hands on a magnetic compass, the ocean spread before him, his voice restrained to a muted excitement, his eyes widening and fusing, telling of the ship's global responsibility, intermixed with visits to palm fanned ports of call. He smiled after the latter, the film cutting to pictures of sailors, arms around long-haired, full-breasted Asian women, all laughing, all walking down a clean deserted beach somewhere in the Pacific. Immediately after the film ended, his recruiter and other strategic Naval personnel then gathered around and began reciting glorious sea stories, their smiles wide, their eyes wider. And at the head of this motley crew, his recruiter, his eyes the widest of all, would sit back like a great baronial bird in his leathered perch and sing of swaying ships, steamy jungles, and smooth, easy women.

After breaking the news at home, his father raved on and on about the virtues of attaining a college education, of how he needed to continue the family line of academic achievement, of uphill accomplishment, pointing to the collage of relatives—scientists, generals, businessmen—tacked neatly down the hallway leading to the master bedroom, how he should not visit shame on lineage by entering the military as an *uneducated* enlisted man. His mother tried to act as a buffer between them, keeping her opinion to herself. If it wasn't for the intervention of his grandfather, who had served two years as a cook on a destroyer, his father would never have consented. "He'll go in young and naive," said his grandfather, "Yet come out a man with respect. Maybe a medal or two. Then college."

His father finally gave in. Daniels thanked his grandfather, as he had done many times in the past. But his grandfather simply nodded this time, his face serious, his eyes drawn, blank. "Just do it," he said, "and be sure to get it right."

They drove down with his parents to the recruiter's office the next day in silence. It was a victory for Daniels, a rare one at that, and it should have bolstered his mood. But it didn't. Something had changed; it seemed different. For all the color and excitement displayed by the larger-than-life posters in the viewing room and corridors, Daniels felt for the first time desiccation creeping through the cracked plaster as he passed through. He wondered if it was just the morning itself, which seemed to impart a dry distance, a cool formality, and stillness that the afternoon's heat had hidden so well. But this was dismissed as he walked deeper into the old brick building; the smiles so bright and wide a few days earlier weren't seen as he walked past familiar heads that now only seemed to mechanically rotate down, arms rising in sync with the slow and swirling ascent of steam from their coffee.

After entering a dim office, Daniels waited quietly with his parents while his recruiter assembled the necessary documents and forms from twelve tall cabinets that seemed to hold up the bare walls. When all were collected and stacked in a neat pile, his father, dressed in a red tweed jacket that had been given to him while studying at Berkeley, picked up a black pen in his right hand, bolted his left securely to the table, and glanced over at Daniels in contempt. He scribbled his signature with restraint, then handed the pen to Daniels' mother, who sat in the corner, her light brown hair curled tight in a bun, a wisp bouncing off her collar. She sat in a blue dress, staring, blank-eyed, out the window into the traffic below.

After leaving the recruiter's office, they all went to Denny's to share their last meal. His mother stressed the importance of writing home, keeping out of trouble, maintaining personal hygiene, and keeping both eyes on the clock.

"Here," she said, handing him a small box. "A gift from your father." She glanced over at him, and he simply shifted and stirred his coffee.

Daniels opened the box and pulled out a Seiko. "A watch?" he asked, puzzled. Daniels, at first, didn't understand and looked to his father for an explanation. But his father kept looking down at his cup. Both Daniels and his mother sank slightly into their seat. Daniels cradled the watch between his fingers, studying the sharp line of the hands, the delicately etched surface of the crown, and the pearl white dial. He fogged the glass with his breath, watched it evaporate for a moment, and then wiped the glass clean with his napkin. His mother folded her napkin neatly and then composed herself. Daniels smiled weakly.

"It will keep you out of trouble," said his mother, her eyes finding her husband's for a brief second. "Let it be your guide home and to

79

college."

"I'll try," said Daniels. "Thanks." He looked to his father again, but his father just continued to stir his coffee, saying nothing the rest of the meal except for a single warning afterwards as they neared their car in the parking lot: "When you leave the service, it better be with an honorable discharge . . . or don't bother coming home."

Daniels looked down at his watch, rubbed its crown with his sheet to shine it up a bit, and then rolled to his right and jumped down from his rack to the deck. A sharp pain from the jolt shot up his heel to his knee. He grimaced and shifted his weight to the balls of his feet, feeling a coldness seep into him. *Africa.* This morning the Midway would be anchoring, and he thought of the safari that Taylor and he had signed up for and that they would take the next morning. He smiled and inhaled deeply, conscious of the perpetual locker room odor.

Life stirred around him. When one man's alarm went off deep in the coop, he heard it. The noise was always a problem. With eighty personnel living in this open space with blasting radios and TV, alarm clocks, snoring, fighting, smelly boots, vociferous JP-5 pump rooms surrounding the coop, clanging feet and banging chairs and tables from the mess deck above, rolling ship, and booming steam catapults on the flight deck, it was astonishing he could get any sleep at all. But he did. He would just shut his eyes, tune out this cacophonic symphony, and drift into a dream world devoid of substance like steel.

Another alarm clock buzzed deep within the coop. Daniels winced. He reached over and shook Henderson, who lay with his face turned to the opposite side of the top rack.

"Hey, Henderson, get your lazy ass up." He shook him again.

Henderson suddenly jumped up, his skinny frame barely filling the space between his rack and the overhead. He took a swing, just missing a vent above him. Daniels quickly stepped backward out of harm's way.

"You idiot, what the hell you doing?" said Daniels.

Henderson sat up and pushed his jet-black hair from his eyes. From the pink folds of the wrinkles wrapped tight around his left eye to the small notch on his jaw, all of the skin on the left side of his face was blotted red. He dropped his arms, stretching and distorting his many tattoos.

"Fuck, Daniels, you woke me in the middle of an awesome dream. I mean . . . I just took out the last guard, grabbed my girl, and dammit, I was just about to lay a lip-lock on her when I was suddenly attacked from behind by some Doctor Strange wizard! Who suddenly materialized into you! How come every time I have a great dream, you have to fuck it up?" He blinked, then flipped his fist into the air and lay back down.

"Sounds like you lip-locked the wrong woman!"

"Wrong woman, my ass!" he exclaimed, rolling back up, his eyes blazing.

A loud piercing whistle sounded over the 1MC, the ship's intercom, followed by, "Now set the special sea and anchor detail."

Yes! Daniels dressed quickly and ran up to the first, or hangar bay deck, where the ship's aircraft were stored and maintained. He scurried beneath long rows of lights and flitted around F-4s, A-7s, Sea King helicopters, forklifts, shipping containers, fire stations, and hundreds of men milling about. As he ducked and side-stepped a swinging wire beneath the tail of an F-4, he suddenly became aware of the shifting deck at his feet, as thousands of tons of steel swayed softly, keeping perfect rhythm to the endless wash of waves passing without. That the wire had to remind him was surprising.

Daniels made his way over to aircraft elevator number three, jutting out over the water on the port side of the ship. The elevator itself was up at the flight deck level, leaving a large hole in the side of the ship like a massive movie screen. Through this opening, he could see the near peaks of the shifting green-blue sea and the dull scratch of the horizon. Gray clouds flickered on and off in the intense blue sky.

81

Daniels lived for moments such as these, moments pure as the breeze that brushed the locks from his eyes. It was great to be up and out from the pits below, to gaze over water and air wrestling into eternity.

He headed for elevator number two on the starboard side. He looked out over the sea to the skin-brown sands, the long sharp shore of Africa. The growth beyond stretched before him like a matted rug. *At last!* His grandfather's words resonated within his ears. He couldn't wait to see his first lion. How exciting and beautiful that would be. He attempted a smile and inhaled deeply, taking in the strange scents that crawled on the wind. But instead of filling him with a sense of wonder and animation, he suddenly shuddered as a clanking roar filled the air.

The sound originated near the ship's prow, a prow no longer slashing into the sea, no longer causing it to pulse up on either side of the hull. *The anchor.* Daniels could picture the boatswain's mates in the forecastle watching the capstans erupting violently, spinning round and round, propelled by a falling 30-ton anchor and massive steel links, sparks of black paint exploding everywhere, filling the air with dark ash.

The Midway was now still in the water. A slight rocking from a restless sea was the only life imparted to her. The ship's whistle sounded again, followed by the announcements, "Anchored" and "Shift colors." The ship's call sign and "steaming" ensign were lowered, and the national ensign and Union Jack were raised.

Another whistle shrieked. "Liberty call, liberty call. Liberty commences for duty sections two, three, and four."

A jubilee of shouts could be heard all along the hangar bay. Daniels' heart quickened. He couldn't wait to get off the ship and drink a cold beer. *Kenya!* Again, a touch of anxiety brushed past him with the wind, but he ignored it and headed below.

Daniels resigned himself to waiting. And it was a long one. It wasn't until around 1600 that afternoon that Henderson and himself finally boarded a local fishing boat by the name of Impala, which pulled up to the boat launch on the side of the carrier. It was a light blue twenty-eight-foot Luhrs with a canvas cover over the upper deck, on which sat two locals, patiently waiting for everyone to board. A strong mixture of salt, oil, diesel fumes, and vomit from already returning seasick sailors hung in the air.

When all was ready, the Impala chugged toward the land mass stretching from horizon to horizon. The sun, now a brilliant orange, was setting low in the sky, just touching the continent. The image resembled a pumpkin set on the back of a long snake. Daniels could almost see within the orange fire two carved eyes, a nose, and a mouth flickering across the sun's surface.

The boat left a long shadow in her wake as she made her way up and over each wave. Daniels turned and looked to the USS Midway. Her large silhouette shrank with each passing minute, finally becoming a gray dot, then almost disappearing altogether as they approached the pier.

They docked and waited in line for a taxi for almost twenty minutes, then jumped in an old beat-up cab and screeched off in a cloud of gravel and exhaust into Mombasa. As they entered the ancient city, they passed beneath four massive elephant tusks curving up fiercely from the earth, framing white the darkening sky.

They passed through the stained, swarming streets, nearly running over a woman holding two screaming children as she darted out from the bustling sidewalk. They soon stopped at the favorite hangout of Weapons Department personnel—the Sunset Club on Moi Avenue. The club was barely recognizable from the street. It was a squat, windowless building with a conical roof that seemed to tilt toward a badly worn hotel on its right. And on its left—an abandoned lot lay littered with paper and splintered wood and the sudden gleam of the eye of a prowling rat. Just in front, on the side with the lot, was a large iron-wrought door. They entered it and quickly hurried down a long, dark, and cool corridor that led to a hot dirt patio in the back of the building.

Daniels scanned the area, and his heart sank a bit. The patio was open to the sky and crossed with long wooden beams from which weak bulbs hung from a crimped wire over tables of sailors and prostitutes. In the far back was a short fence that emptied out onto the street. To his right, a long, frayed plastic bar ran down to an empty wall. It was filled with sailors either standing or sitting on metal stools. There was no fancy woodwork, no hard liquor—just crates of beer stacked to the ceiling behind it and a plump African bartender fumbling at an old cash register. Next to the bar was a door that led into the building from which he could hear the far-off dull murmur and moan of drunk humanity.

They walked over to the bar. Roberts and O'Reilly greeted them as they slid around a table in the middle of the patio. Sanchez was there as well, wearing a large cowboy hat on his head. As Daniels approached, Sanchez leaned over and whispered that he needed to talk to him. It was important. But Daniels had waited almost a month for a drink. He ignored Sanchez and walked past the table to the bar and bought two Tusker Lager beers. He walked back and gave one to Henderson, popped the top off of his, took a long-needed swig, and then nearly blew it out all over the dirt.

"Jesus Christ!" gasped Daniels, "This shit's hot."

O'Reilly, a short red-haired seaman, and Roberts both chuckled as they put their bottles in the air, clinked them, and guzzled.

"Didn't you notice how warm the fucking bottle was," said Henderson, a smile cracked ear to ear.

"No. I had my mind on other things," replied Daniels, fingering the bottle in his hand.

"Well, it might be warm, but it ain't bad," bellowed Sanchez, silhouetted, his body blocking the light from a hanging bulb that was slowly drifting back and forth from a light, intermittent breeze.

All around them, sailors and locals chatted and drank. Daniels sipped his beer. Though he wanted to feel the sharp tinge of cold carbonation funneling down his throat, the warm beer wasn't that bad. A few sips later, Sanchez wiped his brow, tucked in a loose piece of shirt, and made his way over to him. He put his arm around Daniels' shoulder. A moist heat seeped through. Daniels stiffened.

"Look, we need to talk," said Sanchez.

Daniels leaned back. Sanchez dropped his arm and walked several feet from him, stopping under the swaying bulb. He motioned to come over by tipping his hat. Daniels obeyed.

"What's the problem?" asked Daniels, looking down. "You look too serious. This is liberty, for crying out loud."

"Look, this isn't exactly the place or time for this, and I don't know how to say it without sounding like an asshole, but I've been taking a lot of heat lately from you know who."

Daniels took another sip.

"The Chief, needless to say, is nearing his limit. He will only put up with so much. He tends to be exacting, as you well know, a perfectionist at times."

"So what are you trying to say?" quipped Daniels.

Sanchez narrowed his eyes. "Hey, I'm trying to help you, so shut the fuck up and listen." He stepped back and took a sip of beer, then continued. "What I'm trying to say is that you had better straighten your act up, and by that, I mean, you got a watch, so use it. Quit showing up late to muster, setting off alarms, and for Christ's sake, get a haircut, polish your shoes, and iron your fucking clothes."

Sanchez took another sip, and as he did this, Daniels noticed that the table nearest him had become very quiet. He could feel them straining to hear.

"Furthermore, following Sunday night's alarm, your second one, a sailor was taken to sick bay with two broken ribs and a dislocated shoulder after a Marine knocked him down with his rifle."

Daniels looked down. "I didn't know that."

"Well, now you do. And do you remember a month ago, while watching that flick on the mess deck that the alarm tripped off when that M-Division sailor bumped the emergency escape scuttle. You remember that?"

Daniels nodded.

"You bet your leather ass you do. Do you remember five people had to be treated in sick bay that night? Do you remember two people had to have stitches? Do you remember that you were one of them?"

Daniels turned and brushed the hair behind his ear. All eyes were on him.

"For crying out loud, we're on liberty, Sanchez."

"I asked you a question. Now do you?"

"Yes," said Daniels.

"Yes, what?"

"Yes, I remember."

"Good. Enough's fucking enough. Your record isn't exactly glowing. Too much insubordination, too many alarms, too many people getting hurt, too much paperwork and explaining to do. At this point, the Chief honestly couldn't give a shit who's at fault anymore. And neither does the Department Head or Captain." He paused and stared hard at Daniels. "I'm sure you caught a bit of that from the ass chewing over that alarm. But you didn't catch this."

Daniels tensed.

"If you continue the way you've been going, he's going to replace you as team hook leader."

"What?"

"That's right. I just got done talking to him an hour ago. He's done fucking around. He wants the division to pass the upcoming inspection with flying colors. And if that means replacing you with Rogers, he will."

"But, I—"

"Forget it. There's nothing more to say. You know what you've got to do."

Daniels took in another breath. *Rogers!* He tightened his grip on the bottle and swore.

Sanchez glanced back at the others. "Look, think about it later." He smiled. "Drink! We're on liberty!"

"Is he here?"

"Who?"

"The Chief."

"No, no, he left. Only us boys here. That newbie Taylor was wandering around just before you showed up." Sanchez walked towards the group. Daniels waited a minute and then shuffled over. Everyone was quiet.

"What say we get back to the real reason we're here—drinking!" Sanchez smiled. "And you're just in time for the show," he said, looking to his watch. "Let's head in and get us a seat."

"What show?" asked Henderson, eyes wide.

"What show? Who the fuck cares—shut up and get your dumb ass moving." Sanchez staggered slightly as he aimed his large bulk past a few patrons and into the club. The others followed. Then Daniels.

The interior reminded Daniels of the Tiki Room at Disneyland, which he had visited on his fifteenth birthday. Tall bamboo pillars crept up into a thatched ceiling. Smoke from torches drifted up towards a large ragged hole at the top. The diffuse light and a cigarette haze flowed and swirled about the room, as did the sailors, locals, and prostitutes spilling from the many tables that filled the place. The room reeked of stale beer and something unpleasant that he couldn't quite recognize.

In a large dirt ring in the center, four men lit torches, which cast an orange glow across the walls. They were dressed in red skirts, brightly colored grass armbands, and lion claw necklaces.

Daniels and Henderson grabbed some seats near the back and waited, their mood fueled by the infusion of spirits from their bottles. In front of him, to his left, several sailors and prostitutes were flirting and drinking along a long wall next to two windows. Daniels looked behind him. Taylor sat at a table next to the far wall. Daniels started to rise to greet him, but something warned him that now was not the time, seeing that Taylor was preoccupied with two men. Taylor's head was turned away from two large Kenyans, his hand signaling "no" to them. One of the men stood looking nervously around the room while the other leaned across the table, his hand spread flat across its surface toward Taylor.

A voice suddenly boomed into the crowd from the room's center. Daniels sat back down. A heavyset man in a loose white shirt, purple slacks, and beat-up white tennis shoes announced to the crowd that a "world-renowned" local tribal group would now perform for them. Daniels settled in his seat, feeling the warmth of the bottle in his hands.

A low chanting soon filled the air, and the room became still. Drums from a distant corner started beating softly and then quickened at a fast, heightening pace. The sudden increase in intensity started the dancers whirling around and around until grass and flame blended into a solid spinning mass. Round and round, they swarmed to the deep beat flashing red, yellow, and black. Chants and smoke and moving images filled the room's center with an exotic, almost hypnotic suspense. Daniels and Henderson sat transfixed as the dancers moved faster and faster, spinning and circling, darting and weaving to the pounding beat and stirring rhythm of the drum.

Suddenly, a loud shout filled the room. The drums stopped. All eyes and ears focused on a moving mass of men fighting in the back of the room where Taylor was. Daniels swallowed. The dancers shuffled, then stood still, plainly irritated by the intrusion, their torches crackling and sputtering, their jaws hung slightly open. Henderson leaped to his feet and ran toward the pack. Daniels followed, knowing damn well what Henderson's look meant. Henderson had been written up too many times for fighting, and another mishap would mean expulsion from the Personal Reliability Program. That meant expulsion from "W" and hello to G-Division.

As Daniels approached the fray, he could make out Henderson pulling bodies off someone on the floor. Henderson was cussing and prying limbs one from another. When the heap thinned, Taylor lay on the bottom, his arm tightly wrapped around a local whose eyes were shut, face puckered in, and he was trying to breathe. Taylor's lip was bruised, a trickle of blood visible on his chin, and he was growling.

It took three sailors to secure him, and as they did this, he frantically tried to swing at the face of the local, who tried to defend himself, but only ended up tearing Taylor's shirt—revealing Taylor's massive frame with veined arms pulsing and straining and flexed in a fury. It took all of Henderson's might and two others to uncoil his arm, free the Mombasan, and then keep him on the ground.

"Calm the fuck down!" screamed Henderson into deaf ears.

Sanchez shot up and grabbed Taylor. Together, Sanchez and Henderson finally got him up and escorted him out the door to the patio. They let him go, but Taylor quickly started to pace in circles. He was breathing heavily, his hands balled up into tight fists at his side.

"What the fuck happened in there?" shot out Sanchez, his right hand flipping his hat.

Taylor stopped, his jaw sawing back and forth, blood trickling out from a split lip. He lifted his head to speak, paused, took in a tremendous breath, and circled again. He stopped, then simply said, "fuck em." He lowered his head, his eyes fixed on Sanchez's and wiped the blood from his chin with his forearm. "They're lucky."

Sanchez shifted, as did the others, then spoke in a biting tone. "That was not—"

"Shore Patrol!" someone yelled.

"Shit, get him out of here," said Sanchez.

Grabbing Taylor, Henderson bolted for a fence that enclosed the patio. A group of locals parted quietly as the two shot by. They spun around a table of sailors, swung up over the back fence in a tumbling web of fingers and feet, and disappeared.

Sanchez strode back into the bar, and Daniels walked over to a chair set up against a wall. He sat, feeling strangely awkward and troubled, and sipped his beer, a beer that didn't offer him much respite from the heat. He studied the groups of sailors and locals as they thrust out from the shadows. He then focused on the far wall across the patio, on that swaying bulb hanging from a beam, on the small light unequal to the task of keeping the night at bay. *But there's never enough.* A slight wind kicked up, imparting a steady motion to the bulb and its spray of light. Dimmer, lighter, dimmer. The darkness crept before him, in tune with the delicate ebb and flow of luminescence.

The wind blew warmly across his cheeks, and as he studied the gleam from a broken window high up beyond the fence, a long chill ran up his back. It scared him, for he suddenly realized what it might possibly mean. He drank quickly and tried to bury it. But as he stared out over the drinking swarm before him and past the fence into the dark, jagged hole of the window, he started to slowly turn round and round in his head that this city was no different from the countless others. It was just another city. Just another bar. Alcohol and drunks and hookers. No magic or youthful promise in a place that bore the blemishes and scars of so many failed dreams.

He raised his bottle of Tuskers to the small orb and tipped it, "Keep trying." He downed the rest of the beer and made a beeline for the door of the club and the commotion within, all the while thinking, "Tomorrow will be different. Amboseli will definitely be different."

1 Oct. 77

At Sunset club. I lost it. They wouldn't stop—trying to sell me cocaine. Shore patrol showed. Got away. Onboard less than two weeks and almost thrown in brig. Dammit, not using my head.

Went another club. Henderson not so lucky. It's late had a lot—still very drunk. Need to get up early.

What's wrong with me?
Wanted to kill that man. Would have My god, I would have

if

if

Tsavo

Taylor climbed into the Volkswagen bus as the first in a line of six buses started to pull away. Wearing a floppy cotton shirt, Levi jeans, and tennis shoes, he walked back loose but measured as though each step were calculated beforehand in his mind. He sat down next to Daniels, nodded, and stared out past the driver.

A small white mist rolled from the sea onto the split wood of the long pier, covering it in a ghostly blanket. The morning was surprisingly chilly. The sun hid behind slate clouds that had gathered during the night along the coast. Two seagulls shot up above the coned roof of a shack, screeching and fighting over a bright scrap of food. Daniels watched as the two tore at it, wings flapping madly, beating around and around the sloped roof until the scrap flipped through the air and fell into the sea. Both flew down and disappeared from view. Daniels faced Taylor.

"What the hell happened to you and Henderson last night?" asked Daniels.

The engine turned over, stopped, turned and turned, and then suddenly hummed to life. The driver threw it in gear, accelerated, throwing everyone back into their seats, and sped off, the last in the long column of Volkswagen buses. The bus kept accelerating until it reached 70 MPH. The ride to and tour of Tsavo would be long, and they needed to arrive at Amboseli before nightfall.

"Don't want to talk about it," said Taylor, his voice a bit rough.

"What do you mean you don't want to talk about it?" said Daniels. "Henderson's supposed to be here."

"I said I don't want to talk about it." He pointed to his head and then drifted back to the front window. "Hangover."

Daniels let him be and focused on the swarming city roads before him. As the bus left Mombasa, neither talked, and the minutes mounted. The clouds thinned, and the air heated. Soon no buildings could be seen. Outside the open window, the browns, blacks, yellows, and numerous reds of dry savannah blurred past like a film in fast motion. A sea of red oat surged with the gusts of hot wind. Sweat broke out on the palm of Daniels' hands. He swallowed. Again, a touch of anxiety within him surfaced. *Dammit, what the hell's wrong with me?* He closed his eyes for a minute and then opened them to a brown cluster of hills, buckshot with yellow sterculia trees. Low valleys and acacia streamed past the glass in video fashion. Overhead, the sun crouched in the sky, burning hot and fierce. A cloud fled, and a shaft of light penetrated the open sunroof and lit up the top half of Taylor's face. The light seemed to carve out his features in slow motion. From his hair, it leaped down the precipice of his forehead through thick, sparse brows and then raced down and out over the slope of his chiseled nose, kicking up sparks from its tip, leaving his eyes dark and recessed.

In a calm, eased movement, Taylor moved his fingers to his left chest pocket. With a nimbleness surprising for such a large hand, he undid the button and pulled out a pair of Vuarnet sunglasses. He eased them on.

"Hey," said Daniels, "tell me what happened to Henderson. I heard he was arrested."

Taylor stated his position by not stating anything.

"Look, Taylor. You're a newbie. I'm a second class. Now, I have a right to know what happened to a seaman in my division."

Taylor smiled. "Don't pull that shit on me."

"Hey, watch it. Friend or not. I'm still senior."

"I told you, I have a headache."

Daniels sat back. "What are you hiding? I mean, what the hell's so secret about Henderson—"

"Shh."

"What do you mean, shhh?" said Daniels.

"Just what I said. Can't you see? I'm sitting back, just clearing my head." He paused. "It's as simple as that, and you can't read it."

"Read what?" said Daniels.

"Why do you look deeper than what is already staring you in the face." He pushed his glasses up tight against his cheeks.

"Is what stares you in the face always what it seems?" Taylor ignored the question.

"I said, what happened to Henderson?"

Taylor shook his head. "Damn your persistence. All right, I'll tell you. I'll allow you to spoil my peace and tranquility on this fine fucking morning."

"Correction, on this fine Navy day," said Daniels.

"To you, maybe, not me." He removed his glasses. The bus lurched as it hit a large bump in the road. "From the Sunset Club, we made it to the Elephant Bar. Henderson got drunk, and it wasn't long after that he was trading blows with a few Marines."

"Typical."

"Shore Patrol showed, and he took 'em on. I got to admit, for a small man, he can sure handle himself. It took six Shore Patrol and two local police to control him. The man thought that he was the Hulk." Taylor and Daniels both started to chuckle.

"Where were you? How come they didn't drag you in?"

"I stayed low. To hell if I'll ever be dragged to the brig."

"You know it's gonna be a long stay for Henderson. Maybe even suspension from the division."

"The fates lead him who will: Him who won't, they drag."

"Very apt," said Daniels. *The brig.* That was a place Daniels did not want to ever see. The "game" suddenly surfaced. He eyed Taylor and then swallowed, checking himself from saying anything. He had thought about it a lot since their conversation and felt like throwing out some new ideas. But instead, a tinge of anger flicked through him. He really wanted to discuss it. He looked around the bus. But the thought of getting thrown in the brig for discussing how to take a nuclear weapon off the ship scared him. The image of both of them in a long column of sailors with shaved heads, both hands secured to one another in one long human chain, sent another tremor zipping through his body. He had painfully watched as the Marine guards would count off while the "detainees" would sing "Gangway!"—their heads pointed down to the deck as they marched through the passageways on their way to the chow hall and back. And God help the sailor who got in their way and did not move or even stared too long in passing. It was rumored that the Marines, up on their booted toes, would scream at the unfortunate lad. And if he didn't respond, the Marines would knock him down in a blur of rage and make him walk in the unholy procession until they reached the brig—and what horror stories slithered from there—the beatings, the humiliation, the isolation.

"Tell me why you got into a fight last night," said Daniels.

Taylor slid his glasses back on and didn't answer. A fresh scab on his lower lip was easily discernible. It matched in size of an old one on his forehead.

It was hot. And getting hotter. Daniels looked at the beads of sweat on the palm of his hand. A blur caught his eye. A Thompson gazelle burst forth from a thicket behind a fig tree and leaped across a wooden fence tacked over with barbed wire. *Running, that's right, always running.* Daniels glanced at Taylor and wondered if Taylor was also running from something. School, the fumble, parents, himself?

Daniels took in the road as it blurred past in its retreat. The heat of the morning sun beat against his brow as he tried to pick from the waterhole of the memory images of his life before enlisting. But his mind went blank, and again, anxiety reared its head. He tried to concentrate on the African forms running movie sharp past him. *The source, the anger, the answer, here, maybe here, closer, don't dwell, don't think.* He scanned the brush for movement, concentrating on discerning a claw, a gleaming eye, or a tooth. But the memories came.

Scenes of fighting flared. With his father, a man, a stranger to him. Fighting with him and his teachers over poor grades and incomplete homework during his senior year. Fighting with his high school classmates for the first three years due to his academic superiority, for being better than them. No, not fighting—covering, defensive,

95

withdrawing his frame from the incessant barrage of insults and embarrassing pranks. A dumpster. Sharon watching. *Jesus, they threw me in while Sharon watched.*

The bus slowed and came to a halt at a store with gas pumps by the side of the dirt road. It was a small shack with pieces of red plywood in several places covering holes in its side. The driver yawned and climbed out. The men followed.

Daniels accompanied Taylor up the steps, across the porch, and through the doorway. Inside was cool, but he immediately felt claustrophobic. The interior was densely packed and barely lit, with many shelves of dusty canned goods stacked in a haphazard fashion. Boxes of food with strange writing and symbols leaned against the back wall. To his right, across from the makeshift counter, stood an old ice box. He went for it. He grabbed a bottle of Coca-Cola, thinking he enjoyed more the look and feel of the bottle than its contents. It was warm. Fuck it, he was thirsty, and a warm coke was better than none— particularly from a glass bottle. He hated the look and feel of aluminum in his hand and the slight aluminum after-taste left in his mouth. Smooth glass always appealed to him. It was tasteless.

Daniels walked out to the porch and waited. The field across from him was littered with rusted cans and torn paper. Further down, patches of stilted houses lined the road. Low blue-brown hills and smudges of trees trembled in the deep distance. He swatted at the flies that buzzed his head as his driver worked an old pump with a hose biting into the bus. The other drivers sat in their vehicles, waiting.

Daniels smelled him first. He turned, and below, to his right, sat a local native. He stared up at Daniels with a grizzled palm outstretched. A torn and soiled robe clung to his waist. A stump that had once been his right leg was crossed over on his left. The skin was dark red and swollen around the severed bone just above the knee. His lips moved, but no sound came forth. Daniels saw in his eyes the faint spark of a man who had quit running. *Couldn't run.* A man who accepted fate squarely, sitting, hoping, depending on the luck and generosity of others. Daniels slid his hand down into his pocket.

But before he had his fingers wrapped around a coin, a large hand appeared and dropped some coins into the man's hand. It was Taylor. The man's eyes bloomed, and he smiled, and he grasped the coins and placed them in a fold of his robe. He then repositioned his hand up toward Daniels' chest. Taylor walked across the porch and down the steps.

Daniels found a few coins and dropped them into the man's hand. He went after Taylor.

"Hey, Taylor."

Taylor stopped a few feet from the bus.

"Hey, did you notice that guy on the way into the store?"

Taylor gave a quick, loose shrug of his shoulders.

"No, I mean it," said Daniels. "Did you?"

Taylor nodded.

"Well, hell, that's funny. I didn't notice him sitting there at all."

"I believe we tune in and see only what we want to see." Taylor climbed into the bus. Daniels stood there a moment, irritated at Taylor's quick remark and overly cool mannerism. He kicked the dirt and then started to board the bus but suddenly stopped, feeling somehow compelled to look around, knowing that somehow this was connected to the nervousness that he had been experiencing. He looked at the man sitting on the porch and then over to the houses across from him. He studied them, noticing a few features he missed the first time. The houses were clumped, one story each, and pieced together with an assortment of materials, cardboard being one of them. Rotting wood, frayed plastic over windows, blown-out holes, and a fetid smell all targeted him. And to his right, on the shoulder of the road that his bus had passed coming in, a thin native woman stood with two children. She was tall and gaunt, shoeless, a soiled pink dress clinging to her drawn frame, a long string of tangled thread hugging the dirt behind her. With one hand on her hip, curled, elbow out, her other hand holding the upraised hand of a naked child, she stared straight at Daniels with a gaze that was hard and penetrating. The second child had short pants on, stained, and sat staring down the long stretch of empty road. Both were bone thin and covered in a skin of white dust. Their stomachs bowed slightly.

Edema, it was called. Fluids collected in the cells cause bloated distension. Daniels turned away. He swatted at the flies and climbed onto the bus.

Daniels noticed Taylor watching the three figures through the window, but he couldn't quite make out Taylor's expression. It was hard yet soft, revealing yet distant. It spoke of subdued intensity, almost a halting hatred that smothered just beneath furled brows and discerning eyes. It was a hazy questioning look and yet, sharply judgmental. Daniels truly didn't know what to make of it. Taylor's head shifted as the three Africans turned and walked toward the houses. Daniels felt odd, uncomfortable. He wondered what these three Kenyans saw lurking in his eyes. In Taylor's? What did they think? Did they seek to find familiarity or comfort in the eye? A shared gesture of kindness? Of hope? Respect? Or was it, as he had already felt, a shared disappointment of a dream? A bloodied realization that poverty and desire were always at the core of every heart, in every city, in every continent? Or was it deeper, something that could not be shared, something that transcended mere properties of pigment, of pupil, of heart?

The bus lurched forward, and Daniels sank back, deep in thought. The sign at the entrance of Tsavo animal reserve read:

"You enter this park at your own risk. Please do not:
-Exceed 20 MPH 32 KPH
-Disturb the animals
-Leave your vehicle except at the lodge or at official sites
-Drive off the roads
-Enter with dogs or firearms"

The park didn't look any different from the landscape they had just driven through. *It's not what I imagined it to be. But we're deeper, closer into the heart of...* The driver shouted and stopped the bus. *Game*.

The road coiled up a hill overlooking a river. Down in the sand of the riverbank, three elephants drank. At four tons, a large female swayed gently back and forth, her trunk flitting across the surface of the water. Two younger ones stood drinking by her side.

His first reaction was a disappointment as he reflected back on his grandfather's stories. *No lions.* He looked at his watch. The group of buses stopped and idled while sailors stood up in the open sunroofs and shot picture after picture. Clicks could be heard up and down the row of dusty vehicles.

Daniels stood up, squeezing in between two sailors. An uncomfortable presence fluttered on the wind. He turned and scanned the landscape, taking in a swirl of black bees, swollen termite mounds, stripped bark of the Yellow Fever Trees, and a sharp canine wind. It all seemed somehow surreal.

He stood on his seat, head and neck extended out from the open top, camera positioned, and shot frame after frame—wasting an enormous amount of film on the first of hundreds of elephants he would inevitably see.

They drove on and soon encountered and photographed an array of animals—antelope, giraffe, hippopotamus, crocodile, warthog, cape buffalo, eland, bushbuck, oryx, wildebeest, ostrich, and the rarely seen cheetah. But no lions. Approaching a group of Masai, the driver slowed to a crawl, and he asked them if his group could photograph them. They wouldn't allow it. But Daniels snapped a few pictures anyway while they weren't looking, and he wondered if he had indeed somehow captured their soul, or at least a piece of it, as some had mentioned being the case if photographed. He swallowed and concluded he hadn't. If he had, he reasoned, they would have undoubtedly reacted when the shutter descended on the light like shears. But they didn't so much as flinch when he pressed the button. Their feet still fell hard and quick to the red earth in perfect rhythm, their eyes and heads constantly moving ahead of them. They walked on, sticks in hand, and never looked back.

Light, then, he mused, reflected from flesh and stored in the mind or camera, had neither the power to penetrate nor illuminate nor capture the essence of the object. Those levels of observation, he concluded, were left to the pervasive understanding of the heart. For there lay the true shutter, where heated valves clicked, stored, and encoded the dark noble blood of being. Of all being. Blood, darkly deprived or ruddy rich, was the character lining of soul. And light, mother to hue, was only a messenger, and as always, the case was extinguished unfairly with the fire.

By mid-afternoon, they arrived at a safari lodge in Tsavo animal park. After eating an enormous meal of assorted meats and vegetables, Daniels walked outside the lodge and mingled with some female tourists from Australia. As he listened to them talking about the dangers and excitement of Africa, he fingered a lodge pamphlet that he had picked up in the dining hall and tried to keep his attention off the strange taste of meat lingering in his mouth. He couldn't identify it and didn't bother to ask.

But just as he was going to interject on the "romantic" and "coolness" of Africa to these young girls, he was startled to see one of the tour guides walk up and beat the earth next to his feet with a large stick. He jumped back in alarm. The guide casually bent down and lifted a small snake. It hung kinked and crushed, and the trickle of blood running down to its tail contrasted harshly with the dusty black scales. The girls, hands to their mouths, screamed. The guide looked up at Daniels and smiled. "Poison," he suddenly said, bursting the "P" of the word. Daniels felt his stomach turn. The snake had been three inches away from his foot.

The guide walked toward a huge trash pit on the side of the lodge and then tossed the carcass into the heap of trash as he would a cigarette butt—with practiced, refined ease. The Marabou Storks, their pallid legs covered in excreta uric acid, hopped back a few feet at this intrusion, then continued picking at the cans and discarded waste.

Between the strange meal and sight of those strange birds, trash, and a close call with the deadly snake at his feet, Daniels felt a bit sick. He lifted the pamphlet in his hand and studied the clean glossy photo of the building and the enticing, exotic landscape in the distance. The angle was just right to hide the trash pit in the back. He tore the pamphlet in two.

God, it's hot. The sun beat down on him and burned his skin. He wiped away a stream of perspiration crawling down his forehead and walked to the lodge.

He entered and scouted the main lounge for Taylor. He wasn't there. He looked through a huge window set along the length of the room overlooking the plains and a water hole 200 feet away at the foot of a hill. During the dry season, the lodge would fill the man-made hole with water to attract game so that the tourists could sit up high, air-conditioned, sipping drinks, safely discussing their excitement and the animals gathered below. For the slightly more adventurous, an underground passage led into a small barred room next to the water hole. Thinking that Taylor was there, Daniels headed toward it.

Daniels walked past the manicured garden, past the lavish outdoor bar, and down a short flight of steps to the entrance. Looking through the opening, he could see that the tunnel was long and dark. He entered into cool air. He walked forward, scanning for snakes. A sharp movement caught his eye. He stopped. It took a while in the dim light to register. But as his eyes slowly adjusted, short quick movements were visible on the walls. *They're moving!* His eyes adjusted a bit more, and he tried to focus on a slithering mass that covered the walls and ceiling. *What the...?* He peered closer. He could make out thin bodies writhing about and heaped on top of one another. *Snakes—no, can't be—lizards!* He swallowed. *Fucking lizards!* The place literally crawled with hundreds of the large black reptiles. He took in a deep breath, ducked, and, drawing his arms into him, continued on, hoping none would drop on him.

One did.

It swept past him, a black blur. He jerked back in shock as it hit his shoulder, its thin claws digging into his skin, then leaped off, its tail slapping his neck, and quickly disappeared. Trembling, he recomposed himself. Keeping an eye on the light at the tunnel's end, he quickly made for it. He entered a small room set in the earth. Taylor was leaning against the iron bars of a window opening out at ground level. He was watching a group of zebras and two giraffes drinking from the water hole a few feet away. Daniels searched the room for snakes or anything else that wasn't supposed to be there. Nothing.

"Hey, what are you doing down here? I thought you'd be up in the lounge?"

Taylor didn't move. It was as if Daniels had never walked in, had never said a word.

"Fuck, this is awesome," said Daniels, looking out to the water hole and the drinking zebras, giraffes, and other animals to the hills beyond, realizing he had answered his own question.

"Take a good look," said Taylor, "it'll be nothing but pavement and people someday."

Daniels stared out at the landscape. "What makes you think so? This is a protected park."

"Don't be so naive."

"Don't be so patronizing."

"I'm not. Just stating a fact. A hard, cold, fucking fact."

"Well put."

"I just happen to give a shit about tomorrow," said Taylor. "If I could stick every politician into a time machine and zap their fat asses into the future they are now making . . . what do you think they'd say when they got back?"

Daniels shrugged. "It probably wouldn't make any difference."

"Don't you think rubbing shoulders with billions of hungry people living in a fucking wasteland wouldn't kick you in the ass?"

"Just what I said. It probably wouldn't do anything."

"Sure as shit would."

"I don't think so. Because even if they saw and smelled it, they would have to convince the others back here that the future *stinks*. And you know as well as I do that's impossible. You'd have to send every government asshole with a say in the matter."

"Maybe. Maybe not. Someone might make a difference."

"Yeah, it's called parents. They have more influence than anything or anyone. I'm sure your mother instilled positive values in you."

Taylor suddenly turned and hunched over on his elbows. He watched the zebras cautiously drink from the water's edge. The silence was a bit awkward. But at last, Taylor spoke, his voice soft and hesitant.

"Yes, she did . . . before she died."

"Oh, sorry to hear that. How old were you when she passed?"

"I really don't want to talk about it."

Daniels nodded and leaned against the bars. He tried tuning his mind to something more pleasant. He studied for a while the long graceful curve of a giraffe's neck. Amazing, he thought. It could see so high and so far. What must it be like to look down from such a height to the earth below? What a truly remarkable animal. But the realization that someday the only giraffes his distant grandchildren might see would be in zoos filled him with a deep sense of sorrow and loss. And with that, the words of his grandfather suddenly echoed in his mind. *A land of great beasts, great beauty, and great trial.*

"You know," said Daniels, shifting his attention, "this reminds me of when I was a kid growing up in the woods. I always found it exciting to try and sneak up close to animals or try to identify their spoor. How about you?"

"No," said Taylor.

"No, not at all?"

"I said no."

Daniels turned and watched as a warthog and her offspring cautiously made their way to the water's edge.

"Do you know what the word 'spoor' means," asked Taylor.

Daniels looked back to Taylor. "Yeah, I'm pretty sure what it means—a 'track.'"

"Partly," said Taylor, "It's a Dutch word for 'footprint' or 'trail.'"

"Oh," said Daniels. He put both arms up on the sill and rested his chin between his hands. After a while, a small zebra, its flanks muddied, crept up to the water's edge. It lowered its head, and just as it touched its lips to the water, Taylor spoke, the words flowing out slow and awkward. "I grew up poor in the city." He paused. "I never joined the scouts, built a fire, or camped in the woods."

The unexpectedness openness and tone surprised Daniels. He smiled, "How'd you know about spoor then."

"A man doesn't have to travel to the moon to know what it is."

"Hey, I was just kidding."

Taylor closed his eyes for a few seconds and then opened them, looking out past the zebra. "I was always a reader." The words were almost a whisper.

"Oh, I see," said Daniels.

"No, I don't think you can. It's something you have to live, to feel, in order to understand."

"Kinda like the moon, huh."

"Don't get smart with me. Sometimes the only difference between this place and any other is the size and shape of the animals. Maybe not even that." He turned and faced Daniels, his voice rising. "And screw the lounge. I don't give a damn about some rich tourists sipping drinks in plump chairs, all exchanging stories or writing letters about the danger of wild animals from behind glass!"

Daniels didn't respond. He looked out for the animals. For the next few minutes, they watched the small piglets drink from the muddied water; their tiny heads poised delicately over the dark waters. *Clouded, not clear, no danger of captivation, of falling, pulled down by vanity as Narcissus.* The zebra trotted off, scaring the pigs.

Daniels turned to Taylor. "I'm curious, Taylor. Sorry, but I need to ask again. Why'd you leave college? Was it really because of some football game you lost? A fumbled ball with seconds to go, with the whole school putting you through hell. Is that really true?"

Taylor backed away from the wall and stared hard at Daniels. "No, it's not. Not even close."

"Then what?"

"If you were really listening, I just discussed it." He turned and walked out, disappearing into the hole that led up to the surface. Daniels stayed a while, smoked a joint, and then left just as a lone elephant, its ribs and bowed back revealing its age, padded up to the water, scattering the remaining zebras.

In the afternoon, they pulled into Mzima Springs. The driver cautioned them against leaving the path and then pointed to a sign:

"Caution—You are likely to meet dangerous wild animals on this trail. Please proceed quietly and with caution. You proceed at your own risk. The National Park is not responsible for any eventuality."

Eventuality, thought Daniels, they mean dismemberment. The thought of encountering his first lion outside the safety of the bus disturbed him. Yet the thought of lions at a distance and the sight of the springs instilled within him his first real sense of excitement of the day. He smiled. The springs reminded Daniels of an oasis he had once seen in a photo as a wide-eyed child at his grandfather's house. He took in a deep breath. A large meandering pond lay before him. Dense brush around the shore broke off in ragged patches, then tapered and scattered into the bare plains. Bare backs of hippos rose up in the middle of the springs like small volcanic islands, and "Rainbow" lizards and vervets—medium-sized, smoky-gray monkeys—scurried around the paths.

Daniels approached a vervet sitting hunched on a stone fence. The monkey nodded his head and screeched, his hand slapping into his chest. Daniels eased up to it and stopped. The gesture made by the animal betrayed within Daniels an overwhelming need to capture its image, for it struck him as curious, and he couldn't understand why. But he wanted an intense close-up. He put his camera to his eye and cautiously inched closer. The monkey turned and eyed Daniels. With every step, the monkey's face grew until it filled the frame, its flickering white and brown fur a helmet framing brown eyes. The eyes grew larger with each inch till he could make out his own reflection within the glassy surface of the monkey's eyes. This image halted him. Daniels drew closer, intrigued, still quite high from the joint. The pupil of the monkey dilated, opening wide a vast cavern, increasing a dream-like vacuum which gently tugged him forward, absorbing him, pulling him in past the lens, iris, nerve, pulling him further into the blood of artery, of heart. Strangely, he could see now the valves flush, and the blood flow richly in rapid waves, feeding the hundreds of billions of cells crying out within the earthen body. He wanted to touch that heart, to feel its warm fluid pulse across his fingers, to feel it alive. *Alive!*

Instinctively and unknowingly, he moved forward. The monkey suddenly jerked back, the movement sucking Daniels back up into his right index finger. He pressed the shutter. At the sound of the "click," the monkey shrieked and attacked Daniels' leg. Daniels jumped back in fear. Taylor laughed. Daniels tried to shake free from the monkey's hand that was holding tightly to his pant leg. He kicked and hobbled about, and the monkey screamed and barked and twittered, following his every move, one arm still clutched, the other arm shaking wildly in the air.

The monkey let go. Daniels breathed hard and fast, his head turning from the crowd that had gathered. They were all laughing at him. He put his hands into his pockets and walked to the water's edge, the excitement gone once again. Taylor grinned the whole way down.

They made their way over to an underwater viewing tank set up for tourists. They walked across the bamboo bridge and stepped down into the tank. It was cramped, dark, and reeked. But it was cool. Daniels was able to see small, brightly colored fish, which, as they approached the glass, grew large and distorted and then shrunk again, expanding as they skitted by. He was disappointed. He wanted to see a hippo or a large crocodile thrust its snarled and jagged snout by. *Behind glass again.* He could see movement but couldn't make out form or shape. The light penetrated only a short distance before being swallowed completely. He felt uncomfortable and, surprisingly, cold. He climbed out.

They walked to the water's edge. A small sign read:

"Lower Pool—Warning, beware of crocodile. It is dangerous to enter or be close to the water."

A small group of people stood next to the shallows, oblivious to the sign. Oblivious to the danger beneath the placid water. Daniels kept back from the water's edge. The driver had told him earlier that a crocodile was capable of launching out from the water at speed too fast to avoid. In fact, he said that he had seen crocs taking watchful gazelles from the banks as they drank. And if a croc could take an animal as fast and as alert as a gazelle, it sure as hell could take a slow, lumbering human. And it did. Two or three tourists were taken every year at this very spot, he said. It happened so suddenly and so unexpectedly that the victim hadn't time to react. The croc would clamp down with its ragged teeth and drag the screaming, clawing, disbelieving tourist out into the water and drown him. Firmly attached to its victim, the croc would then violently roll its thick body, thus severing an arm or leg, and then bury the rest in a convenient larder below the surface. After the body decomposed and bloated up, the croc would then return to continue feeding.

It was so typical, Daniels thought. Why do people chance it or ignore such danger? They must think it will never happen to them, or it's a one-in-a-million shot that they, singled out from all the others, will be the unfortunate one. But more than ten people are dragged screaming off the river banks and eaten each day in Africa. One croc alone in Central Africa had been credited with killing and eating over 400 people. The villagers must have a fatalistic outlook, Daniels thought. When a family member is taken and eaten by a large croc while bathing, washing clothes, or gathering water, the family will still go back and use the same spot! Crocs are not dumb. They are quite cunning. They will, in fact, sit and wait in ambush at a particular place if the feeding's good. Daniels couldn't understand this at all. It was like playing Russian Roulette or living in a minefield. But then again, with the snakes, lions, hippos, tribal warfare, starvation, disease, and a host of other deadly afflictions, he could see how they numbed themselves and accepted it as a way of life, hostility, chance, and fate.

"I wouldn't stand that close if I were you," said Daniels. Taylor had perched himself on a large flat rock set out on a small thin peninsula. His hands were in his back pockets, and he was leaning over, staring down into the reflective water.

Daniels felt nervous, and he checked the muddy shoreline and green water reeds growing in tight, phalanx patches for any sign of movement.

"Taylor, can't you read the sign? There are man-eating crocs around."

Taylor didn't respond.

Daniels shouted. "Taylor! Read the damn sign."

Taylor stirred and turned towards Daniels, the water now behind him. "I can read well enough."

"Look, Taylor, you're tempting fate."

"Fuck it. Let it lead me. The bus ride down here was more dangerous. Walking home from school was more dangerous."

"Taylor!"

"Join me?"

"Sure . . .Let fate lead me," said Daniels, "but I sure as shit don't want it to drag me. Particularly under that wretched water. Now get your ass over here—now."

Taylor seemed to look right through Daniels, through the Acacia trees, and out into the ghostly red hills festering in the heat beyond. *I don't understand; it's as if . . .* A slight rippling in the water behind Taylor suddenly caught Daniels' attention. He swallowed. A black snout surfaced. Someone screamed.

Everyone near the edge, including Daniels, scrabbled back in a blur of arms and legs. Except for Taylor. He slowly turned and watched the form approach.

People started shouting. Daniels took another two steps back and watched, horror-stricken.

Taylor stood and stared, and no one moved. The croc was about twelve feet long, and it drew nearer.

Taylor's chest moved slowly and easily, and his head swiveled like a radar device locked onto the approaching croc, whose long snout barely made a ripple as it moved. Ten feet, nine feet, eight, seven, six. But at five feet away, the croc suddenly swerved to the right, clamping down on and exposing the frantic tail and pumping hind legs of a smaller croc hidden just beneath the surface. The smaller croc's head thrust up, and its mouth quivered and opened, exposing two rows of needle-like teeth. The larger croc shook his massive jaw and turned toward the center of the lagoon, the small croc snapping slower, slower, and then not at all, its small beady eye fixed open and upward. Taylor kept watching until the two shapes melted into the dark waters from which they came.

Taylor looked down and watched as a small ripple from the two bodies approached and lapped the rock. He turned, jumped to the embankment, and walked up the trail in silence to the buses, his fingers trembling. Daniels followed, his sickness returning.

2 Oct. 77

Pure. That's all I can really say. For how can one express the inexpressible?

I'm sitting next to a campfire right now, drinking a tequila sunrise. Mt. Kilimanjaro, in its white cloak, watches over me. There are no fences here, only wandering, stalking eyes. There is a pure, cutting wildness here, strong and free. You can smell it, touch it. But only with muted sense, atrophied and smoothed over with urban disuse. I wonder what it would be like to have full capacity again, like our ancestors. To stalk and kill, to be intensely alive and alert. The senses were crucial. To live out here as they did and not to smell the scent of a stalking cat, or hear the crunch of a fallen leaf, is to die. To shut one's eyes is to die. They are free choices with bloody deviations.

Yet when I look to the locals, the thin children in layers of dirt and partial dress, the Masai tribesman in western clothes and mannerisms, I look to strangers. As I gaze out, only a sense of sorrow seems to settle around me like the red dust that blankets the beaten land.

At Mzima Springs today, I felt alive for the first time in a long time. I can't explain it, but death brushed by and colored me. It was as pure as God's rainbow. I played a game of death with a passing croc. And I won. It was strange, and I was fearful, but for some reason, I knew no harm would come to me. Not sure why. But fate was my ally and guide today.

Amboseli

The night brought Daniels some solace. It was hot but not scalding. The sweat oozed down his forehead. A few drinks at the bar had quieted his mind and stomach, but he still felt slightly ill. The snake and crocodile incident had shaken him up, and three hours ago, a German couple had reported seeing lions only a half-mile from the lodge—and he hadn't seen any all day. *Damned luck.* He walked in the darkness toward the thin line of the "Kilimanjaro Safari Lodge" huts. He could barely make them out. They looked unreal, like two-dimensional drawings from an encyclopedia pasted into the sky, each a cheap and flimsy fixation to quiet a wandering mind. *Dammit, mine has to be the last one.* He glanced at the dirt. An image formed, condensed, and moved. *Snake.* He jumped. He steadied himself, bent down, and stared. *Shit, a stick.* He swallowed and continued. *Dammit, no fence. There's no fence around these huts.* He stopped and looked back.

The campfire spit and roared, flames leaping and dancing at will, shooting spears of yellow light at the earth. Taylor sat alone, leaning in a chair against the outdoor bar, drink in hand. He took in a powerful breath of the ebony night, his huge chest billowing slowly outward like a great cloud. He held it, held it, let go.

Daniels also took in a deep breath. It tasted hot, sticky, and ancient. He wondered if these molecules racing past his nostrils had also touched the moist lining in his ancestors' lungs. It must be all cyclic, as the atoms that bound his ancestors and his own tight skin were assembled within distant stars. With the passing of his death, they might eventually rearrange themselves in another, perhaps giving a straighter arc to a nose, a different pigment to the skin, a set of feathers or claws or gills. Maybe someday, even traveling back to the stars in reasoning organic form as a witness in the exploration of their fiery birthplace—or, maybe, as waves of dust in the cosmic cycle. *Maybe maybe, maybe. Maybe not!* Daniels turned and aimed for the light of his hut in the distance.

The darkness had now settled into the slopes of Mt. Kilimanjaro, concealing its presence, but he could feel it. Even in the daylight, the mountain was hardly seen. A tourniquet of gray clouds was usually wrapped tightly about its volcanic skin. The best time to view it, said the guide, was in the early morning hours before the heated air rose and cooled and condensed. Just its snow-covered tip was visible when Daniels pulled into camp an hour before sunset. His heart sank. He wanted to see the full majestic image that graced every pamphlet and article on Kenya. But just a huge band of gray clouds that extended from horizon to horizon greeted him and the smallest sliver of a snow-covered cap. And even this small reward seemed imperceptible.

The ground trembled slightly, and he stopped. *Earthquake!* His heart jumped. The only thing solid and secure in the whole world right now rolled in waves under his toes. He looked back toward the fire, at Taylor's upturned head, at his large hands gripping the chair tightly. How odd, Daniels thought, as he tried to steady himself, to look up to the heavens instead of down to his feet as the earth rolled smoothly beneath.

The movement faded, but its energy fueled a nervousness in his body. *It's okay, just a small trembler.* He continued toward his cabin, the grass crunching under his feet.

As he got halfway to the light of his door, a glistening in the dark caught his eye. He stopped. As the curve of light loomed larger, a second one appeared very close to the first. Instinct swept through him. *Move. Now.* He couldn't. Fear seized him. A large dark form materialized in the faint light. The hump of its arched back shifted gracefully from side to side as it silently approached.

A shudder, a rooted tremor launched from the tips of his toes, forced its way violently up his legs and into the pit of his stomach. He tried to release it, vent it, through its proper channel, the vocal cords, but they wouldn't move. They were as still and silent as the great cat poised three feet away.

Okay, don't panic. She's curious, just curious, like the croc and Taylor. Don't run, don't run, or she'll react.

The lion shifted her powerful head. Her three-hundred-pound body expanded with each rank breath making its way past her cruel canines, curved up, glistening and sinister. *Rare events, they clump. Snake didn't bite; croc didn't bite; the lion won't bite. No. Stupid! Don't trust laws. She's standing there waiting, wondering how and when she's gonna kill me. Eat me.*

The two stood close, waiting. Daniels took in deep shallow breaths, careful not to expand his chest too rapidly. He focused on her paws, on the soft brown hair concealing retractable death just beneath. The cat stood still. Long seconds swept by, neither moving. Daniels felt lost in space and time. It was as if the gap that separated him from the lioness was billions of light years away and, at the same time, mere fractional angstroms. As though size and distance evaporated, transcended, into eternity. He and the lioness fused and became one. It was as if he had been standing there lifetimes, since the beginning of creation, the start of time itself—watching hunter and hunted, man and beast, victor and victim, action and reaction, cause and effect. All runners in a world racing against the onslaught of entropy, where all would eventually collide, wind down, and collapse, spent of energy, fuel, of blood. The pendulum stops.

The lioness moved, then halted, if studying him, sizing him up. Daniels flinched and then remained still. Her tail sliced through the air, back and forth, back and forth. The only sounds to be heard—the continuous cumbrous gruff she ejected with each breath—and the rapid beating of Daniels' heart. He had to wait to play it out. Anger seized him. *The stories, the stories—bullshit, nothing here, only chance, only survivors!*

Daniels kept his eyes on her paws, for he had read that a lion never backed down from a stare; rather, it would accept the challenge and charge. He fixated on the tiny brown hairs and spots of dirt littered on her paws. Finally, at what seemed like years, they suddenly twitched and moved to the rhythm of her swaying frame. They lifted off the grass with a soft yet sharp crunch and moved forward and to his left. Daniels took in a large breath, his stomach seeming to plunge toward the center of the earth. Her tail swished by his ears, past his eyes, and moved in the direction of the campfire of Taylor. *Taylor!*

Daniels tried to respond but couldn't. Time stretched painfully. Everything seemed in slow motion. Even his thoughts. The large black shape slowly crept toward Taylor.

"Taylor." It was barely a whisper.

The cat was now only a few yards from his chair.

"Taylor!" This time it was loud. The cry exploded over the tread of the cat. Taylor lifted his head and looked toward Daniels, then to the lion, only a few feet away.

Daniels expected Taylor to stand still as he had done with the crocodile, but instead, with a dexterity rivaling any cat's, he leaped from the chair like a shooting star—disappearing over the top of the bar behind him. The lion froze. Taylor froze. Daniels froze. Daniels then watched Taylor's hand rise up in the glow of the fire and grasp a leather cord running up to a large bell above the bar. The hand pulled. Hard. Then violently. At the first "bong," the lioness, startled, leaped to the right and, with a steady gait that matched the cadence of the ringing bell, ran in the direction of Kilimanjaro.

Lodge officials, drivers, and guests streamed from buildings, some with pots, some with rifles, running about this way and that, all a buzz in the excitement. But the great cat ran on, becoming a thin shadow in the eyes of the men, finally merging with the blackness of the night itself.

Daniels trembled, feeling again a deep sense of loss and sickness. He knelt and emptied his stomach onto the earth. He stood and wiped his lips and chin with his forearm and looked down in embarrassment. The heavy stench drifted up into him. He swore and kicked a stick.

He walked a few feet and stopped, looking back at the contents of his stomach steaming in the pale light. He stood confused. A sense of loss, not explainable, seemed to pervade him, to flow out from his eyes and down his cheek. It was a loss that touched deep, embraced feelings and visions of youthful promise. A promise that seemed to dry and crack as he was picked up and driven out and away from his home to a new one, one that, with time, event, and circumstance, kept hammering home a bit of truth that he had blindly failed to see. *The offing forever an inch away, never nearer, never healing.* He lifted his head to the heavens and suddenly thought of his grandfather, of Conrad, of a passage his grandfather had muttered several different times after drinking, "Our weary eyes looking still, looking always, looking anxiously for something out of life, that while it is expected is already gone—has passed unseen, in a sigh, in a flash—together with the youth, with the strength, with the romance of illusions."

Daniels continued on towards the light of his hut, his eyes scanning the ground, his heart beating strongly, his thoughts on Taylor. Taylor and the croc.

7 Oct. 77

I sail on. The massive propellers turn, tearing into its liquid love, which rears up, churns and bubbles behind, dulls with distance, settles, thins, and integrates, becoming one with a stalking horizon.

Africa is only a memory now.

And like all memory, no longer tangible, a true wake.

Worked out tonight with a Marine named Collins—Lance Corporal Collins. Pretty cool. Erudite, good attitude, married, two kids, Karen, two, and Tina, one. Showed me a picture of her. Beautiful. Plans to leave the service in two years and continue with school. He has an AA from a community college and will go for his bachelor's in some type of science. I wanted to tell him that physics was my major and that, like him, I left school and joined the service. But I didn't.

Collins is not as "gung ho" and "Macho" as the other Marines I've talked to. He's down-to-earth and likable. Will work out with me occasionally if he gets the time (his schedule is irregular. They are constantly busy preparing for inspections or doing some sort of work or training). He's changed my perceptions of the Marine Corps.

Picked up Heart of Darkness *again. Will try to finish it soon.*

Rogers

"Well, up or down?" demanded Petty Officer Second Class Rogers. Mitchel, the division's key and lock custodian, leaned over the office shredding machine and stared blank-eyed at his twenty-dollar bill. Rogers had swiped it from his hand and had set it tight into the teeth of the shredder. Mitchel brushed back his red hair and tightened his jaw. He placed his index finger on the unmarked "On/Off/Reverse" switch. Daniels watched carefully, as did O'Reilly, Sanchez, Stoker, and Roberts.

"You fucking asshole," said Mitchel.

"Well, I guess you'd better put your memory into overtime and try to recall which way you flip that switch." He leaned against the office bulkhead. "If you flip it just right, your bill will shoot up and float back into your pocket. But, if you push it wrong, you'll need a microscope, some glue, and shitloads of time to get your twenty back."

Everyone chuckled except for Daniels.

"Dammit! This is bullshit." Mitchel reached into the machine to rip his bill out, but Rogers intercepted his hand and flung it back.

"Now don't you go cheating on us, you hear. That's the rule. If you want to flash that twenty around like a cheap whore, then it's fair play. You understand, little man."

Rogers poked Mitchel in the chest, pushing him backwards into a desk. Mitchel balled his fist, but he didn't react. He took in a breath and walked over to the machine.

He flipped the switch down.

The bill disappeared into the shredder, cut into a thousand fragments. The room exploded with laughter. Daniels put his head down. The machine had just sliced up Mitchel's only remaining twenty till payday. No more sodas or candy for him.

The hum of the machine cut the air. Mitchel hovered above the whirring teeth, his fingers moving about the switch like a spider wrapping a fly. Sanchez, appearing to sense trouble, walked over and switched the machine off.

Mitchel lifted his head and then suddenly pointed to Rogers' grinning face. "You fucking bastard, I'll..."

He leaped at Rogers. Sanchez grabbed Mitchel's arms below his shoulder and held him. "Calm down—you hear me?"

Mitchel tried to break free. "Stop it!" said Sanchez. He shoved Mitchel back. "Damage is fucking done. Now calm down . . . you hear me?" Mitchel squirmed, but Sanchez held tight. "I said fucking stop!" Mitchel relaxed. Sanchez let go.

"All right, all right, show's over," said Sanchez, straightening his shirt. "Maybe next time you won't be so free-spirited in flashing your money around."

Mitchel kicked a desk, agitated. Sanchez turned and pointed. "Daniels, get your team down below and start that parachute exchange. Now."

Mitchel swore at Rogers, then headed for the door. O'Reilly, Stoker, and Roberts followed in procession.

"I thought we had a component exchange scheduled for today." said Daniels.

"No," said Sanchez. "Chief changed it. It'll wait, but the parachute in that one 57 is long overdue."

A quick one, Daniels thought as he looked at his watch. A component exchange operation was a time-consuming job, requiring special equipment to be set up to warn the team of any potential problem. A parachute exchange, however, particularly on a B57, was fast and easy. Daniels stalked Rogers out the door.

Rogers shuffled over to the opening of the trunk, grabbed the rope hanging from a pulley to steady himself, and climbed down the ladder. The rope swung back. Daniels approached it. *Bastard. Everyone's game to you.* The rope slowed, its undulations transferring to and rocking his eyes, his mind, and his memory. The hook on the rope before him was once attached to a large W-Division laundry bag. Stoker was enclosed within, gently rocking and swaying over the open trunk, a trunk that went down 24 feet. That was how Rogers, with a few friends, wished Stoker a happy birthday while docked in the Philippines last month. After placing him over the open trunk, they took turns slapping the bag. They sang out repeatedly, "Happy Birthday, dear Stoker. Happy birthday to you." Chancing on the scene, Daniels almost went crazy. He rushed over and ordered them to let him go, all the while wanting to punch the shit out of them. Yet, Daniels didn't hear one peep as Stoker had swung back and forth in the bag, broom handles beating into him. Stranger still, Stoker refused to put them on report, nor would he allow Daniels to do it for him.

Rogers always pushed people to their limits to see how they would react. He played, testing and teasing, emotions and frailties his cards. Daniels disliked him. The first day Daniels reported aboard, Rogers met him in the coop. Daniels didn't even have his seabag off his shoulders yet when Rogers walked up to him and extended his hand in friendship. Daniels responded in kind. But as his hand rose, Rogers slapped him hard in the chest. Rogers walked away laughing, saying, "you'll never be senior to me."

Rogers had gotten word that Daniels was a push button and was senior to him. And after that first meeting, things got worse. Because Daniels graduated first in his GMT "A" School class, he was offered advancement to E-4, or Petty Officer Third Class, from E-2, Seaman Apprentice. Daniels declined the offer because of an added extra year he would have to serve in the Navy. Instead, he was promoted to E-3 before Rogers. Rogers took this personally.

Daniels grabbed the rope and quickly descended the aluminum ladder to M-2. At the trunk's bottom, a slight tinge of toluene lingered in the air. He entered the magazine and walked to his left to the division's cleaning bench. The metal bench was set in under a row of white cabinets. It was six feet in length and three feet in width, and it had red splash cans of chemicals lined up against the dented rail that framed its top surface.

His team quickly spread out. They set up the equipment and

prepared the weapon for transit to the parachute workstation just next to the cleaning bench and just before the tool bench and main workstation on the left side of the magazine. Rogers sat down on the cleaning bench and looked at his manuals, fully aware that Roberts was standing next to him, patiently waiting for him to move so that he could finish his work.

Rogers was the team QA, Quality Assurance inspector. His job was to ensure that each step and action was done properly and in the right sequence. And if done so, he would simply check the appropriate box in his QA manual. He also loved to abuse this position. He would always halt the procedure and nit-pick on trivial details, irritating Daniels.

"Okay, everyone, let's get rolling," Daniels shouted to the group. Rogers looked up, put the manual down, and walked toward the back of the magazine. More in protest and contempt than to perform some task.

But just as Daniels turned to check the tool bench, Stoker suddenly let out a howl and raced towards the back of the magazine. He jumped over a double stack of B-61s and grabbed the red protective covers of two B-57 tail fins. He thrust his hips between them, the bomb projecting away from him like a large penis. Rogers stood ten feet away smiling, a B-61 shining out from his own gyrating hips.

"En garde," yelled Stoker.

"And you'll lose you tiny mother fucker," screamed Rogers. "I could fuck the world." Rogers started to grunt and hump the weapon, his hands squeezing and sliding over the silvery skin of the bomb. O'Reilly let out a cat call but abruptly lowered his head as Daniels glanced at him.

"Stoker, get off," yelled Daniels. "Now!"

Stoker reluctantly let go of the weapon, grinned at Rogers, and then shuffled over to the hoist. Rogers continued to pretend to hump the warhead. He moaned and then screamed, his eyes fusing, his hips thrusting tightly into the rear end of the weapon, his arms and body rigid. He then fell over on top of the bomb, panting, his arms limp. Stoker turned, smiled, and said, "Fucking A."

Daniels approached Rogers. Rogers stood up grinning, fanning his groin, and then walked over to a locker in the back corner of the magazine. He opened the door and lifted a B-43 nose cone in the back, exposing a small Tupperware container filled with homemade wine. He stuck his finger in and tasted it. Daniels stepped in between him and the locker. "Almost done," said Rogers. He smiled.

"Look, put that shit away before the Chief shows," said Daniels. "He'd shit bricks just seeing you fucking around with the weapons, let alone this. What the hell's wrong with you."

Rogers smiled. "You know, you'd be a better leader if you'd learn to mellow the fuck out." He put the cover back on and closed the locker.

"Don't be so concerned with me," said Daniels.

"What's wrong? Your stash dried up. I really think you need a good doober." Rogers reached into his front pocket, pulled out a joint, and offered it to Daniels. Daniels swatted it away.

"Fucking mellow, wog."

"Fuck you, Rogers."

"Now, now, woggy. We'd better get a move on. Don't want to piss off the nice Chiefy."

Daniels fought an overwhelming urge to hit him.

Rogers grinned, his head shifting up and down. Daniels tried to control his anger. He turned and studied the weapons stand set up just beyond the cleaning bench for the tail section of the weapon to be placed in and secured.

With a loud hiss, Stoker turned the air on and moved the hoist over to the designated weapon in the middle of the magazine. Daniels walked towards it, and as he did, he ran his hand along the yellow and black striped weapons elevator situated in the aft center of the large magazine but pulled away when a papercut-like pain forced his hand away. He stopped and pulled a chip of paint from his finger. He wiped a spot of blood on his trousers and approached the bomb. Everyone gathered around. The lead shield was removed, and as Daniels called out the commands, the cable with the hook was lowered from the hoist and affixed to the handling tool attached to the bomb. Daniels checked the cable for slack, and then Mitchel and O'Reilly removed the bolts, which secured the weapon in place.

Daniels glanced at Rogers, then started to give the command to lift the bomb but stuttered as the thought of stealing the weapon and pinning it on Rogers suddenly popped into his head. His eyes shifted to the B-57, to its dull white color, its red nose, and tail fins. He'd been thinking of the game more and more lately. *Yeah, steal it, pin it on him, notify the press and then tell them all about Rogers, all about this fucked up division.* He smiled as he thought of Rogers sitting in federal prison, in a small, dank cell, his hands, feet, and mouth shackled with great iron chains.

"Hey, space cadet," said Rogers. "Any day."

Yeah, take it—just to burn you. "Lift her slow and easy"...*and this division.*

With a loud whir, the bomb was eased up out of its cradle and then gently brought over to the cradle set up at the workstation. Curved metal bars with pads were fastened to the cradle with pins, and the weapon was set down carefully on them. Canvas straps attached to the bars were then wrapped around the weapon to hold it tightly in place. With the bomb secured, the hook and hoist were disengaged from the weapon. A large canvas sling was then fixed to the tail of the bomb by running it around and threading it through itself, and then attaching it to the hook under the hoist. Again, slack was taken up. This ensured that the sling would hold the tail if it suddenly slipped down.

As Daniels called out the appropriate steps, Rogers smiled and nodded his approval. *Bastard.* Stoker handed the speeder, breaker, taped screwdriver, and rubber mallets to the two workers, O'Reilly and Mitchel. O'Reilly placed the breaker, an Allen wrench, into the first screw on the tail clamp, joining the tail of the bomb to the warhead.

Two smaller ones at the tip joined it to the radar cone. With a loud snap, O'Reilly broke the torque, loosening the top clamp. He repeated this to the other remaining screw and then handed the breaker to Mitchel, who did the same to the two bottom ones. With the clamps loosened, O'Reilly took the speeder, an Allen wrench with a crank for fast turning, and removed the two top screws as Mitchel held the clamp in place with both hands. Sliding the speeder under the tail to avoid dropping it and damaging the weapon, Mitchel removed his screws while O'Reilly held the clamps.

Mitchel then picked up the taped screwdriver as Daniels marked a check on his plastic-covered page with a grease pencil.

"Insert screwdriver and gently pry clamps apart. If need be, use two rubber mallets to tap loose," said Daniels.

Mitchel inserted the screwdriver into the small slot between the two round clamps that joined one another and twisted. O'Reilly's clamp loosened and fell into his hand. He gently placed the clamp on a piece of cloth, which Roberts had set down on the deck. Mitchel then tugged at his clamp. It wouldn't budge. O'Reilly picked up the mallets, put one mallet against the clamp, and tapped against it with the other rubber mallet while Mitchel pulled. It popped off and out of Mitchel's hand. With a clang, it hit the steel deck.

"Shit," said Mitchel. He leaned down to inspect the damage.

Daniels set his manual down, walked over, and took the clamp from Mitchel's hand. He held it to the light and studied the surface. It didn't appear to have any structural damage to it, just a small ding.

"Any damage, Daniels?" demanded Rogers.

"No, not really, just a ding that a little paint couldn't fix. But we'll still have to file a report," said Daniels.

"What? You can't be serious," replied Mitchel.

"Yep, I am," said Daniels, "We have to. We go by the book. Sometimes the damage is internal and not visible."

"Fuck, it's just a clamp," said Stoker, "Why get the khaki excited and generate a lot of paperwork over just a chip."

"Stoker, cork it. I'm not going to repeat myself, now shut the fuck up, and let's continue."

"Hey, lay off the man," said Rogers, who stood off to Daniels right. Daniels sensed it coming. He took a deep breath.

"I think he's got a point," continued Rogers. "It's just a little nick on a little clamp in a little hand." He smiled, as did everyone. "Don't sweat such a little load, little man."

Daniels felt the anger rise. "Did you idiots hear me? I am not going to bend the rules just to satisfy you." He turned and glared at Rogers. "And you are supposed to be the QA, a man if I could call you that, responsible for the strict adherence to all rules and regulations."

Rogers placed two fingers against his lips and sucked in, pretending to inhale from an invisible joint.

"And," continued Daniels, "if you're trying to tell me to neglect my job and responsibilities while you neglect yours, and my authority, then I swear to God I'll write your dumb ass up, and you can explain it all to the Captain at Captain's Mast." Daniels swallowed and then stood tall, tapping into his pool of anger. "And that goes for all of you. If you don't listen and do well on my team, we'll all end up failing the inspection. And dammit, it is not gonna be on account of me. We go by the book. Now pull your head out of your asses, and let's move— now!"

Roberts moved to the clamp resting on the deck, picked it up, and then took the other one from Daniels' hand. He walked them over to the cleaning bench to wipe them down. Rogers lowered his head and muttered.

"Did you have anything else to say to me, Rogers?" said Daniels.

Rogers leaned back and smiled. "No, I have nothing further to say to you, my friend. Other than the crossing of the line ceremony's coming up real soon."

"Is that a threat, Rogers?"

"No, Mr. Hook, leader, sir. Just stating a fact. Just a fact. That's all." He smiled.

Daniels shook his head, picked up the manual, opened it, and read aloud the next step.

"Pull tail carefully away from warhead approximately six inches. Caution—do not stretch cables attaching warhead to tail."

Stoker eased the controls on the hoist. It sputtered, hissed, and slowly moved the tail backward six inches. Daniels checked off the step.

"Warning--Do not stand behind the tail. All personnel remain clear."

Daniels still simmered. He looked to the tail and thought of Rogers standing behind it as the detonators accidentally fired off, discharging the parachute while O'Reilly and Mitchel disconnected the cables. He saw a picture in "A" school of one that had gone off, lodging itself halfway through a wall. He could see Rogers, wide-eyed, blown through the air with the tail of a B57 nuclear bomb exploding through him and impaling him in the magazine's bulkhead. He grimaced. *Disgusting. What the fuck's happening to me. Never had thoughts like that.* He looked around the magazine, at the rows of bombs stacked up, at his crew, at the deck. The deck plugs shimmered.

"All clear. You may proceed with the operation, sir!" said Rogers, leering down at him.

"Cool it, Rogers." *His look.* Rogers reminded him of someone. It was like a hard kick to his gut. *Who?* The way he stood, looking down at him as a spider would a fly. Hooked jaw, hooked nose, and tall thin features reminded Daniels of someone from his past, from many years ago. He tried to but couldn't remember. He looked at the manual, checked off the step, and continued.

"I mean," said Rogers, "we wouldn't want a parachute accidentally misfiring, now would we."

"Yeah," said Stoker, "cut right through a man."

"What did I just say?" said Daniels, feeling the blood rise.

"Clean through a man," said Rogers. "Bloody fucking mess."

"Remove A1 and A2 cables from the tail," said Daniels, trying to

125

contain his anger but couldn't.

O'Reilly and Mitchel each undid a cable, disconnecting the tail with a parachute from the warhead. They put electro-static proof caps on the ends of the cables. The tail and detonators were safe now.

Daniels suddenly turned, and WHAM!—he kicked the bulkhead, the echo resonating through the magazine. Everyone froze. Rogers shook his head in disbelief.

"The first one to open his fucking mouth..." said Daniels, "...I'm going to fucking kick it in."

Rogers kept his mouth shut.

"Do you hear me? I said, do you hear me?" Everyone nodded but Rogers. "Now," said Daniels, his head cocked with a crazed look in his eyes, "Let's continue. Shall we?"

The hatch opened, and at the sight of Sanchez, the tension eased. Yet, Daniels' voice was tremulous for the next ten minutes, as were his movements, but they eventually calmed as well. The rest of the operation went without incident. They moved the tail, replaced the parachute with a new one, and then re-assembled the weapon.

On the way out of the magazine, Rogers pointed his finger into Daniels' face and shook it slowly but didn't speak. Daniels slapped it aside and continued. As he climbed up the trunk, he could hear Rogers' soft laughter beneath him.

09 Oct. 77

Daniels is in trouble again. Word spreads fast in this division. Rogers, Roberts, and Mitchel complained to the Chief that Daniels is a poor hook leader (which isn't far from the truth), has a bad attitude, and is disruptive to the morale and efficiency of the team. The Chief threw them all out of the office but later "discussed" the incident with Daniels. The Chief told him that he was trying too hard to get respect from his men. That he should loosen up a bit and give them some room. I think it went in one ear and out the other.

I haven't really talked to him since Africa other than an occasional hello. But tonight we had a long discussion over a chess game. Maybe too long. His hands move painfully slow while his mouth moves at 500 miles an hour. We mostly discussed how everyone is "wog" crazy— being that the ceremony is now two days away. I actually would have missed it, as the Midway had sailed down from the Indian Ocean and was supposed to have had the ceremony before pulling into Mombasa. But they hit some really bad storms, and the Captain uncharacteristically postponed the ceremony till after we left Africa and headed back up and over the equator. Daniels also missed the ceremony during the Midway's last Indian Ocean cruise, as he had to fly back home on leave just after the Philippines. Rogers thinks he did it on purpose to escape the initiation. But I'm not so sure. But I'm definitely curious to experience it. I was told that the shellbacks would huddle us all up, then lean back, a wicked spark gleaming in their eye, and recite incident after sick incident, trying to terrorize the hell out of us—how we will experience, loath, the dreaded "coffin." Of all the "tortures" of initiation, they can't seem to shut their mouths about that one. It's some sort of box filled with vomit that everyone rolls in and then adds to it. Can't wait.

The only way out of the ceremony is to win the beauty queen contest tomorrow night. But no one wants to win that. Admission to the contest is strictly by force. I warned Daniels again to watch his back.

127

But he still seems to think he can hide safely. But I'm not so sure.

Other than small talk, I avoid most of the division now. I can't seem to get that incident of "Sword in Steel" out of my head. I can feel their inner laughter, particularly Rogers' and Stoker's. I now believe they set me up so that the Chief and Division Officer would have caught me in the act. Jesus, I feel it's true. They're crazy. And I gave in. What the hell did I get myself into? I should have finished up school and then split. Somewhere, anywhere, but to hell away from such stupid fools. And if those idiots—any of them—lay one finger on me for the beauty queen contest or for anything else—I'll kick their ass from here to Japan. I swear it!

I've invited Daniels to work out with me in the division's armory. Maybe he'll take me up on it, maybe not. I don't care either way. I enjoy the chess, though. He's starting to win a few games.

Armory

Taylor was on a bench, pressing more weight than Daniels had ever seen. Daniels stepped inside the small W-Division compartment in the mid-section of the ship and slammed the watertight door behind him. The space was used primarily for storing equipment and personnel gear, secondarily for weightlifting.

Taylor hissed and groaned as he forced the bar up—continuing this five more times. Sweat poured down his face, and the air was heavy with scent. His eyes collapsed into wire slits as he heaved the bar up and onto the heavy frame, which held steady from the tremendous weight. Just Taylor's weight alone added over 280 pounds to the bench.

"Jesus, that's a lot of weight. How much you got on that bar?" asked Daniels.

Taylor didn't respond. He lay still and breathed heavily, eyes fixed on the pipes and wires overhead.

Daniels walked over to the bar and counted. 50, 100, 200, 300, 350 pounds! "Fuck, that's three hundred fifty fucking pounds!"

Taylor sat up, grabbed his towel, and wiped his face. He chuckled.

"Here, try a set."

Daniels shook his head in disbelief. Taylor stood up and started pulling the weight off one end of the bar. He motioned to Daniels to help. Daniels put his watch to his mouth, blew on it, wiped it clean, and then lay it carefully on a shelf.

"So why don't you work out in the ship's gym," said Daniels, slipping the weights off.

"Too crowded."

They pulled the last two weights from the bar. Daniels tossed the weight to the deck. It hit a twenty-five-pounder with a bang and slid a foot toward a locker. Taylor eased his down, annoyed at the sound.

"Didn't you have a working party today?" asked Daniels.

"Yup."

"And you still came here to work out."

"I need to get my blood going."

"Don't tell me, freezer, right?"

"Yup."

Daniels hated working parties. Particularly freezer duty. His last one had him passing seventy-five-pound boxes of frozen meat over from a naval supply ship to the Midway. "Underway replenishment," it was called. Men were volunteered from the day's duty sections in each division. Taylor was the unlucky one this time. Usually, the newbies and lower rates were chosen. They formed long lines and pitched frozen box after frozen box from the flight deck or sponsons to the hanger bay to the food elevators. From the elevators, they continued the human chain down into the ship's freezers, kept at zero degrees. They were cold and cramped, and he hated every second of it. The only consolation for the discomfort was being alert and quick—not tired and sluggish from the heat and sweat on the other end of the line. But if you stopped working, you froze. No gloves or jackets were provided, nor did anyone bring any, for only a few of the chosen men were unfortunate enough to fill the last bit of chain in the freezer. Everywhere else, the work was hot and grueling. Daniels hadn't decided which he hated more, the heat or the cold.

"How the hell could you come here and lift weights after lugging 75-pound boxes?"

"Easy." He sat down on the deck.

"God, it's hot." Daniels slid down and faced Taylor. The two sat in silence for a while. Finally, Daniels said, "Hey, Taylor, I was just wondering." He paused. "Have you, ah, thought of any other—"

"No."

"Let me finish what I was going to say; thank you."

"I know what you were going to say."

"Well, then," said Daniels.

"I said no."

"I don't believe you. I know you've been thinking about it just like

130

me."

"I thought we promised not to talk about it."

Daniels shook his head. "Yeah, so?"

"So, I don't want to discuss it. You're going to get us thrown in the brig." Taylor leaned against the bulkhead and looked up at the overhead.

"Look, I know you want to discuss it. I keep thinking about it, and I can't seem to get it out of my head."

"Think of something else," said Taylor.

"I do, but it pops up again."

"I can't help you."

"Yes, you can."

"I said no!" Taylor's hand hit the deck. "I will not jeopardize myself over this fucking game. It's not worth it, now don't ask me again. Understand?"

"*This* game?"

"Yes, *this* game."

"You seem to really like games, Taylor. Tell me then, what game *is* worth the risk to you?"

"Did you hear me?"

"All right, all right," said Daniels. "I'll try to rid my mind of it, okay." They sat in silence again, and Daniels fidgeted. "Well, which do you prefer, living in a hot or cold climate," he asked.

"Neither," said Taylor, a trace of irritation still riding his voice.

"Neither, good answer. A warm, moderate climate would do me just fine, too," said Daniels.

"I never said I would live in a moderate climate."

"Well, you said neither."

"If given a choice," said Taylor.

"What are you saying?"

"Remember that village we visited on the way back from Amboseli?" asked Taylor.

"Yeah, how the hell can I forget."

"Does poverty come with choice?" asked Taylor.

"No, in the same way, neither of us had a choice. We have to deal with the shit life throws at us and make the best of it."

"Do we?" asked Taylor. "Easy for you to say, coming from an upper-middle-class family."

"Whoa, slow down. I didn't make the rules, and I sure as shit don't control them."

"But it's a lie to think just pluck away, and all will be peach pie."

"I use 'em to my advantage like you and make the best of it," said Daniels. He smiled. "How did you know I came from an upper-middle-class family?"

Taylor shook his head. "Do you think that those villagers can go back to the way of life their forefathers knew or integrate into Western culture without any outside help?"

"Maybe, maybe not," replied Daniels.

"Maybe not's more like it. They have been enticed by modern ways and now suffer from overpopulation and poverty."

"What's your point?"

"Didn't you see it in the elders' eyes? They hunger for the spiritual happiness and healing they once had when they looked to the earth, the stars, and each other for guidance. Now they rely on the West; it's paper money and gods. Again, people and pavement."

"And their own damn leaders. Look, Taylor, I understand your point, but in all fairness, that's the way of the world. Of what my father used to call the 'Universal Intent.'"

"The 'Universal Intent'?" Taylor smiled.

"Yeah, the Universal Intent. It flowed through all the possible niches in nature. Throughout history, man has always conquered other lands and tribes. Hell, even America butchered and displaced all the Native Americans who lived there, as Weller did to the Yuki tribe in . . ."

"California," said Taylor.

"Look—"

"Hey, cool down. Discussion is just an avenue to knowledge, to truth."

"Oh, and I suppose our game contains no truth."

"Truth? The brig is fucking truth!"

"Truth?" Daniels pulled his arms in. "As long as blood will flow, so will truth."

Taylor rolled over, his face blank. "Okay, so continue."

"Continue what?"

"Your point."

"About the game?"

Taylor took in a breath. "About Weller!"

"Why?" said Daniels. "What's it mean to you?"

"I enjoy a good discussion every now and then." He smiled.

The room was hot and cramped. Sweat crept out from Daniels forehead and hands. "John B. Weller, Governor of California, had companies of volunteers kill Native American men, women, and children and then thanked them for a job well done. The historical list goes on. I'm not saying it's my fault or yours, or maybe even our forefathers; maybe most of those men were just caught up in the groupthink and violence of their own time."

"Bullshit," said Taylor.

"Bullshit?"

"Yes, to those who revise history in light to fit their taste. Every century has borne witness to genocide from so-called conquerors."

"I know," said Daniels. "So, what's your point?"

"The killing keeps rising at an alarming rate."

"Again, what's your point?" said Daniels.

"My point. Don't you get it?"

Daniels leaned back. Taylor continued, his voice hot. "Really think about what we're working on. It's insane! The past does not excuse the present. We are spending trillions on ways to decimate people. You and me included! Tell me, don't you think that just a small fraction of that money could be put in those grass bowls we saw?"

133

"You know, it's more complicated than that. Politics, economics, science, and especially responsibility, individual responsibility, factor in the equation."

"Equation? Fuck that. To uncover mathematical forms is one thing, but to use and interpret is another. There lies wisdom, and very few truthfully possess it. It's *spiritual reason* that counts. Not just almighty science, statistics, and the holy adherence to numbers."

"What the hell are you saying?" said Daniels, leaning forward.

"What I'm saying is science is pure potential. That's all."

Daniels stood up. "Speaking of which, I need to get to class and get me some of that." He felt suddenly hot, and he stepped through the watertight door, his hand clutching the round handle. But as he started to shut the door, he spun around. "What do you mean by potential?"

"A tool. A lens to one, hammer to another."

Daniels eyed him, then shut the door. He quickly headed down to the coop, grabbed his book, and zipped up to the O-2 level to the pilot's ready room where his Oceanography class was being held. He was a bit early, and he grabbed a seat and waited. He really loved being in this room, particularly sitting in the large padded seats, facing a large whiteboard in front of him. He couldn't wait for the class to start.

Daniels fidgeted in his seat, and to kill time, he took in the complexity of the room, with all of its photos, TV, coffee machine, wall plaques, and the fighter squadron patches and memorabilia of VF 151. The pilots of VF 151 met here for their pre-flight and post-flight briefings, among many other things. A smaller whiteboard next to the main one caught his attention, and he tried to figure out the meaning of what appeared to be a status list of planes and pilot names, with another list just next to it of what looked like code. But as he did this, the door banged open, and in walked Professor Blair. He was middle-aged, bony, bald, and wore thick black glasses. He was also quite short. As he made his way to the front of the room, Daniels could see that the back of his plaid shirt was not quite tucked in. He definitely fit

Daniels' image of the scholarly type—which was very much at odds with the highly skilled muscular young officers that regularly used this room.

Professor Blair quickly settled into his usual lecture pose—slumped up against the large wooden lectern—and then droned on for about 40 minutes about the Ekman layer and spiral and the Coriolis force and effect. Daniels took lots of notes and was quite excited by what he heard. When the class ended, Daniels quickly headed for the door, but Professor Blair suddenly called out to him.

"Mr. Daniels! Can I have a word with you?"

"Sure," said Daniels, his stomach tightening. He suddenly felt he was back at high school and was about to be scolded for his poor work or attitude. And he wasn't far off.

"I noticed that your first two papers were outstanding. In fact, exceptional. I rarely see such work among the enlisted men, so I don't say that lightly. Your quizzes and particularly your midterm exam, were also excellent, and you scored at the top of your class."

Daniels could feel it coming.

"However, your last two papers and your last two quizzes really surprised me. As you well know from my grade and comments, they were both substandard and lacked the necessary attributes for passing this course. In fact, both of your quizzes were 'F's, and if you don't get a good grade on the final, which is coming up soon, then I'm afraid you won't pass this course."

Daniels looked down at the foot of the lectern.

"If it was just one paper or quiz, I could easily dismiss it, as you most likely got caught in a work project or something else, which I see all the time. But here, you clearly had time to study and do the work." Professor Blair straightened up, his voice softening a bit. "So what's happening? Are you still planning on passing this course?"

"Yes, sir," said Daniels.

"Mr. Daniels, please. I'm not an officer. There's no need to call me sir."

"Yes, Professor Blair."

"Considering my position and my short stay aboard ships, I try not to get involved in the lives of sailors. But with you, I can't help but ask you if you plan to stay in the service or get out and go to college. The reason I ask is that Oceanography is not a typical general advancement course. It's an elective. So you taking it tells me that you really want to learn and, or, you're really trying to prepare yourself for college."

"Actually, if you want to know the truth, I can't think of anything more important to me than getting out of the Navy and going to school."

Professor Blair smiled and then placed a hand on Daniel's shoulder. "Good, good. Then I ask that you really try to put effort into this course to pass that final. And if you do and get a fairly decent grade on it, I would be more than happy to write you a letter of recommendation for whatever university you apply to."

"Really? That'd be great!"

"Yes. So please try a little harder. I think that you'd fit right into college and really excel there."

"Do you really think so, sir?" He was beaming.

"Yes, I do," said Professor Blair, "Thus, it's important to keep your mind clear and focused on the goal. If you can align your work ethic with your talent, then nothing will stop you from achieving a college education. If you need to talk further about this, particularly about college, please don't hesitate to contact me. I'm always here. In fact, I really have nowhere else to go. I'm stuck on the Midway for a while." He smiled.

Daniels laughed. "That makes two of us. Again, thanks." Daniels turned and headed out of the ready room. For the first time in many months, he suddenly felt a burst of pride and self-confidence. He could do it. He could actually get out of here and go to college. As he headed down the passageway, he resolved that he was going to put in the effort and really study. W-Division and Rogers and Stoker be damned!

09 Oct. 77

Columbus Day.

Beauty Queen Contest is tonight. There's a charge in the air. Every wog on the ship's wondering who's going to get hijacked and paraded around in front of the Captain and Admiral. In our division, I was told it would be Daniels.

A sense of frustration is setting in. While helping Sanchez stow some training gear and cables in one of the division's storage spaces down in M-3, I stumbled on someone's winery—large pitchers of homemade strawberry wine up high on a shelf underneath five B43 nose cones. I discovered them while moving the cones to make room for our equipment. Since no alcohol is allowed out at sea, a few enterprising individuals are taking matters into their own hands. And pockets. That wine would sell for quite a bit, considering how many sailors have drinking problems. Normally, the long voyages at sea allow them to dry out and interrupt what would undoubtedly be a steady stream into their systems. The sea moderates, invigorates. But intoxication at sea is trouble.

Sanchez smiled when I uncovered it and later ordered me to keep my mouth shut. "No need to create big waves in a small pond." Unbelievable! Again, the more I see here, the wilder it gets. We should have reported it, but I shut up.

I find it hard to believe that some of the individuals in the division were given security clearances. A sailor named Linden worked in the spaces for a few months until they found out he had served time in the Marine Corps for trafficking drugs. The man had a prison record, for Christ's sake! Didn't anyone bother to check?

So much for the thirty-thousand dollar background investigation on each individual.

Another guy was sectioned eight and discharged for his mental instability. He constantly got into fights and brawls with the shore patrol and Marines. In Japan (which we'll be visiting soon), I heard he jumped up and down on luggage racks in commuter trains, swinging

137

from the hand straps, his free arm scratching his armpit, all the while screeching out like a monkey to the shocked Japanese. And this was while he was sober.

Insanity really infuses the system. It seems so unreal at times, and I have a hard time believing that everyone has top-secret security clearances and has made it past high school. Yet it seems to work most of the time—everyone becalmed temporarily while engaged in an operation. Then tempest once again. There's a fine line here, and I worry as the pendulum keeps rising. What's to stop a determined or crazy individual with a gun from seriously damaging a nuclear weapon? It's just a matter of time.

0-7 Level

Daniels clenched the steel rail. The bulkheads, overheads, decks, and ladders on this level were all bathed in blue. Intermittently throughout, brass glittered like gold from various pipe fittings, fire nozzles, and switch boxes. He stepped through the open hatch into the Captain's Passageway high above the hangar bay. Buzzing strongly from a joint, Daniels proceeded through it with caution. He needed to reach his "comfort zone," a small nook high up on the ship's superstructure, to find solitude from the torrent of humanity below. And Rogers. Daniels knew he was a marked man, but if they couldn't find him, they would have to dress up another victim.

He passed through the Captain's Passageway, his feet marking the blue tile waxed several times a day, his eyes taking in the dazzling light. He climbed a ladder and then leaped up several black stairwells to the O6 level and found the first of what he was looking for. He opened a door and peered outside the ship. It was intensely black. He gripped the handle. *Black night. A well. In our open-eyed blindness, we fall.* The THC was really hitting him hard. This was the most pot he had smoked in a long while. He stood transfixed, his thoughts churning. A touch of paranoia snaked through his body. This happens every time now, particularly after smoking so much. He thought of the game again. *Dammit.* He gripped the railing. *Don't think, don't think. Don't go to the brig. Something else, something . . . the night. The night, the blackness, an eye. A slick slit of pupil.* His paranoia still lingered. The drug had really taken hold of him. The game melted away into thoughtless caverns. The longer he stood, the deeper he looked, the more his eyes adjusted, and the more he believed he was being studied, dissected, dissolved—rewired into the covert conduits of God. *His eye, mind, one with. Concentrate on the inner, miss the outer. Look to the earth—His body; the sea—His blood.* The water beneath him was still not discernible. *A few more minutes.*

Daniels walked over toward the navigating or captain's bridge, the intellect and controlling force for the crew of almost 4,500 men. He passed a signal light, restrained from rising heavenward, allowing but a horizontal sweep for a distance of eleven point three miles. He stopped in front of a large pair of binoculars used for observing coded messages. He looked inside the bridge.

A sailor on watch leaned against the empty captain's chair. The chair sat up high off the deck and resembled a barber's seat. Immediately in front of it, high overhead, on a shined brass pedestal, was a television. During the day, the Captain could watch flight operations, and later in the evening, he imagined that the Captain would sit here and catch up on the news, sports, or other programs, courtesy of the Armed Forces Television Network that was broadcast from the Midway's television studio.

Daniels walked over to the railing and checked out the flag or admiral's bridge one deck below. A few sailors standing watch talked and walked about. Daniels plopped his arms down on the rail and looked around the flight deck. It was quiet. Air operations had ceased for the day. Everyone was preparing now for the boxing matches and beauty queen contest below in the hangar bay. Earlier, the deck had been swarming with red, green, yellow, blue, brown, purple, and white-shirted men buzzing about as they moved planes, missiles, and bombs and launched and recovered aircraft. *Flight. Of men and mind. Never really up, but out. Forever the fall.*

Daniels noticed the repaired catwalk on the outer edge of the flight deck. Three weeks ago, on a stormy afternoon, a sailor trying to reach a jet walked right into the propeller of a mail cod. He was high on marijuana. The impact threw him over thirty feet and impaled him on a split rail. A medical corpsman, who chanced to see the incident, pulled his belt off and wrapped it tight around the stump of the man's severed arm, stemming the flow of blood. The injured man was flown off the ship to a medical hospital. Daniels, a member of the searching party, spent that tempestuous evening trying to find the man's missing arm. Cold rain and rough seas ate into him. Around and under lockers, on catwalks, and between the rubber tires of parked planes, he searched for the bloody arm and wondered. No luck. The arm was finally written up in the ship's log as lost at sea, rumored to have ended up in the belly of a great white shark or whale.

Five days later, a pilot died when his plane malfunctioned. They never recovered his body. The ship's chaplain announced that he, too, was claimed by the sea.

Just in from this bit of catwalk were the blast reflectors, large rectangular shields laid precisely into the flight deck. They were raised when the planes were launched to deflect the jet engine's exhaust away from the officers and men in the superstructure or island. The heat was intense even from up on the 0-8 level, where Daniels and others would sometimes go to watch the planes being launched. Two steam-powered catapults shot the fighter jets zero to one-hundred and sixty knots in two-and-a-half seconds into the heavens. *But gravity wins, always wins.*

Daniels walked over to the door, scrambled up a ladder, and reached the 07 level. He walked to the other side of the superstructure. Out on the catwalk, he faced the open ocean, the flight deck now behind his back on the other side. A warm uneven wind slid across his face.

He made his way over to his favorite spot on the ship. Running alongside and against the ship's smokestack, the catwalk suddenly jumped inward, creating a small cozy nook that was just above three small steps and just in front of the large "41" adorning the side of the Midway's superstructure. The space had a beautiful, almost completely unobstructed view of the ocean—a high thin rail being the only barrier to the horizon. The floor of the catwalk was a widely spaced thin metal grille. Daniels looked directly down past it into the churning waves below. He sat down, feeling almost at once the heat from the smokestack ooze into him, *like the THC passing through my mind.* He loved it here, particularly in the cold winter months. The heat generated from deep down within the bowels of the ship kept him warm and protected from the harsh breeze that ceaselessly bit at him over ten decks above the moonlit water.

The greatest asset of this spot was its isolation. Nothing—no one but himself and the elements. The dark jeweled sky undulated over a hushed breeze. Waves lapped against the side of the ship, and hum from down in the ship's belly resonated up and through the skin of his back. It was here, here, that he felt free. For here, he was above the flood of humanity that swept into every crack and crevice within the welded maze below.

Daniels felt good to be up from the deep magazines, but he was still angry with Rogers about the clamp yesterday and a bit fearful of what he might attempt tonight. Daniels knew Rogers was probably furious right about now, for Daniels slipped out from the spaces early and made a direct beeline for the 0-7 level, by-passing the coop and chow lines. Rogers and company were probably waiting in ambush deep in the coop. Daniels smiled. *Fuck 'em.*

The game solidified again, and his thoughts turned to how to take a weapon off the ship. *Stop it.* "Forget it, just forget it," he told himself aloud.

His eyes were now fully adjusted to the dark, and eighty feet below him, he watched the sea curl by. He tried to clear his mind. This spot always seemed to have a calming effect on him. A few shafts of light from the moon danced over the small waves. Others seemed to vibrate like dots, then vanish, then reappear and freeze, changing shape and size. And still, others slid sharply beneath. *Beneath! Jennings. My god, six feet a second.* The Chief announced it a few hours after the man overboard alarm had sounded two months ago. Daniels had raced down from the coop to the spaces to muster for a ship-wide personnel count. The carrier had slowed and circled while a helo and two motor whaleboats, each with a sharpshooter to fend off the sharks, were launched to pick up the sailor. But they never found him.

It was later discovered that Jennings and a buddy were throwing some trash off the flight deck, an unauthorized spot. As it fell, a piece of wire caught Jennings by the leg and dragged him. His buddy grabbed him but lost his grip. The pull from the ship and the weight of the wire ripped Jennings screaming from the clawing hands of his friend. The Chief said he was dragged down at a rate of six feet a second—flailing, unbelieving, finally inhaling one last wet breath. His body finally free falling, forced by gravity all the way down to the cold, dark, desolate sand in an unforgiving sea.

A quick sound caught Daniels' attention. He tensed and looked toward the door. Another sound, a faint splash, focused his attention on the water. *Flying fish.* He could see it in the dim light. It hung over the water for a few seconds, shimmering in the moonlight, wings spread like a large dragonfly, and then plunged down. *So natural an instinct. To loosen the grip of gravity.*

Henderson once told him that while he stood watch on the bridge of a small destroyer, the ship accidentally rammed a whale. Daniels asked him what caused the mishap.

"What color is the ship?" replied Henderson.

"Gray," said Daniels.

"And what color is a whale?" asked Henderson.

"Gray."

"So, there you have it."

Daniels stood there with his jaw half open, eyeing Henderson, trying to fully comprehend the meaning of his remark. Henderson couldn't be that naive! Or was he?

The whole sky above Daniels seemed to vibrate. A thin white streak suddenly shot out above him, sparkling as it went. *Shooting star.* It vanished over the ship's superstructure, the antenna and radar blotting it. He eyed the rotating radar dish. A painted, happy face smiled back at him. He watched it spin on its axis, the smile beaming across the ocean and up into the star-filled sky. The smile was one of self-mockery, of an irony forged in steel and blood, of knowing a skull and crossbones would be raised next to it to whip wildly in the wind tomorrow. Daniels smiled. A pirate flag on a United States ship, and with the full consent of the Captain and Admiral. *Grown men playing games, dressing up. But what's the difference?*

A soft sound, like the fall of a foot on tile, made Daniels jump. He looked in the direction of the door but, seeing no one, settled back down. *Just a passing sailor.* Daniels wiped his watch with his shirt, then studied the second hand as it rotated second by second, round and round. The "game" surfaced again. He swore. Sweat broke out over the back of his neck. He tightened his fist. Hard. He suddenly felt the need to go higher. He was too low. He needed to keep moving. He wasn't safe. The 0-8 level would be better.

As he started to rise, he heard the soft clink of metal to his left, and as he turned his head, he saw three dark figures charging him. He quickly turned to his left to evade them, his arms flailing out for the railing, his legs fumbling to rise beneath. But it was too late. He was grabbed and roughly thrown to the narrow grating. Rogers, Stoker, and Sanchez held him down and bound his hands behind his back with a belt. And as they dragged him to his feet, he could hear another faint splash as another fish fell into the sea.

"You motherfucker," said Rogers. "Thought you could get away again, huh? This time you're not on fucking leave, you fucking wog!"

"Trying to hide was not cool," said Sanchez. "You know it only makes it worse."

Daniels kicked out at Rogers, hitting him in the shin. Rogers doubled over, gasping. Daniels took off toward the door, his hands bound at his back, his gait slowed, awkward. As he leaped through the door into the island, Sanchez caught him and wrestled him to the deck. Sanchez then sat on him till Stoker and a teary-eyed Rogers showed.

Rogers raged, hovering over him, his fist balling. Daniels knew it was coming, and even Sanchez reacted too slowly to stop it. Rogers unleashed a tremendous blow to Daniels thigh. The pain shot through his entire body, and his scream must have long echoed through the passageways and stairwells of the island.

They picked him up, and half carried, half dragged him down to the coop. Every shift of weight to his sore leg fanned a fire of flame that swept from the tip of his scalp to the tips of his toes. When they finally got there, they threw him down on top of the laundry bags in the corner. Two other shellbacks from G-Division jumped in with Sanchez to steady him while Rogers and Stoker tore off his clothes. They stripped him bare. Then Rogers, smiling, pulled a straight razor from his pocket and flicked it open, its blade seeming to slice the very light that dared to dance upon its edge. Daniels lost it. If thoughts were sparks, he became an inferno. He screamed, twisted, and kicked, threw his body up toward the overhead, toward the island, toward the black vault of heaven itself. Hands clutched and fumbled and pushed and hit him, and he felt his body rolling and free falling, then hitting the deck hard. Stunned, he watched as Rogers quickly grabbed a hunk of his hair. His head rose, then slammed down hard onto the tile. He blacked out.

As he came to, his first sensations were of a deep, almost muted sound mixed with a high-pitched slapping against his cheek. The sound contained an almost palpable texture, as though he could reach up and touch it, caress it, feel its longing. It solidified. Became his name. He opened his eyes.

Sanchez was hunched down over him, his wide face and matching pupils fixated on his. He slapped his face, turning his cheek each time.

"Daniels. Daniels. Come on, that's it. Come out of it."

Daniels shook his head and swallowed. His mind cleared. Rogers now came into focus. He was leaning over his bare legs, razor still in hand, smiling.

Daniels jumped again, but Sanchez powered him down.

"Stop it! Hear me! We ain't gonna cut you! We ain't gonna cut you!" He relaxed his grip. "Just shave you. Hear? Now calm the fuck down. That's all we're gonna do, is just shave a little hair from you, that's all."

Daniels settled back, fear still snaking across his body, fueling the need to escape. Sweat broke out across his forehead, and he could feel coldness seeping into his skin the length of his body. *My body!* He suddenly realized that he was naked. He struggled again, but Sanchez and the others pushed harder. The pain in his thigh wormed its way into his consciousness again.

"Aren't you listening, wog?" said Sanchez. "You fight, and it's only gonna make it worse. Now mellow the fuck out, let it happen, and maybe you'll even enjoy yourself."

As they spread shaving cream on him, Daniels tried to relax. But as the cold blade fell across his chest, he jerked and felt a sharp sting. "Damn you!"

"Don't move, moron," said Rogers, "or it could be worse."

"Careful with that thing." Sanchez shot a warning glance to Rogers.

Rogers bent down and, with a delicate stroke of the razor, cut a swath of hair and cream from Daniels' chest. The cold scrape of steel sent a shiver through his body. Rogers continued, shaving the chest, then the armpits, then the legs. When he had finished, he leaned over Daniels' crotch, the razor twisting above it, and he smiled.

"Now, now, woggy, woggy. What'd we have here? A pecker that's in need of a heart." He laughed. "What'd you think, royal shellbacks? Shall we carve out a little heart of hair, see'n that he has none in that poor excuse you'd call a chest."

The others laughed.

"No, not a heart; why not a mushroom?" said Stoker.

Rogers' eyebrows raised, and his lips bloomed out. "Hmmm. Good idea, but I couldn't do it. Not enough to work with." He laughed.

Daniels took in a deep breath and shut his eyes. "I'll hunt you down like a dog."

"Oooooh. I'm trembling, little man. Or should I say, little wog?"

"Hey," said Sanchez. "None of this shit. It's all part of the ceremony. Just someone had to be unlucky. That's all."

"Look, Daniels," said Rogers, "this is gonna happen. Now we can do this the easy way, or we can do this the hard way. And if you

146

choose the hard way, that razor might slip, and as far as you're concerned, you might as well keep wearing a dress and a wig cause you'll have nothing to prove that you're a man anymore. Hear me?"

At this, Daniels gave in and relaxed. He turned his head toward the coop. A group of W-Division and G-Division sailors stood gaping, smiling down at him. "Go to hell," he muttered and shut his eyes as the first stroke cut away a swath of his pubic hair. Each stroke sent a cold flicker of anger and fear through him. He fought the instinctive urge to tense, to fuel, and to gratify and reward their effort. He tried to relax and succeeded in partly loosening the muscles of his arms and legs as he breathed deeply in and out. But the idea of being watched and held and humiliated gave rise to terrific hate that only seemed to intensify with each stroke. He balled his fists and clenched his jaw, and swore silently again and again in the dark and solitary recesses of his mind. In time, he thought, in time. *I'll get even.*

When the heart was cut out of his hair, they stood him up and dressed him. Pantyhose, high heels, lingerie from a Frederick's of Hollywood catalog, bra, dress, make-up, a blond wig. He was now numb to it all, complying but silent. The men standing around watching started to whistle and make catcalls.

"Damn," said Sanchez, "If I didn't know you. Shit, you'd make a *fine* woman."

"Hell, you just might be lucky after all, Daniels," said Rogers. "You win; you won't have to go through the coffin. Hear me?"

Daniels remained silent. The deep-cut furrow of his brows doing all the talking.

They called down to the spaces, informing them that Daniels was ready, then they marched him up to the hangar bay, the rest of the division at his heels. They sat him down on top of an empty crate, and for the next twenty minutes, he watched a series of boxing matches— the filler between the main course. The Captain and Admiral had front-row seats. Two sailors, one white, one black, danced in tight circles around one another, each pumping fists furiously to force to the surface the red fluid that coursed through both. They succeeded equally well, and it was judged a draw. As their chests heaved and their gloves were drawn together, blood dripped to the bowed canvas, dotting it as easily and freely as one would the "i" in Midway. The crowd booed the decision; they thought the African-American won the fight.

After the matches ended, the Beauty Queen contest began. Daniels was paraded up on stage with all the other unfortunate sailors shanghaied from each of the ship's divisions. At this point, everyone went willingly, and most even seemed to enjoy it as they were paraded around, some with pimps, strutting their stuff to the Captain, Admiral, and most of the entire ship's company of men. The hangar bay went crazy. All the men jumped up and down, whistling, screaming, and screeching out propositions to their favorites.

Daniels kept his head and eyes fixed on the wooden stage, watching and counting the knots in the planks. His head felt like it was no longer flesh and bone but soft rubber fitted over heavy lead. The weight of his skull pulled him down, his backbone straining under pressure, and the skin of his cheeks and eyebrows seemed to slide down his face. He wanted to just rip everything off of him and run. *Should I?*

Rogers held his arm tight as he pulled him around and around, the shouts and screams spiraling into his mind like screaming gulls. And all the while, he wished he could just stop in the center, just fixate himself on the axis, being neither left nor right, nor up nor down. Eternally removed and hidden deep within the midway of the Midway.

No, just play along. Play the game. . .

10 Oct. 77

Daniels got hammered tonight. I tried to warn him, but he wouldn't listen. Most of the others seemed to accept their fate and go along with it. In fact, most even enjoyed it. But Daniels fought and paid the price. His thigh is badly bruised, as is his pride. And he wasn't even chosen for the queen or royal court. All of that, and he'll still need to face the coffin tomorrow!

Mulling over the initiation, I can't understand why it exists. In heaven's name, why do grown military men suddenly step outside the rigid social dictates of a formal system to engage in the informal, wild, hazeful activities that would make the average citizen cringe? Hell, that would make the fraternities at UC Berkeley cringe! Why the need for such a ceremony? Is it for the maintenance of adult male cohesion? The symbolic death of the child and the rebirth of the man? That was then; this is now. I mean, just how important today are passage rites to the modern mind? Are they really needed for proper psychological functioning? Did they evolve with the brain tens of thousands of years ago to serve and satisfy some deep-seated archetypal purpose? It all sounds so childish, so strange.

My clearance came in. I am officially a green badge now. I no longer have to be escorted and can stand duty as a Tech.

Crossing the Line

0500 the following morning slammed into Daniels. Shellbacks dressed in pirate shirts, leggings, eye patches, and cardboard or wooden cutlasses threw him out of his rack with the other wogs. He was forced to dress backward. His pants were put on first, inside out, and then his underwear went over them. After putting on a T-shirt, he was made to get down on his knees, a position he would be in for the next six hours.

Daniels was then herded up to the mess deck with the hundreds of other sailors for the "wog breakfast." He was served green eggs, purple hash browns, and a blackish, greenish drink that was filled with a blistering sauce. He protested, but his hands were bound behind his back, and they forced him to bob down, nose fully immersed in his plate, and eat. The remaining food on his face was left to dry.

During the next hour in the spaces, grease, oil, shaving cream, and other appropriate body lotions were smashed, rubbed, and injected into his hair and various body parts. Rogers took great pleasure in singling him out, and Daniels hated every minute of it.

Daniels was then packed onto an aircraft elevator with the first group of wogs, and as they rode up to the flight deck, shellbacks from above blasted him with stinging salt water from fire hoses.

From the elevator, he was forced to go through the shillelagh line. The pain was intense. He had to run through crouching as a long line of shellbacks with wet cut-up fire hoses smashed his rear and thighs. Tears blended with the salt water on his cheeks. If they didn't like the way you ran, or if you covered yourself with your hand, they would grab you and make you do it all over again. Daniels went through twice.

From the shillelagh line, he was brought to the royal dentist, who injected a scorching pepper paste into his mouth and then brushed it around with a toothbrush. His tongue flamed, and he spat out the liquid into a barrel next to him.

From the dentist, the royal baby, a Shellback especially chosen due to his large weight and bulbous belly. Daniels sat down in front of him, his body held fast by strong legs, and was made to pick a cherry from the Crisco oil-filled belly button with his teeth.

Then the pillory, or stocks, a large wooden device with holes for a head and hands, which was used to lock up prisoners during medieval times. He shut his eyes as shellbacks fired salvo after salvo of eggs at the top of his head.

From the stockade, the dreaded coffin. Of all the stories, this one dominated the most. No wog spoke in this line, not even Taylor. Every eye was locked on the giant wooden crate, on sailors stepping in and struggling out, faces contorted in sickness, their whole bodies covered in a thick green-brown paste of rotten food and vomit, part of which fell thickly like paste off their clothes and shoes and onto the flight deck. Retched fumes drifted over, making their stomachs twist.

When his turn came, Daniels stepped into the wooden crate. His foot sunk into the ooze. It seemed to sink forever. The smell of vomit was overwhelming. A Shellback with a clothespin over his nose screamed, "Sit your fucking ass down, wog. Experience the beauty and wonders of ritual." He grinned and lifted the lid up over Daniel's head, forcing him down into the pit. His thighs and waist sunk deep into the oozing wretchedness. He felt claustrophobic and sick. He tried to breathe through his mouth. It didn't work. The stench was too much. As he emptied part of his stomach, adding to the pile and his pain, the sides of the crate suddenly exploded as two shellbacks beat it with fire hoses. He put his head down and clenched his fists. All he could see in the darkness was Rogers holding a razor over him, twisting and turning the blade, the light reflecting in a shower of sparks.

The lid was finally pulled off, and he started to rise. "Get your slimy ass back in there. You ain't leaving till you're covered in vomit. Roll wog, roll!"

They forced him back in. They beat the sides and screamed, "Roll wog, roll you, cursed creature, roll in the filth you create. Roll! Roll!"

151

He rolled. He cried out. He emptied the remainder of his stomach.

From the coffin, they marched him to a long black cloth tube. It reeked as well. Daniels could barely breathe, constraining himself, as he inched his way through the slime of the narrow tube towards the light at the tunnel's end. Like the coffin, this, too, was filled with vomit.

Exiting the tunnel, he was led to a giant metal vat of water, and he was ordered to jump into it. It felt cool and refreshing. He wanted to stay submerged, to extinguish the pain and the rot. He closed his eyes, and his arms and legs went limp and free-floated, turning on their own inertia. He could feel the pressure quickly build in his chest. But it felt so good to be free from weight, from gravity, to just float, to drift. His lungs cried out, and he surfaced.

"Are you a pollywog or shellback?" screamed a Shellback. Scared to say the wrong answer, Daniels played it safe and said, "pollywog." Wrong answer. They forced him through the ceremony again.

During his second time through, he was taken to the Royal Court to see the Queen—a thin, makeup-caked man with just enough soft round facial features combined with a bouncy walk to be the winner. Sitting on the Captain and Admiral's lap and stroking their chests helped him as well. Now sitting on a thin aluminum fold-out chair high above the proceedings, the queen and his court leaned forward and listened to the accusations with a smile.

Daniels was charged with treason, for written on his shirt in large letters were the words, "The queen is an ass." Rogers had written it along with various other comments. The queen and her court immediately sentenced him to be thrown into the coffin twice. With a flick of her wrist, eyes drawn, the queen simply gestured, "Take him away."

Daniels was furious. It took all he had to keep from losing it while locked in that foul box again. While sitting inside, he swore out sentence after sentence, spitting out his hate for the service.

He was finally led back to the tunnel and then jumped in the pool again. "Are you a damn pollywog or shellback?" asked the Shellback.

"Shellback," screamed Daniels. "I'm a fucking shellback!"

The Shellback smiled and let him out. He shuffled over to the showers set up on the flight deck and tried to wash the oil and grease from his body. It wouldn't come off. His clothes were tossed overboard, and he hobbled forward, one drop among a filthy stream of naked men flowing down into the heart of an immense warship.

20 Oct. 77

I'm alone in the storeroom, listening to them babble away in the pub room. I'm feeling a deep sense of alienation, frustration, hatred. It's over. A bunch of brainless idiots forcing me into a fucking meaningless ritual that has been watered down and softened into something that is fake and unhealthy. The ceremony was a failure. It is, and all it will ever be, just an impotent version of an ancient ritual that still calls to us from somewhere deep in our psyche.

I worry about Daniels. They beat him pretty badly. I tried to talk to him, to cheer him, but he's keeping it in. He won't talk. It's just a matter of time before he explodes. But then again, what comes around, goes around.

Aft Cage

Daniels followed Rogers through the aft mess deck. Rogers hunched every now and then to avoid the low vents that choked the passageway. Hundreds of sailors filled the area. Heads bobbed up and down as sailors walked back from the chow line and ate. The shouts, shuffling of feet, and the clanging of forks and knives against aluminum trays all blended together with the smell of mashed potato, green peas, steak, oil, and JP-5 jet fuel. Elevator doors with bright stencils stood out on both sides of the compartment. In areas where there were no pipes, wires, equipment, or tables lined with milk dispensers, fruit punch fountains, silverware, and napkins, there were large spaces littered with gauges and water valves for filling or emptying the numerous voids needed to stabilize the ship.

Just next to a passageway, Roberts sat eating his dinner by himself. He waved his knife, which dripped with butter. Daniels nodded and continued on.

The aft cage was situated in a small nook ten feet down the passageway from the mess deck. Rogers and Daniels stopped in front of it. Rogers then kicked the door with his steel-toed boot. The echo shot down the corridor, turning the heads of several sailors.

"Fucking Marine isn't here yet." He glanced at Daniels, disgusted, then leaned up against the padlocked cage.

Daniels eyed him and trembled in a controlled rage. He could still see a hovering Rogers, razor in hand. *Yeah, pretend it didn't happen, you fucker. Just keep pretending.* Stoker had switched today's duty day with Rogers. *Why?* He rubbed his watch. He was now going to have to stand and wait with Rogers until the Marine showed up. Daniels gritted his teeth as he thought about how much he hated spending even a single second standing in the same compartment, breathing the same *air* as Rogers. He now had to do rounds with him, log the temps, and then spend the rest of the night together until lockup. *Fucking Stoker!* Daniels spun his keys quickly in his hand. The tension ran high between them.

Two minutes passed, and Private Dell materialized from around the corner. He stood five foot two inches, had beach sand hair, green jittering eyes, and talked with a watered lisp.

"Sorry, fellas, running a bit late."

As his hand reached up with the key to unlock the door, Rogers grabbed and twisted it.

"Look, jarhead, we've been waiting here for over fifteen minutes because of you. Don't you ever, ever do that to us again. You hear me?" The small Marine trembled.

"Hey, I said I'm sorry, Rogers." Dell jerked his hand back, but Rogers held it. "Shit, man, let go!" Dell jerked his hand harder. No good. Rogers smiled down at Dell.

"Leave him alone, Rogers," said Daniels, stepping forward.

Rogers glared at Daniels, then at Dell. He let go. "Don't you ever show up late again," said Rogers, "or I'll break your fucking arm. Hear me?"

Dell flexed his hand and, with his other one, reached into his shirt pocket and pulled out a key affixed to a chain. A small identification tag hung limply from it. He inserted the key in the lock and then peeked up at Rogers, who stood straight, back now to Daniels. With a quick twist, Dell opened the lock and pulled it off. He then opened the door, walked in, and slammed it shut behind him. A loud "clank" reverberated throughout the passage as the inside door bolt thundered into place. Rogers and Daniels walked up and inserted their military ID cards into the slot below the window. Then waited.

Rogers stood hunched over, looking at his feet. Daniels eyed the cage. *Poor Dell.* He was the smallest Marine on the ship, and the Marines took turns picking on him. Even the sailors. Rogers particularly liked to push him around because he was so small and a bit slow in grasping things. And when attacked, he never defended himself. Daniels had seen Rogers on a couple of occasions throw Dell up against a bulkhead and scream in his face, "you're the sorriest excuse for a Marine I've ever seen." Daniels often wondered why would anyone that small join the Marines and subject himself to such abuse. He couldn't figure it out. *Like figuring out how to take a weapon.* The thought popped in unexpectedly, almost scaring him. He clenched his fist. *Stop it!*

But the mental "game" would not stay locked away. Too many times a day, it would surface. *Stop it, stop it!* But he knew it was no use; the more he tried to keep it out of his mind, the more it challenged him. He decided enough was enough. The next time he met Taylor alone, he would speak to him. *I don't give a fuck what he says; I know he's thinking of it as well.*

Daniels suddenly thought of the story of the emperor and the blue elephant. A man condemned to die told the emperor that he was a great wizard and would give the emperor two chests of gold if he was released. He said the chests were buried in the royal garden under the fountain. But if the emperor thought of a blue elephant *just once* while the treasure was being dug up, the chests would vanish, and the emperor would still have to keep his word and release him. The emperor agreed, thinking it would be too easy. The fountain was moved, and men started to dig—the condemned man watching it all with a slight smile on his face. But no sooner than ten shovels of dirt had escaped the ground when the emperor let out a large scream. He glared hard at the now-free man, spun, and stormed off into his palace.

Okay, think the opposite. Dwell on the game, and the mind will drift to other things. He tried, but this didn't work either. The more he thought about it, the more he got excited about the possibilities. He forced himself to think of the brig. If causation fueled the fire, then maybe consequence would smother it.

Another violent "clank" split the air. The door opened. The two men walked into the red-lit compartment, and the door slammed behind them. Dell's hand trembled as he handed the phone to Daniels. Daniels quickly gave the correct number and passed the phone over to Rogers. Rogers identified himself, paused, and then said the number "three" into the black phone. He then waited a few seconds and then turned around, the black cord stretching over Dell's shoulder. A few more seconds passed. Rogers motioned to Daniels, the phone cupped tight to his ear.

"It's dead. No response."

Dell's head shot up. "What'd you say?"

"I said it's fucking dead, you moron," said Rogers.

"No way!" said Daniels. "You gave the wrong number!"

"Fucking 'A' I did. I screwed up."

"What the fuck!" Daniels leaned back against the bulkhead, his eyes shut tight. Rogers handed the phone to Dell. Dell banged it against the holder as he hung it up.

"This can't be happening," said Daniels, his anger growing. *The Chief's gonna kill me.* Rogers tried to keep a smile from forming. Daniels stepped toward Rogers. "You fucker! You did this on purpose!" He grabbed Rogers by the shirt and pushed him up against the bulkhead.

Rogers grabbed his hands and pushed them away. "What's your trip? It's an accident, man, an accident."

"Bullshit!"

"Bullshit nothing. Get your fucking hands off me." He pushed Daniels back. Daniels banged into Dell but quickly turned, his fists balled, ready to hit him.

"Stop! Now!" Dell stepped between the two, one hand raised, the other one on the holster of his gun.

Rogers leaned back, clearly amused. "Now, Delly, you wouldn't dare put a gun to my head, now would you?" He grabbed Dell's arm. "It's not a fucking rule; it's entirely up to the Marine. And this was an accident. Accident! Do you want me to spell it out for you? A-K-S- I-D-E-N-T!" He let go of Dell's arm and smiled.

Dell glanced nervously at Daniels and then back up at Rogers. His fingers fidgeted on the black leather of the holster. Rogers capitalized on Dell's indecision. He thrust his finger into Dell's face. "Plus, you know me, and I swear to God, if you do something stupid, I'll find your dumb ass in the Philippines and whip it." Dell's lip twitched. He looked at his gun and then up at Rogers'. His hand fell away. He sat down in the chair, clearly distressed.

Rogers peered out the window, and Daniels leaned up against the bulkhead. *You bastard! You fucking bastard!*

A faint smile curled across Roger's face.

That's right, revel, you fucker. You'll pay. I swear to God, you'll pay. Daniels knew he would take the brunt of it, even though Rogers caused the alarm. Stating that Rogers did it on purpose would go nowhere. And he knew Rogers was fully aware of that. This was Rogers' first alarm in at least a year—this was Daniels' fourth alarm in a month. Daniels was in deep trouble. *The Chief's gonna grow critical and detonate. He's definitely—*

A sound caught Daniels' attention. He peered into the passageway. An armed Marine flashed through an open door at the far end of the corridor. Daniels turned. Rogers stays stooped, a cat-like arch to his back. His face was propped up, forehead touching the glass, a smile widening across his face. The heavy sound of boots filled the air. *Shit, they're coming.*

The words "Hit the Deck!" exploded through the mess deck like a tidal wave. Shouts and the sound of heavy boots on steel filled the air. Someone started screaming. Daniels took a deep breath. It sounded like Roberts.

23   Oct. 77

Can't believe it. Was told to take the trash to the sponson. All I did was just drop it down a chute into the water, one plastic bag bobbing on the sea, joining an irregular line stretching to the horizon, to the setting sun. What incredible waste. Some of the bags dumped, according to the sponson watch, are never punched with holes to make them sink. A Russian ship just over the horizon stalks in our wake, picking up and then sifting through our waste, trying to find useful scraps of information. It's shocking to think of all the trash dumped overboard. Oil, equipment, banding wire, paper, pipes, paint, solvents, and anything you could think of is cast into the sea from the aft sponson or, against regulations, from other sponsons or the flight deck. But no one really seems to give a shit. The Marines even set up their M-60s on the ship's stern every so often for target practice, even giving the sailors a chance to shoot—a rapid fire of lead aimed at the drifting dots of plastic. The watch said that he heard from his Chief that the Navy dumps over 60,000 tons of garbage a year into the ocean! No wonder trash is being found washed up on uninhabited islands. Besides trash, the world regularly dumps nuclear waste and toxic chemicals into the sea as well. After World War Two, both the US and Russia dumped all of Nazi Germany's chemical weapons into the Baltic. No protective containers were used, and no maps were made of all the dumping spots. And corrosion is splitting the containers apart, spreading the chemicals, washing them up in hellish clumps onto beaches. What will happen when all that poison finally seeps up into the Baltic, and then by currents, into the Atlantic? Enough poison was dumped into the Baltic to kill every man, woman, and child in Europe.

As I was about to leave the sponson, the watch lowered his head to the water and shook it, his eyes fast to the bags of trash cutting the surface of the sea like fat fins. "You know," he said, "I swear to God. The world's just like that there movie, 'Jaws.' When Brody, that cop,

160

said to the mayor, 'You aren't gonna realize that we have a shark problem until it swims up and bites you on your goddamn ass.'" He spat. "Or words to that effect."

I nodded and left.

Worked out with Collins again. He finally got some time off. Am really changing my opinion about the Marine Corps. Collins has a good head, and he has a definite plan for his future. But he takes his job seriously. Deadly seriously. Talking with him in the "cage" while he's on duty is a very different experience from talking with him in the Armory off duty. In the cage, he keeps his words to a minimum, almost forgetting he knows me, his head constantly shifting and scanning the far passageways while he moves the phone or badges. But tonight, outside of the cage, he was a different person. Loose and casual, speaking freely and laughing at everything. He apologized at one point, with a slap to my back, about his military manner. He said that it was important to keep up a strict attitude. The Sergeant of the Guard would periodically make unannounced spot checks on the cage, but more importantly, his careful and precise behavior was driven by a deep sense of honor and commitment. He wants to feel proud of his accomplishments when he leaves the service in a couple of years and passes this pride on to his two children. I like his attitude.

The Chief

The Chief sat securely in his chair. He pored over a stack of paperwork on top of his desk. His dark arms splayed out before him like a stem post and stern, bracing the paper from a stream of air blowing from a torn vent just above him. On his left forearm were visible the scarred remnants of a tattoo. Specks of red and blue ink intermixed with scar tissue testified to an angry, alcohol-infested night years ago when he burned off the name of his ex-wife with a steaming iron. Just above it was a new tattoo—a small wooden warship with the words "Navy" written in script below it.

Daniels stood at attention. His hands slid along his pants, brushing the sweat off. The waiting was making it worse. No one, absolutely no one, ever crossed the Chief. Warrant Officer Hempel presided over the division, but "sure as shit," Chief ran it. Even when Lieutenant Commander Fremont was sent down from Air Department, VA 115, for a week to run things until Hempel reported aboard, the Chief operated things his own way. The backbone of the fleet were the enlisted chiefs—and this everyone knew. They ran the Navy. And most "boot" officers fresh out of college gave them a wide berth. Friction finally built between the Chief and Hempel, reaching overload on the third evening. No one watched the ship's movie that night in the pub room. The yelling was intense. All had their ears perked up, and their heads turned to the office bulkhead.

The Chief was fed up with the way Fremont was running things. Fremont was an A-6 pilot and had no experience running a nuclear weapons division. Normally a chief petty officer—a noncommissioned officer, would leave alone any officer above the rank of lieutenant. Such officers usually had earned enough respect by then—that is, they had a "full seabag" of naval knowledge and experience. Fremont was given the respect owed to an officer of that rank, for he had definitely earned it, but he had no inkling of the protocol and procedures inherent in a nuclear weapons environment. That knowledge was the Chief's domain.

Thus with all of the tradition, experience, and gumption that he could muster, the Chief broadsided Fremont in hearing range of Daniels and the division, who listened with the excitement of kids. Individual words were hard to make out, but the high-pitched expletives weren't. After the first salvo was fired, the Chief slammed shut the office door with such force that the metal stripping bent. Fremont put up a good fight but, in the end, was hopelessly outgunned. The Chief tacked, cut, bellowed, and blazed, easily sidestepping "direct orders." Fremont retreated out of the office, scuttled up the ladder, and was never heard to argue with the Chief during his remaining days.

The Chief stirred. He lifted his head and stared up at Daniels, taking in a breath, his khaki shirt expanding outward like a great canvas sail. He drew his arms to his body as a ship would draw in its anchor. Daniels swallowed.

"I really don't know what to do with you," he said in a calm voice. "I tried talking with you. I tried encouraging you, giving you valuable leadership advice, and I even sent you to Petty Officer Academy." His voice started to rise. "Then I started to lose my patience. You know, I really liked you when you first reported aboard. Your fierce determination to learn. Your college classes. Sailor of the month. Your pride in yourself, your shipmates, and your unwavering pride in the Navy."

Pride?

The Chief's anger now came through in flashes. "How many goddamn times is it going to take to get through that fucking head of yours that this division cannot, will not, tolerate your bullshit?"

The Chief's forehead knotted—a feature that earned him the name "Madman." Daniels grimaced at the thought that all the ears in the pub room now strained to hear his ass chewing.

"You can't seem to be a leader. Even when I order the men to listen to you, they don't. Do you know why? Because they don't respect you.

You can't seem to understand that. Respect is earned—not fucking given away like welfare. Do you understand?"

"Yes, Chief." The reply was barely a whisper.

"Shut the fuck up. I didn't say you could speak. Don't you cross me, Daniels, or so help me, I'll tie your dumb ass from the highest yardarm. You hear me?!"

Daniels nodded.

"This was your fourth alarm in only a month. A month! The Captain wants a full report of not only this incident but the other three on his desk by tomorrow morning. All because you can't seem to get a full fucking seabag together. Well, I've had it! I am going to make an example out of you. Do you understand?" The Chief was furious. Daniels wished he were under the small trash can in the corner.

"You will be confined to the ship the whole time in the Philippines pending investigation."

"What!"

"Shut up! Furthermore, I am considering taking you off as hook leader and replacing you with Rogers."

"Rogers! He was the one who—"

"I said shut the fuck up! I don't care whose fault it was. You were in charge, so you are accountable." The Chief pushed his finger into Daniels' chest. "Do you know what you caused? Do you?"

Daniels didn't move.

"Do you know? Well, I'll tell you. Your alarm not only put the Executive Officer of the ship, Captain Simmons, face down on the deck with the head of Weapons Department, Commander Nelson, but the latest is Roberts' back is broken."

"What?" Daniels reeled.

"That's right." The Chief lowered his voice. "He's partially paralyzed from the waist down because a Marine ran him over while responding to your alarm. We hope it's only temporary."

The light just above Daniels seemed to pulse in its glass tomb. Water pipes and electric cables hung like a web. The small room compressed in on him. He swallowed and decided on a different approach. "When did you hear about this?" he said.

The Chief relaxed a bit, and his words came out semi-controlled. "An hour ago; I haven't told the division yet."

"Chief, I'm sorry. I honestly didn't—"

That was it; the Chief exploded.

"This isn't a fucking game! Do you think the Captain and Executive Officer gives a royal fuck who caused it! No, you idiot! No! They've had it, and they want someone's head. Mine!"

The Chief brought his fist down hard on the desk, and his eyes locked onto Daniels'. "Now get the hell out of here!"

Daniels didn't move quickly enough. He glanced at his watch and then stood for a moment before deciding that he shouldn't try to defend his actions anymore. Those few seconds cost him.

The Chief leaped up and catapulted him out into the hall. Daniels bounded across the deck, tripped, and fell into the ladder, smashing his hand on a bolt. He let out a sharp cry and stared down at the blood on his hand.

The Chief stood in the doorway, his face blank. Daniels glared at him, holding his right hand, blood curling around his palm, dripping. The blood blended in with the ripple of grooves on the step and started to pool. Daniels' body slowly rocked back and forth, back and forth, in sync with the waves of pain sweeping up his arm. The Chief stepped forward into the hallway and spoke in a calm voice.

"Get out of here and have that hand looked at." He turned to walk back into the office but stopped. "Sorry about the hand. We'll need to get that hoist fixed. You understand?"

Daniels avoided the Chief's eyes but nodded. The Chief would be in serious trouble if he reported this altercation. Maybe even thrown out of the Personal Reliability Program. He would lose his security clearance, his division, and, no doubt, his temper. *No, it wasn't worth it to write him up*, Daniels thought. Things would only get worse. He let out a breath and climbed the ladder. *Yeah, much worse.*

24   Oct. 77 (AM)

Last night I dreamt that I approached the edge of a large black hole. I felt like I was being pushed into it, and I tried to stop myself from moving, but I kept advancing, inch by inch. Finally, I was swept over and into it like a mountain stream over a ledge. I then fell, and kept falling, and suddenly woke, my head full of sweat.

I think that dream was precipitated by Heart of Darkness, *which I had finished reading yesterday evening. Kurtz shouldn't have let his desire control him. Thus Marlowe in the Buddhist pose at the story's beginning and end. To kill desire is to kill suffering. Kurtz's fall could have been avoided.*

Need to take this to heart. My thoughts seem to somehow rule my passion.

Path of Least Resistance

Daniels made his way down to the Armory. Both his head and his hand protested in pain. He hoped the aspirin the corpsman gave him would do the trick. His right index and middle finger were only sprained, not broken, as Daniels had feared.

He opened the door with his left hand and stepped in. Taylor was lying on the weight bench, his eyes fixed on the division lockers on the far side of the compartment. Rivers of sweat ran down and along the sides of his head and arms. The air was abnormally hot and humid. Taylor's gaze settled on the bandages.

"Bad luck, huh?"

"Yeah, I guess you can say I'm swimming in it," said Daniels. "It tends to pool, and about right now, I can honestly say that I'm not holding up very well." He leaned against the door. "Before Africa, I was beginning to think things were looking up. But now there's a good chance I might lose my position." His voice trailed off as he sat down on the deck next to the door.

"What are you going to do about it?" asked Taylor.

"I don't know."

Taylor leaned back down, placed his wide hands firmly around the bar, and lifted. He pumped out a set of ten reps with short, explosive breaths.

The bar looked heavier than the last time Daniels had seen it. It amazed him that someone could lift so much weight. Taylor put the bar down, his muscles rippling out from his body, stretching his T-shirt to its limit. Daniels studied his bandaged hand. "Why do you think they're fucking with me?" He seemed to already know, but he didn't quite want to accept it.

Taylor sat up. "You tell me."

Daniels shook his head.

"Look, Daniels, the answer is as plain as the cut on your hand."

"Tell me then."

"Can't you see, dimwit? He wants your job."

Daniels tensed. "I know he wants my fucking job! I've always known that. But I refused to believe that he would put people at risk over it."

"Then you really are an idiot."

"Jesus, Taylor, Robert's back is broken." Daniels slid down the wall to the deck, his anger rising. He could see Rogers hovering over him, his face twisted in satisfaction. *Razor in hand.* His teeth glistened, eyes vulture-like, staring, penetrating. *I've seen it before.* That head cocked back, the eyes staring down at him. Defiant, calculated, hateful. Yes, hateful, as though reveling in it. Pride in it. *Who?* Suddenly it surfaced. An image as hot as the sun.

John Kilazzi. Tall, thin, bleached hair, oversized canines, and a large black mole growing on his jaw just under his right ear. He hovered over Daniels with that same look. Sharon screamed, but her cry sounded distant, echo-like, as Daniels looked up from the stench at the bottom of the trash bin. Flies buzzed around his head, then disappeared into the darkness of the corners.

"Think you're smarter than us, huh," said Kilazzi, holding up the metal lid. "Think you're better. Well, I'm gonna tell you the truth, moron. You'll never amount to anything. You hear me. Nothing. Just a dumb old janitor in school. That's it."

Kilazzi pursed his lips together and blew softly, sending out a stream of spit that slowly made its way down toward Daniels' face. Daniels instinctively jumped and landed on the trash heap. When he sat up, a foul-smelling remnant of a banana hung down from his nose. Kilazzi jumped off, laughing, which soon swelled into a chorus as others joined in all around him. Daniels wiped his face. The sound of scuffling feet and mocking cries soon faded and then disappeared. Daniels lay still, breathing in the stench. A few seconds passed. Soft footfalls could now be heard. Sharon. But instead of increasing in their delicate pitch and rhythm, they too receded, blending into the background—

"Daniels, give me a hand," said Taylor.

Daniels jerked. He inhaled sharply to clear his head and anger. It didn't work. He looked at the bandages on his hand. 'Very funny."

"I didn't mean it that way." Taylor stood facing one end of the barbell, hands gripping an end weight.

Daniels walked to the other end of the bar. "Fuck, I need a joint."

"Not in here, you don't. Do that shit somewhere else, you hear me?"

"Hey, it's cool. I just need to calm down."

"No, it's not fucking cool!"

"What the hell's with you? I meant I wasn't going to."

Taylor slid a weight off. Daniels did the same. They took enough weights off each end until four twenty-five-pounders on each side remained. Daniels walked over to the bulkhead and sat down. Taylor did ten quick military presses, then put the bar down and sat next to Daniels.

"Heard anything on Roberts?" Taylor asked.

"No, just what the Chief announced to the division."

"Hard to believe what happened."

"They'll be flying him off the ship tomorrow."

"Heard Henderson got beat up pretty bad in the brig a few days ago," said Taylor.

"Yeah, I heard that too. He doesn't know when to quit."

"When's he out?" asked Taylor.

"Wednesday."

"Day after we pull in."

"Yup. Just in time for our division party at the Buffalo Beer House Wednesday night," said Daniels.

Taylor sat down on the bench. "No way the Chief will let you off the ship tomorrow or attend the party?"

"No way in hell. But no big loss, anyway. I've got Yuki now, and I'm sick of those raunchy parties. You'll see; it's only a matter of time before you do too."

169

"Who said I wasn't sick of them now."

"Sorry, I should never assume anything. As the Chief says, 'If you divide up the word 'assume,' you'll see that it makes an ass out of—"

"'—you and me,'" said Taylor. They both grinned. "What brings you down here," asked Taylor, eyeing Daniels.

"Well, I've been thinking about our thought experiment, and I came up with an interesting idea." He carefully watched Taylor's reaction.

Taylor put the towel around his neck and rested his arms on his thighs. "Remember what we agreed."

"Hey fuck that. I've got a really good idea. I think you'll like it." Daniels smiled.

"So," said Taylor.

"So, I'm fucking tired of keeping it locked up in my damn head, and so I'm going to tell you no matter what you fucking say."

"So."

"So, acetylene," said Daniels.

"Acetylene?"

"Yeah, acetylene."

"A colorless, highly flammable or explosive gas that is used for cutting or welding," said Taylor. "So what."

I knew it. He's itching to talk. "Well, if someone went down one of the escape trunks with a welding torch, they could cut a hole in the emergency escape hatch."

"Not possible."

Daniels smiled. "Thought about it already, huh?"

Taylor ignored him and continued. "The tops of the trunks are alarmed. Plus, the heat and flame would set off the magazine sprinkler system. They have thermal fuses, and the solder would melt out at either 110 or 130 degrees."

"But those trunks are opened all the time for maintenance, and if you can slip in—"

"No," said Taylor. "There's a Marine sentry posted. Didn't you read your manuals?"

"Yeah, but as I told you before, that was a while ago." Daniels paused. "Yeah, you're right; the Marine would smell the smoke."

Taylor cracked a smile.

"Well, did *you* think of anything, smart ass?" said Daniels.

"Nope." Taylor leaned back and stretched.

"What about another magazine surrounding our magazines," said Daniels.

"You could gain access to them fairly easy while on a magazine night watch," said Taylor.

"Yeah, or gain access long enough to bring in the equipment."

"Or fellow members of your team, if needed. You could continue making rounds and not raise any suspicions."

"Good point; no one would know," said Daniels. "Those damn watches are done alone. Open the door, throw the equipment in, let the rest of your team in, and presto, weld city."

"What about smoke, heat, and getting the warhead out."

"Hold on; I'm thinking."

"Maybe—"

"Got it!" said Daniels. "Do it slowly, in timed patches; that way, the magazine won't heat up enough to set the alarms off. Cut a small part of the circle, stop, wait a while for it to cool down and the heat to disperse throughout the room, and then start again. It might take a bit longer, but you wouldn't have to worry about the sprinkler system."

"Hmm, one problem, the flame from the torch. All magazines have insulation covering the bulkheads; it's fire retardant, but heated to such high temperatures it will probably burn."

"Water."

"Flooding sensors."

"CO_2."

"Might work," said Taylor, "if you can control the smoke and heat. But there's a second watch later in the evening."

"Problem."

They paused for a while, then Taylor spoke. "Either have him in on it or get out in time...which would be an impossibility—the smoke would linger around all night. He would report it immediately."

"Good point," said Daniels.

"Path of least resistance. We need to keep narrowing."

"A void or another compartment surrounding our magazine."

"Mmmm. If there are any."

"Come to think of it, I think there is at least one void next to M-2," said Daniels. His eyes lit up.

"Assume there is. If there is a void, red tag it so that no one enters or floods it."

"And there are thirty-six nuts that need to be removed to enter it," said Daniels. Pop them off with a wrench, throw your equipment in, and seal it up. With it red-tagged, no one will go near it."

"Problem. If you seal it up, it's a small space with a limited supply of air. With the smoke, you'll need air packs to breathe."

"Piece of cake. Scott air packs, you can breathe for an hour, more than enough time to cut a small hole. They're in every coop on the ship."

"Another problem. Explosive vapor. Jet fuel or something else."

"Another good point," said Daniels. "You would have to think of a way to get rid of the vapors or find a void without them."

"Smelling's not good enough. Have to test for them first."

"Well, do what some of the old coal miners used to do. Put a bird in a cage and leave it," Daniels started to laugh. "If it lives, no vapor; if it dies, find another void or compartment."

Taylor stared coldly at him.

"Hey, just kidding."

"A bigger problem."

"What?"

"Cut a hole into a magazine and hit a power line, or worse, a vent. A fire could endanger the ship."

"Good point," said Daniels. "A vent fire would be dangerous. But if you cut a small hole first and stuck in a stick or something, a mirror or telescope tube, you could check out the area."

Taylor stood up, grabbed his towel, and wiped his face down. He paced the room for a few minutes, finally sitting back down next to Daniels.

"Wait." Taylor paused. "We are presupposing that the exact location of the magazine is known. If known, and an adjacent compartment is known, then they would most likely know enough about the interior of the magazine to avoid a vent or power line."

"And that wouldn't be hard to do," said Daniels. "After a weapons offload at sea, anyone, including shore workers and civilians, has access to the spaces. There are no weapons and no Marines. Anyone of them could map out the entire inside space as well as the surrounding compartments."

"Get the information during an offload, then carry through with the operation the next time in port with weapons."

"Shit, it's scary that two enlisted men can figure this all out. I wonder if the Marines have?"

"I doubt it," said Taylor.

"Yeah, so do I. To them, it would be unthinkable—wait, a terrorist group might get the area mapped out all right, but who's to say they know the arrangement of weapons and equipment. They could cut into an area where it would be difficult to squeeze in or get a warhead out—there could be a stack of B43s in the way."

"They would have to move them," said Taylor.

"But that would take time and make a lot of noise, particularly if they had to use the hoist."

"Plan carefully, and be lucky."

"Or, something we haven't mentioned yet—a contact with someone inside the spaces."

"Good, good, the path of least resistance," said Taylor. "That's *very* good."

"Watch it; I sense a slight tone of condescension." Daniels shifted.

173

It was hot. He wiped a stream of sweat inching its way down his cheek. "Let's take it a step farther," continued Daniels. "It seems the whole damn system is set up to prevent someone on the outside from getting in, not for someone on the inside getting out."

"Meaning," said Taylor.

"Meaning, in terms of this mental exercise, or game, it might be easier for someone on the inside—being inside is half the battle—to sneak a weapon out than a group of people isolated on the outside trying to get in and then out."

"Least resistance. Good point." Taylor suddenly stretched, signaling that he was getting tired of talking.

Daniels was also tired. The heat was sapping his strength. He was amazed at how Taylor could work out here, particularly alone, without anyone to spot that amount of weight for him. He yawned and then also stretched.

"It's getting to be about that time," said Daniels looking at his watch. "I need to study anyways. Got an important final coming up just after the Philippines." He opened the door and turned to Taylor. "The next step, when we meet again, is to again find the weakest link in the system. Define and refine."

Taylor didn't respond. Daniels stepped through the door and slammed it shut. He walked back to the coop, alone in his thoughts.

25 Oct. 77

The ship is docking right now. Everyone is running around like idiots, their tongues and groins steaming in lustful anticipation. Olongapo. A sailor's Paradise, they call it. The Garden of Eden. I haven't seen it yet, but from the lurid stories and strange smells sullying the breeze, I could suggest a better name.

Philippines

Daniels laid his letter from Yuki on top of his Oceanography book. He took in a deep breath, his head spinning. He had just received it at mail call. He picked it up again, studying its last few sentences: "I want to marry you Chris!!!!!! I love you!!!! But mother don't like America. She really hate. My father died a five years ago from wound in War II. She's health also very bad. Alone in Tokyo. I don't think she will allow. I'm sorry.

PS. Please keep send me penny. I love poem very much!"

He couldn't believe it. He kept staring at the word "sorry." The "y" of that tiny word had transformed itself into the head of a massive hammer—a hammer that hit him in the head and heart a thousand times.

"Hey, Daniels," said Sanchez, startling him. "The Chief wants to see you." The shadow of Sanchez's hat hid his eyes. *Shit, not again.* "Move it."

Daniels had no problem jumping down to the deck. He actually wanted his fall to keep continuing. *To the bottom of the fucking bay!*

He followed Sanchez, and they walked over to the cage and inserted their cards in the slot, and waited. The bolt exploded back, and the door slid open and away from the sides. Sanchez stepped in, the soft red light swallowing him. The door slammed shut, the echo shooting down the passageway, leaving Daniels alone to wait his turn. He pulled a pen from his pocket and drew an eye on the cage, just up from the deck, directly beneath the mirrored window. He studied it, amused, wondering if anyone would notice this improvement.

The bolt rang out again, and the door swung open. He entered, and a small arm reached up and slammed the door shut.

"Heyyy, ease up on the door, huh," said Daniels.

Dell smiled and handed Daniels his badge. "Nope," said Dell, "enjoy it too much."

Daniels clipped his badge on, opened the inner door, and exited the

176

cage. His boots clicked on the tile. He opened and closed his hands, his mind still ringing from Yuki's letter. Pain shot up his right arm from the wound on his finger. When he reached the office door, he tapped softly, then again, louder. He was fully expecting this day to get worse exponentially. Implode.

The door burst open. Daniels stepped back. The Chief filled the frame of the door like a tongue in a monstrous mouth.

"How's the hand?" the Chief said.

The soft tone caught Daniels by surprise.

"Good." He was still nervous. *Must be the calm before the storm.*

"Step in."

Daniels walked in, feeling like a fresh piece of fish. The Chief closed the door behind him. He picked up his cup of coffee, studied it for a second, and then took a sip, a wisp of steam curling up into his nose. He sat down. Daniels sweated, wondering.

"I've changed my mind. I'm willing to let you go ashore for the remainder of our stay."

Daniels' eyes lit up. It sounded too good to be true. The Chief was actually changing his mind! *What's the catch?* He waited.

"Missing the first day in was more than adequate. Now get the fuck out of here."

There must be a catch. He must be feeling guilty for his bloody deed. Afraid I might report it? Both? It didn't matter. The room suddenly glowed. His thoughts turned to cold bottles of San Miguel beer and the division party that evening. His luck had changed.

The Chief suddenly hit the desk. "You're still here! Get the hell out before I change my mind!"

Daniels spun and raced for the coop. His luck had changed, and he was going to try to make the best of it. Maybe a few beers and some fun would ease the pain of the letter. At the least, a cold San Miguel would put a smile on his face. *A substitute for an Asahi Super Dry with Yuki.* But that was for another day, another battle. For now, he needed to try to forget.

177

He quickly changed into jeans and a nice shirt and then made his way to the afterbrow and off the ship. The sun perched directly overhead, biting into his skin. The pier was filled with swarming sailors, large pipes spurting steam, vendors selling hot dogs, and several bare-legged women standing around the afterbrow. A moist breeze swept across his face.

Daniels wanted to stoop down and kiss the concrete. It felt that good to be on land again. He quickly made his way through the base, settling in behind a group of hormone-intoxicated sailors headed to Olongapo City on the other side of "Shit River." As he approached the gate to the base, the wind shifted, and he winced. It was christened "Shit River" for a good reason. The city vomited all of its waste and raw sewage into it. If a sailor fell in, it was rumored he had to be medically quarantined for three days and given every shot in the book.

He passed through the gate and walked slowly up to the top of the bridge. The stench of the bathroom brown water flowing beneath was heavy. He walked further along the bridge and stopped next to two sailors throwing coins. He looked down. Short dug-out canoes overflowed with small children. They jumped and swarmed about, eagerly holding up wire baskets to the staring white faces above them. One of the sailors threw down a peso. It plopped into the roiling water and disappeared immediately, spiraling down unseen to the bottom. Three naked children, one with a rubber face mask with no glass, dove in after it. They surfaced seconds apart, gulped air down, and dove again. The one with the face mask surfaced and let out a cry, his hand and coin held high. The other two appeared, and doggy paddled back to their small canoes.

Daniels grimaced. *Poor kids. So much to give, and the world gives so little*. He watched as a small girl with large pretty eyes and a long ponytail clung nakedly to the boat with one arm, the current tugging her, while her wide brown eyes and free hand pleaded. She carried no basket. *The world turns and walks away from the flowing filth as I will*. He made out the top of a wooden chair that was slowly floating towards him. A smorgasbord of cans, bottles, paper, the stew of progress, and what looked like clumps of human excrement bobbed here and there, every now and then bumping into a child.

Beneath him now, the chair swirled slowly and then sank from view. Daniels reached into a pocket and, grabbing a handful of coins, including several pennies that he had been saving for Yuki, threw them down. He aimed for the boat, but most splashed into the river. The children screamed, scrabbled, and dove, disappearing quickly beneath the dirty surface. The small girl released her grip and quietly sank out of sight.

Daniels turned and walked toward Magsaysay, the main boulevard and entrance into Olongapo. He wanted desperately to stop and drink a few cold beers before heading over to the division party that evening.

Daniels made his way down the street, past swarming people and blaring Jeepneys decorated in an assortment of styles and colors. A yellow jeepney screeched by him, silver plates riveted all over its surface, three small statuettes of horses gracing its hood, and a small plastic sign on top, wings on each side, with a royal crown that said "Lovable" in large red letters. A woman leaned out and flashed her tongue at him. He ignored her and moved on. *Keep focused.*

Sailors and locals filled the streets and sidewalks in a moving symphony of color and sound, and a cluster of half-naked girls hung out from the windows of a building with a sign "Massage-Very Cheap!!" They smiled and yelled down to a group of taunting sailors in the street. Both groups howled and gesticulated to one another for a few minutes until the sailors suddenly slipped inside.

Further on, the scent of barbecued chicken fluttered in the air from the many stands lining the boulevard. All along both sides of the street, cement hotels with yellowed, cracked interior walls seemed to moan softly from within as Daniels walked by, almost all infested with the biggest cockroaches Daniels had ever seen in his life.

He had once mistaken one for a small mouse as it raced out from the water-filled shower drain at his feet. His heart skipped, and he leaped back against the wall in fear. He inched up to it as it tried in vain to climb the slick tile. He raised a huge bedpan over his head and smashed it down. One half of the monster bug scurried toward the drain and disappeared; the other half scurried defiantly toward him, its two antennae cutting into the air like French foils.

Music blasted into the street from the hundreds of clubs, and there were clubs to cater to everyone's needs and tastes—country western, hard and soft rock, disco, and other styles. But by far, the main draw was the alcohol and bar girls. The sailor's motto was that you could get drunk, laid, and a room for the night for less than ten bucks. The San Miguel beer was cheap and cold. The women, many and willing. They spilled out from every club and bar in the city, luring drunken, horny sailors inside. Once a sailor had chosen a girl from the swarming multitudes, he would then have to buy her many drinks in order to stay with her in one of the rooms at the bar or to leave with her to his hotel or her house. Or he paid her very cheap bar fine. Often, a sailor would buy a girl out of the bar for the whole length of stay in port.

Daniels walked past bar after bar filled with beautiful girls, and the temptation was tremendous. *Need to keep focused. Forget.* But Daniels quickly realized that trying to forget a lover or anything to do with love and sex in Olongapo was too tall of an order. The girls giggled and smiled and blew kisses to him, sometimes exposing a breast, sometimes grabbing an arm to drag him in. He walked past the sex houses or "massage parlors" littering the streets. It was rumored that a few specialized in dipping, spinning "basket" sex, a drinking oral sex game called "smile," multiple partners, or some other type of kinky or exotic sexual act.

Daniels stepped into one of his favorite bars, the Florida Club. Aside from the many bar girls, it looked like a normal club from the States, which is what really appealed to him. It was dark, and the cool air immediately calmed him. He sailed past the girls who called to him and sat down at one of the many tables. The band on stage was doing an excellent rendition of Jeff Beck's "Cause We've Ended as Lovers." Thin girls in scanty G-strings stood on small round platforms next to the dance floor, swaying and moving their hips to the music and lights. Many of the eyes in the audience were locked onto the soft shifting breasts of the girl's bodies and not on the band.

A bar girl sat down next to him and slid her fingers up his arm and around his shoulder. She leaned into him. Her long black hair cascaded down her bathing-suited body and flowed across his thigh. She fingered his shirt sleeve and peered deeply into his eyes. "Buy me drink?" A badge with the number "Forty-eight" floated over her breast. He gently picked off her hand and slid it a few inches away.

"No," he said, "I'm taken." And to reinforce this, and as a reminder, he reached into his top pocket and pulled out a picture of Yuki, and stared at her warm and waiting smile. He smiled back. *We will marry. I swear it.* The bar girl glared at the picture and then vanished as silently as she had come.

"Beer?" asked a waiter.

"One, please." The waiter sped off in the direction of the bar. *One can't hurt. Just one, and that's it.* He wanted his reasoning abilities and physical reflexes intact for that evening.

Six beers and four hours later, he staggered towards the division party.

26   Oct. 77

This is bullshit! I was going to meet Collins at Grande Island for a small barbecue tonight, but Sanchez laid into me a few minutes ago and ordered me to go to the division party! The Chief wants everyone not on duty to attend. "We're a team, and you're part of it! They've spent a lot of money and time on this, and both the Division Officer and the Department Head are going to be there with their wives." Wives? Why would anyone want to fly his wife to this God-forsaken city, to the Buffalo Beer House, to watch a bunch of drunken sailors slobber and drool over a couple of kinky strippers paid for from the division's rec fund? Why the hell should I be ordered to attend this freak show like some damn dog? There is a fine line where authority ends and my freedom begins. They've crossed it again.

Buffalo Beer House

"Yeeeehaaa." It was Henderson. He strode into the bar, beaming. Everyone cheered. Daniels perked up at the sight of his friend. He leaped to his feet, slipped, jumped up again, and staggered over to greet him.

"Henderson! How's it feel to be a free man?" said Daniels, his speech slightly slurred.

Henderson looked down at him. "It feels great, you drunk motherfucker. I need a beer; hell, make that two."

"Two it is," said Daniels as he tacked over to the bar.

The room was teeming. Girls were prancing about and falling off the shoulders of loud, drunk W-Division personnel and other sailors from Weapons Department. Sanchez and O'Reilly sat drinking with bargirls glued to their sides. Warrant Officer Hempel and his wife sat next to the head of Weapons Department, Commander Nelson, and his wife at another table. All four were drinking heavily and laughing. An old jukebox in the corner with a brick for a missing leg blasted out the Deep Purple song "Smoke on the Water." The Chief sat at a table in the corner, drinking with a cute bar girl.

Daniels bought beer for Henderson and himself. He shuffled over to the table where Henderson had sat down with a bargirl named Patsy and another girl who Daniels had never seen before.

"Hey, partner, I hear you're in some hot water," said Henderson. Daniels ignored the question and handed him his beer. Henderson eyed the bottle as if he were a crazed soul in the Sahara chancing upon water. He threw the bottle to his lips and guzzled, beer frothing down both sides of his chin. He sucked the bottle dry. Wiping his face, he slammed it down and screamed, "Where's my other?!"

Daniels quickly gave him his own and sat down. He then looked around the cramped room at the faces of the many sailors and bar girls, at the long bar running parallel to a cracked wall, at the large painting of a buffalo filling the wall and at the old black and white photos sagging in their frames. A weak light cast itself out from the middle of a spinning fan. *Damn this place.* For the first time in ten visits, he suddenly felt hatred for it.

A bar girl slid in next to Daniels, surprising him, and she put her arm around his waist, her long black hair hiding her eyes. "I'm Maria. Buy me drink?" Her smile was soft and fleshy, and the heat from her body pressed into him. Her hand ran up and down his leg. Tremors rippled through him. His mind shut down, and his alcohol-infused body took over. He instinctively leaned in her, inhaling her perfume. *So sweet.* The strength of his desire surprised and shocked him. Some inner instinct called out to him to kiss her long and deep, and he suddenly felt that he somehow needed her. Needed to hold her, needed to—*What the hell am I doing? Stop!* He pushed her away.

Henderson nudged him. "Damn . . . now that's commitment, brother. A rare thing these days. Especially here. She must be one fine woman." An ear-to-ear smile filled his broad face. Maria looked offended, and she turned and glanced up at the light leaking in from the boarded windows.

"Yes, yes, she is," said Daniels. "You could say she's my . . . my little angel."

"Must be to keep your legs locked in this place." Henderson took a long swig of beer.

"So what the hell happened to you," slurred Daniels. "I heard you got popped in the head . . . at that plush suite they prepared for you . . . the hole."

"Fucking Marines," said Henderson, his smile fading. "I have never seen anyone want to fuck with you so much, to shame you to no end . . .and enjoy it, I mean, really, really enjoy it. They're like fucking Nazis, for Christ's sake." Henderson took a long swig from his beer. "Jesus, did they mess with me. If I did even the slightest thing wrong, even so much as to cock my head an inch while eating or scrubbing the deck, they jumped on me like fucking banshees. If you complained or resisted, they beat you. They sound their little piss ant alarms, and ten to fifteen jarheads come flying at ya with billy sticks, beating the living shit out of you. Then they tack on more fucking time!"

Henderson jumped up on his seat, lifted his head high, and shouted out to the bar, "I would have kicked all their fucking asses if they hadn't sent in reinforcements." He flexed his wiry arms, his bald head shining like the radar cone of a B-43 bomb, and let loose the Marine call, "Oooraaahhh, Ooooraaahh." Everyone joined in and then laughed. Hempel, Nelson, and their wives smiled.

Maria turned and tried to tempt Daniels again. She eased into him warm and silky like a cat, rubbing his leg and purring into his ear. "Please, buy me drink," she said. Her eyes shone. "You come room me. I make happy." Her fingers slid over his crotch. "Buy me just one drink."

Daniels leaned back, pushing her hand away. "I said no."

"Please." She tugged at his shirt and bit her lip. "One drink. I like you, no bullshit." She smiled.

Daniels took in a breath. "Don't you. . . don't you understand. I have a girlfriend that I love."

"What!?" said Maria, her eyes wide. "You crazy! No one here think like you. Look around." She scanned the bar, looking at all the sailors with girls, some married. She turned back. "You not marry? You too young, handsome." She grabbed his hand and looked at his bare ring finger. "See. You free sailor! She not here, so no worry!" Daniels looked away, and as he did this, the music suddenly stopped. A Weapons Department sailor stood holding the plug to the jukebox. He dropped it as Division Officer Hempel stood up and walked up to him, his bottle of San Miguel cradled in his hand. Hempel turned and addressed the group.

"I hope you're all fully enjoying yourselves!"

The room burst into cheer. Bottles clinked, and feet stamped the wooden floor.

"Good, that's what I like to see. Now, I think we need to get this show on the road."

185

Yells and screams filled the room.

"Hold on . . . Quiet, please . . . Just settle down. I think you guys might have spent a little bit too long at sea." He took a swig of beer amongst the chorus of shouts.

"As you all know, at every W-division party, we like to do it up good and raunchy, hopefully topping the last one. And so for your benefit, pleasure, if you like, Mamasan got us a pretty young lady who's going perform . . . ahh, something *special* for us tonight." He looked around. "Is she ready? Yeah, okay, she's ready, willing, and able, so let's clear a circle here in the back for her."

The men and bargirls all got up, hollering and shouting, and formed a large circle at the back of the room next to the jukebox. After a few minutes of stomping, whistling, and shouting, a tall thin woman in a tight pink bikini, made her way up to the front of the crowd and walked over to the jukebox. Sailors whistled and called to her as she passed. She plugged it back in, reset it, and inserted some coins. She selected a few songs, walked into the middle of the floor, stood in front of the chanting sailors, and waited. A thin smile crept across her face. She seemed to relish the attention. A light above her switched on, highlighting her features. Her black hair swirled past her pretty but hard-edged face and flowed over her high breasts and her soft curved waist, finally stopping just above her knees. A butterfly tattoo on her belly fluttered as her flesh rippled.

The music kicked in, a slow, deep beat. Her body responded, moving, blending passionately to the rhythm. She swung her hips and arms smoothly as she danced and taunted the sailors who howled like dogs before her.

Maria again put her arms around Daniels. "Sailor man, you handsome." Her fingers ran up and down his stomach and chest. "No short time. Buy me drink. All night, I with you."

Daniels pulled back. "I said no. There's something I, I need to do."

"What?"

"Business." Daniels looked at his watch and then around the room.

186

His eyes settled on a large sailor at the far end of the crowd. *Rogers.* Daniels made his way to the middle of the crowd and waited.

The stripper slipped off her top, exposing perfectly rounded nipples on large brown breasts. Necks craned, eyes bulged, and grunts and catcalls echoed throughout the room. Amid loud screams of "Take it off," she undid the G-string of her bikini and slipped the garment off, exposing her body and driving the sailors into a frenzied state. She grabbed a bottle of beer from a sailor and placed it on the dirty floor, and motioned to the crowd to throw her coin pesos. The stripper bent down, teasing the men as she picked up the coins and stacked them on top of the bottle, each with a distinctive "clink." When she finished and had a stack five inches high, she slowly danced around the bottle. She then stepped over it, both legs forming a fleshy arch immediately above the coins. Slowly, she gyrated downwards in synchrony to the pulsing beat of the jukebox, taking the whole stack deep inside her.

The room howled. She spun around and shook her hips violently; the coins showered down, glittering to the floor, a river of metal. The crowd panted and swelled, excitement and daring promiscuity floating over their sweaty faces. They taunted and cheered and threw her more pesos, begging for more. Warrant Officer Hempel, Commander Nelson, and their wives laughed, swayed, and joined in the chanting.

Daniels eyed the wives' reaction in disbelief. He turned to Maria. She was smiling in amazement. She quickly slid in behind him again, wrapping her arms tightly around him. He shook his head. Her hand slid down to his zipper. He grabbed it and held it. Soft kisses pressed into his back, then her teeth.

He pushed her hand away, and he suddenly felt angry. He wanted to leave but couldn't. He slid out and away from Maria.

"I need a volunteer," the stripper yelled forth as she twirled around the room.

The crowd surged. Someone struggled. Rogers, Stoker, and Sanchez had Mitchel by the arms. They forced him down to the ground. As they held him, the stripper pulled his pants and underwear down to his ankles. Mitchel stopped struggling; his head bobbed about from intoxication and disbelief. The men let go, and the crowd cheered as the woman started dancing around the exposed body of Mitchel. He lay staring up at the circling fan above him. The dancer stopped and bent down, arousing Mitchel with her mouth and fingers. Satisfied, she picked up a peso bill from the floor, tore a slit through the end of it, and stuck it on Mitchel's erect penis. The crowd went wild. She slowly descended on top of him and forced him into her. The bill disappeared. The crowd exploded. The officer's wives pumped their beers in the air in amazement. Daniels looked into the eyes of Mitchel. Mitchel looked down at his exposed body, then away, not sure how to react to everyone staring at him.

Daniels was furious. *The humiliation!* Rogers stood hunched, laughing at the sprawled figure below him, his eyes slits, nose pointed, hooked like his chin. Daniels balled his fists. An image of Rogers holding him down, razor in hand, flashed out frame by frame in his head. *Bastard. You fucking bastard. I'll kill you. You'll pay for Roberts . . . for Mitchel.* His thinking stopped, collapsed in on itself. Only blind hate remained, steaming, clawing, rising with each beat of the music of his own heart.

He tore through the crowd, an image of Rogers burning through his head. The walls seemed to bleed in towards him, threatening to crush and consume him. Rogers leaned against the jukebox, smiling down at the exposed body of Mitchel. The rotating cross of the fan above him blew down a hot wind from its blades.

Daniels slammed into him. Knuckles cracked into skin and bone. Rogers flew into the jukebox. Glass broke, the metal gave, and the music stopped. Rogers' body twisted completely around, rebounded off the shattered machine, and spun to the floor. All eyes turned.

Daniels leaped on him, swinging, kicking, screaming—"You fucking bastard! Paralyzed . . . over a job! Over a fucking job!"

He kept swinging.

Sailors and women screamed and shouted, running into each other, some approaching, some abandoning the fray. Rogers and Daniels flopped and rolled onto the floor. Someone yanked Daniels' collar, pulling him up from Rogers, but he suddenly jerked to a halt as Rogers held a handful of Daniels' hair. The pain was intense. He thought he was being scalped. He kicked. Hard. His shoe blasted into Rogers' groin. The pressure and pain in his head ceased.

Rogers fell screaming to the floor. Daniels struggled to free himself from the many hands holding him. He screamed and kicked, trying to get at the man he hated more than anything in the world. Rogers rose and disappeared, swallowed momentarily by the crowd.

He didn't see the bottle coming. Too quick, unexpected. He didn't hear it shatter. The broken piece slashed across Daniels' forehead, splitting it open. Blood ran down, filling his eyes, almost blinding him. The bodies before him blurred, but he saw the glint of glass as it swung back, then rushed in, targeting his throat. Daniels looked in disbelief as the shard approached his throat. He tried to move but couldn't—he was still being held from behind. He jerked his head back in a desperate attempt to ward off an almost certain death but realized in horror it wouldn't be enough. The glass raced in. But suddenly, a huge hand reached in and intercepted it. It was Taylor.

Taylor quickly threw Rogers to the floor, his huge arms pummeling the screaming body beneath him. Blood pulsed down from Daniels' forehead, blinding him. The yelling continued, and the Chief's voice could be heard thundering in the distance. Henderson howled immediately behind him. Hands loosened. Someone quipped, "lucky to be passing," and yanked him hard, dragged him into and past moving bodies through a doorway, and stopped on what appeared to be the cool open street. Arms circled his body, lifted him off the ground, and then threw him onto a metal surface. He lay in pain, his head and hand throbbing, a warm thick wetness seeping over his chest and sleeves.

A few minutes passed. The door opened again, and a large body landed next to him. He recognized the grunt. *Taylor*. The door slammed, the metal vibrated as an engine started, and he felt the pull of acceleration.

Taylor moaned. Daniels grimaced as Taylor rolled and sat up. "You look fucked up," said Taylor. "You okay?"

Daniels tried to wipe his eyes, but it did no good. Blood filled them again. Taylor ripped off his T-shirt and wiped the blood from Daniels' face. He then tied the shirt around Daniels' head to stop the bleeding.

"God, my head," Daniels said.

"Just be cool. They'll fix you up."

"We headed to . . . to medical?" Pain radiated out from the wound.

"I don't think so."

"Shit." Daniels shook his head and closed his eyes. *Military Police*. The truck rumbled on.

At the main gate, they were yanked out and marched over to shore patrol. They were ordered to stand in line and wait with the other drunk and bruised detainees, a typical night's roundup.

Taylor assisted Daniels as they approached the line.

"Hey, this man needs medical attention," Taylor said to a large petty officer second class. He pointed to Daniels' forehead.

"Keep your mouth shut and keep walking."

"I don't think you understand. He's hurt pretty bad."

"I said keep your fucking mouth shut." The sailor pulled out his nightstick and swung it low, hitting Taylor in the thigh. Taylor cried out as his body buckled in pain.

"You fucking idiot, what'd you do that for?" said Daniels. Though he couldn't see him very well, Daniels swung and surprised himself when his fist impacted the shore patrol's chest.

The second class stepped back, shocked, then screamed, "That's it! I've had enough of this shit all evening." He stepped forward, the club raised, "Your fucking bloody head is going to be the only decent part left when I get through with you." He swung at Daniels, but before his club hit, he was down, Taylor smothering him. Daniels dove to pull him off but was torn up and away, billy clubs hammering down on his own arms and legs from the other shore patrol who suddenly materialized. He screamed as the blows rained down.

Taylor went mad. He tore at them, his huge arms tossing men around. A large group of Military Police joined in and, combining forces, proceeded to slowly pound him into submission. A particularly large policeman kicked Taylor in the head as he crouched on one knee. Taylor stopped moving. Handcuffs were placed on his still body. They picked up Daniels, handcuffed him, and then sat him down next to Taylor on the side of the street. A short while later, shore patrol came over and bandaged his forehead, then left without saying a word.

"Taylor?" Daniels gasped, his head throbbing. Taylor didn't respond. Daniels looked at Taylor's chest. It expanded slowly upwards. He was still breathing.

Daniels was nearly in tears from the pain. He could feel the blood oozing out from his forehead.

Taylor took in and expelled a huge blast of air. *Must be conscious.*

"Taylor, you all right? Taylor! Goddammit, Taylor, they can't do this to us. This isn't fair!"

Taylor took in another huge breath. And then another. His breathing soon slowed and quieted. They lay still. Daniels stared up into the moonless night. He couldn't make out a single star.

Taylor finally stirred. "Man," he said. It was almost a whisper.

"What the fuck are you talking about?"

"Man."

"Man, what?"

"Man . . . man. Is always the weakest link."

"What do you mean?"

" . . . in any system." His voice trailed away.

Blood crept down into Daniels' eyes from the swollen bandages, blinding him again. "This is Bullshit!" he said. "I've been assigned to shore patrol before; I know the rules, and they can't fucking do this to us. I'm going to write that son of a bitch up."

Footsteps approached. Stopped. Someone kicked him hard in his sore thigh, the exact spot where Rogers had walloped him the night before the crossing. He screamed as pain shot through his body. Someone kicked Taylor.

"I said keep your goddamned mouth shut."

"Fuck you!" screamed Daniels.

A boot slammed into him again, much harder. The same spot. A tsunami of pain surged through him, drowning all remnants of conscious thought. Hoarse shouts filled his ears, but they made no sense to him. Thoughts came, went, fragmented. He fought, trying to make sense of where he was and what had happened. A warm liquid seeped into his mouth. Pressure came to his chest, a twisting, and as he was yanked to his feet, he fought to remember.

A tall petty officer first class stood before him, bracing him up. Daniels shook, then tried to balance, pressing down, testing his legs. The pain grew sharper. He grimaced, his head clearing. He eyed the first class, noticing his shore patrol insignia, his lips moving. He suddenly realized that the words floating far off around his head were somehow being directed toward him. He pulled them down, dreamlike, guiding them. Fragments became half-sentences, then became complete.

"Hey, hey, you okay? Wake up. Snap out of it."

Daniels nodded. His vision sharpened. He looked around. Taylor was standing a few feet away to his right, his hands handcuffed behind his back, his head down, his body leaning slightly forward, almost touching a sailor in front of him—one of ten in a long line waiting to march back to the ship.

"Talk, man. You okay?" said the first class.

"Yeah, I think so," Daniels muttered. "Yeah, I'm okay."

"Good." The first class straightened up and put his hands on his hip. "Now get the fuck over to that line and keep your goddamn mouth shut."

Daniels nodded, then attempted to wipe the blood from his mouth. But he realized both hands were still secured behind his back. He swore, suddenly remembering and feeling the mass of sticky bandage strapped across his forehead.

"Did you fucking hear me? I said move!" The first class grabbed his shoulder and pushed him toward the line. Daniels, his feet still unsure, staggered into Taylor, who bumped the sailor in front. The sailor in front of Taylor swung around, cussing, but froze upon seeing the size of Taylor. He apologized and turned back around. Taylor slumped down again and closed his eyes.

"All right, ladies, single file, groin to ass, mouths shut, march!" The first class pointed into the darkness toward the ship. He stepped forward, one hand on his billy club. The men grumbled, then moved.

They shuffled through the winding streets of the base, feet clomping against tar, past dark and silent buildings, echoes winging down alleys and up into a moonless night. Each step was agony for Daniels, but he grit his teeth and hobbled the best he could.

They finally reached the pier. Up the gangway they marched, the smell of jet fuel and oil permeating the air, the faint lap of water against piling slipping up and past. Not stopping at the afterbrow, they kept moving, heading down a ladder, then another, down into the bowels of the ship, finally stopping at the brig.

Two Marines, with boots polished to a spit shine and billy clubs in hand, dismissed the first class. Then the taller Marine of the two, his eyes gleaming, stepped forward. "You're mine," he whispered, continuing down past the men, his billy club softly falling on his outstretched palm. "All mine."

[Taped into journal]

31 Oct. 77

Halloween.
Am in ship's brig/cell. They gave me some paper, but not much. Not sure how much more of this I can take. Just want to smash these assholes. The screaming, yelling, humiliation, physical training, and beatings are too much. I tried to control myself today. Three Marines ordered me to keep doing jumping jacks on the flight deck. Laughing at me. Not giving me any water, rest. I couldn't stop, wouldn't stop. Kept going, finally dropping from exhaustion. They ordered me to my feet, but my body wouldn't respond. They called me a weakling. A pussy. I tried to ignore them, to stand, but I couldn't. One kicked me in the side. I tried to hit him. They piled on top of me and pummeled me. I passed out.

I fear them.

I fear myself.

The Brig

"Mother, why are they beating me?"

"Because it is good."

"Because it is good?"

"Yes, because it is good."

"Does that mean that they like me?"

"Yes, that means that they like you."

"Love me?"

"Yes."

"Why?"

"They are teaching you."

"Teaching me?"

"Yes, teaching you."

"Teaching me what, mother?"

"Administration, son."

"Is that all, mother."

"No, son."

"What else?"

"Obedience."

"But I don't like obedience."

"You will learn to like it."

"Then will I learn executive ability, mother?"

"If you want to, son."

"And do I want to?"

"Yes, you want to."

"Is pain good, mother?"

"Yes, it is good, son."

"Why, mother?"

"Because without it, you shall hold within your heart no appreciation for what is painless."

"Can I rest now, mother?"

"Yes, you can rest now, son."

"But, the time, mother."

"At two fifteen sharp, son, they will administer three blows to your back, one blow to your neck, and one to your groin. Do you hear me, son?"

"I hear you, mother."

"Look at me when I am talking to you."

"Yes, mother."

"As I was saying, at two fifteen sharp, they will administer three blows to your back, one blow to your neck, and one to your groin. Do you hear me, son?"

"I said yes, mother."

"Look at me when I am talking to you."

"Mother?"

"Now, as I was saying, at two fifteen sharp" . . . Daniels! *"They will administer three"* . . . Daniels! . . . *"blows to your back, one blow to your neck"* . . . Get your fucking ass up! *"And one to your groin"* . . . Daniels!

"Mother?"

Daniels!

"Mother!"

Clank! Clank! Clank!

Daniels jerked and opened his eyes. The sound of wood hitting the iron bars sent a sharp tremor reverberating through his body.

"I said get your stupid ass up, squid." A Marine stood on tip-toe, his baton beating the bars of his cell back and forth, back and forth. Daniels jumped down, the image of his mother wisping into fragments, then nothing. He stood dumbly, staring at the large figure swinging against the bars, trying to piece back together the dream. But he couldn't. He only knew, only felt, that it was somehow significant and had left him with an awkward feeling of uncertainty and terror. The Marine stopped.

"You got exactly three minutes to towel up and stand sharp. Hear me, squid?"

Daniels nodded and quickly made for his towel hanging on a hook in the small four-man compartment. He was alone. The other three racks hung empty from the bulkhead, the sheets and blanket perfectly folded and tucked. He stripped bare and wrapped the towel around his waist. A chill wormed up his spine. He grabbed a bar of soap and stood next to the door, and waited, his head down, his thumb sliding up and down the greasy bar in his hand. He didn't wait long. He heard an all too familiar voice screaming into the cells along the corridor, the clink of metal as the doors were flung open, the scurry of bare feet upon the deck. The Marine approached his cell. Lance Corporal Butler unlocked the door.

"Morning, precious." His voice was soft and low. He was tall but thin, and his jaw came to a point, as did the corners of his ears, which were tattooed in a large spiderweb. One hand fingered a billy club at his waist. He smiled, as he always did before screaming.

"Get your ass in line now, now, now!"

Daniels kept his head down to his chest and his eyes down at the deck. He made sure his hands were kept tight to his thighs, his back arched down just a bit, and his steps small but quick.

The first morning he had failed to move quickly enough, and he paid the price. Events snowballed. He was grabbed and thrown into the hallway, his towel flying off. He then made the mistake of swearing and talking back to the Marine. The Marine hit him in his sore thigh with a billy club. His leg buckled in pain, and he collapsed to the deck. As he held his leg, naked, sprawling, two other Marines stood over him, taunting him, calling him an "exhibitionist," a "faggot," and screaming for him to "resume the position." He finally managed to climb back to his feet, wrap the towel back around him, put his hands to his side, and place his head down. They then screamed to move, and he quickly shuffled down the hall, joining the others.

Now, five days later, his leg still throbbing, he scurried down the dim corridor and joined a small line of towel-clad sailors. All stood rigid, heads down, each butted up close to the other. Daniels inched behind the last in line and could make out the strong scent of body odor creeping up from the man inches away. He knew he must smell just as bad, or at least his hair. Because of the short time allowed to shower and the fact that he couldn't get the stitches and bandage on his forehead wet, he couldn't maneuver delicately enough within the few seconds allotted to wash his scalp.

Another three sailors filed in behind him, then another four, and then another four, followed by the Marine.

"Okay, squids, move!"

They shuffled down to the end of the corridor, knees and thighs clipping into one another. A cold breeze blew past them. They stopped at the head, the bathroom. The Marine pulled from his pocket a stopwatch and stood by the door.

"First eight, sound off and move!"

One by one, each sailor hollered a number and zipped it into the small compartment. Daniels yelled "six" and ran in. He quickly found an empty shower stall, placed his soap in a small dish, stood at attention, head down, and waited. The Marine then screamed, "Undo towels!"

Daniels unraveled his and hung it. He shivered. "Water, on!"

Knowing that a slight delay or hesitation would cost him and fully aware of how long it takes for the hot water to flow, he tensed and flipped both knobs at the same time. A cold stream slapped into his chest, sending a huge shiver through his body. His muscles tensed, and he found it hard to move. He turned, feeling the skin numb across his back. He straightened up, letting the water hit his neck, then the bottom of his skull, then the back of his head, mindful of keeping his forehead dry. His whole body seemed numb.

"Water, off!"

He flipped both knobs, then immediately grabbed the soap and lathered up his body. He worked fast, feeling a slight heat generated as his limbs coiled and uncoiled. He rubbed the soap across the stub of hair on the back and top of his scalp, kneading up a thin paste.

"Water, on!"

He swore softly, threw the soap down, then braced, then flipped the water back on. Another wave of cold water slapped him. He spun around, carefully rinsing off, the cold water needling down his chest, arms, and legs. He cupped the water and quickly ran it over his scalp, doing this a few times till most of the soap was removed. He then let some of the stream hit his chin, and stepping back, he wiped his face. As the water streamed down his legs, he sensed a slight increase in its temperature, then a greater one. The hot water was just now starting to flow.

"Water, off! Out, out, out! Now, towel!"

Daniels swore again, picked up his towel, and stepped out of the stall. He grabbed his towel and vigorously rubbed his body and scalp till most of the moisture was gone. He padded the bandage on his forehead, absorbing the few stray drops. The muscles in his neck tensed from the cold, and his limbs trembled.

"Okay, squids, exit! Now!"

Daniels hastily wrapped the towel around his waist, put his head down, and ran out. But as his foot lifted over the baseboard to the door, the towel fell from his body. He quickly bent down to retrieve it.

"Don't move!"

Shit. Daniels stood back up at attention. The breeze from the corridor swept into him, making his body shudder.

The Marine walked up to him and circled. "What's your problem, Precious? Can't seem to keep your towel on?"

Daniels kept silent, his head down, knowing full well that to answer would only bring trouble.

The Marine smiled. "Are you a faggot, squid? Did you drop that towel on purpose to show us your lame-ass pecker? Huh, did you? Did you!" The Marine stared down at Daniels' exposed body, then laughed.

Daniels could feel the lowered stares of the others on him as well. He tensed, humiliated, feeling the anger rise.

199

"I said, are you a fucking faggot squid? Are you a fucking faggot?"

"No, sir," whispered Daniels.

"What did you say, squid? Huh! Huh!"

"I said no, sir!" yelled Daniels.

The Marine put the tip of his billy club lightly into Daniel's chest, leaned in, and whispered, "Don't you ever raise your voice to me again, faggot. Or I swear to heaven I'll fuck you up. You hear me?"

Daniels nodded, trying to control the urge to lash out.

The Marine pushed the billy club into Daniels hard. "I said did you hear me?"

"Yes, sir," whispered Daniels.

"Good." His voice softened. "Now put that towel back on." He smiled, his eyes remaining tight. "And cover that poor excuse you call manhood and get the fuck back in line."

Daniels closed his eyes in anger. The Marine exploded. "I said now! You hear me faggot. Now! Now! Now!"

It took everything he could to keep from lashing out. He leaned over and picked up the towel. No longer shivering, his head down, he wrapped himself and ran to the back of the line. From the corner of his eye, he could make out Taylor's huge body pressed in between two smaller sailors.

"Next group! Sound off and move! And there better not be another faggot among you!"

The remaining sailors scuffled in and showered as the Marine called out the commands. Daniels stared down at the drops of water clinging to his toes. He started shivering again.

After all the sailors had showered, he was marched back to his cell, and he dressed. He then lined up again for breakfast. Head down; hands balled to his side, he marched with the others up the ladder and into the main corridor of the ship.

"Sowwwwnd aaaaaaawff!" bellowed Lance Corporal Butler, marching in front.

"Gaaaaang waaaaaay!" they all yelled.

The sound echoed throughout the corridors of the ship. Anyone in the vicinity cleared out of the way.

"Sowwwwnd aaaaaawff!"

"Gaaaang waaaay!"

Daniels shut his eyes each time he yelled, humiliated, still shocked, still not quite believing that he was actually saying the very words he had always said he never would. With each step he took, with each yell that seemed to pitch higher and higher, his heart seemed to sink further and further into the belly of the ship. How much lower can I go, he thought. *How low is low? How much more of this can I take?*

He was told that he'd need to go to Captain's mast in the next day or two, and the Captain could easily add on more time and even take a stripe from him. *Shit, this could even affect the type of discharge I receive. My father!* And just as he thought this, just as he thought he had sunk as low as low could go, his body tensed as he suddenly heard his name being whispered from a side passageway. He shifted his eyes and made out the dim outline of Rogers and Stoker standing behind a large pipe. They ran their hands across the tops of their head, poking fun at his shaved skull. And though he couldn't see their faces, he knew they were smiling.

[Taped into Journal]

2 Nov. 77

It's dark. So tired. A struggle to keep my eyes open. It's morning. They'll be here any minute banging the bars. Couldn't sleep last night. I need to get out of here. Each second seems a day.

Mother, I miss you. So much. An anger festers within me each day here. How can they treat me and others like this? It's barbaric and sub-human! I know you'd counsel otherwise, and I know in my heart it's wrong, but I really want to smash them. Kill them.

How dare they.

How dare He!

Captain's Mast

Daniels stepped past his Marine guard and through the door and into the one place all sailors dreaded—Captain's Mast. It was the Navy's process of non-judicial punishment, according to Article 15 of the Uniformed Code of Military Justice. Different captains chose different rooms to hold mast in, such as the chapel, wardroom, hangar bay—or even the ship's bridge. But the Midway's Captain chose this small compartment just next to his quarters on the O-2 level. It had a large table that had a green cloth on it at the far end. Sitting at one end of the table was the Executive Officer, or XO, of the ship, Captain Mulligan. Just in front of the table stood the legal officer, a lieutenant. He wore his at-sea khakis and stood rigid at a small aluminum lectern, his arms at his side. Next to the table and standing silent along the starboard bulkhead was the Chief. Daniels shuffled over next to him. The Chief ignored him.

A side door to the Captain's quarters suddenly opened, and an armed Marine corporal entered, followed by the Captain. The Marine yelled, "Attention on deck!" The XO quickly stood, and everyone straightened up, chests out, Daniels included. The Captain sat down, as did the XO, and the Captain studied a clipboard in front of him for what seemed like an eternity. The Marine stepped back and stood at attention next to the door that they had just entered. The Captain finally looked up and said, "Petty Officer Second Class Daniels." Daniels jumped. "Come forward."

Daniels walked up to the front of the room, just in front of the legal officer, and faced the Captain. Captain Carmen was a tall, well-built man with a stern and steady gaze. His height and bearing exuded an immediate sense of authority and confidence. Daniels swallowed and started to sweat.

"Lieutenant Simmons," said the Captain. "Please read the charges."

"Petty Officer Daniels, you have been charged with assault. You struck a petty officer while on liberty in Olongapo, and then you struck a shore patrol petty officer. I see that you . . ."

"Thank you, Lieutenant Simmons," said the Captain, taking over. "That will be all." The Captain turned to Daniels. "How do you plead?"

"Guilty, sir."

"Do you have anything to say?" asked the Captain.

"Yes, sir. First, I had a few too many to—"

"Alcohol is no excuse, sailor," said the Captain, cutting Daniels off. "If I took a penny every time I heard that, I'd be retired by now." The Captain looked irritated, and the veins on his neck pulsed out.

Not good. Daniels leaned forward, and for some reason he couldn't explain, he suddenly blurted out, "Forgive me, sir. I know it's just one lucky penny at a time, but isn't taking money from sailors for personal gain *against* Naval regulations?" He smiled.

"Daniels!" yelled the Chief. "That's no way to speak to the Captain!"

The Captain leaned forward and looked deeply into Daniels' eyes, his face devoid of any humor. *Shit!* Daniels realized that he had made a major mistake. One that would cost him dearly. The XO sat up straight, his eyes wide, and it looked as if the Chief, with his fists clenched, was about to detonate.

But to his surprise, the Captain suddenly looked down, half-smiled, and fumbled with his pen and paper for a second or two. "Now, I've got to admit. That's balls." He turned and smiled at the XO, who, in turn, slumped down a bit and forced a smile in return. The Captain then continued, "In all the Captain's Masts I've presented over, you're the first to challenge me . . . in a positive way, mind you. I take money from sailors all the time, but the Navy gets to keep it. But you're right, Petty Officer Daniels. I'd never do it for personal gain, even if it *was* just for luck."

"Yes, sir!" Daniels relaxed a bit, as did the Chief.

"Now, continue, Petty Officer Daniels. You have my full

attention."

"Well, sir. At our Division Party, I saw that some sailors grabbed Mitchel . . ."

"Who's Mitchel?"

"Sorry, sir! Mitchel is a fellow member of our division."

"W-Division?"

"Yes, sir!"

The Captain glanced over at the Chief. "Continue."

"Well, sir. They pulled Mitchel to the ground, pulled off his clothes . . ."

"His clothes? All of them? Against his will?"

"Yes, sir."

The Captain looked back over to the Chief, who quickly looked down.

"Continue."

"Then a bar girl came over and . . . ahhh . . ."

"And what?"

"Well, sir, she got him hard and went down on him in front of everyone."

The Captain didn't seem fazed by this revelation at all. But he once again looked over at the Chief. "Continue."

"Well, sir. I looked down at Mitchel, and I could see the humiliation in his eyes. He looked so . . . so . . .helpless."

"And . . ."

"And so . . . so I lost it, sir. I hit out at the one man who caused it."

The Captain looked at his sheet. "I don't see a name here. Who was it?"

"Petty Officer Rogers," said the Chief.

"Chief, why isn't Petty Officer Rogers listed here?"

"Sorry, Captain. Rogers was just one of several sailors who grabbed Mitchel. And we really don't know who it was that cut Petty Officer Daniels after the fight started. It all happened too quickly, and then people just scattered after the police showed."

Bullshit!

The Captain turned back to Daniels. "Okay, I've heard enough. I understand you were only defending a fellow sailor, and I applaud that. I will not remove you from the PRP program, where you serve a vital role, particularly for the upcoming NTPI inspection, which *you will pass*. Isn't that right, Chief?"

"Yes, sir," said the Chief, straightening up. "Daniels is an integral part of the team. And *we will* pass that inspection with flying colors."

"That had better be an affirmative, Chief. If we fail and this ship is decertified from carrying nukes, that means I stand a good chance of not making admiral. And God forbid, if that ever happens, I'll make sure that you sink with me. Do I make myself understood?"

"Yes, sir!" said the Chief.

"Now, Petty Officer Daniels. In light of what the Chief has just assured me, you are a valuable asset to your division and to this ship, and thus to me. So I'm going to be lenient on you starting a fight and assaulting a fellow sailor. However, you did strike a shore patrol petty officer, and I can't dismiss that. That type of behavior is unacceptable. I find you guilty of assault, and I sentence you to two more days in corrective custody. Furthermore, you'll be docked one stripe. You are now a petty officer third class, and you *will* retain your PRP status in your division. I am also going to dock you half pay for two months, which is . . . what? I believe that's . . . let's see . . ." He looked down at his sheet. "You make about $625.50 per month. Yes, so that's over 62,000 pennies for Uncle Sam if my math is correct." He looked over to the XO.

"I believe that's correct, Captain."

The Captain turned back to Daniels. "Good. Let it be noted that this proceeding will also be a permanent part of your military record. Dismissed."

"Yes, sir!"

Shit. A stripe. And my record! And my father! And two more days in the brig! It was the latter that really shook him. Daniels didn't know

206

if he could take another minute of the brig, let alone two more days. His body suddenly felt like it weighed a ton, and he struggled to move his legs towards the door and the waiting Marine, who smiled at him like he was merely a cold bottle of San Miguel after 90 days at sea. *God help me!*

Daniels was quickly led back down to the brig, and it wasn't long before the Marines were back where they had left off—screaming at him and humiliating him. It didn't take long before they ordered him and several other men out of the brig and marched them over to a ship's passageway to clean some brass fittings.

Daniels stood in front of an already-shined brass wheel. He studied it. Its surface glimmered mirror-like, reflecting distorted pipes, cables, and hatches of the passageway. He checked his watch. Almost time for chow. He placed the cloth around the fitting, smothering it, and vigorously pressed and pulled back and forth, buffing it. He stopped and again studied his work. It looked the same. It sparkled. A dot in the brass moved and rapidly grew, elongating into human form and staining the surface of the fitting.

"Precious," Lance Corporal Butler said softly. Daniels tensed.

"Is that fitting shined? Well, is it!" The abrupt, high-pitched yell startled and shook him. Daniels turned his head. *Shit.* The Marine screamed again into his ear, louder.

"Did I tell you to look at me?! Did I, precious! Did I! What the fuck's wrong with you, sailor. You an idiot! You a moron! Put your fucking head back in position now! I said now!" With his billy stick, he pushed Daniels' shoulder hard. Daniels lowered his head, his chin almost touching his chest. He gritted his teeth and softly swore.

"Did you just say something, Precious? Don't fuck with me! Did you say something? Huh, huh, did you?! Did you?! Answer me, you fucking squid did you?!" Daniels' eardrums hurt as the Marine screamed into his ears. Daniels drew his arms in and lay them flat against his sides, his fingers butted tight together as he was trained to do when addressed in this manner.

207

"Did I tell you to move?! Did I tell you to put your hands on your legs?! Did I?! What the fuck's wrong with you, Precious?!"

"But, we're suppose—"

"Did I say you could talk?! Did I say you could talk, huh, did I?! You're a fucking moron! Now, get your ass down to the deck and assume the position! Now! Now! Now!"

Daniels didn't move. This was too much. Nothing he did was right. He closed his eyes. His heart pounded against his chest, which was expanding further and further out with each breath. He couldn't take it much longer. He felt degraded by the continual barrage of verbal abuse, of standing, sitting, lying for long hours frozen in one position as the Marine now wanted him to do. The only bright spot in all of this was that the Captain didn't kick him out of the division and the PRP program. If the Chief hadn't intervened and put in a good word for him, such as how valuable a team member he was for the upcoming inspection, it could have been much worse than two days.

Two more Days! This was going to be hard to take. The conflicting orders and chaotic actions upset Daniels the most. He had been scolded many times for not bringing his arms to his side while being reprimanded for something petty. And yet, though he brought his arms in just now, as he had been instructed to do, the Marine wouldn't stop punishing him. Catch-22, play the game, and this happens. He was miserable while the rest of the ship was now preparing to pull into Hong Kong.

"I said assume the position!"

Daniels still didn't move, and with that, the Marine didn't wait long this time. He slammed Daniels down hard to the deck. But instead of falling flat as he was supposed to, Daniels hit the deck and rolled, swinging his feet around. He swept the Marine's legs out from under him, bringing him down. Another Marine at the end of the hall, seeing this, screamed out the distress alarm. Daniels readied himself. Lance Corporal Butler climbed to his feet, his face twisted.

"So, Precious, you want to play now, do you." He smiled, then charged.

Daniels side-stepped him, slipping his right arm under the Marine's outstretched arm. Grabbing it, Daniels bent down and twisted the Marine's arm in a counter-clockwise circle, flowing with the Marine's forward motion, flipping him down to the deck. It was a technique he had learned in Beginning Jiu Jitsu in his junior year of high school. The Marine rolled into a bulkhead. *Wow, it actually worked!* Footsteps boomed behind him. Daniels turned. Three Marines pounded into him.

Daniels fell backward; the wind knocked out of him. His right arm hit the deck first. Falling, he watched in horror as his watch smashed into the deck and shattered, pieces of glass skimming across the tile surface. His eyes followed in slow motion what appeared to be the hour hand sliding across a sea of blue. It hit a combat boot and stopped. Daniels' head smashed into the deck. Then all went black.

4 Nov. 77

Released today. Daniels too. The Captain didn't let us off the hook at all. Like Daniels, I lost one stripe, was fined, and was kept in the damn brig for an extra two days. However, my PRP is still intact, as I'm needed for the upcoming NTPI inspection. Very lucky to be assigned to W-Division, which is charged with such an important inspection for the ship—and its Captain. I understand that not passing will cripple the ship and destroy the Captain's reputation. The Midway is the forward arm of the Navy, and for it to be stripped of the ability to carry nukes would be a disaster for everyone.

Except me.

I'm sore, bruised, angry. At what I've been subjected to. What I've now become. I looked for justice and found pain. I save a friend and have been myself condemned. They beat me again, and again, and yet again. I really wanted to kill them. All of them!

To my mind flows truth, mother. I feel I need to address the injustice somehow, to give vent to my feelings—to give breath to words.

I want to flush the filth away. And yet there's so much of it. Too much.

Maybe Daniels will help me.

I feel with the right enticement; he'll somehow commit. He just doesn't know it yet.

The Dialogue

"Push harder," said Daniels. "That's right, do it again; come on, give me one more, one more, good!"

Taylor put the bar down on the bench and grabbed a towel. Daniels pulled the weights off one end of the bar until just a few remained. Taylor removed the others. Daniels lay down on the bench and gripped the bar. Pain shot through his hand.

"Now, let's get your blood flowing," said Taylor. "Think about the Marines."

Daniels took in a huge breath and lifted. The weights clinked together as the bar ascended and came down. *Marines!* The beatings, pain, and humiliation. The nights in isolation after the passageway incident. The barred room in the pit of the ship—never seeing the waves, the sky, the sun.

"Aaarrrgggg."

"Now, think of the Marines again, and give me another."

An image surfaced of walking through the passageway, head lowered, shaven, yelling "Gangway," walking past fellow shipmates. Past the eyes of Rogers.

"Aaaaarrrrgghhh."

"Now think of Rogers."

Rogers. Now hook leader and senior, and Daniels now his junior. Even more infuriating, Rogers was not put on report for attacking him. The report never mentioned Rogers breaking the bottle. The ten stitches to Daniels' head were attributed to rolling on glass. Since no one really saw it nor wanted to report it, Rogers simply denied it, Stoker backed him up, and the Chief kept silent about it, as he knew he'd need Rogers to be hook leader after Daniels was sent to the brig. Daniels' outbreak during the "Dancing Number" embarrassed and upset both the Division Officer and his wife and the Department Head and his wife. So the riot and the alarms in the past month were nicely explained away to the Division Officer as having their origin and cause in one screwed up second class petty officer named Daniels—now a third class.

"Bullshit! Aaaarrrgh."

"Good, now one for the Chief." Daniel's brow's knotted.

"Aaaaarrrgghhh."

"Now think of the division."

Fools. Hypocrites. Rogers and Stoker recently got high marks in their evaluations, while he got poor ones for failure to lead properly. *High marks for what?* They were animals, inhuman. They, as all men, were blessed with the uncanny ability to transform a person into non-human operatives, garbage, badly needing to be burned and buried.

"Aaaarrrgghhh."

"Now, give me one for your "F" in Oceanography."

Damn them! Of all things, this one hurt the most—he failed his Oceanography class because he missed the final! And now, no recommendation for college from Professor Blair. He felt he really let the professor down. And his father.

"Aaaarrrgghhh."

"And that's not just an 'F' you got. That 'F,' like your Captain's Mast and military record, is now part of your *permanent . . . academic . . . record.* It will be a huge red flag in your Chapman University transcript that you'll need to explain away to any college that you want to attend. And trust me, I know . . . they won't miss a *thing* in my transcript—particularly my shitload of 'F's for dropping out. So we're both screwed. So give me another!"

"Aaaaarrrgghhh."

"Good, good. Now give me five more. You can do it. Think of how good it would feel to get revenge on the Marines, Rogers, the Chief, the division."

Daniels pulled the bar down, feeling its weight. *Just five more.* He gripped tightly, pain shooting through his right hand. *Yeah, it would feel good to see justice served. This division could use a cleaning, an enema of the soul.* He pushed up and let the weight drop hard to his chest. He tried again but couldn't lift. He strained, sweat dotting his face. It moved, then stopped. "Taylor!"

"You can do it. Push!"

Taylor helped him ease it up a little. "Push, dammit, push." The weight crept up, inch by inch. "Come on, almost there. You can do it." Taylor leaned over and whispered "Rogers," into Daniels' ear. Hearing this, Daniels suddenly felt fury and extended his arms. He did it! Taylor took the bar and placed it on the bench.

Daniels sat up. "Shit," he said, breathing fast. "It's amazing what a few dirty words can do."

Taylor handed him a towel. "And teamwork."

"God, I needed that. I'm so fucking angry!" said Daniels.

Taylor sat down on the deck. His forehead glistened. Sweat dripped onto his chest.

"If you could get a weapon off this ship," said Taylor, suddenly serious. "What would you do with it and why?"

"Why do you ask?"

"Just curious," said Taylor.

"I already told you a while ago what I'd do. Besides, I thought you were uncomfortable talking about it."

"People change."

"I don't know."

"Answer me."

Daniels was nervous. *Why is he asking now?* Yet a tinge of excitement flickered within him. "If I was able to get one off the ship, I would probably sell it for a million dollars." He grinned.

"What happened to 'demonstration'?" said Taylor, annoyed.

"Hey, it was just a joke. I wouldn't do something that stupid."

"And stealing a weapon isn't stupid?" said Taylor.

Daniels looked to the deck. No, he thought, he would never sell it for money; that would be the last thing in the world he would do. It would most certainly end up in the wrong hands.

"Don't you realize that that is exactly what is happening now in the

213

real world? It's called MAD, or mutually assured destruction."

"Yeah, I know all about MAD. So what."

"Even if the world had only two missiles left, they would both be pointed at cities—not military bases. Children are being held hostage to the superpowers." He wiped his face. "The innocent."

Daniels nodded.

"Nagasaki," said Taylor. "Did those children deserve to die? Did those innocent children deserve to feel that intense heat, radiation, and blast that scattered their bone fragments across the city?"

Daniels' nervousness increased. He wasn't sure where Taylor was going. *Or do I?*

Taylor continued. "A double standard. Truman could have destroyed a military base. And if that didn't work, then another and another. Children should have been the last targets on their list. Jesus, can you imagine children and women? *Mothers! Innocent mothers!*" Taylor's anger sent a shiver through Daniels.

"Taylor, I'm not in the mood."

"Well, you should be. This is important." Taylor stood up. "We work for mass murderers. Dealers in death."

Daniels leaned back. "Yeah, yeah. We both signed up for that." It was barely a whisper. He lowered his head.

"But did we know?" Taylor continued, his voice hot. "At the beginning of the war, when Hitler accidentally bombed London, the world was outraged. 'Barbarians' the world called them for killing defenseless civilians."

"Heard it."

Taylor continued. "England should never have retaliated, but they did; they bombed Berlin. The London blitz ensued, killing over 20,000 people! Non-combatants! Children and mothers!"

"What's this thing with mothers you seem to have? I'm sorry you lost yours. Truly, I am. But I asked you to tell me something about her, and you remain silent."

Taylor sat down and wiped a bead of sweat from his eyes. "Don't misunderstand me. What happened to my mother is not relevant. So don't go there. What I'm really talking about is the degradation of progress and morality. War does this."

"All wars do."

"But this was different. Our technology finally eclipsed the humanity of the heart. Did you know that at the end of the war, killing massive amounts of innocents was touted as the American way of winning?"

"Yeah, I know. Jesus, you sound just like my father." Daniels straightened up, eyeing the door.

Taylor continued calmer. "That same thinking was applied to our current strategic policy. They fuck with us, nuke the cities, make the millions of innocent people pay for the rashness of their leaders."

"But the people elected them!" said Daniels.

"Did they," said Taylor. "Easy to blame the people instead of the leaders, leaders who get elected through political action committees, rich interest groups, ten-second sound bites, false campaign promises, and blasting the opposition's character to make themselves look good. And who's to say that the people are educated and informed?"

Daniels suddenly thought of the carved letters running down the north side of the Boston Public Library: "The Commonwealth Requires the Education of the People as a Safeguard of Liberty and Order."

"Look," said Daniels. "I see your point. But it's more complicated than that. Who's to blame, the lion that lies or the lamb that lies down to listen? The listener is *supposed* to be able to see, as you said earlier, through the froth, to the core, the heart of every issue. Do his homework, weigh the evidence, and then make an educated choice."

"Dammit, Daniels, listen. Ease of physical and mental exertion seems to be the norm today, causing a fundamental breakdown on both sides. The speaker and listener both become deaf and blind, both feeding a starving ignorance and apathy that has taken root in the selfish self." Taylor sat down. "The public wants quick and simple answers to difficult and complex problems."

"So, what's your point?"

"If a crisis develops and an ill-informed, irrational leader makes a bad call, that decision could multiply. Forces beyond the people's control, beyond the leader's control, could then unleash a nuclear catastrophe. Events themselves could become a powerful force in their own right."

Daniels fingered his towel.

"So again," said Taylor, his voice now calm, "what would you do with a weapon if you got the chance to take it off the ship? Tell me exactly."

Daniels thought about it for a few seconds.

"I would probably take it somewhere and ditch it, notify the press as to what I did and where the bomb was." He grinned. "I mean, could you imagine the press showing up, cameras blazing, a nuclear weapon unguarded, just sitting naked in the sun for all the world to see? It would embarrass the hell out of the military. And it should. Could you imagine us telling the world about our division?"

Taylor nodded.

Daniels continued, "every news station in the world would prick us with microphones till we looked like a fucking porcupine. And we'd tell 'em about the idiots who work on their precious nukes." *Tell 'em about the drug use, the craziness, the dresses, and the shaving of pubic hair into hearts, into mushrooms.* His brows fused. *Fucking asshole.*

"Is that all?" asked Taylor.

"It would also send a message to the world to stop the nuclear madness—that proliferation and terrorism is a reality with fatal consequence."

"Is that all?" Taylor asked again.

"What?"

"I said, is that all?"

"What else do you want me to say?"

"Well, what about some recognition? Accomplishment. Being

216

looked up to. Can you imagine the world looking up to you? Your father."

"What the hell do you mean by that."

"Nothing. Just think about it."

"I'd rather not." Daniels fidgeted and looked up to the overhead, then to the deck. "What about you?"

"What about me?" asked Taylor.

"Why would you do it?"

"Why? Why is it so important to kill millions instead of feed millions? If we rid the world of weapons and their parasites, then the money could go to the cities, to the poor, to the innocent children and mothers! Let 'em fucking arrest us, me—"

Jesus. He's just crossed the line. Daniels felt his stomach turn.

Taylor continued.

"—Let's show the world's cupboard to be what it is—shamefully bare."

"'Me'?, 'Let's'?! Now I'm in on it too?"

"Hypothetically. Remember, it's just a game."

"Okay, hypothetically, then. Could you imagine what would happen to someone, anyone, us, if we're caught," said Daniels, acknowledging the indescribable. "And, of course, we'd be caught. That's an absolute given." His fingers tapped the bulkhead next to him. "They'd lock us up and throw away the key. If we thought a few days in the brig was bad, could you imagine spending the rest of your life in federal prison? That means goodbye college! Goodbye Yuki! Forever!" Daniels instinctively grabbed his wristwatch, but it wasn't there. "I mean, we're lucky as it is that they didn't kick us out of the fucking PRP!"

"They didn't because they need us for the upcoming inspection. They'd be two men short, and they can't afford that right now."

"Neither can we!"

"Daniels. You should really think about taking the game to its natural conclusion. It would be a small price to pay for the many."

"The many!" Daniels leaped to his feet. "Do you really think that stealing a weapon would make a significant change in anything other than our own miserable lives? I mean, let's cut the bullshit." Daniels paced the deck. "This conversation is not hypothetical anymore. We're actually talking about doing it! I mean, come on, we're talking in covert terms here. It's us, us, me, and you stealing a bomb because of the events in our own miserable lives, not some abstract twist fuck." He sat down on the bench.

"Yes," said Taylor softly, "But it all depends on where and how you do it."

"What do you mean?"

"If you do it in the States or at sea, it probably won't amount to much. The military will most likely cover the incident up and pass us off as a couple of psychopaths. Even if we got to the press, the impact would be marginal. News one day, gone the next."

"Probably," said Daniels. "The government would downplay the incident in its investigation, show a solution, say it's to be fixed immediately, and then forget about it."

"So that's not the way to do it."

"Then what is," said Daniels. "No, no, forget I said that. I don't want to hear it. The apple is before us, Taylor."

"The way to do it is by stealing a weapon in a place *so* sensitive, *so* outrageous, it will cause an enormous upheaval of emotion and pain. Enough so that even if the military tries to cover it up, it couldn't—the public outcry would be so great. Then and only then would governments and institutions react. And change."

Daniels wiped his brow. Sweat seemed to flow from every pore in his body.

"You know the place I am talking about," said Taylor.

"No, dammit! I don't want to know." He covered his face with his hands. But he couldn't help himself. The answer surfaced. "Japan."

"Bingo."

"Jesus!" said Daniels. He suddenly thought of Yuki and how she would be so disappointed to know what they were talking about right now. *And her mother!*

"I see you have taken this game to its logical conclusion."

"It's not a game anymore!"

"Oh, yes, it is." Taylor's voice softened, barely audible. "The stakes are just more serious."

Both sat down and remained quiet for some time. Finally, Daniels spoke. "I really haven't taken it to its logical conclusion." He lied. He had entertained the notion of what he would have done and where he would have done it once he smuggled the weapons off the ship. But in another country, not Japan. *Her mother would never forgive me.*

"Japan," said Taylor. "What better place to make a statement, an impact on the world, than in a country that had two of its cities full of innocents vaporized."

Daniels nodded. He thought of Yuki's warm smile and how much he missed her.

"We pull into Japan, Yokosuka, four days from now," said Taylor. "They are always protesting. Their country strictly forbids the entry of such weapons onto its soil."

"Okay, say you steal one, and it does send the country and the world into a panic that still leaves us sitting in jail—probably for life. Any dream we've ever had of getting out of here and going back to school and getting married is fucked!"

"Maybe, maybe not. We could be viewed as heroes, particularly in Japan, for we exposed the great lie and cared enough to do something about it in a world gone nuclear mad."

"The great lie?" said Daniels. "What about their lies! Their unwillingness to come to terms with their own history—the rape of Nanking, the death marches, and Korean sex slaves—"

"Hey, and what country has? Ours included? Remember your discussion of the Native Americans."

"Okay, okay." Daniels lowered his head. "But we could also be viewed as traitors."

"To some yes, to some no. They would view it as a great accomplishment, a noble attempt to rectify the wrongs of a world run astray."

Daniels again reached for his watch, but again his hand touched exposed skin. This startled him. He rubbed his fingers along his wrist.

"I don't know," said Daniels. "I really don't know how my family would react, particularly Yuki. And her mother. She hates Americans, and if I can't change her mind, she'll never let me marry her daughter."

"First, how could your father not applaud and respect your honest convictions? He would really feel proud of you, of what you accomplished. And second, Yuki and her mother are Japanese! Come on; they would applaud that you took a chance to expose the illegality of nuclear weapons in Japan. Japan, Daniels! A place where nukes are strictly forbidden! Where they had once caused so much pain and suffering. And still do. You'd be a hero here. Particularly to Yuki's mother!"

Taylor's words hit him. He leaned back.

"I don't know. Maybe Yuki, possibly her mother. And that's pushing it. But my father's never respected my own actions before or taken an interest in anything I've ever wanted to do outside of academics."

"Yes, because you never listened to what he wanted you to do, whether that was right or wrong. You were just as hard-headed as he was. Always doing your own thing once you left the glare of his eye. You told me so yourself. And felt proud of it!"

Daniels leaned back. Taylor continued. "Didn't you tell me that he told you to come home with at least an honorable discharge? Well, this is more than that. You are not only listening to him for once, but you will make him proud. And famous. Your name and picture would be flashed to every country in the world, in every newspaper, and on every TV in every home, including his. The great hero, the great leader. If viewed in the light of a humanitarian act for the world, how can he possibly ignore it, ignore his son."

"I don't know." Daniels looked nervously around the cramped room. "I mean, this could get us killed. It could backfire, and we could be the scorn of the entire world, and then what would we have? Nothing! Do you hear me? I want to get the fuck out of here, marry Yuki, and go to college. What part of that do you not understand?"

"Daniels, listen to me. I hear you. Look, considering the anti-nuclear sentiment in Japan and the rest of the world, this is a chance of a lifetime. A chance for you and me to do something about the injustices of the world. Not many people are given that kind of chance in life."

"And a chance to spend the rest of their life looking out windows with bars. Never to gaze at a forest or stream, to hear a sparrow, a university lecture, or feel the warm kiss of the woman you love!"

Taylor slapped the deck. "A lot of children won't either! In Cairo, for Christ's sake, they live in cemeteries, in tombs, with no electricity or water or sewers."

"I don't know. I mean, I am already being considered for suspension from the division. And it would have been if Saxton hadn't gone to bat for me. And that is trivial compared to this. Have you really grasped just what the fuck we are talking about here—what you are really trying to tell me! We are talking about *stealing a nuclear weapon off a ship*! Jesus!"

"For humanitarian reasons. Good reasons."

Daniels got up and paced around the room. "I don't know, Taylor, it sounds too risky and dangerous, even if good does come from it. Besides, we have only talked about others on the outside trying to get in, not two crazy people on the inside getting one out."

Daniels lay down on the bench and did five quick reps. *My god, he's really thinking about stealing one. Is he crazy . . . am I?* He thought of Rogers, razor in hand, then the Chief cursing at him for being such a poor petty officer, and the Marines screaming at him like he was a dog. He put the bar down and sat up.

"I know how to get one off the ship," said Taylor.

Is this for real? Are we actually talking about it, going to do it? Yet, for all the anxiety, the game still excited him. He wanted to outwit, get back at, and outsmart the system. But it was more. It was the thought process itself. No matter what he did, however, he tried to keep it out of his head; his mind would always dredge the game up. In addition to the moral imperatives, it was the secrecy, the illegality, and the excitement of playing a game where a nuclear weapon was the prize that stimulated him. The game was challenging. The harder he tried to shove it out, the easier it was to pop back in. It was like trying to still the small waves of a pool by slapping them down. It was hopeless. However, he now faced "action"—quite a different entity altogether.

"Did you hear me," said Taylor. "I know how to get one off."

Daniels lifted his head. "I heard you. I'm not sure I really want to know."

"I think you do. And if you say you don't, you're lying. Eventually, that head of yours will arrive at the same place mine is. You can't help it; you'll be intrigued and figure it out."

"Don't fucking tell me what I think!" said Daniels. He eyed the door again.

"Another thing. If we do it and it goes well, a full investigation into the division and Marines will take place. With your input, goodbye division, which means Rogers, Stoker, the Marine Corps, and all of the illegal, highly insane bullshit in this place. At least think about making the military safer and drug-free."

"Are you fucking nuts? Help stop nuclear proliferation and the illegal activities of fellow sailors by stealing a nuclear weapon and breaking every law in the book. I do say it sounds appealing."

"It's not funny!" Taylor stood up.

Daniels tensed. Taylor loomed before him, angry.

"Sorry," said Daniels.

Taylor wiped his forehead. "Look, this isn't easy for me either. It's just that I feel the need to do it. I think it's right. Morally right."

"Morally, right? There must be something else." Daniels leaned forward. "Why are you so obsessed?"

Taylor pressed himself against the wall with his face towards the deck. "I'm not obsessed. I just think that we could make some kind of a difference, that's all."

"I don't know," said Daniels. "You haven't really told me a fucking thing about *your* reasons."

"Promise me you'll give it some thought. I think we have a chance of righting a lot of wrongs both in the world and in this division. The Navy doesn't need people like Rogers."

Rogers. Every time Daniels thought of him, his blood raced. Yes, it would certainly be better off without people like him. "I don't know, Taylor; it's just too nutty. Let me think about it."

Daniels attempted to rise, but Taylor stepped in front of him.

"Do you believe in God?" The question surprised Daniels. He slipped back down.

"Taylor, I'm warning you, don't even start. I said I'll think about it, and I'm fucking leaving."

"Do you believe the 'in God we trust' on American Currency?"

"Taylor. Don't."

"Did you know that the 'God' from 'in God we trust' was not the God from the Bible?"

"No, dammit!"

"It's true; our founding fathers were Deists. Do you know what Deists are?"

"Yes!" Daniels moved to get up. "I've had it."

"Stop!" The command was loud, cutting. Daniels froze. Taylor hung over him, knotted. For the first time, Taylor scared him.

Taylor seemed to sense Daniel's fear. He backed off. "Daniels." His voice calmed. "Hear me out. You said you wanted to know what was driving me. Well, I'll tell you. Just give me a few minutes. This is important to me. Please."

"Three minutes, tops. And I mean it."

"Good." Taylor leaned on the weights. "Deists believed that the mind of man was open, intimate, with the mind of God—by way of reason." He paced around the room. "Thus the universe and God was open to man, to Democracies. Especially the ability to reason without the help of divine intervention and religious institutions. That premise drove the founding fathers of this country," he paused. "Very smart men."

"Look, I think we're out in left field," said Daniels, "and I really don't see how this has anything to do with stealing a weapon."

"Again, hear me out. Reason gave us the light bulb and put us on the moon. Or, to put it another way, reason drives the theories and experiments that carve out the mask of truth."

"Who says which face finally represents truth."

"Bernini's Apollo and Daphne," said Taylor, "will always be marble, no matter how perfect and finely carved the skin and leaves are. It is only a model—not real, not absolute."

"So."

"So truth, as an absolute, might never be known, but the process of getting there, do you hear me, of getting there, remains alive, free flowing, through the endless currents of argument, reason, and discovery."

"Emphasis on argument."

"And that is why I am a deist, a 'Modern Deist,' who feels that reason can carve out the future. My future, the world's. Yours'."

Daniels didn't respond. He shut his eyes. *Shadow. Shotgun night. Blast into form with fire and light. Sit still. It moves. Sun cycles round. Stronger the rays. Stronger the edges found. But to touch. Oh, to touch. Vanishes. As truth.* He opened his eyes. Taylor shimmered above him.

"I don't know, Taylor. It's all so relative."

"Yes. But there is absolute truth in action," said Taylor. "And *leadership. Academic* leadership."

224

Daniels eyed Taylor.

"Yes, that's right. You can correct that 'F' and fix your fucked up and permanent academic record. Just think of it! As a hero, a world hero, all those universities would be clamoring to get you to attend. Free! With grants and scholarships. Just imagine you giving talks and attending conferences on the nuclear arms race and world peace. Particularly here in Japan. They'd be begging you to go. Me too! Again, think of it. How would that all feel? To you? To your father? To Yuki? To her mother?"

The latter words hit him. Hard. Daniels stood up and walked out the door, not looking back, leaving Taylor leaning against the bulkhead, his eyes studying the deck. Daniels swore. An image of his father hung in his head like an old portrait. And looking down just above his father was Yuki, her smile seeming to fade.

10 Nov. 77

Soldiers serve their country. Farms neglected. Men discharged from service. Drift to cities. Become dependents of "well-to-do." Look to politicians for security and entertainment. Small independent farmers disappear. New social class rises. War profiteers blossom— contracting with the army and dealing in booty. Buy up of ruined farms, restocking, using for other means. Small plots merge into huge tracts of pastureland, vineyards, olive groves. New capitalistic owners forget displaced farmers. Cheaper means sought to run farms. Hired hands fired. Gap between rich and poor increase. Senators, upper class, perverted. Honesty, simplicity, high-mindedness, gone. Riches pour in from overseas. Virtues erode through temptation. Austerity, discipline, give way to indulgence, corruption. Patriotism, respect for law and order, decline. Promotion, spoils, personal gain, privilege, compel. Leaders mock tradition, enlarge influence. Civil strife ensues. Legal procedures violated. Personal power prevails. Old political arrangements become obsolete. Armies rise, class warfare ensues. Thus the fall of the Roman republic 2000 years ago (recounted from A Brief History of Western Man by Thomas Greer.)

I fear the spinning spokes of time.

The Decision

With one hand, Daniels grabbed the ladder. The aluminum felt cool and damp against his fingers. He placed his other palm onto grooved bars set into the cascading metal, the metal that ferried the men up and down each level in the ship. He descended down the trunk to M-2. Stoker followed.

They quickly removed the locks and entered the warm magazine. Stoker walked around the corner before Daniels put the khaki lock on. *God, he can try my patience.*

Daniels scanned the magazine, taking in the maze of pipes, vents, cables, and weapons. He took a few steps to his right. Stoker stood a few feet away on a ladder, checking an air valve on the hoist used to move the weapons. "Goddamnit, Stoker," Daniels yelled, "there's a two-man rule. How many times do I have to tell you? You've got to respect at least that, or we're both gonna be shit-canned out of the program."

"Don't sweat the load," Stoker shouted back. "You're the one who stopped. And watch your mouth." He grinned. "At least respect the Lord's name."

"You knew I was behind you, and if I wasn't keeping up, you damn well know to stop and wait! It's both of our responsibilities."

"Well, where the hell were you?"

"Look, I'm in no mood to take any shit right now," said Daniels.

"Well, don't worry, Mr. PO, sir, I'll be on my best behavior."

Stoker turned a small valve on the bottom of a glass bulb protruding from the hoist. A trickle of dirty water appeared and flowed out into a bucket that he held up to it. It carried a sickly bitter smell. "You know, Daniels, you really do sweat the load too much, you know that."

"Stoker, cork it."

"Yeah, yeah."

The water sputtered and began to hiss as the air needed to drive the hoist sliced out into the compartment. The steam swirled about and covered Stoker's head in a light film of water and oil, giving the skin on his face a varnished plastic look as it glistened in the light.

Stoker screwed the valve shut and then wiped his face with a cloth he grabbed from his back pocket. His bloodshot eyes turned to Daniels.

"Daniels, why don't you make your ass useful and go read the temps."

"Listen, Stoker, don't fuck with me. You know that's your job. So get your ass down and do it. You hear me!"

Stoker shook his head and climbed off the ladder. "You know, Daniels, you can be such an asshole sometimes."

Daniels took in a heavy breath.

"I mean it, Mr. Peeon," said Stoker, "I mean PO third class, one . . . big . . . pain in the ass." He walked towards the temperature gauges on the far wall, his back straight, head high.

Daniels could almost see, *feel*, the grin now washed across Stoker's face.

"What the hell's your problem?" said Daniels.

Stoker stopped. "Not my fucking problem," he said. "Yours!"

"What the fuck are you talking about?"

"You! You're your own damn problem. You don't know what end's up or down."

"Watch it, Stoker."

"No, you watch it." Stoker stepped toward Daniels, one arm cocked at his side, the other pointing forward. "You're so lost. Don't you realize that you'll never get the respect you want? Never."

"Stoker, I'm warning you."

"Give it up," said Stoker. "Everyone looks to Rogers, not you. No matter how hard you try, you'll never be a leader, you hear me? You'll never get nothing from no one." He paused, "Maybe your mother if you're lucky." He turned and walked toward the back of the magazine. "But I don't think you're that lucky."

"Stoker!" it was more scream than command. "Get your ass over here."

Stoker kept walking. "Fuck you," he yelled. "You're only a fucked up third class now. Why don't you go shave your pubes into a heart again or open up one of your sissy school books to page zero? Yeah, that's right. Cause that's all you'll ever be. One big, fat, fucking, zero!" He laughed.

The plugs at Daniels' feet vibrated. The orange of the deck seemed to change before him into red. The plugs were now eyes, baleful and blinking.

Something snapped. Daniels bolted forward and shoved Stoker up against a stack of weapons. Stoker cursed and spun around. For a second, they both stood, eyes soldered together, pupil to pupil. Then Stoker stepped forward, grabbed Daniels by the shirt, and shoved him against a stack of two B61s. With a thud, Daniels' head bumped the shield on the top weapon.

Ignoring the pain, Daniels lunged into Stoker. He slapped his face, diverting Stoker's attention upward, and then grabbed his hand. Daniels then twisted Stoker's arm up and around in a downward arc, spinning Stoker's body into the weapon. Keeping his right hand secured to Stoker's bent arm, he grabbed a handful of Stoker's hair and pushed his face up against the skin of the bomb.

"Stoker, don't you ever, ever, say shit about a razor or my books again, you hear? I swear to God I'll smash your fucking face in. Do you hear me? Do you?"

Stoker groaned.

"Answer me!" Daniels pushed Stoker's arm up higher. Still no answer. Daniels pushed harder.

Stoker groaned, his teeth clenched.

Daniels forced the arm a bit more. It was ready to give. Stoker cried out in pain.

"I said answer me, or I swear to God I'll rip your fucking arm off!"

"Damn you."

Daniels pushed harder.

"Okay, okay," Stoker gasped as his arm reached the breaking point.

Daniels released his grip and stepped back, anticipating a retaliatory strike. Stoker spun around, his eyes barely discernible beneath fused brows, his jaw slack, his lips quivering. He breathed deeply in and out. He rotated his shoulder round and furiously rubbed his arm.

But Stoker was no longer pale as when he first attacked—the blood shunting away from the skin to the muscles and brain for action. Now red-faced and angry, he passed that stage. Stoker shook out his arm and walked to the temperature gauge and log book.

Daniels paced the aft part of the magazine, trying to cool down. He felt only fury. He looked around the magazine at the weapons splayed out before him. *Fuck 'em, fuck 'em all!*

He walked over to Stoker, who was still recording the temperature. Stoker wrote down each number from the gauge meticulously and slowly. Daniels stood two feet behind him, his fists clenching and unclenching, trying to control the impulse to hit him. He needed to calm down. He turned and put his right arm up on top of a B61 shield and tried to relax. *What's wrong with me? Never felt this angry before.* He wiped his forehead and threw back the hair from his eyes. *It's this place, this fucking place.* He glanced around at all the weapons before him and then down at his spit-shined shoes. He kicked at them and scruffed them up with the bottom of each foot until the glossy finish had completely vanished.

He looked up. Stoker was gone. His anger returned. He walked back to the entrance of the magazine and ignored Stoker, who stood turning his lock in his hand, ready to close up. Daniels stepped to the 30MC and flipped the brass speaker switch.

"This is Daniels in M-2. Coming up."

Daniels stowed his keys, headed down to the coop, and walked up to Taylor's rack. He appeared to be asleep. Daniels reached up and touched his shoulder. Without opening his eyes, Taylor said, "What's up?" His face was covered in shadow.

Daniels tensed, climbed up, then leaned over and whispered one word. Taylor nodded, his eyes still shut. Daniels then jumped up into his own rack and lay still, taking in the hum of the JP-5 pump rooms, the muted murmur of men playing Spades in the far corner, the bottomless smell of boots tied to the tops of racks, and the gentle sway of the ship—a cradling set in motion by the ceaseless wash of wave roving in rank over the surface of the sea, driven in turn by winds originating from a difference in pressure caused from the tremendous heat emanating up and out from the gravity fed fusion deep within the heart of the sun. His eyelids grew heavy, soon closed, and like the soft siren call of gravity itself, he was gently pulled down into the dark and warm depths of sleep.

15 Nov. 77

Pulling into Yokosuka in a few hours. Daniels can't stop babbling on about seeing his girlfriend, Yuki, whom he wants to marry. I really don't think he fully understands, which is good. I'm truly sorry for him, for them—but it is necessary and inexorable in light of my decision. Our decision.

I was told to expect a whole flotilla of boats to greet us, mostly protesters. I was told by Sanchez that not only do they know what we carry, but they even know the locations of the magazines. Though their government knows what is stowed in our magazines and knows that to bring one on their soil is a blatant violation of their own laws, they still deny the presence of American nuclear weapons on our ships— ships which rest upon the world's waters, not Japanese soil. But that will all change.

Japan

Daniels raced up the ladder to the hangar bay, the cold air slapping into him. It was only a matter of a day before he saw Yuki again. He knew she must have gotten his letter with the time and place to meet. His pace quickened as he made his way over to the side of the ship—and to the shoreline of Japan! But before he could reach the door to the sponson, he could hear people yelling through bullhorns, screeching up at the giant carrier easing into Yokosuka harbor. He stepped through the door and walked towards the forward five-inch, 54-caliber Mark 16 gun on the ship's starboard side.

He walked around it and into the sun, and he peered out at hundreds of boats of all sizes and shapes. They clumped in rows. Most had large paper banners strapped across their sides, some in Kanji, most in English. One read, "Keep Japan Nuclear Free. No weapons." Another, "Yankee, go home, and take Nuclear Weapon with you." A small news boat packed tightly with cameras and long-range microphones zipped in and out the sailboats and the slower motor boats. Above the mass of the churning wake circled a news copter, a long camera jutting out from its open door.

Daniels looked at the catwalk above him and at all the sailors manning the rail, a custom when pulling into port. He hoped that Rogers would be directly above it as he heard he would. He quickly scanned the men he could see, but he didn't see Rogers. But surely, he was somewhere up there standing next to Stoker, both at parade rest, dressed in their whites, legs stretched shoulder width, with both arms bent behind their backs. Daniels could imagine Rogers leaning over slightly and whispering to Stoker and then both spitting at the boats below them. Rogers would then flip off the news boat. And Stoker, taking a cue, would do the same. Then both of them would laugh like little kids.

Daniels swore and slipped back into the hanger bay. He headed down to the division's landing force locker, a space the division uses to store extra clothing and belongings. He waited outside the door. Mitchel finally appeared, key in hand.

"They up there," asked Mitchel.

Daniels smiled. "I'm sure they are. Let's do it."

Mitchel grinned and jingled the key. "You're going to owe me one hell of a dinner."

"Surf and turf's your favorite?"

"Damn straight it is," said Mitchel.

Mitchel unlocked the door, and they stepped into the compartment. Daniels flipped on the light and searched the room. He found what he was looking for. He motioned to Mitchel, and they both walked over to a group of travel bags hanging from a pipe in the back. They found Roger's and Stoker's and unzipped them.

Daniels pulled out a small bag from his pocket and studied its contents in the light. "Boy, are they going to be surprised."

"I'll say," said Mitchel. "Can't wait!"

"Fucking A," said Daniels. "I'd pay anything to see their faces come next month's "surprise" inspection. Pilfering weapons cables might send them to the brig for a while. Rogers should never have fucked with the division's key and lock custodian." He smiled.

"They'll find the cables gone from the supply cabinet, and he's gonna get what he deserves," said Mitchel. "Should never have shredded a man's last twenty dollar bill."

"That's all you're mad about? What about the Buffalo Beer House?"

"Naww, actually, in retrospect, kind of enjoyed it." He smiled.

Daniels shook his head in disbelief. "You're crazy."

Mitchel peered out the door. "Let's do it and get out of here."

Daniels placed one bag in Rogers' front pocket and then the other one in Stoker's. He kissed his fingers and patted the pockets, then zipped up the travel bags and left. Mitchel returned his key, and Daniels hummed the whole way back to the coop.

At ten o'clock, the ship docked, and at twelve o'clock, Daniels and

Taylor walked off the ship and headed for the main gate of the base. The sky was clear, but the air was surprisingly cold. As they neared the gate, they could hear a chorus of shouts. A large crowd of sailors stood just within the tall chain-linked fence, another crowd of Japanese protesters on the other side. The protesters marched in single file back and forth, many carrying signs, all echoing the shouts of a man standing on a small crate. Two police vans, riot water cannon aimed, idled on either side. Inside, to the front of the sailors, stood a row of helmeted military police.

"Fuck. What do we do now?" asked Daniels.

A sailor standing to Daniels' right leaned over and spoke. "Overkill."

"Excuse me?"

"Overkill. The Japanese are amazing. They'll leave pretty soon."

"How soon?" asked Taylor.

"Ahhh," the sailor looked at his watch. "They're scheduled to leave at twelve-thirty."

"Yeah, right," said Daniels.

"No, they'll leave," said the sailor. "Like I said, they're amazing. Seen it before. They started their protest at exactly twelve as they said they would, and they will leave at exactly twelve-thirty."

"I'll believe it when I see it," said Daniels.

Fifteen minutes later, the protest leader looked at his watch, shouted a command, and the protesters dispersed. Daniels and Taylor looked at one another in awe. "Told you," quipped the sailor. "Pretty amazing. You can set your watch by 'em." Daniels glanced at his bare wrist.

The police opened the gates. The crowd burst through. A Japanese film crew sat on the opposite corner, panning the rush of sailors heading into the "Honch," the infamous district just outside the gate that was bristling with bars. They passed through the gate and approached an old woman standing next to a table stacked with pamphlets. A paper banner draped across the front said "Yokosuka

Citizens' Group." The woman's face and hands were scarred. She stood wrapped in a traditional Japanese Kimono; the pink flowers and leaves of cherry blossoms were stitched around the pearl-white fabric. Her eyes were shadowed, and her lips moved as if by a breeze. She leaned on a crutch, her one hand gripped around it, the other thrust out with pamphlets. Taylor took one, nodded, and slipped it into his front pocket. They walked in silence for a while, finally stopping in an alley. Taylor pulled from his pocket a list. Daniels did the same.

"Let's split here," said Taylor, "We'll meet at the Zig Zag Club tomorrow at four thirty as planned. That's plenty of time. Make sure you find a tailor that speaks good English, and just be sure to find a shop that has a whole pig. Remember, it has to be big enough. Time is of the essence, and we don't need any fuckups."

"Don't worry, I will," said Daniels. "And don't you forget the travel and news agency."

"Hey, I know what the fuck I'm doing. It's *you* I worry about."

"Well, don't. I'll see you later." Daniels turned and walked forward, his eyes taking in the neon Kanji signs above the many bars and small restaurants, his fingers folding and refolding his list. He knew he had to hurry, but for some reason, his feet felt like lead. He would be seeing Yuki tomorrow at five o'clock, and his stomach turned at the thought of what he needed to tell her. But what that was and how he was going to say it, he wasn't sure. All he really knew at this point was that he needed to tell her that it was most likely going to be a very long time before they saw each other again, with a small chance of not at all. But she had to trust him. It would ultimately be worth it.

I hope.

15 Nov. 77 (2030)

The Pueblo Indians believe that all life comes from the mountain. Jung wrote of these people, ". . . he is equally certain that he lives upon the roof of an immeasurable world, closest to God. He, above all others, has the Divinity's ear, and his ritual act will reach the distant sun soonest of all. The holiness of mountains, the revelation of Yahweh upon Sinai, the inspiration that Nietzsche was vouchsafed in the Engadine—all speak the same language." I, too, speak it. On Thanksgiving, I will seek that solitude at the world's roof, its holy peak, its gateway into the immeasurable mind of God, and bring back a little light and understanding to the shadowed and suppressed sediments of humanity.

I have been very busy preparing for my quest. Daniels as well. He is taking care of a few essential items. He will buy a pig for the upcoming division's picnic and softball game the day after Thanksgiving. I also had to use the black market to buy an item that we might need.

The Midway pulled into Yokosuka, Japan, this morning. The protesters were out and plentiful. They sailed with the ship in the harbor and marched at the gates of the base. After leaving the gate, I took a pamphlet from an old woman in the Yokosuka Citizens' Group. From her scars, I believe she was a Hiroshima or Nagasaki survivor. The pamphlet was a plea to the American sailors and went as follows:

"To the sailors on the Midway. We don't want the Midway here, in our country. Please don't misunderstand. We would not object to you coming here, if you came as a civilian to travel, to study, to visit, or to work. It's the Midway we don't want. Why? We know that the Midway carries nuclear weapons. For more than twenty years, we have been lied to about this. We have been told that the US had promised not to bring nuclear weapons into our country, and that the promise was being kept. Now we have learned that the promise is not being kept, or maybe that no such promise was ever made. It was all a lie. If some foreign government brought some dangerous weapons into your

237

country, weapons that you particularly hated, without ever telling the American people about it, would you be angry? If so, you should be able to understand our anger. Maybe you think that you, or your officers, know more about nuclear weapons than we do. But that's a mistake. All you know is how to store them, load them, and drop them. But we know what they do. Two of them were dropped on us, and we have not forgotten and never will. In Hiroshima, and again in Nagasaki, a city full of people—little boys and girls, their aging grandparents, workers, mothers, everybody—was changed in an instant to the bottom of hell. Some were vaporized, some broken and torn to bits, some burned to ashes, some poisoned by radiation, and some left to wonder for the rest of their lives why they, alone of their families, had been chosen to survive. How many 'Hiroshimas' does the Midway carry? If World War Three begins, your nuclear weapons will protect nothing. You will fire yours, Russia will fire hers, (no one will ever know who fired first), and then you will die, we will die, the Russian people will die, and your families back home will die. That is all. Nothing will be protected. But maybe you know these things, you sailors who live every day under harsh discipline on a ship that carries even its own jail, and who sleep every night next to the most destructive weapons on earth. Midway sailors, all that we ask is that you think about these things, talk about them with your buddies, and try hard to understand what we are saying and doing. You might learn something. In the meantime, don't be surprised to find us demonstrating against the Midway every time it comes, and again every time it goes out again. That's right: We don't want the Midway coming here, and we also don't want it sailing out of here on military maneuvers, threatening the lives of our neighbors. Where should it go then? You figure it out. It might look nice filled with concrete and planted in a park somewhere as a monument to the stupidity of war."

The Zig Zag Club

Daniels zipped along the sidewalk of Dobuita Street within the Honch. It was full of dark-lit bars, massage parlors, tattoo joints, "buy me drink" women, cheap food, and silk embroidery jacket shops that were all mostly concentrated on what the old timers called "Thieves Alley." Regrettably, many sailors who had visited Japan could only say that the Honch was the only Japanese soil or territory that they had actually ever set foot on. But they were also the same sailors who prided themselves on not having seen the sun for a month on a carrier.

Daniels stepped into the Zig Zag Club, his favorite bar in Japan. He loved it here. In front of him was a large open space filled with a clean bar, large booths and couches, plenty of pool tables, and an assortment of table hand games, such as soccer. But the main draw of the club was, without a doubt, the large glass booth to the right as you entered. A Japanese DJ sat behind the glass and took requests from sailors for albums to listen to. But only one side of the album was the rule, and they played every song on it. Thus, every fifteen to twenty minutes, the sailors got to dive deep into a favorite album of their choice. And they cherished it. Once the DJ received a request, he quickly nodded, spun around, and flipped through 2500 records that were lined up in boxed shelves behind him. Once he found the album, he placed it behind the glass in a line at the front of the booth, so the sailors could see what was coming next.

Daniels made his way over to the DJ, as he knew he needed to wait a while to hear his request. Tonight's DJ was a young Japanese kid, maybe 18 or 19. Unique among the Japanese, he had very long black hair with a very sparse mustache and beard.

"Montrose," said Daniels to the DJ. "*Paper Money*. Side two." And to emphasize this, Daniels lifted two fingers and shook it at him. The DJ nodded and quickly found the album and placed it in the window just next to the Genesis album already playing. He couldn't wait to hear one of his all-time favorite songs, "We're Going Home."

239

Every time it came on at the Zig Zag Club, the sailors would perk up and sing along—as it struck a nerve in that they were so far from home.

Daniels looked around and saw Taylor sitting in the back of the club on a large blue couch behind a small wooden table. He waived to let him know that he was there. He then walked up to the bar, bought a cold Asahi Super Dry, and then joined Taylor.

"Cheers!" Daniels said as he plopped down on the couch.

"Let's hope so," replied Taylor. "Were you able to check off our list?"

"Wow, you don't waste any time. Straight to the point. Couldn't we just relax and enjoy some Genesis for a bit?"

"No. It's too important."

"Well, if you must know. Everything's cool. Except . . ."

"Except what?"

"The pig. I ordered it but can't pick it up till tomorrow."

"Shit, we don't have much time; that's the most important piece." Taylor put down his beer.

"Yeah, yeah, time. No worries, I'll have it done tomorrow."

"Good. Don't fail me. Everything depends on that."

Daniels nodded, a bit irritated at the remark. He knew what he needed to do, and there was no way he was going to mess this up.

They sat in silence for a while, taking in the music and the beer. The Genesis album ended, and then the first song of Montrose, "I Got the Fire," suddenly kicked in. For once in a very long time, Daniels felt like he could really relax, just melt into nothing. No cares, no worries. *Just be.* Daniels stretched out, took a few sips of beer, closed his eyes, and enjoyed the music for a while.

"Hey," said Taylor suddenly. "Isn't that your girl?"

Daniels looked up. Standing next to the door at the front of the club was Yuki.

"How'd you know it was her?"

"Easy. The Japanese are right on time, and, bingo, it's exactly

240

five." He looked at his watch. "Her name also means "snow," right? And guess what color jacket and pants she's wearing?"

Sure enough, Daniels could see that she was wearing a thin white coat and white jeans. It was the same outfit that she had worn to the Santana concert in Yokohama stadium.

"Lucky guess," said Daniels, standing up. "See ya tomorrow." He started to make his way toward her, his heart racing.

"Yo," said Taylor.

Daniels stopped. "What?"

"Aren't you going to introduce me to your girl? Have a drink or two. Relax?"

Daniels looked down. "Actually, no. After I tell her that I won't be back for a while, I'm going to have to do some serious damage control. That could take some time." He looked around. "Something we're both short on right now."

Taylor nodded.

"If everything goes right," continued Daniels, "We'll all meet back here to toast our success."

"Sure, sure. We'll do that." Taylor took a swig of his beer. "Go ahead and enjoy yourself. And good luck. From the sounds of it, you're really going to need it."

Daniels ignored the comment, turned, and headed towards Yuki, his heart racing. At seeing Daniels, Yuki's eyes immediately widened in delight, and she yelled, "Chris!" She jumped into his arms, burying her head in his chest. He instantly collapsed around her and held her tight. Her perfume drifted up, and he could feel her body shaking. She was crying. His eyes watered, and he held her tight, not wanting to let her go. *Ever.*

But he knew that he needed to. Had to. At least for now. And the thought of that suddenly made him want to collapse and die. And as if on cue, the song "We're Going Home" suddenly kicked on, filling the room. Daniels looked over to Taylor, who was sunk deep into the couch in the back, and he waved goodbye to him. Taylor lifted his beer in a salute and then gulped it down. Daniels grabbed Yuki by the hand, zipped out the door, and guided her over to their regular hotel in the Honch, the Sea Star, a "Love Hotel" that was rented out by the hour.

There was no one in the lobby, which, as usual, was impeccably clean and smelled of perfume and cleaning solution. They quickly looked at the lit panel on the side wall that showed the different styles of rooms that were available—traditional Japanese, contemporary Japanese, contemporary western, cowboy-themed, space-themed, bondage-themed, etc. They chose their favorite, contemporary Japanese. Daniels walked over to the counter and rang the bell. Almost instantly, a short Japanese woman with long gray-streaked hair appeared and bowed. Daniels quickly paid her for two hours, and they hopped on the elevator and settled into the room.

It was a small room with a very large bed with a black leather padded wooden console bordering it on all sides. At the head of the bed, the console had sets of buttons that controlled all of the lights in the room, as well as the TV and stereo system. Just above the bed was a large glass mirror, which matched a series of mirrors that lined the black walls. The room was dark and heavily shaded, and a small but exceptionally clean bathroom was just next to the door. Yuki immediately made for it.

Daniels plopped down on the soft comforter, turned on the music, dimmed the lights, and waited. About ten minutes later, the bathroom door opened, and out walked Yuki, her hair wet and combed back, a towel draped around her lovely body. Their eyes locked for a brief second, and then Yuki let out a soft squeal, threw the towel off of her body, and jumped on top of Daniels.

He had made love to her many times now, but this time, it felt very different. And Yuki understood the change immediately. He was not all smiles and a whirl of energy and emotion, which she seemed to cherish and build on. This time he was solemn, patient, careful, and caressing. He touched her softly, and afterward, he kept hugging her, not wanting to let go.

"Are you okey-dokey?" she suddenly asked. Her smile disappeared into concern.

"Yes, I'm okey. Maybe not dokey, but I'm okey." He attempted a smile.

"Mmmm . . . Chris. What wrong? Please tell me."

"No, it's all good. I'm just tired. Too much on my mind." He rolled over and stared at his face in the mirror. At hers. But her long and frizzled, wet black hair was hanging over her face, obscuring it. And this suddenly scared him. He turned and gently brushed her hair back.

"Yuki." He looked deeply into her eyes.

She tensed. "Yes?"

"I'm not sure how to say this, so I'm just going to tell you."

She sat up and took his hands. "What? Your ship leaving soon?"

"No, my ship is not leaving. But . . ."

"But, what? What? Tell me!"

He grabbed her fingers tightly. "But I am."

"What you mean?"

"I will have to go away for a while. Maybe a long time. And . . .and I'm not sure when . . . when I'll be back. It might be years or never at all if I'm unlucky."

"Away?! Years! Oh, no, Chris! No!"

"Oh, yes."

"Why? You upset that we not marry? Because mother?"

"Actually, yes."

"Oh, Chris. Don't. We still see each other. You can live here, in Tokyo."

"How long, Yuki? Can we get married?"

Yuki looked away. "I'm, I'm not sure . . . My mother . . . she needs me."

"I know. You told me."

"But why you leave? And years? That crazy!"

"I can't talk about it. It's a top-secret US mission that I've been assigned to. Okay? It will make both you and your mother proud."

Yuki looked at him, her eyes searching his. She then looked away and was silent for a while. But then suddenly, she exclaimed, "Top Secret mission? I *don't* believe. Don't lie to me, Chrisgopher!" She got up and went into the bathroom again, and slammed the door. Daniels leaned back and whispered, "It's Christopher. Christopher." He rolled over and went over to the bathroom and raised his voice so that she could hear him, "Yuki, you'll need to trust me. When I get back, I going to marry you! Do you hear me?"

But Yuki remained silent. The only sound that Daniels could hear was the soft whir of the bathroom fan. He waited at the door for a while, then gave up and lay back down on the bed. A few minutes later, the door opened, and Yuki stepped out. She was fully dressed in her white pants and coat.

"I need to go," she said.

Daniels nodded and quickly dressed. They walked in silence to the train station. After getting her ticket, they stood on the platform, the clean white walls of the station gleaming in the light. Daniels took her by her hands.

"Look, Yuki. I'm sorry. You're right. It's not a Top Secret mission. That was stupid."

"Then what? What, Chris?" she said, her eyes searching his.

Daniels looked down to the rail track and the soot-covered rocks just beneath it. "I can't . . . I can't really discuss it."

Yuki pulled away and then slapped him softly in the chest. "Why, Chris, why? Is it some other woman?"

He grabbed her and pulled her over to the far wall, then held her tight. "No, you silly girl. It's because I *love* you. Don't you understand!" He kissed her and pulled her even tighter.

"You really love me?"

"Yes! My God . . . You should know that."

"Really?" Her eyes lit up.

"Of course . . . it's, it's like you're the sun. The sun is female here

244

in Japan, right?"

Yuki nodded.

"Okay, then. When we're separated, it's like night. Blackness. You're hidden beneath the earth. Understand?"

Yuki nodded.

"And I'm," said Daniels, "I'm a mountain. Dark, dumb, and cold. But when we're together. . . ." He looked around him and swept his arm out before him. "Bang! Sunrise! Instant light and beauty!" He smiled. "The start of a new day."

Yuki smiled, clasped her hands together, and started to hop up and down in excitement.

"See," said Daniels. "What I'm doing is for you. For your mother. For us."

"My mother?" She stopped moving and looked up at him, puzzled.

"Yes, *especially* your mother. Though I seriously think she misnamed you, I want her to be happy, to allow us to get married."

"Misname?"

"Yes."

"I don't understand."

"Your name is Yuki. Snow. Right?"

"Yes."

"Well, you're many degrees from that. She should have named you something beautiful and warm . . . like the sun."

Yuki smiled.

"What's the Japanese word for sun," asked Daniels.

"Ahh. . . taiyou. But Amaterasu was Japan sun goddess."

"Amaterasu? That's what she should have named you. That's infinitely more appropriate. In fact, when we get to America, I'm going to give you the nickname of Sue."

"Sue?"

"Yes, Sue. It will be short for Amaterasu. So every time I say your name, I'll be conferring on you the beauty and majesty of Japan's sun goddess." He smiled.

Yuki softened, then wrapped her arms around him. He leaned back, and then he gently placed his hands on both sides of her face. He looked her in the eyes and said, "I love you so much. Please, please, don't forget that. I'll be back."

"Promise?"

"Yes, I promise."

She reached into her pocket and pulled out a penny, and pressed it into his palm. "Don't forget."

He nodded, stared at the bright penny, and then slipped it into his pocket. He then pulled her close and pressing his mouth against the side of her face, softly whispered her name. Again, and again, and again. *Yuki, Yuki, Yuki . . .*

But all he could feel was her body shaking and a warm wetness starting to spread across his chest where her head was buried.

23 Nov 77

All is set in stone. Tomorrow is Thanksgiving—a day of thanks. It most certainly will be.

God help us.

M-2

Taylor and Daniels approached the cage, their boots softly pressing against the deck. The air was hot, humid, and heavy with the scent of fresh paint. They stopped in front of the cage and glanced at one another. Sweat beaded across their brows. They inserted their cards and waited, both eyes on the red glow creeping out from the bottom of the door. Each fidgeted with their keys. A sneeze blew out from behind the mirror of the cage, and Daniels instinctively twitched.

He looked at his wrist. *Shit*. He had forgotten to replace his watch. But he knew it was late Thursday night and that they were re-opening the forward spaces. He also knew it was also November 24, Thanksgiving. They had kicked everyone out and closed the spaces a half an hour ago in order to make rounds in the aft spaces before going to bed. Daniels had called the Corporal of the Guard from the aft office and asked that a sentry be posted again so that they could re-enter the forward spaces.

The bolt thundered, and the door swung open. They stepped inside. Dell looked up, his round forehead red in the light like a beach ball.

"Damn. I was just ready to hit the rack, and I get called here. What gives, fellas?" Dell sounded as if he were speaking through a long tube. He raised a handkerchief and blew his nose.

"None of your business," said Taylor, his voice wavering slightly. Daniels glanced over at him, surprised.

"I try to make everything my business," said Dell looking up, his eyes bloodshot.

"You're gonna find out soon enough," said Daniels. He attempted a smile, trying to mask his own nervousness. Taylor coughed, showing his disapproval at the comment.

"What do you mean?" said Dell. "I hate surprises."

"Just as we were gonna hit the rack," said Daniels, "the LPO, Sanchez, told us to do something about that pig we brought down for the division picnic tomorrow. Apparently, everyone complained about the smell. You remember us bringing down that pig, don't you?"

"Of course. It's not often a fella gets to see something like that slide by him here."

"Well, it's gone bad," said Daniels.

"Then hurry it up, will you," said Dell. "I need to get some— Ahhhchooo! Sorry, damn cold. Need to get some sleep."

Dell handed them their badges. He then passed the phone to Daniels. Daniels gave his number and handed the phone to Taylor, who had traded duty days with Stoker. Taylor gave his number, removed all the alarms to the forward spaces, and then handed the phone to Dell. They undid the locks. With a loud clank, Taylor opened the door and bounded through it. Daniels paused, then followed the smell of rotting meat.

They descended the ladder and walked into the division storage room. Taylor looked at his watch. His hand trembled.

"It's late," said Taylor. "We gotta be quick."

Daniels moved calmly as he made his way toward the back of the storage room. The odor grew worse. He grabbed the padlocked laundry bag sitting next to a locker, opened it, and dumped out some pillows, a custom-made seabag, and a massive pig's head wrapped in plastic. The large head wobbled, and a wave of rot rose up. Small holes had been cut in the plastic over an hour ago to help clear the spaces of lingering personnel—an excuse to bring Taylor and Daniels back. The head stopped moving, its dry eyes vacant and wide, its mouth opened as if straining to speak.

Daniels went into the pub room and grabbed his keys from the safe. When he came back into the storeroom, Taylor hadn't moved. "Hey, Taylor." Taylor turned from the desiccated eye of the pig and walked over to the trunk.

"Got your keys?" said Daniels.

"Shit."

Taylor jogged into the pub room, got his keys, and bounded back to the trunk. Daniels grabbed the seabag and they climbed down to M-

2.

They opened the magazine and walked over to a stack of three B57s. Both stared at the warheads, a pale white.

"Well, this is it," said Taylor.

Daniels didn't respond right away. It was hard for him to believe what they were just about to do. Daniels lifted his hand. It trembled slightly but was dry. This surprised him. *Should be nervous as hell. Taylor is.* A thin line of sweat on Taylor's forehead crept down into his eyes. He wiped it away.

"Fuck it, let's do it; we don't have much time," said Taylor. He turned and walked over to the tool bench. Daniels set the seabag down and walked over to the hoist, turned it on, and positioned it above the bomb. He lowered the hook. Taylor dumped the H-gear and tools onto the deck, picked up two ratchets, handed one to Daniels, and in unison, they quickly undid the four bolts of the cradle that held it tightly to the two warheads below. With the bolts gone, Daniels raised the forward lug nut, inserted the handling gear lift, and attached the hook. With the hoist, he raised the weapon and its cradle up into the air and moved it out away from the stack.

"We've got to hurry," said Taylor, glancing at his watch.

Daniels lowered the weapon to the deck. They quickly undid the hook and H-gear, removed the bolts on the cradle, and popped the top half of the cradle off. The bomb sat exposed.

"Fuck," said Daniels, "we're really going to do it."

"Yes. Let's move." Taylor threw Daniels a speeder wrench. They quickly removed the screws holding the nose cone. They popped the clamps off without a hammer, only using their fingers. While Taylor held the nose in his hands, Daniels undid the cable attached to it. Taylor set the nose down by the bulkhead.

Daniels quickly removed the top tail screws. Taylor followed and undid the bottom ones.

"Brace the tail; if it falls, we're fucked," said Daniels. "A jolt or torn cable could detonate the parachute."

"I'm well aware," said Taylor. He leaped over and cradled the tail in his arms. Daniels pulled off one clamp. He positioned his fingers around the second one.

"Ready?" asked Daniels.

Taylor nodded. Daniels pulled. Nothing happened. He pulled again, but it wouldn't come off.

"Fuck," said Taylor, "get the goddamn hammer. Hurry."

Daniels bolted upright, scrambled over to the tool bench, grabbed the rubber mallet, and scurried back. He looked to Taylor.

"Do it!" said Taylor.

Daniels swung. The clamp flew off, and the one hundred-and-twenty-five-pound tail dropped gently into Taylors' massive arms. It didn't explode. Taylor hugged the tail tightly, like a child, and then moved it back away from the warhead six inches.

"Come on, dammit, move before someone comes," said Taylor.

Daniels bent down and reached his hand inside the tail. He found the first cable connector and twisted it. It wouldn't loosen. *Shit, they come off so easy during a normal operation.* Taylor grimaced. "Move." Daniels locked his arms, used his body as he would in removing a deck plug, and twisted. It loosened. He grabbed the other cable end and twisted it. It came off easy.

"They're off."

Taylor moved the tail back gently and swung it around. He placed it on the deck. A soft metal clink shot up.

"Caps, we need to put on caps," said Daniels.

"Fuck it, no time."

"Jesus, those connections are exposed; any static could set that parachute off."

"I said no time. It's not going to fucking explode."

"It might, and I am not going to be responsible for someone's death or blowing a hole through a bulkhead." He ran over to the tool cabinet and looked around for a cover.

"Goddammit, Daniels, grab the ones off the trainer."

Daniels ran over to the training weapon and pulled the covers off the parachute cables in the stand. He quickly placed them on the tail of the real weapon.

Taylor picked up the seabag, but Daniels jumped over and grabbed it.

"Here, let me get that while you lift the warhead," said Daniels.

Taylor let go, irritated, then jumped over to the warhead.

With a grunt, Taylor stood the warhead up on its end. Daniels slid the customized seabag over it, the extra length added to the seabag fitting the warhead just perfectly. Taylor then grabbed the straps to the seabag, set the warhead down carefully on the deck, and then rolled the warhead over to the door.

"Fuck, we've got to hurry," said Taylor.

Taylor heaved the warhead up over the door frame and set it down with a loud clang against the deck in the trunk. He leaned it up against the bulkhead. As Daniels was about to step through the door, Taylor leaped back inside the magazine, nearly knocking Daniels over, and ran over to the bulkhead above the cleaning bench. He pulled out a black grease pencil and wrote on the wall:

"Know then, O waiting and compassionate soul, that is to fear which has the power to harm, and nothing else is fearful even in Hell."

Taylor spun and jumped back through the door. Daniels followed. *Of course, Taylor wrote the Dante passage on the door in the cage.* Daniels felt stupid for not realizing earlier that Taylor had been its scribe. *No. Wasn't allowed down to the spaces yet. Then who?*

They threw the locks on the door. Daniels pulled the cover of the seabag down, exposing the warhead, and, snatching the grease pencil from Taylor's pocket, scribbled "Rogers" on the side of it.

"I baptize thee in name," said Daniels.

With a swipe of his thumb, Taylor smeared it so that the word was no longer recognizable. "This weapon cannot be named." His eyes were intense. "It's woven from blood—not name." He turned and climbed the ladder.

Daniels closed his eyes for a second, recalling in his mind a passage in a letter from Melville. He then spoke softly to himself as Taylor neared the top of the trunk. "What's the reason, Mr. Hawthorne, that in the last stages of metaphysics, a fellow always falls to swearing so?"

Taylor lowered the rope and hook. Daniels stepped back and grabbed it. He then ran the hook through the carrying straps that were reinforced to hold the warhead. He nodded to Taylor.

Taylor hoisted, and foot by foot, it rose. *Hope it holds.* The warhead swung as it moved over Daniels' head, a huge cloud blotting the light above him. *Should have gone up first. Has he lost it? Have I?* He swallowed. The warhead stopped at the top and swayed back and forth. Taylor grabbed it and, with a great heave, swung into the passageway. Daniels followed.

As his head cleared the top of the trunk, the smell hit him. His stomach churned, and he gripped the rail in support.

"Good heavens," gasped Daniels.

He climbed into the passageway. In the middle of the deck, next to Taylor, was the grisly head of the pig, out of its plastic tomb. Taylor was breathing through his mouth, his face contorted.

"You okay?" said Daniels, now breathing through his mouth.

"Yeah, yeah, I'll be fine."

Taylor picked up the foul head. "Open the seabag."

Daniels rolled down the edges of the seabag, exposing the top of the weapon. The smell was unbearable, and he fought the urge to vomit. Taylor placed the head on top of the warhead and then moved it about so that it covered the edges completely. A disgusting fluid crept down the sides of the bomb. Daniels pulled the sides of the bag up around the top of the weapon and foul head, leaving just the nose, the brownish snout of the pig exposed.

His mouth watered as he fought the urge to throw up. They had set the head in the sun for several days before bringing it down past Dell.

"Let's go," said Daniels. He raced over to the ladder.

Taylor crouched down with his back to the bag, put both arms through the straps, leaned forward, and with a loud grunt, stood up slowly. Daniels started up the ladder, trying to keep his stomach from emptying. Taylor followed. Daniels stopped at the bathroom and checked on Taylor. Taylor's eyes showed the strain of the weight, his jaw hung slack, and he was breathing heavily. He suddenly bent over and threw up on the deck. Daniels grabbed the magazine keys from Taylor and stepped into the head. He stashed Taylor's and his own set of magazine keys into a vent in the overhead. *Buy a little more time.* He handed a bunch of paper towels to Taylor to wipe his mouth and face with, then walked over to the door of the cage. *Poor Dell.*

Daniels felt sorry for Dell. He would probably get court-martialed and maybe do time. But he was the only Marine they could trust to blunder, to let them out of the spaces with a nuclear weapon. It was easy enough to find out his duty schedule for the past week and even easier to convince him that they had a whole pig in a bag when they brought it down into the spaces a few days ago. Instead of closing the bag, they left the top open. Dell just looked at the snout and waived them through, remarking all the while on how he hated the taste of pork. Poor Dell, he thought as he opened the door and stepped into the cage.

However, it was Corporal Collins who greeted him.

Daniels froze. *Holy shit.* Taylor entered, the seabag on his back. His eyes widened at seeing Collins.

"My God!" yelled Collins. "What the hell is that!" Collins put his hand to his nose, waving the air frantically with his other hand.

"A pig for our division picnic," said Daniels quickly. "It's smelling up the spaces. Didn't Dell tell you? Where is he?"

Collins looked at the crusty nose sticking out of the bag. "I think I'm going to be sick." He gagged, not throwing up but spitting a stream of saliva on the deck. He coughed, cleared his throat, and then wiped his mouth with his sleeve. He turned. "Dell was relieved just a minute ago, whining about a fucking cold—will you please set that thing outside the cage." Collins threw up. At the sight of Collins doubling up, Daniels fought hard to keep from doing the same. Taylor handed him an extra paper towel. Collins wiped his face and uniform and then tried to compose himself. He opened the door. Taylor's face was sweaty and blank. He stared at Collins. Collins looked up. "Out. Now!" Taylor jerked, then stepped out. He set the bag next to the cage, easing it gently down, careful not to betray himself with a clink of metal on metal. He re-entered.

"That's the most disgusting thing I've ever smelled my whole life," said Collins. He lifted the phone.

"Obviously, you're still a wog, not a shellback," said Daniels, "or this would smell sweet to you compared to the coffin." He looked for a reaction from Taylor, but Taylor just stared at the deck, clearly troubled. *Jesus Taylor, don't blow it now.*

"I sure as hell know what the coffin smells like," said Collins. "This is worse." He handed the phone to Daniels.

Daniels gave his number to the Corporal of the Guard. Collins watched him intently, his face wrapped in a sickly pall. Taylor did the same, asked that the alarms be put on, then hung up the phone. Collins leaned toward the door and slammed the bolt back.

Taylor groaned, causing Daniels to shoot a look of caution at him. The door swung open, and they left the cage. Taylor slung the warhead on his back, his head shaking in distress. *What the hell's wrong with him?*

"You okay?"

Taylor straightened up. "Yeah, I'm okay." They walked away from the cage. Just past the mess deck, they stopped in front of a hatch. Daniels reached behind a large vent and pulled out a small sea-bag. He opened it and took out two work jackets to protect them from the cold outside. He handed one to Taylor. Taylor set the warhead down with a dull thud and put on the coat. "I'll be right back," he said, "I forgot something." He bounded off.

"Taylor? Where the . . . hey! Where're you going?" Taylor ignored him and disappeared through a door.

Daniels glanced nervously about and resigned himself to wait. A few minutes later, Taylor returned.

"Where the hell did you go?" said Daniels.

"I told you I forgot something."

"What?"

"Never mind."

"What do you mean, never mind. What's wrong with you?"

"I said never mind! Hear me?" He lifted the warhead onto his back. "Consider it a good luck charm in case we're stopped. Now let's go." He walked down the passageway. Daniels kept his mouth shut, picked up the seabag of clothes, and followed.

They stopped at a stairwell leading up to the hangar bay. A blast of cold air hit them, sending a shiver racing up Daniel's spine. They climbed up to the hangar bay, Taylor laboring under the weight, and they headed towards the stern of the ship, towards the afterbrow. A thick band of sweat broke out across Taylor's forehead. Two sailors walked by and suddenly jumped as the smell hit them. Daniels squeezed the shoulder strap to his seabag.

"Daniels—"

"Don't call me Daniels anymore. I'm not just a last name and social security number."

Taylor slowed and started breathing heavier. *Shit, he's tiring already. How we ever going to make it?*

"What is it?" said Taylor.

"What is what?"

"Your first name?" said Taylor.

"Don T."

"Very funny. What's your name?" asked Taylor.

"Christopher," said Daniels.

"Christopher."

They walked past the hangar bay doors. "What's yours?" asked Daniels.

"Joseph."

"All right, Joe."

"I said Joseph." Taylor bent, trying to adjust the weight evenly.

"Okay." Daniels tried to grin but didn't quite make it. "Just don't call me Chris."

They approached the afterbrow. Daniels' nervousness increased. The afterbrow didn't have the security checks the cage had and, in fact, required no searches at all on leaving, but there could be problems. Daniels walked up to the Junior Officer of the Deck and swallowed. The JOOD. He looked ancient. In fact, he was the oldest-looking Chief Daniels had ever seen in the Navy. But he had a stern, majestic face, and his hair and beard were streaked with white. He stood tall, broad, and vigilant beneath the overhead lights, which cast a soft glow over his watchful face. He sniffed the air, his nostrils flaring at the horrible smell. He coughed.

The JOOD's name tag said, "Marcus." Daniels saluted with his right hand, his left bracing the seabag as it sagged down his shoulder. "Permission to go ashore, sir."

The JOOD studied him, his face blank, then turned to Taylor.

"Permission to go ashore, sir," said Taylor. He also saluted with his free arm, the other supporting the bottom of the bag. The nose of the pig pointed up toward the lights. Taylor's knees bent slightly, almost as if the metal on his back were magnetized, pulling him towards the center of the ship.

"Who approaches with the scent of Hell itself?" The JOOD's eyes narrowed to sharp slits; he glared at the quivering nose of the pig. He stepped back.

"I was told by my Chief to get this pig out of the spaces," said Taylor. "It was supposed to be for our Thanksgiving picnic tomorrow, but, ah, as you can see, it's gone bad."

"See?!" His eyes widened, and he inhaled sharply. "You mean smell!" He studied the bag and then Taylor. He took in a great breath and held it. He then stepped forward towards the seabag. Daniels clenched the strap of his. The JOOD stood on his toes, leaned over, and gently pried back the top of the seabag in a curious attempt to take a peek at the pig. Daniels and Taylor glanced at one another in fear.

Taylor acted quickly. He leaned into the JOOD, bumping the pig's nose against the Chief's forehead. The Chief stepped back and gasped. A string of brownish slime stretched from the pig's nose to the Chief's forehead. The Chief looked horrified, and he quickly pulled a handkerchief from his back pocket and frantically wiped his face. He then quickly stepped over to the phone on the podium, forcing a sailor on the brow watch to step back. Daniels put his head down, shocked that it would end so suddenly, never having set foot on dry ground. *Damn! He saw it. All in vain.* Taylor also lowered his head, his knees shaking under the weight, his fingers pulling softly at the straps, betraying his thought.

Daniels fought the urge to panic, to flee. He eyed the gangway leading to the pier and lowered his body, setting himself to spring. The Chief dialed a number and put the phone to his ear. He stared at them in contempt. Taylor's eyes seemed to focus far beneath the deck.

Fuck this; I'm history. Daniels started to move, his eyes on the empty gangway, but as his foot lifted, to his utter surprise, the Chief lifted his head. "Still here! Get that fucking thing off my ship—now!"

"Yes, sir." The words came from Taylor, weak but adequate. Daniels was in too much shock to say anything. They turned and walked over to the gangway. The Chief watched them walk off, then yelled into the phone for an "immediate replacement" so that he could wash "the devil himself" from his forehead. Daniels smiled nervously. Taylor showed no emotion as he lumbered down the gangway.

The night was chilly. As they neared the bottom of the gangway, Daniels could feel the thick wooden planks swaying beneath his feet, the combined weight of Taylor and the bomb moving them. When they stepped off, Daniels breathed easier, and his pulse slowed. *Come on, just a little more. A little more.* He looked to the water and thought of the kids he had seen in the Philippines. *Falling metal from the West.*

Over 250 pounds of it. He stepped down onto the pier and smiled as Taylor followed.

"That was close," said Daniels, letting out a large breath. "But we did it."

"Not yet. Keep moving."

"Oh, shit," said Daniels, looking past Taylor toward the large pier they were headed towards.

"What now?" said Taylor.

Walking up to them was the Master Chief Petty Officer of the ship.

"You're kiddin' me," said Daniels, lowering his head so that his face couldn't be seen clearly. "Now? Now?! Of all times? Now?!"

"Shhh . . . ," whispered Taylor. "Be cool. It's just a Chief. Just walk calmly past."

"No, you don't understand. It's the ship's Master Chief, and he's been looking for me since I did a stupid thing on the fantail! If he stops us, it could be trouble."

Taylor suddenly grabbed Daniels and turned him towards the sea. "Don't move; keep your eyes on the water and just keep talking."

As the Master Chief approached, Daniels and Taylor made sure that they kept their backs to him. Taylor pointed to the dark profile of a distant destroyer that almost blended in with the night, and they discussed if it was Japanese or American. But as the Chief passed, he suddenly caught a whiff of the pig and quickly turned, his face clearly contorted in disgust.

"Jesus," said the Master Chief, "What the hell is that?"

Daniels started to turn, but Taylor's hand and arm kept him facing the ocean.

"Sorry, Chief," said Taylor, turning his head toward the Chief. "Just a pig gone bad for a division party. We're getting rid of it now."

"Damn well better! That stinks!" He glared at them for what seemed like an eternity.

"What division you in?" he asked.

"'W,' Chief."

"That's 'Master Chief.'"

"Sorry, Master Chief."

"Saxon's your Chief then?"

"Yes, Master Chief."

"Good man."

Taylor nodded.

"Give him my regards, will you?"

"Sure will, Master Chief."

The Master Chief stared at the seabag. He grimaced once again, turned, and made his way toward the gangway.

Taylor swung Daniels around, keeping his back to the Master Chief, and they slowly walked off.

"That was close," said Daniels, breathing easier. "And unbelievably bad luck. Shit, I mean, what are the odds of that happening? Other unlucky events might clump now . . ."

"Clump?"

"Yeah, according to the Law of Rare Events, incidents like this tend to clump. So maybe we should . . ."

"Should what?" said Taylor, cutting Daniels off. "You need to change that damn thinking of yours! As you change your nature, the attitude of the world changes with you. Gandhi said that was the damn 'divine mystery supreme.'"

"Gandhi said, 'damn'?"

"Yeah, or words to that effect."

"Definitely words to that effect then."

Taylor ignored his comment and, suddenly picking up the pace, he swept past Daniels, plowing through the cold air. He walked ahead, his body rigid with the weight, and then stopped in front of a large wooden piling. He put the bag down next to a faucet and, bending over, carefully removed the pig's head from the top of the warhead. He studied it in the dark for an instant and then lowered it to the surface of the sea. He let go. It hit the water with a muted splash. Colored reflections snaked across the top of the ripples rolling away from the point of impact.

Daniels brushed past Taylor. He pulled out a towel from his own seabag and proceeded to wipe Taylor's bag and the weapon off. He fought the urge to throw up. He reached over to the faucet to wash his hands, but Taylor's foot intercepted his hand. "No."

"What the hell do you mean?" said Daniels.

"I said no." He paused. "No water can wash away that stain."

"What, are you crazy!? I can still smell it. We can't smell that shit all the way up . . ."

"I said no!" Taylor grabbed the towel and threw it into the water. "We might need it. It could be our best defense right now."

"Oh, yeah. Like with the Master Chief? He stopped because of it!"

"And he left because of it, too! And didn't we just get past the Marines and get off the afterbrow as well? Looks like lady luck has been with us, not against! Now stop it!"

Daniels swore but shut up. It wasn't worth it. Leave Taylor to Taylor. Besides, almost all of the grime was wiped off, and Taylor would be carrying it. *Just stay a few feet back from him.* Taylor bent over, picked up the weapon, and ambled off.

The wind bit into Daniels. He shivered and zippered his jacket. He reached into his pocket and pulled from it a small plastic bag. It was the rest of his marijuana stash. He walked over to the water and, opening the bag, released the contents in a shower of green. He balled up the plastic and threw it as far as he could. It went ten feet and fell to the ocean, where it unfurled and slowly filled with water till just the tip of the plastic cut the surface like a fin. He looked around to see if anyone heard the splash from the pig's head. Seeing no one, he picked up his seabag and started after Taylor. As he hurried, he looked up but could see neither the moon nor the stars. Just blackness.

A white speck zipped past his eye. The concrete before him started to pop with black dots, each of varying sizes. *Shit, rain.* It was as though the blackness all around him was melting. He wrapped his arms tight about himself and hurried through the drizzle toward a pair

261

of lights approaching fast, silhouetting the huge body of Taylor and the bomb.

24 Nov. 77

Made it to a taxi. This is for you, mother. Your life cut short at so young an age. I will never forget. Please forgive me. Put in a word for me; take my hand. Guide me up the rough slopes of Fuji.

I have stumbled already, condemning a friend, Collins. We must succeed now. It is our only hope of redemption.

Mt. Fuji

Daniels grinned. He watched the neon signs rainbow out into the rain-filled night as the taxi cab sped through narrow streets. The water snaking down the window distorted the color—warping, stretching, and elongating the pulsing signs. A tiny, almost toy-like truck zipped past him, sped out in front of oncoming traffic to avoid a parked car ahead of the cab, and flashed back into his lane, narrowly missing a head-on collision. No horn sounded. Amazing, he thought. The oncoming driver slowed down from his Indy 500 speed, swishing in and out past this and that car on the endless city street—fully expecting and allowing for the blitzing in of opposing traffic. Japan was truly amazing. Millions of petite people, tiny cars and trucks, all driving rocket speeds on needle-thin roads.

Daniels checked his seat belt. A few minutes later, the cab swerved onto a small side street in the Ota ki cho district of Yokosuka and screeched to a halt in front of the Yomiuri building, an editorial office of one of Japan's major newspapers. The building was fully lit, and even at this very late hour, several people could be seen bent over desks. The lobby was empty and dark, and a small light fizzled just above the company's name over the front door. Taylor jumped out of the cab and hopped past a Japanese couple with matching lime-green umbrellas, causing them to step back in alarm. He bounded up the steps and slid an envelope through a large mail slot next to the door. He then raced back to the cab and gave Daniels a thumbs-up gesture as he slammed the door shut.

They soon entered a ramp and drove up onto a freeway riding high up over the city. The driver relaxed, his white-gloved hand up high on the steering wheel.

Daniels looked around him. The cab was intensely clean. Frilled lace floated over both front and back seats. The burgundy satin-like upholstery combined with the lace gave the interior an elegant pale glow. It was just so damn clean, he thought. Remorse, with a touch of

264

guilt, filled him—the weapon in the trunk was soiling such a clean vehicle. But the look was worth it. The *look* on the driver's face when the scent of the seabag drifted up into his nose. His reaction seemed typical of the response most foreigners gave Americans when they did something stupid—the driver narrowing his eyes, his head slightly drawn back, then he closed them, fusing his eyebrows inward in disgust, shaking his head. That said it all and was justified. The driver then straightened his back and walked quickly to the rear of the cab, opened the trunk, and swept the floor with a small pocket brush. Taylor then set the seabag down with a metallic clunk. The cab sank down an inch. The driver studied the bag, then the two sailors then shook his head.

The echo of surprise still rang in Daniels' head when they had asked to be taken to the Yomiuri building and then to Mt. Fuji. The driver's eyes went wide, his finger waving in front of his mouth, as Japanese with chunks of English gushed out. They understood him to mean the distance was too far, that he wouldn't do it. Taylor then pulled out a wad of money, 75,000 yen, and counted it out in front of him. He placed the money in the driver's front pocket. It bulged outward, matching the driver's eyes.

Off they sped.

Daniels chuckled. It's amazing what money would do, even in Japan. The taxi ride should have been only 30,000 to 35,000 yen, considering the distance. *Paper power. Funding the soft click of a button.*

A sudden movement startled Daniels. Taylor stretched, then pulled his small black journal from under his shirt and started to write again.

"25 Nov. 77.

Still in cab, now headed towards Fuji. Thanksgiving ended a short time ago in Japan but is still being celebrated in America because of the time difference.

265

The language here . . ."

"Hey, Joseph."

Taylor put his pen down. "What?"

"Why are you writing?"

Taylor fidgeted with his pen. "I don't know. Why are you breathing?" He glanced out the window and then picked up his pen. He tapped it against his journal.

Daniels turned away. The brightly lit buildings, street lights, and rain all blended into a colorful cacophony as he sped past. He couldn't focus on one particular thing. Aside from the smattering of eastern shingled roofs and rarely seen traditional architecture, the endless city, Japan, had become in many respects similar to America in its structure and modern look but extremely different in its feel. Its encompassing compactness. Its written language is sprinkled on signs. Its clean, high-tech gloss, cement and steel, western design, and glitter meshed itself into the very fabric of this ancient culture that still retained, through its language, rituals, and business dealings, a prominent influence in the life of the Japanese people. It was all so interesting to him.

" . . . is very interesting. There is no equal in Japan. When two Japanese are introduced, they quickly assess each other's status and arrange their grammar appropriately. Each person spoke down to, or up to, another through an intrinsic differentiating structure of their language, that is, in the conjugation of the verbs. Aside from an occasional "neutral" language spoken between close friends of usually equal age, the Japanese people configured their sentences on whether you are of a higher or lower position or rank than themselves, a trait dating back to the highly structured Samurai periods.

Businessmen in sharp suits will draw a business card when first meeting, each with a resume of accomplishments on the back to distinguish status. That is, who will bow lower and longer and who will talk up or down to the other.

266

The very polite language is spoken to elders, between businesses, first greetings, and to upper class (Thus, 'When did you come to Japan?' would be spoken, 'Nihon ni itsu kimashitaka?'). Polite language is spoken to someone senior to yourself, first greetings, and to men from women ('Nihon ni itsu kitano desu ka?'). The neutral language is spoken between close friends and in literature—publishers do not know the social standing of the reader—and sometimes between spouses when alone ('Nihon ni itsu kita no?'). The not-polite, or insulting language, is spoken only by men; women are forbidden to speak it, and indeed are often times the recipients of it ('Itsu kita?'). The way the Japanese speak to foreigners depends on race, nationality, position, and skin color. They might get the polite or very polite language if a respectful white American, or plain form or insulting language if Iranian or dark Brazilian Japanese."

Amidst all the pleasantries and order and discipline, Daniels sometimes sensed a tinge of anger. *Contained. Waiting.* He saw it in the eyes of the old, scarred woman who had handed him and Taylor the pamphlet as they walked off the base on their first day.

All of the Japanese Daniels had encountered so far were very friendly and well-mannered, and though he had certain reservations about some of their history, as with his own country's, as a visitor, or rather guest, he found their culture, work ethic, and sense of honor quite fascinating. *The stretch of skin that webs the world.*

25 Nov. 77

Chaos—The tempest of knowledge. Order—The manageable pieces.

Each piece of order contains within itself the seed of chaos, each fractal, each reflecting the realm of uni-dimensional truth.

Truth is not contained nor restricted to one dimension, to one scale—it's an eternal state, breaching abruptly and unexpectedly within the flow of time and space.

Man is fractal.

Man is an imprint of a process through time.

Man is a function of the fractal output of mysterious and hidden systems within his cells.

Fractals manifest between transition states of order to chaos. Man sails within that boundary.

Man hunts within that boundary.

Man is increasing in number, like cancer.

268

Takizawa Forestry Road

The eagle screeched, its gold feathers ruffling in the wind. It plummeted earthward, razor talons extended, its form missile-like, growing larger and more threatening as it came at him. Daniels threw up his arms, a futile gesture, for the great bird snatched him up and carried him aloft, high above the volcano's rim. Daniels looked down into the fiery pit, the heat rising, blistering his flesh. He screamed. The talons opened, and he dropped effortlessly through space, tumbling end over end, down into the molten mass and flames of the volcano's mouth . . .

Daniels sat up and opened his eyes. *A dream.* He took in a breath and placed his trembling palm on his lap. It was just a dream. *Just a dream.* The driver motioned to Daniels that Mt. Fuji was near. He nudged Taylor. Taylor yawned and peered forward, trying to locate the volcano. The rain had stopped. Daniels could see nothing, only the blur of buildings and dark forest. The volcano's sacred silhouette lay hidden in the night.

Daniels leaned over and tapped the driver's shoulder. "Can you drive us up to the fifth station? Fifth station?"

The driver shook his head and replied, "Kitaguchi Hongu Fuji Sengen Jinja."

Taylor inched forward. "What's he talking about?"

"Fuji Sengen Jinja," said the driver. "Shrine! I drop off you."

"I think he's referring to the ancient Sengen temple at the base of Fuji," said Daniels. "That means we're in or close to the city of Fujiyoshida right now."

"Look," said Taylor, sitting up, "We don't want to be dropped off at the Sengen. We need you to take us up to the fifth station."

The driver raised his hand and waved it abruptly.

Taylor pulled out from his pocket another large roll of yen. He counted out another 20,000 yen and placed it in front of the driver. The driver shook his head no. "Fuji Sengen Jinja."

"Shit." Taylor counted out another 10,000.

The driver lowered his hand, staring at the money. He grabbed it and stuck it into his shirt. "Fifth station, okay."

The taxi exited the freeway and sped along a road at the base of Mt. Fuji. Minutes later, the driver turned onto the Subaru line, a road that would take them up to the fifth station. A few minutes later, they stopped. A large steel gate was blocking the road. A sign dangled from the middle of it.

"Hey, this road is supposed to be open," said Daniels.

"Tsukoodome," said the driver. He paused, staring intently at Daniels and Taylor. "Yuki. Yuki, ahhh, snow. Snow!"

"Shit. That's all we need," said Taylor. "Didn't count on snow." He put his hand to his mouth.

Daniels peered out the window toward the summit. He still could see nothing. "Damn," he said, "while it rained in Yokosuka for the past couple of days, it snowed up here. Now what, do we get out here and walk?" Daniels leaned back in his seat in disbelief.

The driver put the cab in gear and started to turn around. "Wait!" they both yelled at once.

The cab stopped. "Now just hold on, we haven't. . . hey!" Daniels pulled out from his pocket a guidebook he had gotten from the ship's activities office. He opened it up and quickly flipped to a small map of Mt. Fuji.

"Here, there are two roads. Take us to the Takizawa Forestry road; maybe it's open, and we can get at least part way up the mountain."

The driver reached over and grabbed the book. He studied it for a moment. Taylor gestured to the driver and rubbed his thumb against his fingers, indicating that he would pay more. The driver knotted his eyebrows and tossed the book into the back seat. He turned the cab around and raced down the road.

The taxi sped east along route 139, passing the Fuji Sengen shrine—dedicated to the Goddess of fire and safe childbirth,

Konohanasakuya-hime, to ease the fears of the local inhabitants who were afraid of the volcanic mountain. Daniels peered into the narrow opening between the trees but could only make out giant cedars flowing back into darkness. In his mind, from a picture he had seen, he penetrated the gloom and saw the ancient stone monuments leading up to the red arch hovering over a bubbling stream. Behind the arch stood the main structure, fiery red, with its stout wooden beams, its wind-blown leave carvings, and hissing golden dragons. To the left of this building stood a covered fountain that held mineral water from Mt. Fuji's thawed snow. The water within it trickled from the mouth of a dragon and was used to purify the hands and mouth before praying. The picture had been so beautiful to him. So peaceful. So still.

The taxi zipped past, turned right, and passed Fuji Pines park, arriving a few minutes later at Nakano chaya, the starting point of the Yoshidaguchi, or old climbing trail. A large sign with a picture of the mountain showing all the stations and corresponding elevations stood on the shoulder between the entrance of the trail and the road. It also stated that the drive to the fifth station was twenty-one kilometers.

The Takizawa Forestry road veered off to the left. The gate was open. They drove on, speeding past snow-covered pine trees blending into the night. Up and around, they raced, climbing higher and higher. Soon they could see in the dim light a thin white blanket of snow covering the road.

Ten minutes later, the taxi hit a large bump and started to shake. The driver stopped. The paved road had ended. The driver got out, looked around, and climbed back in. A blast of cold air hit them. "Stop. Dirt road. No can go. Please out."

Taylor pulled out another wad of yen, but the driver yelled and shook his hand vigorously.

"I think this is the end of the line," said Daniels.

Taylor put the money back into his shirt. "Shit." They opened the door and stepped into sub-frozen air. The snow crunched under Daniels' feet.

"Shit, it's cold," said Daniels, his breath a cloud, his arms wrapped tightly around him. "Hey, can we get that trunk open?"

The driver quickly complied. A huge puff of condensation filled the air as Taylor strained, lifting the warhead up. As the bag came out, the cab lifted back up. The driver slammed the trunk and walked toward the door. The smell of rotten meat hit them. Daniels stepped back a few paces and took in a cold breath of pine. It refreshed him, but he was freezing. All around him were tall pine trees. A small abandoned hut was just visible to his left. Just in front of it was a small untended garden with some old equipment and a fallen wheelbarrow. Directly in front of the taxi, the dirt road curved into the gentle slope of the mountain.

"Excuse me, sir," said Daniels. The driver turned.

"Stables? Do you know where the stables are at the fifth station?" said Daniels. The travel agency he called had only told him which area to go to but couldn't give him the exact location.

The driver looked puzzled.

"Stables, stables, you know, donkeys, horses," said Taylor. He placed his hand on the roof of the car with four fingers down, the middle one up in the air, and moved it about like an animal, his upraised finger straining back and forth like the neck of a horse. The cab driver started laughing.

"Hey," said Taylor. "It's not funny."

The driver laughed even harder, holding one hand on his belly, the other pointing to Taylor. The two stood for a minute until the driver quieted down, and then all three stood in silence. The driver scanned the road.

"Follow, white," he said, pointing up the snow-covered road. He muttered something in Japanese and then put his fingers in the air, gesticulating wildly like a running horse, and started laughing. He climbed in the taxi, revved it up, turned it around, and drove off—the soft glow of its tail lights soon swallowed by the dark.

"Well, let's follow white," said Daniels as he rubbed his hands together. "No, let's change. I'm freezing."

Taylor nodded. Daniels pulled from his bag a couple of pairs of thermal underwear, pants, hiking boots, shirts, sweaters, gloves, hats, and two large-size down jackets. He shook so hard he could barely dress. If he survived this, he thought, he would move to Tahiti. After dressing, they chucked their military clothes and the bag over the side of the road. Daniels could feel the warmth quickly building.

"All right, let's follow 'white,'" said Daniels. "We'll warm quicker if we walk for a bit. We still might have a hell of a long way before we hit the fifth station and get a horse. If they're open, that is."

"You're not the one lugging this thing, now are you," said Taylor. He bent down and picked the warhead up. "And what do you mean, 'if they're open'? I thought you checked up on it."

"Well, the lady I talked with told me the stables would be open till the end of the month. But sometimes they close for odd things, such as holidays."

"Might? Might ain't good enough. You told me they would be open."

"Look," said Daniels. "I tried to find out from a bunch of people the exact dates but got nowhere. She was the only one who really knew anything about it. She said they should be open and even gave me the prices. From the fifth station, where the trail begins to the seventh was 12,000 yen, one way."

"But you didn't tell me she said 'might.'" Taylor kicked the snow.

A few stars blinked at Daniels from a small gap in the clouds. "I hope it doesn't start snowing again," he said. The cold wind blew his hair into his eyes.

They started walking up the road, Taylor carefully placing his boots to avoid sliding on the snow and tripping over many of the rocks. His feet, under the combined weight of his body and warhead, sank through the thin layer and grit against the volcanic rock.

Daniels reached into his pocket and pulled out a small flashlight, spilling a few coins. He bent over and picked them up. He would need them. After descending back down to the fifth station from the summit, they would call Tokyo's biggest news agencies. It was vital that they be interviewed and photographed by the press before surrendering to the authorities. He didn't trust the news agency that they dropped the letter off. It was just one of many, and they could have easily regarded their letter as just a joke. Better to follow up to be sure.

Daniels shuddered. He flipped on the light, the beam defining the rocks and holes. They continued on. The section of road they walked was almost level, with a slight incline, and with the heavy breathing and slow pace of Taylor, Daniels wondered if they could make it up to the fifth station, let alone the summit. He figured they were somewhere past the fourth station, around 2100 meters, and still had a few kilometers to walk before reaching the fifth. At this rate, to make it up past the seventh level, he thought, would be paradise.

"What time is it?" said Taylor, stopping to catch his breath.

"I don't know," said Daniels. "I don't have a watch. But it must be around four or five in the morning."

"With luck, they won't discover it gone for a while. Once they find that cab driver . . . it won't be hard to locate us. They'll just use the radio."

"Number one," said Daniels, "As we went over before, I really don't think they'd want to open the spaces, considering past experience. They're all sound asleep. The odds against someone getting up in the middle of the night to open are extremely low. Number two, even if they did want to open it, they couldn't since we hid the keys. They would have to cut the locks, and to do that would require waking the Department Head, which I don't think they would want to do. They would simply wait till morning to see if we showed. Stealing a weapon would be the last thing on their minds. AWOL, absence without leave, yes; fucking around on base or downing a few drinks on the Honch, yes. Warhead heist, no. And lastly, we can't hurry because we have a long way to go and the road is dangerous. If you trip, the weight of that thing could kill you."

"Listen," said Taylor, "No mess-ups, or we're both history." He started forward again.

"Hey, you'll need the flashlight. No mess-ups, remember." Daniels smiled and followed him.

A mere two minutes later, Taylor stopped. He was taking in great heaps of air and was just barely able to walk. He looked ready to collapse.

"Hey," said Daniels, "you've barely made it this far, and—" He looked back at the spot where the taxi driver let them off. "Let's find a spot and rest for a bit. When the sun comes up, we'll be able to see a bit better, and the going will be a little easier."

"No. Gotta keep movin.'"

"Look, don't be stupid; you're shaking and can barely stand. You're going kill yourself before we get halfway up the damn mountain. The sun will be up soon, so let's just kick back till then."

"Listen . . . Daniels, Chris, Christopher. Can't stop. You stay. Got to keep moving."

"What the hell are you talking about? You can't keep lugging that thing up the mountain right now; look at you; you're fucking half dead as it is."

"Jesus, I'm just a bit . . . out of breath. I can make it." He wiped a bead of sweat from his eyes. "If you want, you can sit here; if you want to rest, I'll meet you further on up the road."

Taylor turned, and as he lifted his right leg, it caught on a rock. He flew forward, swearing, his left leg hopping and shooting out in front of him for balance. But his boot hit the snow and accelerated, catapulting his body down and to the left. Taylor tucked his head and twisted as he fell so that the warhead hit the earth first. He hit hard on his side, grunting loudly, and lay still, only his chest and fingers moving.

Daniels ran over to him. "Are you all right!? You all right?"

Taylor swore and slammed the earth with his fist. He crawled out from the straps and sat on the road, looking down at the seabag. A small rock lay exposed where he had fallen. He placed his hand to his side and grimaced.

"You okay?" said Daniels.

Taylor glanced up and then slowly rose to his feet. He took in a deep breath and stood the warhead upright. He grabbed the straps and then, with a loud grunt, dragged the warhead to his left. Daniels reached over toward the straps to help, but Taylor yanked harder.

Taylor took a step forward, still determined to keep moving. But he suddenly winched in pain, and he grabbed his side.

"Look," said Daniels. "Let's rest. You're tired and hurt. Please."

Taylor looked at him, took in a deep breath, and winched.

"Please, Joseph?"

Taylor just stood there in silence, breathing heavily. Finally, he looked to Daniels and nodded. "Okay," he whispered, "We'll rest."

Taylor dragged the seabag over to the side of the road, pulled it over the embankment, and carefully slid it down the snow to a large boulder butted up against a tree. Daniels cleared a small patch of snow and Taylor set the seabag beneath a small overhang of the rock.

They scouted the area, picking up branches, leaves, and sticks, and built a crude protective enclosure. Satisfied, they climbed in, huddling for warmth, and tried to sleep. The wind had picked up, and the cold seeped into Daniels' feet and hands. He pressed his back against Taylor's and drew his arms into his own body, trying to keep warm. Taylor pressed back, responding to the needed heat. Daniels peered through a hole in the branches. No stars were visible. The nearby trees pulsed in the wind; their tips vanished, like reasoning itself, swallowed by the gloom. His eyelids felt heavy, like dead weight. His thoughts slowed, and his breathing eased. He tried to keep his eyes open. They wouldn't obey. Lulled earthward, he descended into a deep sleep as the wind howled above and around him.

25 Nov. 77

Can't sleep, mother. Think I busted a rib. Every time I take in a deep breath, pain shoots through my side. Daniels is snoring like a buzzsaw. Too much on my mind. Sky is starting to lighten.

0550. Mountain range across from me on the horizon is now visible. It stands out in tin relief, the sky a heavy pink just above. Above that, black.

0600. Sky above mountains now bright orange.

0605. Sky now yellowish orange. Can now see outlines of trees.

0610. Glow has finally reached half of the heavens above me. Which cloud are you on? Wave. Do something. Let me know you're watching. Speak to me. Remember me, your son? How about you, Sis? Remember the time we all went to San Diego? Remember? The Wild Animal Park? That tiger waltzing right up to the fence, jaw agape, a line of saliva dripping, the other kids falling back, and you standing there, leaning forward, just a ball of wonder. Yeah, just beautiful ball of unbounded wonder.

I miss you both so very much.

0615. Yellow sky above mountains now. Very peaceful. Quiet. You must be still asleep. Sky overhead still growing brighter. Has a blue-gray tint to it.

0623. Can see the trees and bushes around me now. The roundness of the rocks press out at me. Hands freezing. Body okay. Sky is white above the mountains. Dark gray tint overlaying this—buttressing the blackness just beyond.

Ascent

Her voice! O shame! A passion seized him, a passion borne on waves of hunger, of pain. She stepped closer, her voice rich and sweet as honey, calling, singing, caressing the flesh of his body, his mind, his heart. Temptress! He couldn't resist. His mouth opened, and he drank from her golden lips the soft song. Down it poured, filling and filling, his stomach growing, extending, distorting beyond reason. He couldn't stop, each sip firing the need for another. The taste soured, but he couldn't stop. He could feel the heaviness, the weight. He teetered, and slipped. He screamed as he fell, but no sound came, just the slosh of liquid within his belly. Down he went, rolling and rolling, splashing into the sea, its depths, his spirit dragged under, tossed and torn by the flush of current . . .

Daniels opened his eyes. He shook, as did the branches and the rock. *Earthquake!* Pine needles, snow, and a small stick from the enclosure fell down on him. He grabbed the seabag and clung. The quake stopped. Taylor laughed.

"What's so funny?" asked Daniels.

"You. Just a small trembler. Common here."

"Well, I'm glad you find it amusing." Daniels brushed the bits of bark, snow, and pine needles off his chest. He threw back the hair from his eyes. His hand still smelled of pig. He wiped his hands on his pants and grabbed a branch that had fallen from the roof. He tossed it aside and crawled out into the sunlight.

He stood up and looked directly into the sun peering through a gap in the dark gray clouds. A warmth oozed into his face and body. He closed his eyes. A yellow spot vibrated before him. He opened his eyes and looked around, not quite sure of where he was. Patches of earth and brown grass bobbed on a sea of snow. Bristled trees long since shed off of their colored coats interwove tall pines. The snow sloped down from where he stood, steeply, spreading, then fading into the valley and city of Fujiyoshida. In the distance, a string of mountains stood in sharp relief on the horizon.

Taylor emerged from the shelter. He rubbed his eyes and stretched—then quickly pulled his arm to his side. Pain flickered across his face. Daniels scanned Taylor's body for any cuts. There were none that he could see, but the pain was obvious. He had bruised himself bad, or worse, had broken a rib. *Shit.* He thought of the dream, the earthquake. *Don't like this, things not right. Dammit, why now?* He rubbed his hands to warm them.

Taylor studied the light filtering through the trees. He took in a great breath, then stopped. His lip curled from the pain.

"Look," said Daniels, "From the looks of those ribs, you aren't in any condition to carry that warhead any further. What's done is done; why don't we just leave it here, go back, and place the call."

"No. We'll continue."

"Joseph, that's crazy; both of us together couldn't carry that thing all the way up. You barely got it this far, and it's only been a few hundred feet! The road right now is nothing compared to the long trail and steep switchbacks later."

"We'll rent a horse, remember?"

"Yeah, but after that?" said Daniels. "We can only take it to the seventh station. And that's assuming that we can get to the pack station by this road and it's open."

"No."

"Dammit, with you injured, we won't even make it to the station. Why don't we just count our losses and leave it? We'll still accomplish what we've set out to do."

"I said no!"

"Okay," said Daniels, "why don't I bring a horse back here?"

"And split up? What the fuck's wrong with you?"

"Hide the warhead and come with me."

"What were you just telling me?" said Taylor. "If we took off, how long would it take to get there and back? How far is the station? Do

279

you really know? Is it open? Will they let us take a horse off the trail and down a mountain road?"

"I don't know! It was just a suggestion!"

"Well, it's a stupid one."

"Watch it, Joseph!"

Taylor stepped forward. "Watch what?"

Daniels leaned back. "Look, Joseph, arguing like this is crazy. It's not going to do either of us any good. Our responsibility should be to our final objective—an interview with the press."

"So."

"So. Some moron could have tossed our letter at Yomiuri news by now thinking it was some practical joke."

"Not the Japanese."

"I'm not so sure about that. Or even worse, they could call the military to cover the whole thing up. Remember, we went carefully over this. Nukes are not allowed in the country. So one letter's not enough. We need to call the other agencies, remember? Interviews? Photos?"

"There's plenty of time."

"But we could get caught by the authorities first. So what the hell does it matter if we take it to the top or not—the end result is still the same."

"No it's not. Are you with me or not?"

"Dammit, Joseph, what's with you. We're a team, remember?"

Taylor took a step forward, his voice trembling slightly. "I made a promise to complete this task. Any deviation would leave the impact marginal."

"Marginal? You call stealing a nuclear weapon marginal? What we've already accomplished, marginal?"

Taylor ignored him and pulled the seabag out from the enclosure and dragged it back over to the road. Daniels followed. Taylor stood the seabag up, squeezing the straps between his fingers. He looked to the earth, then up past the pines. The sun disappeared behind a heavy

280

blanket of clouds. A cold wind blew. Taylor pulled the straps toward him and lifted them.

A strap ripped.

"Shit, it's tearing."

A one-inch tear in the top of one strap was plainly visible. A few stitches on the other had been torn out as well.

"Pull out the repair kit," said Taylor.

"What repair kit?"

"What do you mean 'what repair kit?' The one I told you to make."

"Didn't do it."

"Why the hell not!" Taylor slapped his thigh.

"Didn't think it was necessary. The tailor convinced me those straps and stitching would hold a tank."

"Well, he was wrong!"

"Hey, we're getting riled again," said Daniels. "Calm down. What's done is done. It's only a tiny tear, nothing to worry about if you're careful."

"Oh, nothing to worry about? Bullshit! You carry two or three hundred pounds on your back with a torn strap."

Daniels stepped back and took in a deep breath. "Hold on," he said, "I have an idea."

"What?"

"I said, hold on. Just give me one minute, okay?"

Taylor swore and looked down at his feet. Daniels turned and ran back down the road to where they were dropped off. He ran into the garden next to the hut and quickly made his way over to the wheelbarrow. He set it upright and inspected it. I looked okay; the tires still had air. Satisfied, he quickly pushed it back up to Taylor.

"This should help," said Daniels, out of breath but smiling.

Taylor eyed it, then bent down and checked the tires. He stood up and nodded. He then picked up the warhead, and while Daniels steadied the wheelbarrow, Taylor gently set it down into the barrow. The tires bulged out a bit but held. He then turned the wheelbarrow around so that he'd be pulling it instead of pushing it.

Daniels looked down at the weapon and the wheel, and he suddenly felt relieved. "Good. I think we can now do this. We still have time; there's no sign of the military or police chasing us. We'll take it as high as we can and then alert the military and news. Okay?" He extended his hand towards Taylor. "I said, okay?"

Taylor glanced at his watch and then carefully eyed Daniels. "Okay." He shook hands. "Let's do it."

Taylor stepped forward, adjusting his grip. The wheelbarrow followed along with ease. They continued up the road, silent but for the sound of footfall and a squeaking wheel. Above them, the trees flowed up the slopes a distance and then stopped. Above this, the snow-covered slopes of Fuji shot up into a bank of dirty gray clouds constricting the summit. The wind picked up. Snow was imminent.

The road before them cut back and forth through the canyon. They marched for several minutes, then stopped when they heard the sound of cars approaching. Daniels imagined authorities scrambling out, guns drawn, throwing them down to the earth. Or worse. *We're not going to make it. They'll stop us dead in our tracks.*

The vehicles approached. Daniels swore. They rounded a bend and came into view. They were civilian trucks. Daniels sighed but still felt nervous. He moved with Taylor to the side of the road. Two trucks sped up to them, each with a sole driver in a colored jacket and hat. The lead truck suddenly flipped on its wipers, shooting a stream of drops up into the air, which softly fell onto the car behind it. As they sped past, the lead driver yelled, "Uphill, uphill." Daniels and Taylor shook their heads.

"Maybe we should hitch a ride," said Daniels.

"No. Don't want anyone asking questions."

"Okay, if you say so."

"What do you mean by that?"

"Nothing. Just nothing."

Another three trucks passed, the middle ones honking to the others to speed up. Pulling up the rear, two followed at a distance, slow and unsure, weaving around every pothole and rock as they made their way up the mountain.

The two sailors continued on. About ten minutes later, they stopped for breath. Daniels suddenly felt very tired. His enthusiasm was waning. He looked to Taylor, to the enormous weight he pulled.

"Joseph?"

"What do you want?" said Taylor, breathing hard.

"You ever wonder what would happen if all motion stopped?"

"No." Taylor started pulling the warhead forward again, slowly.

"I remember a large picture of a Japanese shrine," said Daniels, marching forward in pace with Taylor. "Hell, it might have even been Fuji Sengen Jinja. It was incredible. I was fascinated by two large carved dragons over it. I must have been around ten or so."

"I said no." Taylor wiped away a thick layer of sweat from his forehead. He slipped in the snow but caught himself. His chest rose and fell.

"I looked up at this dragon on the shrine. His left claw was raised, his right was down, his mouth open and tongue shooting out. And then, I quickly shot my eyes over to the dragon on the right side. It had just the reverse."

"So." It was almost a gasp.

"So, its left claw was raised—"

"His right."

"His right. Thank you. His right claw was raised, his left was down, and his mouth was shut. Now flipping my eyes quickly from one to the other turned out to be fascinating. The two dragons seemed to blend into one animated creature. It blew my mind. It seemed *alive*! So then I got to thinking."

"Shit."

"Now, hold on a minute," said Daniels.

"We don't have a minute." He stopped, wiped his eyes, and then continued on again even slower.

"All right, let me just finish. So I got to thinking. What if you moved instead of the object? That is, instead of sitting and watching a moving film animate before you, what if you moved quickly while the film or object stayed stationary."

"What?"

"Just what I said. What if you were confined to a chair in a round room with pictures of a man in varying stages of motion hung all around you, and you started spinning with your eyes fixated straight ahead? What would you see?"

"Puke." Taylor attempted a smile but never made it. His hands held firm to the handles.

"No, really, if you could control the sickness, I wonder if you'd see the exact same thing as if you sat in a theater. Motion being relative and all. I mean, look at a pigeon with his head bopping up and down all the time. That would make us sick and confused, but it's perfectly natural for the bird. That's his world, with motion taken an extra step from us."

"Enough." Sweat glistened over his skin. "And then I thought . . ."

"I said enough. I need to catch my breath." He stopped, let go of the handles, and then walked around slowly, taking in deep breaths. He grimaced in pain with each step.

"And then I thought, what if all motion stopped? The earth, solar system, Milky Way, everything. What would happen? Would all motion, everywhere cease? Would life? Us? Parents, authorities? Everything?"

"I said stop!" Taylor swatted Daniels' shoulder.

Daniels leaped back. "Taylor, don't ever hit me again."

"Well, if you don't shut up, I'll throw your dumb ass over the side."

"Don't threaten me!"

"I swear to God," his breath laboring, "I will."

What the hell am I doing? We doing? "Look, Joseph, we've got to stop this shit. We'll never make it."

Taylor's breaths were loud and heavy. His face was empty of emotion, and his head hung heavily toward the earth. His body swayed and rocked as the wind whipped around him. He seemed ready to collapse.

"Let's stop," said Daniels. "We've gone far enough."

Taylor ignored him. Instead, he straightened, gathering some inner reserve, and trudged on. *He's crazy. Jesus, am I?* Daniels walked a few paces behind, tired, wondering at Taylor's strength and determination. They continued for another few minutes, the wheelbarrow bouncing slightly as its tire engaged the bumps. But after another minute or two, Taylor slowed to barely a crawl. He struggled to control the wheelbarrow as it hit small holes and slid, the barrow struggling over each rock and rut in the road. It was war. Taylor's feet fighting, lifting, dragging, throwing themselves out in front of his body, the warhead following. Taylor's chest heaved in great barrel-fulls of cold and dry air but then spouted it back out hot and moist, a sparkling mist. His eyes targeted the ground before him.

Daniels had had enough. He stepped in front of Taylor. "Look. Let's at least rest a while." Taylor stopped. Daniels glanced down the road, looking for any signs of being followed. None. A quiet "No" dripped from Taylor's lips as he shuffled forward around Daniels, his huge frame moving awkwardly and slowly. He drifted next to the shoulder of the road.

Daniels swore and followed, listening to Taylor's rapid, heavy breaths. Taylor's feet moved a few inches at a time. Sweat streamed down his face. It seemed to Daniels a miracle, a superhuman effort, for him to have made it this far.

But as Taylor dragged his right foot on the road, the lip of his boot suddenly caught a rock. He tripped. Falling, he threw his arm under him to protect his injured rib. The wheelbarrow toppled over and the warhead hit with a heavy thud inches from the steep side. He lay gasping, not moving.

Daniels raced over. "You okay?"

Taylor was too exhausted to speak. Sweat flowed in streams down his face.

"I said are you okay? Anything broken?"

Taylor didn't reply. He just sucked the air and clenched his fists.

"Look, just nod. Are you all right?"

Taylor nodded; he was not hurt. He lay panting, looking up at the stormy summit. The cold wind blew hard. Small snowflakes started to fall, swirling in white dots all around them. That's all we need. *Snow* . . . Taylor rolled over and slowly rose to his feet. He grabbed the strap to the weapon and, with a loud, sweaty grunt, lifted it. The veins on his forehead swelled dangerously out. The seabag rose up to his knees, his body shaking with the weight. With a huge breath, he set it back down in the wheelbarrow.

Daniels kicked the ground. "Dammit, let's just leave it. Roll it over the side and set it up behind those rocks there. You're in no condition to carry it anymore."

"No." He inhaled. "We must go on." His voice strained.

"Look, don't get crazy on me; we haven't even made a dent in this road. The fifth station is still a long way off, and then it will take us hours to climb to the top. Let's leave it. We would still accomplish our objective." Taylor didn't respond.

"Come on, Joseph, it's on the mountain, for Christ's sake."

Taylor swung around. "But not the top."

"I'm fucking freezing, and we're running out of time," said Daniels, wiping a snowflake from his eye. "If the authorities catch us, we'll be in deep shit. And then the press will look at that letter as bullshit." He kicked the ground again, then paced in a circle. "Joseph, will you listen to reason! Reason! Remember?"

Taylor didn't respond. His gaze seemed far off, removed from the present.

"Dammit," said Daniels, "what's so special about the top? They could show any minute, and we're fucked. Without media support, we won't have a chance. They will cover the whole thing up and dump us into the coldest cell imaginable. Then there goes our shot at college! Remember?!"

Taylor stirred. "The top is everything," he said. "We must make it through the gates at the summit."

"What gates?" said Daniels. "Are you mad?"

"No, I'm not mad. There are sacred arches."

"Arches? You mean that cement arch from the brochure? The one that looks like a fucking goal post? Are you crazy? This isn't a game, and you're not carrying a fuck'n football! We'll never make it, you fool!"

Taylor suddenly reached over and, grabbing Daniels, threw him to the ground. Daniels hit hard and swore. He jumped up and flung himself on Taylor. The two collapsed and rolled away from the warhead, Taylor easily swinging Daniels under him, pinning him to the earth.

"You son of a bitch," said Daniels. "Let me go!"

Taylor remained silent, his chest heaving in great breaths of air.

"Goddammit, Taylor, don't be a fool!"

At this, Taylor raised his fist, his knuckles huge and twitching. "Just say it again," said Taylor.

"What the hell is—" But before Daniels could finish, a loud "clang" rang out. They both swung around and looked toward the warhead. The wheelbarrow had fallen over, and the seabag was now slowly rolling away from them—toward a steep face of the mountain.

"Taylor!"

Taylor jumped up and raced toward it. The warhead was sliding lengthwise down a steep slope toward a sharp drop-off, and Taylor pounced on it, grabbing a strap. Daniels jumped in front of the bomb, slowing its momentum. Both of them dug their feet into the ground. It stopped—a few feet to spare from the edge. Each grabbed a strap and pulled the warhead up to the trail; then, both collapsed around it.

They sat in silence for a moment, taking in what had almost happened. They turned to one another and smiled at the near mishap, at the whole crazy situation. They both started to laugh, then fell silent again for several minutes, each exhausted and lost in thought.

"Look," said Taylor suddenly. "I know we can make it."

"No, Joseph. Please."

Taylor leaned over the warhead, his eyes staring at the earth. "We need to continue."

"My god, what's driving you?"

"It's complicated." His voice suddenly softened.

"So, what isn't," said Daniels, throwing his hands up and looking around.

Taylor glanced up at the sky and then spoke, his voice surprisingly soft. "I was home from Berkeley and was watching my sister. It was not long after that UCLA game I fucked up and the bullshit that followed. She was only ten." He shut his eyes tightly, then opened them. "I, I was a bit depressed. My mother was in the hospital undergoing cancer treatment. At the time, she was working at a university lab that dealt with radiation samples. She told me there was no connection, but I knew that was a lie. Had to be. She was too young to get cancer. So that day I smoked some dope to mellow out, strong stuff, then I drove my sister to the store."

"And?"

"Thought I had more than enough time to catch a yellow light. Swerved to avoid a car . . . lost control. She . . . she was crushed."

"I'm sorry."

"Should never have done it." His eyes watered. "Jesus, she was everything to me. To my mother." He wiped his cheek of tears. "She never forgave me." He shut his eyes for a moment, his body seeming to fold in on itself. He looked out to the dark distant peaks cut sharply against the white sky. "She died not long after."

"So that's why you left school," said Daniels. "Everyone thinks it's from you fumbling the ball."

Taylor glared at him, "Yeah, well fuck them! What do they know." The wind picked up, rustling the trees. "But I sure as shit know that it all starts here," said Taylor, suddenly pointing to his chest.

"What do you mean?" asked Daniels.

"What do I mean? Haven't you figured that out by now? Of all people you aught to know."

"Sorry, I don't."

"I keep making the wrong fucking decisions! That's what I mean!" He shut his eyes and slammed his fist into the snow. "Fuck!"

Daniels jerked back and shuddered from the sound of the impact.

"So, if I don't make the right decision now," continued Taylor, "then nothing will change. You understand?"

"No," said Daniels. He shut his eyes and took in a deep breath, startled by Taylor's confession. "I, I trusted you."

"And you still can. It's the right thing to do. I feel it!" He hammered his heart with his fist.

Daniels looked up at the road snaking its way up the mountain into the dense cloud that hid the summit. "I'm sorry, Joseph. I can't. This is bigger than you."

"Bullshit! It's the game—and it's personal." Joseph stood up.

"No. No, it's not."

"Dammit, why won't you listen to me!" Taylor stepped forward, his body hovering over Daniels, blocking out the sky.

"This isn't a game, Taylor."

"It has to be, dammit!"

"Why! Why does it have to be?"

"Because it's survival, brother. And the survival of our species is a challenge. A game."

"A game?"

"Yes. It must be. Don't you understand? It must be! And I, we, must win!"

"You're deluding yourself." Daniels stood up. "You're not playing against the powers that be. Nor Berkeley, nor UCLA, nor me! You're playing against yourself."

"No. I'm not playing against any of 'em."

289

"Then who? Your mother?"

Taylor leaned forward, his eyes intense, burning. "No," he said, his finger pointing up. "God." He looked up at the dark clouds threatening above them. "I'm playing against God."

They stood still for a moment, only their breaths betraying themselves as it blended with a cold wind cutting across their skin.

Taylor leaned over the warhead. He set it up, and then with great effort, he stood up and gently set it back down into the wheelbarrow. He looked to Daniels, his face wracked in pain, his chest still heaving.

"Now, will you follow me or not?"

Daniels stood in silence for a minute, taking in Taylor's words. "No," he finally said. "I will not."

"Then take care, Christopher." He turned and started up the road; his huge body bent forward, his breaths quickening, the warhead obediently following behind.

Daniels stood up. He swore and looked down the mountain, then back to Taylor.

"Joseph!" yelled Daniels. The echo rang through the canyons.

Taylor struggled on, not looking back. *Dammit.* Daniels turned and started down the mountain, but after a few yards, he suddenly stopped. The Gazelle he had seen running in Africa leaped from his memory. *Running. I'm still running.* He shut his eyes, feeling the scrape of cold air slide across his cheek. His father suddenly loomed before him; his eyes blank yet watchful, his form pale and misty.

Daniels opened his eyes. *Jesus.* The wind picked up. The tips of his ears burned. He clenched his fists and turned back towards Taylor. He looked to the dark clouds and then to the lumbering form receding away from him. *No more running.* He suddenly thought of Yuki as he had walked away from her at the train station, the white of her jacket blending in with the white wall, her tears streaming down her soft pale cheeks. His heart sank at the memory, and the sudden sense of loss was immediate and jarring. He wanted to see her again. *No, must see her again!*

Daniels spun and screamed up at Taylor, "No more! Do you hear me!" But Taylor ignored him and continued on. Daniels ran towards Taylor. He quickly closed in on him and, grabbing the wheelbarrow, yanked. Taylor stopped and then fell backward, but with a momentous heave, he righted himself, pulling Daniels and the wheelbarrow forward.

"Stop," yelled Daniels, clutching the barrow.

"Let me alone."

"No." Daniels gripped tighter and yanked again.

"I said, let me alone!"

"I said no. Do you hear? No!"

"Damn you!"

Taylor tried to move forward, but Daniels held tight. "I swear to God, Taylor, don't do this, don't."

"I said . . . let . . . me . . . go!" Taylor sprung forward. But as he did this, the wheel of the barrow slipped into a large hole in the road. The tire popped from the tremendous weight, and the barrow jerked violently forward and then tipped over. The warhead in its seabag launched towards the steep shoulder of the road. They froze. It picked up speed, gaining momentum.

In front of them to their right, a dry ravine ran down, stopping at a pipe that angled under the road. The ravine exited and continued down into the side of the canyon, its snow and grass-covered embankment falling off sharply a few hundred feet down to a dry river bed. Toward this slope, the warhead sped.

Both Taylor and Daniels didn't move; their feet were frozen to the earth. They watched in horror as the warhead rolled over the lip and then over the side.

"Holy shit," whispered Daniels.

The warhead rolled down the mountain, spinning furiously, pounding rock and snow and flattening grass leaning in the wind. They watched as it hit a large bush, its trunk flattening as it passed. The warhead rolled on, picking up speed. At the edge of the slope, it hit a

291

jagged rock, tearing the warhead loose from its seabag and catapulting it into the snow-filled sky, a large white swan, its pinions bound, twirling downward in a graceful arc. It disappeared from view. A few seconds later, a metallic concussion thundered up.

The two looked at one another, eyes wide. They leaped over the side and bounded down the mountain. They tripped and rolled, got to their feet, and raced to the edge of the ravine. They peered over it. Far below they could make out the crumpled body of the weapon lying exposed on the jagged floor of the streambed. White, silver, black, and bits of red color dotted the rock around it. A small cloud rose up from the warhead and splintered in the wind.

"My God!" said Daniels. They continued down the side of the mountain. They circled around, fighting their way through the maze of trees and rocks. Daniels tripped and fell, and Taylor flew past him. Daniels rolled on the ground holding his ankle, grimacing in pain. He climbed to his feet and hopped down to Taylor, who stood on a ledge overlooking the bomb. Taylor seemed in shock. His whole body was rigid, his head locked on the scene below him. Daniels peered over. Scattered below him floated pieces of the warhead on a river of rock and snow. The main body of the bomb lay split and crumpled around a sharp boulder. The upper part of the metal skin was torn off, exposing the fibrous pit. Its detonators and wires pulsed out from the jagged wound. Snow flitted down onto the bomb, its fine crystals forming a thin white layer.

Taylor's fingers gripped his pants, forcing veins out from the back of his hand. His jaw tightened, sawed back and forth. Daniels trembled. His mouth hung slack.

"My God, what have we done," said Daniels softly. Taylor didn't respond. His body stood hunched, his face slack, his jaw extended out, still slowly moving. His eyes looked vacant, lifeless.

"Joseph, talk to me." No response.

"Joseph. Taylor! Come out of it. We need to get the hell out of here."

Taylor's breaths deepened. The hollowness in his eyes seemed to widen and spread across his face.

"Joseph, listen to me! Snap out of it, and let's go!" Daniels moved to grab Taylor's arm, but Taylor swatted it away. Taylor then turned and reached into the back of his shirt and then pulled something metallic out. He straightened up; his eyes focused tightly, the metal object he had pulled out hidden at his side. He took in two great breaths and then slowly aimed a gun at the warhead.

Daniels swallowed. A tremor shot through his body. "Joseph, what . . . what the hell are you doing? Put that thing down."

Taylor didn't respond. His arm extended steel straight before him. The tip of the barrel trembled slightly. A snowflake landed on the blue metal and quickly melted.

"Joseph, have you gone mad? Put it down, and let's get the hell out of here. For all we know, we could be breathing in particles of radiation right now."

Taylor didn't respond. He stood solid as a rock. Not a muscle moved, rippled. It was as though time had stopped. His massive frame loomed larger than life, statue-like in its stillness, towering above all humanity. From his great bulk, his head thrust upward, his face blank of all emotion, only the flicker of an eyelid betraying the inner agony of mind, of soul.

Daniels sensed it before it came. It was sudden and loud but expected. The echo from the blast reverberated around the canyon, sending two birds up in flight. A small spark flew from the skin of the warhead.

"You're mad. Stop it!"

Taylor fired another round, the flash a bit closer to the open pit.

"Dammit, give me that thing." Daniels reached over, but Taylor's free arm suddenly pushed him to the ground. The gun stayed locked on its target.

Daniels quickly jumped back to his feet. "I don't believe this. If you hit a detonator, we're fucked. The blast from the high explosive could kill us."

Taylor stood rigid, focused on the weapon before him. "Even if we survive the blast, the radiation could kill us."

Taylor remained motionless. Daniels tensed. Taylor seemed to inhabit another world. He appeared asleep as if in a dream.

"Joseph? Joseph!"

Taylor's lips quivered. Then moved. He tried to speak but lapsed into silence again.

"Joseph, Taylor, come out of it. Damn you!"

Taylor's lips moved again. He finally spoke, the words cutting out slow and strong, turning the blood within Daniels' veins cold.

"From hell's heart—"

Daniels sprang. The gun fired. Daniels' body smashed into Taylor's as the blast hit. A tsunami of color crashed into him, spinning, drowning, blending all in a maelstrom of light.

Then the echoing ebb of night.

Descent

Daniels opened his eyes. Dots of falling snow shimmered above him in a haze of gray. The flakes flashed and blinked and touched his skin, and the scent of smoke drifted dully into his mind. Trembling *tips of* trees shot up on one side of him. A thin denuded bush on the other. His head cleared and became strangely calm. No thoughts rippled his *mind*. He watched the snow swirl *in the* wind, fluttering and falling in and around and on the pines. A patch of snow, loosened by the *br*eeze, powdered to the earth from a branch.

He suddenly *remembered*. Taylor, the weapon, falling, falling, a blinding light, and then a crushing cloud of black. He closed his eyes. It detonated, he thought, detonated. *But Jesus, still here, I'm still here.* He tried to move but couldn't. Panic seized him. He breathed hard and fast, concentrating on sensing his body, but couldn't feel *any*thing except his face and head. He opened his eyes. "What have I done," he said, the words flowing out soft and low. "Forgive me."

A thin sound *rose* up a short distance away. "Joseph," he said weakly. No response. *He* closed his eyes again, thinking of the tumbling warhead and Joseph. A cold wetness flowed down his cheek, and *in h*is mind, he watched it hit a blade of grass. The water streamed down its razor edges, *nudged* on by gravity's indifference, and *sl*iced into the sn*ow* to the earth, staining it dark, sinking down, dow*n*, past the roots.

A cold wind blew across his face. *Still alive.* He wondered if there was any radiation, and if so, would it drift into Fujiyoshida. *But who will know? They're going to cover this up somehow. Our bodies if the radiation is strong enough.*

"Joseph." *H*is voice trailed off. Another sound rose. He opened his eyes. It m*ust be him*. His nervousness started to fade, and a calming, accepting mood washed over him. He bli*nked to rem*ove the falling snowfl*ak*es from his ey*es*.

A bird s*creeched and fl*ew overhead, disappearing up and over the jagged line of trees framing the smoke. And then all was silent. Only the whisper of his breath reached his ears. He *listened* carefully, trying to hear the sound of a single falling flake. But couldn't. The stillness broke as a distant dull thumping drifted into his ears. At f*irst,* he thought it was his heart, but the rhythm, and intensity, changed and then grew. *Helicopter.* He shut his eyes. *They found us! The media found us!* His heart started to pound, giving the stream of liquid coursing down his cheek a *s*light bounce. *They'll get the story out.* The thumping from the helo grew, an increasing pitch first coming upwards from his left to his right, then *swing*ing lazily back. The sound g*rew* intense. He opened his eyes as the craft flew slowly past h*im,* heavy gusts rippling across his face. In the thick s*now* and tr*ace* of smoke, he could just b*arely* make out the helo's body, its black belly tattooed in l*arge* numerical ste*nci*led markings, its outline *indeterminate* and phan*tom*-like in the sharp blinking lights, its skids and horizontal stabilizer cut out in black. The copter flew past and hovered near. *Daniels clo*sed his eyes and then opened them, straining to sharpen his image of the craft. He sti*ffen*ed. He could barely make out the figure of a Caucasian man in a U.S. Marine unif*orm* leaning out w*ith* an M-16 rifle pointed down toward him, the *barrel* aimed towar*ds* the landing light cutting through the snow and ha*ze* to an area below *him. No. It can't be.* They must have followed the smoke. A wave of sorrow suddenly washed through him, and his breathing and pulse smoothed and slow*ed. No one will know. It was all in vain. In vain.*

He shut his ey*es. Need to let this go. Just let it go. He suddenly* saw his father standing there on the stairs in the basement of his old home in Dorchester. He w*as* moving upwards towa*rds* the ki*tch*en door. He s*u*ddenly stopped and turned around. He moved his lips as if to say something, but no sound emanated. He *star*ed down at his *son,* his brow furrowed, his eyes focused. Daniels returned his *gaze,* locking his eyes on his father's. Several seconds passed, but it seemed like hours. F*in*ally, his father's countenance softened. He nodded, th*en*

296

smiled. It wasn't a large sm*ile*, and in fact, someone other th*a*n Daniels wouldn't h*a*ve perceived it as such. It was just a slight up*tur*ning of *t*he corners *of* his thin lips. But it was *enough*. His father turned and headed up the stairs, dar*kness* replacing his father's form.

Daniels tried to open his eyes but couldn't. Everything was black. Bla*cker* than the stairwell. But, strangely, *he wasn't afraid anymore. His mind* was clear for the f*ir*st time in his life. The sound of the circling helo seemed to fade, then vani*s*h, though its *presence thump*ed and *reson*ated through his body, loosening and rel*ax*ing his muscles and or*gans*. A r*oo*ted tension, shame that had *wrapped itself mother-like* around his veins *eas*ed itself up and out. Time seemed to slow, to stop, and he suddenly thought of his watch. *Broken.* But that too *slowly dissipated* from his mind. He felt now as if his body would r*is*e *u*p and float, a white snow*flake* floating *in* an empty and curr*ent*-less sky.

He opened his *eyes*. The *chopp*er shimmered. The snowflakes materialized and s*ee*med to come fr*om* nowhere, just appearing as dots fr*om* the swirling *haz*e, increasing in size as t*hey fell. The cold seeped into him, and he* thought of *Yuki's* w*arm penny tu*cked *deep within his* po*cket,* and for the first time, *Christopher P. Daniels* could feel so*me*thing *warm and wet* wind*i*ng its way down the s*id*e *of his face. The drops felt strange but intense. He could* see th*is all* now, very clear, *very sharp*—*a*n image *of Yuki gazing down from the axis of his mind, her face* em*otionless, blank, a pale sun that was set snugly round damp discerning eyes, watching his blood seeping out and around him, mixing with the elements, flowing, stopping, freezing, then slowly being covered over by a sheet of virgin snow. In a few months, it would all thaw in the new light and then flow with the spring rains—rolling, racing, and plunging, mixing in with the brooks, rivers, and tributaries. Like the silent waters moving immeasurably beneath the tottering talk of Sather Gate, it would all sail down, down . . . down to the siren sea . . .*

Epilogue

It wasn't long after I finished writing the rough draft of this book that I received a late and final note in the mail from Mr. Griswold at the State Department. The note just simply said, "I can help no further. The rest of the files on the incident are sealed. But don't let that be an impediment. It was only through faith and perseverance that enabled Daniel to walk away from that den. Keep the faith!"

At first, I was puzzled by the note, and I mulled it over and over in my mind. But then it suddenly hit me that it just might be a hint. A hint that Daniels just might have somehow survived the conventional explosion, the radiation exposure, and, most certainly, federal prison. But I wasn't sure.

It wasn't until a few months later, while trying to put the finishing touches on the book, that I suddenly recalled something peculiar about the incident that the Chief had told me several years ago before he died. I had bumped into him at a W-Division reunion that was held on the USS Midway in San Diego, as it was now a public museum. We were both clearly surprised and excited to catch up. At first, we shared a few stories and laughs, and then I discussed what I had done after the Navy. Though I really wanted to bring up the story he had told me, I kept my mouth shut due to the promise that I had made him. But just after we said our goodbyes, and as I started to walk away, he suddenly asked if I had ever gone back to Japan or planned to do so. I told him, no, not at all.

"Good," he said. "That's good. Maybe it's best if you don't."

"Why, Chief?"

"Let's just say that you should just let things lie. Do you get my drift?"

I said yes, but didn't quite understand.

He continued, "There are some that make it their job to never forget. They have eyes within eyes."

I was a bit shocked at hearing this, and I nodded. And as I was about to follow up on his remark, he suddenly added, "They say the snow blanketing Fuji is quite beautiful to behold at sunrise. Particularly for young lovers." He paused but then spoke slowly, carefully choosing each

298

word. *"And that holds true even for the old ones. It's best to just leave them . . . it be."*

"Sure, Chief, I think I understand," and I said my goodbyes to him and left the ship, never to see him again.

And now, recalling what he had said, particularly in conjunction with Griswold's note, I feel that I have been sanctified in a way with a new understanding of the Chief's words. I have been given a new sense of hope, or faith, if you will. Thus, I now dedicate this book to the lions. That's right, the lions. May they continue to lead and safeguard that which is worth saving. But, more importantly, it's equally apt for them to so let live when living so allows it.

So sows a sower . . .

Author's Note:

A reminder that this story is pure fiction. That is to say, the Chief and his tale of the *Fuji Jiken* incident, the FOIA request, the diary of Taylor, Mr. Griswold and his note, the "Trial of Sword and Steel," the Brig, Captain's Mast, and Daniels' illegal drug use, etc., are all from the author's imagination. Furthermore, all names, characters, and incidents are the products of the author's imagination. Any resemblance to actual persons, living or dead, or actual events is purely coincidental.

And just in case the reader is wondering if I actually went through the Shellback initiation -- I did, and had a great time! I went through it once as a Pollywog and twice as a seasoned Shellback. In regard to the Beauty Queen Contest, I was not unlucky enough to have been chosen to participate -- that distinctive honor went to a fellow and junior sailor that I served with on the USS Midway. Other incidents in the story, such as sunbathing on the fantail, the Peeping Tom, the poisonous snake and close-call with the lion, the Marine's severe treatment of sailors in the Brig, and the anti-Midway pamphlet from the Yokosuka Citizens' Group, were based on real events that I personally witnessed or experienced.